D0829328

Susan Fromberg Schaeffer

Love

PUBLISHED BY POCKET BOOKS NEW YORK

POCKET BOOKS, a Simon & Schuster division of
GULF & WESTERN CORPORATION
1230 Avenue of the Americas, New York, N.Y. 10020

Published by arrangement with E.P. Dutton
Library of Congress Catalog Card Number: 80-15438

ISBN: 0-671-43780-1

First Pocket Books printing April, 1982

10 9 8 7 6 5 4 3 2 1

POCKET and colophon are trademarks of Simon & Schuster.

Printed in the U.S.A.

For Benjamin and May

". . . for to possess a ghost is a distinction above titles."

GEORGE MEREDITH,
The Ordeal of Richard Feverel

"Let us now praise obscure men."

IRVING HOWE,
World of Our Fathers

Contents

Two Dreams

Emily

In the dream, they were all in the living room. I knew they were poor; everything in the room said they were poor, but everything in the room was so clean, and the sunlight poured in as if the sun intended to set light in that room. "We went everywhere," my grandmother said, "on these six feet." She turned her head so that her glance took in her two daughters and her husband. "We had no cars, we had no money for horse carriages or trolleys. So we walked. We went everywhere. To the RKO Brunswick, to Prospect Park, to the Brooklyn Public Library. Everywhere on these six feet," and she looked down at her feet with pride. Her shoes were sturdy brown leather shoes; they had thick brown laces and their soles were sensible. They inspired confidence. "Everywhere," she said again, and the others nodded. The setting sun poured in through the window behind them, outlining them in light. How ladylike was my grandmother's posture as she sat on the edge of her chair, her long, graceful legs pressed together, her hands folded neatly in her lap. And so her daughters sat too. My grandfather sat back in his chair, one hand on each knee, his face in shadow. He said nothing. He never had much to say to them. Then, unexpectedly, he said, Yes, and the girls nodded. They were sitting in an incandescent room, a room of molten gold. I was so happy I began to cry. But they no longer noticed me.

The next night, they were again in the dream, but they were in a back room. I couldn't see them.

I had been so happy since they had come the night before. But why had she said we could go anywhere on these six feet? There were four of them sitting in the room. She should have said we went everywhere on these eight feet.

Someone walked into the room from the hall. I told him about the dream. I wanted to tell everyone about the dream, it was so shining and beautiful and it made me so happy. "Six feet?" he said; "six feet underground." And that was where they were. They were all dead.

Were they trying to tell me that they were still here, although I could not see them? Or were they trying to tell me to forget them because they were gone, beyond reach? They had been dead so long. One of them had been dead for almost thirty years. And suddenly it seemed as if six feet was not very much earth to move, as if I could have them back. And then I realized that one could move the whole world and still not move those six feet, and when I thought that, I was terribly lonely.

I decided to buy a dog and I named it Vidal, after my grandfather's dog. And it was a wonderful dog, protective and jealous and intelligent. But I did not have it long. It was shot by a hunter during deer season. But while I had that dog, I felt as if I had my grandfather back again.

After the dog died, I had the same dream again, and no matter how I thought about the dream, even when I told myself the six feet were just the six feet of ground which covered them, I felt terribly happy. And just then, the clouds blew down the sky and the sunlight filled my room and I saw my ankles and toes at the foot of the bed and each foot was like a sleeping animal which I had never before seen, and each one was golden.

Lucy

I very rarely dream, and when I do, my dreams are terribly boring, which is probably why I never remember them for very long. But one night, I did have a peculiar dream, and every so often the dream comes back, and it is always the same. I dream that I am sitting around Grandma's kitchen table as usual. She had an old-fashioned kitchen and it had old-fashioned open shelves and the cups and saucers were stacked in the old-fashioned way, a pile of saucers, and then the cups, stacked one inside the other. I must have said something about the window. The color of the sky outside was the color of the white tile walls. Every now and then, a blast of wind would throw a handful of snow against the windowpane. Inside, the window was beading with little drops of water. It was very cold.

I must have been looking at the window, and Uncle Sid said to me, "Don't worry, we'll take care of him. When he gets here, we'll give him something to eat." Uncle Koppelman was smiling, and Grandfather was smiling, and my two glamorous uncles were smiling, and my dear, regal grandmother waved her hand at the table as if to say, "Look how well we'll take care of him. We have seltzer and beet jelly and a whole plate of little crabapples."

I wanted so badly to take one of the little crabapples by its stem and pop it into my mouth, but the snow was hitting the window and then sliding down as if it had been hanging onto the windowpane as long as it could, and could hold on no longer. "Don't worry," said Uncle Sidney, "he's going to get tea and cookies like everyone else, if he makes it home." It wasn't until later that I realized everyone I was dreaming about who was sitting around that table was dead. There was nobody alive around that table. But I felt sure that they would take care of him.

The next day, we got the call saying that my father had

been shot. The resident told us to go home. He said he would call us if anything happened. He said we should not wait, there was no point. We were standing and talking in front of the hospital door when he followed us out and told me Dad was dead. Then I knew that they had come to tell me not to worry, that they would take care of him.

I hope that dream was a true dream. I do not believe in an afterlife, although I would like to. Sometimes I do not believe in this life, it passes so quickly, as if it were a story written on a sheet of paper by one hand while the other follows behind it, erasing the beginning of the sentence even before it ends. I adored my father, and I never knew anything about what his life was like before I was born, and so much had happened, so much I still find hard to believe. Dad talked to my sister, but not to me. And as I see my own past fading, it seems more and more important to find out his past and hold it. But perhaps time passed is gone, irrevocable.

It was always such fun sitting around that table. They were all so funny and kind. And there was always something good to eat. It was such fun around that table.

BOOK ONE

RUSSIA

Chapter 1

It was the month of Elul, and for two months, it had been snowing every day, so that the small village of Pobrosk had been isolated from the rest of the world for many weeks. Every morning, the villagers would come out, stand before the doors of their small houses, and think the same thing: the earth is cold, the snow falls, the potatoes freeze, the chickens are thin, the ducks are tough, and soon we will have water for soup. Every morning, the villagers, dressed in black, would stand like crows beneath a sky which was icy gray and differed little from the sky which vaulted over the village at night. Every morning, they hoped to see something new: a wagon arriving from a neighboring town, a vendor bringing swatches of cloth, a farmer bringing a milch cow to the market. But of course it was impossible. As the morning ticked more quickly, people could be seen moving from one house to another, the children to school, the men to their prayers, the women to gossip, all proceeding cautiously along the narrow wooden planks which had been laid down as walkways atop the packed snow which had obliterated the village streets.

In spite of the cold, the people were often outdoors, since inside the houses were gloomy and dark. The sun was so high it had long ago blocked out the light, and the shutters, closed against the cold, were now buried beneath the snow and impossible to open. Recluses and children enjoyed this weather. The only road out of the town, if it could be called a road, was a narrow path dug between the great drifts of snow. So high were the drifts that when the men worked, shoveling the path after each new snowfall, they were invisible. All that revealed their presence were the little storms of snow the men's huge, square shovels tossed rhythmically into the air. The men's work was made harder by the children, whose favorite sport was climbing the walls of snow which enclosed the path; then they slid or jumped down to the hard-packed snow beneath.

The children and the men digging were the only ones who usually saw the woman they called the zenshina, which, in Russian, means woman. They called her that because to call her any other name was to conjure her up in the dangerously familiar way that one might conjure up a demon. The townspeople feared her, avoided her, and feared offending her. She had appeared in their tiny town some twenty years before, driven up in a magnificent carriage which had stopped before the domed church on the edge of town. She had arrived on Thursday, Market Day, and within minutes, the news of her arrival spread through the field from stall to stall, and there had been a stampede from the market to the church. Everyone wanted to see this woman who was dressed, some said, like a queen. Everyone wanted to see the queen. The merchants were the last to see her for they would not leave their wares unprotected, and it was a profitable day for the less curious children in the town who were given two kopecks to stand guard near the makeshift tables in the market. The villagers still talked of the magnificence of the zenshina's dress, although, after that day, they were not to see her in such attire again.

The woman took a room in a small boardinghouse run by a family in the Jewish section. She sent one of the family's sons out for woolen material, and the next time she appeared, she was dressed like any other woman in the town, in a heavy, black, formless skirt, a heavy, loose blouse, a shawl over her head, which she tied under her chin. She differed from the other women in two respects: she had all her teeth, and the shawls which she wore tied under her chin in the ordinary way were of magnificently rich cloth whose colors hypnotized the people in the town: Persian blues, deep-hued crimson shot through with heavy gold threads.

It was soon common knowledge that she had ordered a house to be built for her twelve versts from town, and when warned that the winters made it dangerous to live in such isolation, she raised her eyebrows and said nothing. The owner of the boardinghouse felt it was his duty to remonstrate further. The zenshina told him that she would not be isolated. She would have her dogs and her dogsleds, and in the winter, she would have her serfs.

The villagers who heard this assumed she was a meshuggeneh, shook their heads, and expected to see her buried by the next spring. While her house was under construction, she wandered the fields carrying a large basket of woven reeds, which she filled with leaves and roots. Now the villagers were sure she was a meshuggeneh. Of course, this was before she cured the boardinghouse-keeper's son of epilepsy and the shoemaker's son of scarlet fever. After that, the villagers did not believe she was crazy, but they did believe she was a witch. One day, standing on the porch of the boardinghouse, she saw the water carrier laboring under his two huge wooden buckets, each at one end of a thick branch, and remarked that the man would be dead by the end of the week. His wife found him two days later in the field in front of their house, blood, which had streamed from his nose and ears, caking, flies settling on his distorted face. And so it happened that the people came to believe that the zenshina could cast powerful spells and could kill whenever she would.

At the same time, it became clear that she had ties with the government, since officials regularly arrived with little scrolls tied with red ribbon, all addressed to her. The officials would wait, in gigantic splendor, on the little porch of the ramshackle house until she came back from the fields. She would take the scrolls and go inside. Occasionally, she would give them a letter to deliver to no one knew where. A woman with such powers, who knew officials, who might even know the czar, was no woman to meddle with! On the day the zenshina moved out into the fields and into her house, there was jubilation in the village. It was as if an evil eye had closed, or moved on to other lands.

Yet there were daily reminders of her. Shortly before the snows began to fall, a group of peasants arrived in the village asking for directions to the zenshina's house. To the terrified villagers, they appeared to constitute an entire regiment. They came in wagons that were packed full of sleighs, and tied to the back of each wagon were twenty howling dogs. The villagers had never seen such large dogs, nor so many dogs together, and it was some time before Ely the Burier, also known as Ely the Reckless, came out to talk to them. He found it was not possible to talk to them. As the villagers discovered, these peasants came from Georgia and spoke neither Russian nor Yiddish. But they had a piece of paper which they gave Ely the Burier, and when he read it, he knew what they wanted.

Ely pointed and drew maps in the dirt with a stick. The peasants grumbled ever more loudly. Finally, the leader of the group picked up Ely by the collar and pointed at the map and then in the direction Ely had tried to indicate. Shivering and blue-lipped, Ely sat on the plank that formed the wagon seat, and guided the peasants to the house twelve versts from town. He was escorted home, even bluer, by one of the peasants, who jumped out of the wagon before Ely's house, bowed to the ground before him, and jumped back into the wagon, leaving the stunned Ely staring open-mouthed after him.

The villagers swarmed around the reckless man like wasps, but he could tell them little. Apparently, the peasants were to stay in the zenshina's barn for the winter, and their dogsleds, which they had brought in their wagons, would provide the zenshina with transportation. Thereafter, the winters in Pobrosk were spoken of for miles around. While all other villages were surrounded by impassable drifts of snow, Pobrosk's snowdrifts were the playfields of the zenshina's dogs and her dogsleighs, which could be seen moving like rapid, black dreams across the wide, seamless, white landscape. And those who walked out into the fields along the narrow path the zenshina had dug every winter at her own expense, did so at the peril of coming upon the dreaded woman herself, hunting through the snows for the feathers of birds, or waiting for the dead leaves that the peasants would retrieve from the frozen trees.

The zenshina herself did not seem to appreciate, much less encourage, chance encounters with the villagers, apparently regarding any conversation as useless conversation. She would nod at anyone she met, look them up and down, and walk on. If one of the villagers had a sick child, and the remedies of the local doctors and the prayers to God and the child's ancestors, and the visit to the cemetery's beloved dead failed to cure the illness, the child's mother would set out into the fields, and when she saw the zenshina, would make straight for her and stop.

"What illness?" the zenshina would ask, and the mother would answer her. The zenshina would turn, march briskly through the fields to her home, with the mother of the child following, as if by agreement, approximately ten paces behind her. Once inside the house, which was really a huge kitchen, the zenshina would ask more particular questions. When she was thoroughly satisfied as to the nature of the child's ailment, she would measure out various herbs and roots and place them on a clean white cloth. She would give the mother detailed instructions regarding the grinding and boiling of the roots and herbs. Some were not to be either ground or boiled, but were to be worn in a little pouch which rested on the chest of the afflicted one. To frantic demands of reassurance, the zenshina would invariably answer, "Some live, some die."

She was not a sympathetic woman and was known for her terrible curses. To one particularly distraught mother who kept garbling her instructions, she exclaimed, "May your head rot on your neck! May your tongue rot in your throat! May you grow like a potato, with your head in the ground!" The villagers, who were terrified of her, were constantly on the alert for signs of her essential benevolence, for it was a hard thing to have to believe that a woman who might be a witch, and who lived on the outskirts of their village, was an evil witch. Many believed her interest in curing the children of the town was such a sign. But once, a grandmother, so old that only her shadow remained in this world, asked the zenshina why she was willing to get up at any hour to treat a child, but would awaken muttering curses, if indeed she awakened at all, when a grown person fell ill. And the zenshina answered that the others were already half-dead. "Half-dead is not all dead," said the grandmother. "Look at your hands," said the zenshina. "Corpses! You are cold even in the summer, aren't you, Grandmother? Why fan the flames of a dying fire?" "Because," said the grandmother, "in the winter when the earth freezes and ice settles on the rivers, and a deep breath is like a swallowed steel sword, any fire is better than none."

"It is because you believe that," said the zenshina, "that I give you these things." "Life is always better than death," said the grandmother. "There is no death," said the zenshina; "there is only life turning into life." "I am soon to die," the grandmother said. "You will not die," said the zenshina; "you will only change." "Into what?" asked the grandmother. "If I knew that," said the zenshina. "You know more than the rest of us," said the grandmother angrily. "I know these herbs were once alive, and they give their life to those who do not have enough," said the zenshina. "You know no more than the rest of us!" said the grandmother angrily. "Then I shall give you nothing for your grandson," said the zenshina.

Standing in the zenshina's kitchen, the old woman appeared to shrink. She wrapped her shawl around her and wrapped her head in a long, woolen scarf. The zenshina watched her leave the house. "Old woman!" she called; "take these!" and she threw a little bag out onto the snow. "Make tea out of it," she said. The old woman turned to pick up the bag, then hesitated. The zenshina knew what she was thinking. If it was God's will that the child should die, nothing could cure him. Nothing *should* cure him!

The zenshina waited, a little smile stretching her thin lips, while through narrowed eyes she watched the old woman and waited for her to come to the only conclusion to which she could come. If it was God's will that the child be healed in this way, she was only his instrument. If, by coming to the zenshina, she was disobeying the will of God, the child would die, she would be chastized, and her last days would be lamentation and ashes. The old woman picked up the bag. "God works in mysterious ways," said the zenshina in a thin, flat voice. She folded her arms over her breasts and stood, watching the old woman. The old woman turned and began trudging back through the crisp, crunching snow.

The zenshina never accepted payment unless the invalid she treated was cured. Then she would accept whatever payment the family decided to give her. She never argued, she never questioned. Her outbuildings were filled with feather pillows and feather beds, earthenware pots, ground, dried bones to be used for fertilizer. No one knew where she kept the sums of money which she had accumulated over the years. When her cures failed, the villagers never rose against her because she never treated an invalid who had not already been given up for dead, although she was often contemptuous of the people whose lives were saved. Over the years, the rabbis had lamented her presence, inveighed against the villagers and their unholy faith in her powers, but sooner or later, every rebbitsin found herself on the path to the zenshina's house, and the rabbi, shamed in his own home, was silenced.

The zenshina accepted no thanks. She offered no explanation of her origins, or of the presence of her Georgian peasants who served her like serfs. She did not explain the arrival of liveried messengers bearing scrolls. Rumors about her swelled and died and swelled: that she was a princess, that she was to have wed a member of the royal family, that she was a Hapsburg and would have married a member of the czar's family, but had run away. When she was still new in the village, a woman from the burial society asked her if she was, as people said, a princess. "Why a princess?" asked the zenshina; "why not a duchess? Or a countess? You people know nothing. To you, everyone from the world beyond the village is a princess. Call me a princess if it suits you!" But they did not. They called her the zenshina.

Today, the zenshina and her dogsleds were the only moving things on the horizon. Gray clouds filled the sky and the fields of snow were gray also. It had been twilight all day long. "She moves about the fields like an evil wish!" murmured one of the villagers. When she disappeared, all were relieved. The zenshina was looking for a certain blue feather and she had been unable to find it. Her mind had gone over the problem of the blue feather so often that it had emptied itself of everything else, and now, it had emptied herself of the blue feather as well, although her eyes still sought it without her awareness. As she walked down the narrow pathway between the walls of snow, she stumbled over something. It was soft. The snow, which had been falling lightly all day, had covered it. She kneeled down and began sweeping the snow off the small mound. Something that appeared to be the shoulder of a patched, black coat made its appearance. She dug faster. Her hands, warm inside the rags which wrapped them, moved the snow easily. She recognized the child immediately. He was the only child in the village who had courage enough, or had been desperate enough, to run errands for her. Had he been coming out to see her when he had fallen? Had he fainted from hunger? Was he alive or was he dead? She picked him up and carried him into her house. He was breathing.

She unwrapped the rags binding her hands and feet and began to take off the child's outer garments. As she took off his cap, some snow, warmed by the heat in the room, fell from the cap, and in the dark place left on the cap by the falling snow, she saw a blue feather. The child must have fallen on the feather, she thought to herself. She stopped a moment to consider this, pressed her lips together, and nodded her head as if acknowledging a sign of some kind. She finished removing the child's outer garments and placed him in front of the hearth. He was bluer than the feather and cold. She saw that his hands and feet were frostbitten and she began to rub his skin with snow. She took a clean rag and soaked it in salt water and then twisted the rag so that warm drops went slowly down his throat. Finally the child opened his eyes. He looked at her, seemed to nod, and fell asleep. The zenshina watched his body grow pink and she began to cover him. Slowly and carefully, she moved him closer to the hearth. By morning, he was sleeping peacefully, and the zenshina got up and pulled her pallet over to the child's and fell asleep.

When she awoke, the child was not only awake, but busy. With one eye open, she watched him take a coal from the oven and place it in the little grate under the samovar. She saw him take some wood chips from the hearth and put them on the grate and then blow into the samovar. The chips took fire from the coal, and the glow lit the child's face. There, in that poor, blue room, he shone like solid gold. The zenshina saw the child turn in her direction and hastily she closed her eyes. She watched him carry in logs and place them in the wood stove. When he went out for more logs, she got up and sat down at the bench near her plain table. "So," she said to the child, "what were you doing out there, frozen half to death?" And the child told her, and of course, she was not much surprised by his story because she was not much surprised by anything anyone did in the village, or, for that matter, anything anyone did anywhere.

Chapter 2

The boy's name was Esheal Luria. He seemed younger than he was because he was so short. He appeared to be seven or eight, when in fact he was almost ten. He was the only son of the teacher who ran the village cheder, and he had two younger sisters. Like every child whose home had not been visited by calamity, his life had been uneventful, governed by routine and the surprise of familiar faces, and therefore it had been wonderful. Even when the village endured three hot, dry summers, and the crops were scant, the gardens scraggly, the roads dusty, the dogs thin, the potatoes all eyes, and the onions more scarce than diamonds, his family had been happy.

Even if they did not pay on time, his father's twelve pupils continued to come to school, which was the large space in front of Mr. Luria's hearth, and even if they did not pay all they ought to have, still they paid something. Esheal attended his father's school, swaying back and forth with the other boys, reciting passages from the Bible. He liked to sit in the back and watch the boys sway back and forth as the wheat swayed in the fields. While the boys chanted, he could hear his mother preparing dinner in the far corner of the room, his sisters chirping in the yard, while overhead, thousands and thousands of larks were trilling, and the sky was high, the house was warm, and his parents loved each other, and they both loved their children.

Catastrophe can arrive quickly, like a tornado which winds down from the sky and, within an instant, tosses an entire town into the surrounding fields, or it can arrive slowly, hobbling closer and closer like old age. For the Luria family, catastrophe arrived both ways at once. One Wednesday, the entire town came to a halt. The fires in the blacksmith's forge went out, the needles stuck fast in the seamstresses' cloths, and the children did not come to school. A new edict concerning military service had been handed down by the czar. Suddenly, many men were eligible who had not been before; the czar was now calling up older and younger men than he ever had before. The goys made it clear that this time only the most extraordinary bribery would lead to exemption from service and explained wretchedly that they had a quota to fill and if they did not fill it, *they* would be sent to Siberia. Adult males who were not yet fifty would certainly be taken unless they were unhealthy.

Good health suddenly became a misfortune. The healthy young boy with red, round cheeks and a loud shout brought tears to the eyes of his mother. The husband who chopped wood after a hard day's work saw the shadow of the czar's hand like a cloud over his head. He looked at his children and saw orphans. He looked at his wife and saw a widow. A new kind of traffic sprang up between the village and the zenshina's house. Now, the villagers wanted powders, roots, anything that would make their hearts race or skip beats, their eyes redden and hollow, their chests thicken and rumble with wheezes. They did not want to, God forbid, pass the czar's physical examination, be sent from their homes to die, or to live in an unclean world. And just as the zenshina had made the villagers well, she now proceeded to make them unhealthy.

Nothing worked on Moses Luria, the teacher of the cheder. Whatever draught he took increased his strength. Whatever powder he ground into his food reddened his cheeks. He ate some of the lime the villagers sprinkled on the road to keep down the dust, and his appetite improved. He did not have enough money to bribe the officials, and winter was bearing down on the village. In a week, he would have to take the physical examination given by the Army. He would pass it and he would be conscripted into the Army.

One night, after the children were asleep in their corner near the hearth, he and his wife discussed what to do in their corner of the room. When Moses Luria looked at his children they seemed very far away, as if they were already in another world and he was peering down at them from a cloud. When his wife's hand touched his, he imagined he could no longer feel its warmth. So this is what it's like to be dead, he thought.

The pitiful way in which he now saw himself gave him a daring idea. The cemetery of Pobrosk had a fearful reputation as a gathering place for vengeful spirits, and only the desperate would venture into that cemetery on a gray day. At night, no one had ever been known to enter, there to plead with his ancestors who, being dead, were closer to God and hence more likely to get His ear than one of the living. Moses Luria determined to hide in the cemetery at night. "But what about the spirits?" wailed his wife. "Never mind the spirits," he said; "what about the cold?"

Weeping all the while, his wife considered the type of flask he could carry under his shirt, the type of brandy that would fill it, and how Esheal could bring him more food and more brandy in the dead of night. "I forbid it!" hissed Moses. "The child is to sleep in his bed like any other child. If, God willing, he grows as strong as I am, the czar's Army will already have whatever it is the czar is now trying to get, and this will all be over." "And if it is not?" asked his wife. "Every day the talk is worse. There is talk of taking children into the Army." "Then he will run away," said Moses. "He is more intelligent than I am and he has no family to which he must cling." "He has no family!" exclaimed his wife. "He has no children," said Moses. "And where," asked his wife, "will you hide during the day? When the sun shines brightly, no one fears the vengeful spirits. The graves are covered with sobbing women asking the dead for favors. Someone will see you hiding behind a stone and shoot you for a thief!"

As if his mind moved naturally from the lowest point, the ground beneath his feet, to the highest, the roof and the sky over his head, Moses Luria answered without hesitation. "During the day I will sleep on the roof!" "Whose roof?" asked his wife; "just because you are on a roof, you are not invisible." "On a thatched roof, I can make myself invisible," he said. He began to think it out, while his wife, weeping soundlessly, watched him. "I will ask the zenshina if I can sleep on her roof," he said. "Worse than the cemetery!" wept his wife. "Is it worse than the cemetery?" he asked her. She looked at him sadly. "What makes you think she will let you sleep there?" she asked. "Nothing makes me think it. Tomorrow I will go and ask her." His wife sighed. "Do not sigh!" he shouted. The children moved in their sleep. "What must be done must be done," he whispered.

The next day he walked out to the zenshina's house. "What is it this time?" she asked him; "you are too healthy for me. I have no more tricks up my sleeve. Unless, perhaps, you would like one of my peasants to shoot you in the leg?" "God forbid," sighed Moses. "Do not sigh," said the zenshina; "sighing does no good." She watched him curiously. What plan could he have dreamed up? When Reb Luria asked her if he could sleep on her roof, the zenshina was surprised. The way she raised her eyebrows and nodded at the same time expressed her respect. "And what will you do at night?" she asked. Reb Luria explained his plan. "Why stay in two places?" she asked; "stay on the roof during the day and during the night, too." "But," stammered Reb Luria, "it is said officials of the government come to visit you at night." "Is that your concern?" the zenshina asked him; "are you their concern? If I say you can sleep on the roof, you can sleep on it. You can even fall off. No one will go out and look to see who or what has fallen off the roof. You will be safe up there."

Reb Luria looked up at the roof, which suddenly seemed as far from the ground as the sky itself. "You have a ladder?" he asked dubiously. "I have a ladder," she said. "Someone," said Reb Luria, "will have to walk all around the house and beat down the snow so that there are no footprints going up to a wall and then disappearing. My son will come out here and trample down the snow and shovel off my part of the roof." "Let him trample down each new snow," said the zenshina; "it is not necessary. No one will bother you here. It is not necessary to shovel off the roof. Dig yourself a little trench. The snow on the róof keeps the house warm and it will keep you warm, too. You ought to know that." "I do know that," Reb Luria answered, flushing. "And when may I expect you?" asked the zenshina. "On my roof, that is." "Within ten days," said Reb Luria. "My wife is not used to running a household alone. I must tell her some things."

"I would not wait ten days," said the zenshina; "I would not wait five." Reb Luria was silent. "How many would you wait?" he asked at last. "I would wait four," she said. "Four," he repeated. "Four," she said again, holding up four fingers. "On the third day," he said, "I will send my son, Esheal, to trample the snow." "It is not necessary, but if you wish to send him, send him," she said; "we are not strangers, your son and I. He comes out here to break up the bones for the fertilizer." "My little boy comes out here alone?" asked Reb Luria. "Some children are born old and brave," the zenshina said; "probably you can remember some story or other your wife told you about how the eggs suddenly became plentiful, or the ducks plump, or the potatoes many. These things happen when a child earns money." Reb Luria sighed. "There is much to sigh about in this world," said the zenshina, "if one *will* sigh."

Chapter 3

The villagers were not curious about Reb Moses Luria's many trips out to the zenshina's house. They assumed he was seeking a cure for his good health. When, one day, he was no longer to be seen in the village, his wife let it be known that he had run away in order to escape conscription. She also let it be known that her son, Esheal, had obtained work cutting wood and running errands for the zenshina. The people shuddered but said nothing. There was nothing to say. None of them could afford to support her and her three children. Everyone gave whatever he could, but still the teacher's family was half starved. The little girls were too young to work but they were old enough to eat. The mother ate little and when the children were out, hoarded her small supply of wood.

Reb Luria's wife pleaded with the families of the students to allow her to continue teaching the school as her husband had done, for her education was good, and she had learned as much as her husband had to teach her about the Bible. For a time, she was permitted to continue the teaching. Then, on an evil day, a young man came to the village. He was a teacher, and he had letters of recommendation from an important rabbi in a neighboring town. The wife of Moses Luria was desperate. The rebbitsin, to whom she went, hysterical, had a solution. The new teacher should board at the home of the old teacher, and the students, who were accustomed to coming there, would continue to do so. What could be more natural? Between the income from the boarder, the new teacher, and Esheal's daily earnings at the zenshina's, the family could live until the father returned. And so it was arranged. Anyone peeping into the teacher's house would think that nothing had changed. The children swayed back and forth, the teacher's wife moved about the kitchen preparing meals, and the two little girls ran in and out. Only the teacher had changed. It was as if Moses Luria had died and been replaced by another man, who, what's more, resembled him! Moses Luria's wife saw this and shuddered. Esheal saw this and felt fear.

It was not long before Esheal came to hate the newcomer, who, because of a lame leg, was not endangered by conscription and who so easily seemed to take the place of his father. Esheal watched him as he moved about the room, hoping he would stumble on the rough plank under which his mother hid her small pile of money. He listened to him chant the Bible, hoping he would stumble and reveal himself to everyone as the ignoramus he was. At night, Esheal, who had moved his pallet over to his mother's, watched the new teacher until he could stay awake no longer. He lived in fear of closing his eyes and then opening them again and seeing his mother together with this new teacher, who seemed to have erased his father from the Book of Life. Perhaps at night, thought Esheal, she would dream, and in her dream she would believe this man was her husband.

Esheal would not let this happen. If the man snored, the boy awakened. If the man moved in his sleep, Esheal was wide awake. Esheal watched him as he would a dangerous animal.

Once a week, he would climb up the ladder and pretend to shovel off the zenshina's roof. Then he would tell his father how he suspected the new teacher of every possible sin, and what an evil man the new teacher was. "He is not an evil man," his father admonished him in a hoarse voice; "he was sent by heaven. The rabbi's wife herself suggested he board with us. The rabbi decreed he should stay. Where would we be without him?" "Better off!" insisted the enraged boy. "We would not be better off!" shouted his father, forgetting himself; "we would be starving!" What he was going to say next was interrupted by a fit of violent coughing. "It is not healthy for you up there!" exclaimed his son. "Is a bullet healthy for me?" his father asked. He heard the boy start to cry. "I'll come back," Reb Luria said; "the zenshina will know when I can come down. Then I can come home and get rid of this cough and we will all be back where we were." In an effort to cheer his son, he continued talking. "Do you know what she's worried about? She's worried about my wetting her ceiling. She says she doesn't want to look up and see urine dripping through the roof. So when it gets dark, I get down and walk around. Sometimes I go in and sleep with the peasants. They don't bother me and the dogs are used to me. It's not as bad as you think." The boy said nothing. He went in and asked the zenshina what work she had for him now. She told him to go and groom the dogs.

When he went home, he stared at the new teacher. He studied his face; he studied his movements. There was no question about it; the man was handsome. He had a dark beard and fine dark eyes. He had heard one of the women tell his mother that the new teacher had tragic eyes, and the two women had laughed together. He studied the man as if he intended to impersonate him the next day. He asked him questions: Did he have a wife? Did he want a wife? If he wanted a wife, why didn't he have a wife? The new teacher laughed and said that things were not always that simple. From that instant, Esheal no longer expected the worst. He knew the worst had already come.

One morning in the month of Shebat, the town was startled by the cries of a peasant, and the barking of many dogs. One of the zenshina's dogsleighs had driven up in front of the teacher's house. Another sleigh soon arrived, and the two men in it got out and carried someone inside. By afternoon, everyone in the town knew that Moses Luria had returned and that Moses Luria was dying. "So he was here all along," said one of the townspeople sadly. "The czar will not get him now," said one of the women, dabbing at her eyes. "It was foolish to take such chances just to remain near his family," said one of the men in a hard, bitter voice. "Guessing what should have been is always a good game," said another man. The people stood outside the house for some time, and then drifted home. When they saw Ely the Burier start toward the teacher's house, they knew he was going to wash and dress a body. "Moses the teacher has died," said one woman, turning to her husband, who said nothing. "You should send such news to the wilderness," said the woman's mother-in-law.

Inside the house, the lamentation was terrible. Esheal made no noise but stared at the new teacher as if he himself were the angel of death who had claimed his father. But during the succeeding weeks, when calm returned to the house, Esheal's attitude toward the new teacher did not soften, and the neighbor women spoke to Esheal about his unyielding and improper attitude toward the boarder, who had, as they pointed out, nothing to do with the czar's edict, and even less to do with his father's decision to hide near the village.

Gradually, everyone in the house seemed to accept the new state of affairs. If Esheal resented the new teacher, this was no longer apparent. If Esheal knew that the border sometimes lifted the rough board in the floor and added some of his money to his mother's, he said nothing about it.

A year passed and a second year began. Soon, everyone knew that the new teacher had asked Moses Luria's widow to marry him. Everyone was surprised because the new teacher was younger than Moses' widow, although not much younger. On the other hand, the match seemed reasonable. She had already proven herself to be an excellent teacher's wife, one who could make a teacher's small income stretch further than a man could dare hope it would. Still, for a man to marry a woman who was older, although not, it is true, much older, was remarkable. But to marry a woman with three children of her own! The townspeople were astounded both by the power of the widow's charms and the generosity of the new teacher's heart. The women who had talked to Esheal congratulated themselves on their wisdom and their expert handling of a difficult situation. They did not congratulate themselves for long.

The new teacher was to marry the teacher's widow, but he had two conditions. First, he wanted to return to his own town. Second, he would take Reb Luria's daughters, but he would not take the son. The son would have to stay behind "on the town." The mother cried, the mother beat her breast, she tore her hair, she clutched Esheal to her, but in the end she decided to give him up. She had three children and two of them would have a good home if she married the new teacher. If she did not, three children would starve and she would starve along with them. Pobrosk was a poor village and there was no work for her in it. In the end, she felt she had no choice. When she told Esheal what she had decided, he did not cry. He offered to help her pack her things.

Perhaps the child did not believe that such things could really happen. He assisted his mother with the packing. He listened to the neighbors give advice about which towns were preferable to Pobrosk and why. He listened as his mother promised again and again to come back and get him. "Someday," she kept saying, "we will go to America and we will come back and get you. *I* will come back and get you!" she swore. The child nodded his head.

Finally, the appointed day of departure arrived. Esheal was up early. His eyes were wild. He could not find enough to do to help his mother and the new teacher. He knew he was to stay with the Levys for the first month, and that the second month he would stay with the Sikorskys. All this had been explained to him many times. When there were orphans in the town, and there were always many orphans, or when there were abandoned children, the families who could afford to do so took them in for a month at a time. Each month, the child lived with a different family. If he was lucky, he got a room in the house. If he was unlucky, he slept in a shed with the chickens. At last, it was twelve o'clock and the sun's weak arms began struggling to break through the heavy, silver-edged clouds. Esheal's mother kissed him goodbye and his sisters kissed him goodbye.

Slowly, the wagon carrying his mother and his sisters, the new teacher, and some sticks of furniture from the old house, began to move down the dusty road. Suddenly, the dust swirled up and hid the wagon from sight. Esheal began to run toward the wagon. "Take me with you!" he cried again and again, holding onto the back of the wagon as he ran. "Take me with you! I'll be good. I won't cause any trouble! I can earn money! Take me with you!" He heard the new teacher shouting to the driver, asking him to hurry up. He looked up into his mother's face. It was dusty, streaming with tears. The tears ran down through the dust on her cheeks as rain runs down a dusty road. "Let go!" she screamed at him. But he did not let go. He kept running with the wagon, holding onto it.

Then he saw his mother pick up a big wooden spoon. He saw her lift it into the air and saw her bring it down on his hands. Again and again, she lifted the spoon, beating his hands. It was as if he felt nothing, as if he did not see the red blood beginning to trickle down the back of his bruised left hand. But when he realized that his mother was beating his hands from the wagon, his hands gave up their hold on the rough wooden board. He stood there in the road, motionless, sobbing wildly. For a moment, the dust whirled about him and, to the villagers, it seemed as if a dust devil had caught him and was shaking him. He heard someone say, "Let him cry. It's good for him." Finally, he felt someone take his hand and he let himself be led off. Later, he was told he had been standing in the road, staring after the cart, for almost two hours.

Chapter 4

There was something terrible in the child's silence. The Levys, with whom he was to have stayed, could not stand it and sent him on to the Sikorskys. Silence was no stranger to the Sikorsky house. Morris Sikorsky, the blacksmith, was a large, surly man who would fall silent when angered. He had been known to remain silent for over three months. So Mr. Sikorsky saw nothing unusual in the child's silence. The rest of the children saw the child on the street and knew that he wanted an explanation for this outrageous development in his life, and everyone tried to give him one. It was as if the child had become a little Job, and the villagers, like Job's friends, tried to persuade him that, in spite of appearances, things were as they ought to be.

"Sometimes," said Mrs. Sikorsky, "a mother has to leave her son. Or child. Or children." She faltered under the child's gaze as if she heard him asking, "Would you leave your son?" Her heart beat faster; her cheeks grew hot. "You should thank God that you're well, that you have two good hands and can do a good day's work. When she comes back to get you, you'll go to America and work and have children of your own." "And leave them?" the child's eyebrows seemed to ask; "and leave them?" The child was soon sleeping in the shed with the chickens and the goats. Whenever he looked at Mrs. Sikorsky's own children, Mrs. Sikorsky seemed to see as if she had the child's eyes; she heard as if she had the child's ears. In the background, she heard the sound of crying. She saw her children sitting on rough wooden boxes. She and her husband were nowhere visible. "I feel unwell," she said to herself and went inside to sit by the stove.

Villagers came to see the young boy as if they were petitioners waiting their turn to extol the virtues of his mother, who had been forced to take this terrible step. They reminded him of the virtues of his father, whose son he was,

and whose memory he must honor throughout his life. When
he went into the butcher's on an errand, the butcher wiped his
bloodstained hands on his apron, and said, "You must cut her
from your life like this!" and he brought the hatchet down on
a piece of boned meat which immediately split in two. "Like
this!" said the butcher, slamming the hatchet down again.
The child said nothing. "Some mother," muttered the
butcher, "to go and leave a son like that. What kind of
mother would leave a son like that?"

Frequently, the boy went to the cemetery, where he sat
upon his father's grave because there people left him alone.
He looked at the wooden tombstone, but he had nothing to
say to his father. One day, he was surprised to find an old
woman prostrate on his father's grave. "What are you doing
here?" he asked her. She got up, brushed some twigs from
her skirt, and wiped some tears from her cheeks. Perhaps,
thought the boy, his heart beating wildly, he had a relative he
had not known about. "In Dubno," she said, "I was a paid,
professional mourner. Then I got too old for even that. I was
so old I was getting more sympathy than the corpse. So I
came home." The child nodded. He found nothing strange in
a paid, professional mourner practicing her old profession on
his father's grave. "It is always good to mourn for anyone,"
said the old woman. "There is always enough to mourn
about. Who did you come here to see?" The child pointed at
his father's grave. "Oh," said the old woman, "I'm sorry. I've
taken your place." "Sit there," said the child, who sat down
next to her. "Your father, eh?" she asked. The boy nodded.
"You are the boy whose mother went away and left you
behind?" He nodded again. "It is a rotten world," said the
old woman; "they tell you it isn't, but it is." "Why is it a
rotten world?" said the boy. "Because it is filled with men and
women," said the old woman; "if they kept the men in one
place and the women in another, it would be different." She
saw the spark of interest in the child's eyes. "It is a rotten
world," she said again, averting her eyes.

In the weeks that followed, the child became more and
more expert at whatever tasks were given him. He seemed
like a person hungry for work. He could not get enough of it,
and when he had no more work to do at the Sikorskys, he
would walk the twelve versts to the zenshina's house and then
walk back to the town in the middle of the night even though
the dark wolves howled and the spirits flew about. He feared

one thing only, and that was idleness. He slept when he could no longer keep his eyes open and he would have preferred to go without sleep altogether. After his first week alone, he no longer went to the dry-goods store to ask if any letter had arrived for him. He seemed to have taken the butcher's advice and cut his past life, which was only three weeks gone, from his new life, which was three weeks old. But during the second week of the second month, when he was boarding with the Berchinskys, he woke up late at night, thought about his father's grave and the old woman who visited it, thought about America and how he would like to see it someday, and about his mother, whom he would also like to see someday, and about the new teacher, whom he would like never to see again. The more he thought, the longer the list of things he never wanted to see again became. He decided that he would walk out into the fields, and when he was far from town, he would throw himself into a snowdrift. The townspeople would think he had lost his way.

But when he began walking, perhaps because of the tricks of moonlight, which made the vast, snowy fields seem to roll like a sea, or perhaps because he was so tired, the boy lost all sense of where he was. A sharp wind was blowing from the dark forest on the horizon, and its rattle in the dead leaves of the willow bushes was dry and papery. He stood still to listen to the leaves rubbing against each other like thin, parchment hands. Poor trees, he thought, they are trying to warm themselves. He sat down in the snow to keep the trees company. His back rested comfortably against the wall of snow surmounting one side of the zenshina's path. The rustling, papery leaves began to sound like the rustling slip his mother sometimes wore. I am far away from the town, he thought. I can go to sleep here. The trees kept rubbing their hands together. Their hands were cold, he thought, as he stuffed his own into his pockets. The sharp, dry wind blew some soft snow down from the drift and onto the boy's cap, and in the distance, the great pines bent and moaned in the wind, but the boy was already asleep.

Chapter 5

"So," said the zenshina, when the little boy finished his story, "first your father left you. Then your mother left you. What now?" The boy stared down at his feet. "I'm staying here," he said. "What?" asked the woman. "I'm staying here," the boy said again. The zenshina got up and walked once around the room. Then she stopped in back of the boy's chair. "First," she said, "the father sleeps *on* the roof. Then the child comes and says he's going to live *under* my roof. What," she asked, turning to the child, "am I to make of it? Where will it all end?" "With my staying here," Esheal answered stubbornly. The woman sat down on the bench and faced the child. "With your staying here?" she repeated. "And what will you do here?" "Work," he said. "The peasants do all the work," she said. "You always had work for me to do before," he said. "I always *found* work for you to do before," she said. The child flushed.

The two of them sat, staring at each other like old antagonists. "You cannot sleep in the house," said the zenshina finally; "this house is no place for a child to sleep." The child stared at her and remembered some of the women in the village talking together. "She sleeps with the peasants," he had heard one of them say, and then his mother caught sight of him and chased him into the house. But once inside, he had crawled along the wall until he found himself below the open window. "With the peasants!" the baker's wife exclaimed. "Of course, that's only what they say," said his mother. "They say her grandmother married a Jew," said the baker's wife. "Who married a Jew?" asked the tailor's wife, stopping in her tracks and joining the others. The boy saw her shadow fall across the shining, planked floor. "The zenshina's great-grandmother," said his mother. "So?" said the tailor's wife; "that's so remarkable? To marry a Jew? The men in this village do it all the time." "But she's supposed to be descended from the royal house of Liechtenstein," said his mother. "I thought she was a Hapsburg," said the tailor's wife. "Whoever she is, they say she sleeps with peasants," said the baker's wife. "She didn't get that habit from her Jewish great-grandmother," said his mother. "Is that smoke I see coming out of my window?" asked the baker's wife; "it *is* smoke!" All the women ran down the street to help her put out the fire, if it was a fire. Usually, smoke and gossip went together. Gossiping women let dinners burn.

Inside the house, Esheal remained sitting under the window, his legs stretched out in front of him. He watched the sunlight shrink across the kitchen floor and slowly approach his toes. The zenshina's great-grandmother had married a Jew! She was a Hapsburg or a Liechtenstein or both! And she slept with peasants. Now *there* was a mystery. Why hadn't the women wanted him to hear them talking about that? His own mother slept in a house with a new teacher who was not even a relative. He had turned it over countless times, but could make nothing of it, and so he had given it up.

"If you found work for me before," said Esheal, who had decided that, if it was time to sell his life, he would sell it as dearly as possible, "you can find work for me to do again."

"Listen to me," said the zenshina, turning on him; "didn't you keep your ears open in the village? I'm a witch! I have powers. I can cast spells. When the living die, I do not cry for them. I say good riddance. Your rabbis call me evil. They say I am possessed. I can see into the future. When it is quiet, I can hear people talking even though they are miles away and their doors and their shutters are closed. Why do you want to live here?"

"Why not?" asked Esheal; "you can teach me magic. I want to listen to people talking even though they are miles away."

"No, you don't," said the zenshina; "you don't know what you're talking about. All those voices. It's like living without a skin."

"You only think you hear them," said the little boy; "you really *don't* hear them."

The zenshina stared at him in astonishment. When had anybody last spoken to her like this? "If you stay here," she said at last, "you have to do something. A boy like you should be in school." She said this slowly, her eyes on the boy, as if her ideas concerning children were hidden behind a door with a rusty key, which she was now turning slowly and painfully.

"I'll never go to school again!" he said.

"You should learn to read," she said, her eyebrows furrowing. The sound of her own words seemed to puzzle her.

"I can read," said Esheal.

"You should learn to read Russian. And English."

"Do you know English?" the boy asked her.

"I do," she said. "You must learn English because your mother said she was coming back to get you and take you to America. In America, they speak English."

"Who," he asked, "is going to teach me to read English? Or Russian? I have no money."

"I will teach you," the zenshina said. "In return, you must do some things for me. You must study certain things. Like the onion. You must study the onion until you can see inside the onion. At least, you must try to see inside the onion." The little boy considered this and concluded that the zenshina was indeed a meshuggeneh. "I do not want to study the onion," he said, "but I want to learn how to give people leaves and teas and make them well."

"That," said the zenshina, "is out of the question. To cure others, one must be grown-up and responsible. What do you say to my conditions?" she asked him.

"I will study the onion, but not English," the little boy said solemnly. "I will not study English because my mother will not come back and get me."

"She may come back," said the zenshina.

"If she comes back, I will not go," he said. "My father's sister is already in America. My father wrote her before he ran away from the Army. She said she will send for me."

"She had better send for you before you get much older," said the zenshina; "the czar is hungry for more recruits. Soon people will know you are here. They will send you off to draw in the lottery because then their sons will be less likely to go. You cannot stay here long. Only until the coming summer's end."

So it was arranged. The zenshina found Esheal a very quick pupil, and it seemed to Esheal that the zenshina found his rapid progress disappointing. Within weeks, he was reading simple stories; within a month, he had progressed to books. He did not proceed so quickly with the onion. Every day, at three o'clock, the hour when he had been accustomed to attend cheder, he sat on the bench facing the zenshina's table. Every day, at three o'clock, the zenshina set a peeled, whole onion before him. The boy had to sit before the onion, staring at it, for two hours. He was not permitted to eat while he contemplated the onion. Squirming while watching the onion was not permitted. Days passed. When the outer, cloudy layer of the onion, which in some lights seemed to resemble the ice on a wintry river, began to yellow and separate from the body of the onion, the zenshina would replace it with a new, carefully peeled onion.

After several weeks of staring at onions, Esheal was able to say that it not only resembled the icy surface of the river, but was also the color of a winter sky which seemed to have hardened and diffused through the translucent onion flesh. The zenshina did not seem pleased. "Go out and help the peasants patrol the fields!" she ordered. "What am I supposed to say about an onion?" the boy demanded desperately. "Go out and help the peasants patrol!" shouted the zenshina, sweeping the onion from the table with the side of her hand. Esheal watched the hated onion roll into a corner of the kitchen where, like a mouse, it hid itself in a dark corner. This did not cheer him. The zenshina's cupboard was full of onions. "I'll try again tomorrow," he said hopelessly. "Out and patrol!" she said, turning from him.

The inhabitants of Pobrosk, like the inhabitants of many other snowbound towns, feared the encompassing winter snows into which many a man ventured and from which many a man did not return. The zenshina, whose peasants on dogsleds were constantly searching the fields for feathers, seeds, and dead leaves, ordered her peasants to inspect anything unusual in the snow. In particular, they were instructed to inspect anything that looked like a hole through which someone might have fallen; they were to investigate anything large which seemed to have stopped moving in the snow. During the many years that the zenshina had lived twelve versts from the town, only one man had frozen to death, and he had frozen to death within the town limits.

Before Esheal's arrival, following the zenshina's orders had tried the courage of the peasants who were often too heavy to walk safely on the snow toward the suspicious object. Since Esheal was light and small, he was sent to inspect anything unusual in the snow. But when he had twice fallen through the snow, and twice been hauled out by the peasants who threw him a rope from their sleds, a new method was devised to ensure his safety. He had been provided with a metal rod, to which the peasants attached heavy iron weights. Now, when Esheal left the sleigh, he dragged this stick along the snow behind him, and, before venturing onto more dangerous ground, would throw the weights before him. If the weights sank through the crackling surface of the snow, the peasants sighed, shouldered their shovels, and began digging a path to the object in question. Esheal had found one dead goose and one dead dog, and he dreaded finding what the zenshina had sent him out to find.

One morning when the wide blue sky vaulted over the wide fields of snow, tinting them blue, Esheal returned from one of his patrols and sat down at the table. Although it was still early, the onion was already in its accustomed place. He began to stare at the onion. Perhaps because his eyes had grown so accustomed to looking at the snow, so that, even when he closed his eyes, he saw drift after drift rolling into the distance before him, perhaps because the blue walls of the zenshina's kitchen were reflected in the polished surface of the onion, the onion looked more than ever like the color of snow. No, thought the boy, it looked like the *spirit* of snow. He was cold and tired, and waves of heat pulsed from the huge stove. The air outside was so cold, and the air just inside the walls was so cold that the heat caused all the familiar, spare objects in the room to waver, as if everything material had suddenly become immaterial. The chair in the corner of the room wavered as if it were not yet solid, but was about to become so. The iron stove itself wavered as if it were about to change its shape.

The sleepy child stared from one thing to another; the chair was doing its slow, wavering dance. The candle on the shelf was undulating as if it had just remembered that it was a snake. Esheal stared at the onion. It stared back at him. It was the only thing in the room which remained stubbornly, silently the same. He sighed, and leaned his head on his hand. "Do not sigh," he heard his father say, and he smiled. He was falling asleep. Soon he would be dreaming. For once, he was not afraid of his dreams.

He was inside the onion looking out from its center. He was surprised to find that he could see out through the onion as easily as he could see through glass. Perhaps that was because the onion was so large or because the layers were not pressed so closely together as they were in a smaller onion. He saw that the outermost layer of the onion was the sky and that it wrapped around everything. It wrapped around his father's grave, and around his mother's new village where she was living with his two sisters and the new teacher. It wrapped around the zenshina's house and all the houses the zenshina had ever lived in. In different layers, different figures moved as if they were floating; a little boy who resembled his father, and who he immediately understood was his father, an older boy with his hair parted on the side whose mouth was pulled down at one corner into a silly grimace, whose eyes were two soft brown smudges, and he knew that he was looking at himself, as he had existed several years before. Other, distinct figures tried to approach him, and as they came closer, he saw that they were trying to talk to him. As he sat in the center of the onion, he saw that he could move easily from one layer to another, and he also saw that wherever he went, all the layers of the onion would always be around him. He saw that the longer he lived, the further toward the center of the onion he would travel until finally he would remain there forever. So, he thought, my outermost skin is the rain, and the mists and the snow, and the earth is the marrow of my bones. He saw that his mother had not gone far from him and he saw that he would go far from others and would not move from them at all.

He began to cry. The zenshina, who had been watching him from a corner of the room, sat down on a bench opposite him and examined him carefully. "Did you like what you saw?" she asked. "I don't know," he said; "I think I liked it." "Do you have any choice?" she asked. He did not answer her. "And if your mother came to get you now? Would you go?"

"If you have only one relative, and she comes and gets you," he said, "you go. In the onion, I saw you dancing."

"You were dreaming," she said; "I do not dance."

"In the onion," he insisted, "you were dancing."

"I was dancing in the onion?" she asked him; "and your people call me the meshuggeneh? Stop crying and bring in some wood. Bring your book. One half-hour of reading aloud."

Weeks passed and slid into months. Spring came, and then summer, and still the zenshina did not suggest that it was time for the boy to leave. The many couriers who came to her house said nothing to alarm her about the boy's safety. Every week, she wrote a letter to the boy's aunt, had Esheal sign it,

and then sent him into Pobrosk to mail it. Every week, he
posted the letter to America, but he expected no answer.
During the day, he groomed the zenshina's dogs; he weeded
the zenshina's garden. He worked with the peasants in the
zenshina's fields. When she sent him into town, the townspeople smiled at him sadly, and did not mention his mother. They
did not seem to see him as clearly as they saw one another.

It was as if he had become a very vivid, but nevertheless
insubstantial ghost. It was as if he had already left for
America. Whenever he walked through the crooked little
streets of the town, he noted who had painted his house, who
had mended his fence, and whose wooden walkway was in
need of repair. He would walk past the house in which he had
lived since his birth and in which strangers now lived. He saw
that the loose shutter had been securely fastened to the house
wall. The cracked pane in the window nearest the door had
been replaced. He returned with relief to the zenshina's.

The zenshina now set the onion before him for only one
hour a day. Consequently, he had more time to himself and
often found himself wandering in the fields just at twilight.
One night in the month of Elul, he was walking in the fields
near the village. The wild grasses began not one hundred feet
from the outermost house. The sun was setting, and in back
of the jagged, black outline of the forest, the sky was a striped
garment of rose and silver. The larks had begun singing
madly, as they always did at twilight and before the coming of
a storm. Because Esheal was staring at the horizon, he did not
immediately notice the groups of black-coated men hurrying
from the village. They were walking in the direction of the
forest. Esheal followed, out of sight, walking through the tall
grass.

He knew that the men were following the ancient command
to greet the new moon, which would tonight be reborn in the
heavens just as if God had that instant made it with his own
two hands. Esheal followed their black, familiar, anonymous
backs. When they were out of sight of the town, they stopped
and looked up at the heavens. They opened their worn prayer
books, and the pages gleamed like white moths fluttering in
the darkness. The town seemed far away, as if it had sunk into
the wide land. The men moved close to one another, forming
a tight group, and in soft voices began to read the prayer of
greeting to the moon. The wheat swayed back and forth in the
wind; the men swayed back and forth as they prayed. As

they swayed, their prayers became louder. The wind rose and the wheat rustled. The distant trees rustled and swayed. In the distance, a wolf howled and another wolf answered. The dogs heard the wolf and began barking loudly. Finally, the men concluded the blessing and closed their prayer books. They wished each other a healthy, prosperous month and began drifting to their homes.

Esheal, who was watching the men, stayed where he was. He saw the men disappear, one by one, within the enfolding curve of the village. He heard door after door slam, shutter after shutter slam into place. The new moon was bright and curved like a scythe. By its light, which sifted down like a fine powder, Esheal could see the metal fence around the cemetery. Its glint was visible between the houses which were set apart enough to reveal the fields on their far side. It seemed to him that he saw someone enter the cemetery as if he were, like the other men, returning to his home. The boy waited, as if he were waiting for something very important, but nothing happened. The wind died down; the wind rose. The grass bent to the ground; the grass rose as the wind passed by. In the distance, the dark forest waited as it had waited for centuries. The forest expected no miracles. The boy sighed and began to walk the twelve versts to the zenshina's house.

That night, he woke out of a deep sleep as if someone had called his name. He listened until he was sure he had not been awakened by the peasants' peculiar alarm clock. The clock consisted of a long candle and a string which was stretched between two sticks. A weight was suspended from this string, and when the candle burned down, it burned through the string which dropped the weight with a clatter into a metal pan. Esheal knew that whatever peasant was awakened by this clock got up and went to the zenshina's house and spent the night there. He was no longer ignorant and knew why the peasants went to the house for the night.

One of them had asked him if he wouldn't like to have a woman of his own, and he said he would. "What kind would you like, little Jew?" the peasant had laughed, slapping him on the shoulder. The boy did not answer him. He wanted someone like his mother, but he also wanted someone who would not leave him. He wanted someone like the zenshina, but he wanted a woman who would be faithful only to him, like the widow of Zecheriah the tailor who refused to let even her own sons touch her flesh. When he walked into the village with his weekly letters to America, he would see one girl after another, and each one made him happy. They were so delicate and so quick! But it was impossible to know if they could be trusted. Certainly, they did not trust him, a Jewish boy who lived in the unclean home of the zenshina, who had shaved his curls and wore peasant clothes. In America, he thought, he might find the woman he wanted. Young as he was, he knew he might be looking for something which did not exist, something impossible. But I will make it exist, he told himself, and that thought brought him comfort.

Esheal peered into the depths of the barn and saw the candle still burning far above the string and the weights. He got up and went outside. The night was dark, the stars bright, and the forest an inky outline far away. The dogs heard him, recognized him, and did not bark. He walked along the edge of the barn until he was close to the zenshina's house and then followed the darkest shadows until he reached the window to the left of her door. Pressing himself against the open shutter, he looked in.

The zenshina had lighted every lamp in the room. The rusty tin reflectors behind each chimney sent the light of the flame spiking back into the room so that the room seemed to be filled with thin swords of light. In the middle of the room, the zenshina stood at the head of the table. She bowed to it as if she were bowing to a partner. He saw her raise one hand above her head while she placed her other hand lightly on her hip. Then she began to twirl. The twirling dance flowed smoothly into a complicated dance in which the zenshina, her feet bound in rags, advanced toward the table, her feet twinkling in intricate steps. Then she would raise her left foot in the air, twirl it, lower it, raise her right foot, twirl it, lower it, and retreat from the table. She did this many times. Then, still with one hand on her hip, the other curving above her head, she began twirling again, but faster and faster. Esheal was sure she would fall, but she did not fall. She stopped suddenly, as if at a signal, curtsied deeply to the expressionless table, extended her hand in its direction, and as if someone were leading her by the hand, allowed herself to be led to the table where she sat down on the bench. Her cheeks glowed bright red under her beautiful red shawl and each of its golden threads sparkled and seemed to jump up from the fabric like little golden snakes.

As Esheal watched, she removed the kerchief. Her heavy

coils of hair were pinned securely to her head. He watched
her remove the pins from her hair and then shake her head
violently as if she were terribly impatient to free it. The heavy
hair fell suddenly. It spilled right onto the table. Esheal was
astonished to see how blackly it shone in the lamplight. She
looked so young. As he watched, she lowered her head onto
her arms and began to cry, a low, inconsolable cry that rose
until it rivaled and matched the wind moaning around the
house. He felt a lump forming in his own throat. He
wondered why she was crying and what he could do to stop
her. But the woman he watched was beyond consolation.

It occurred to him that she had probably suffered at the
hands of men. All women seemed to suffer at the hands of the
men whose lives entwined with theirs. He thought of his
mother and saw her crying, tearing her clothes, begging her
new husband to take all her children with them when they
left. He saw his mother crying hopelessly over his father's
body. Once again, he heard his mother trying to dissuade his
father from hiding on the zenshina's roof. But his mother had
not been able to influence either man. In an ideal world, he
thought, women would not be dependent on men. Their
circumstances would not force them into ill-considered mar-
riages; their circumstances would not force them to abandon
their children.

But the world was not ideal. Esheal looked up at the stars,
which seemed to be watching him. He felt the wind touch his
cheeks and his hands and saw the fine rain which had begun to
fall scatter the smoke coming out of the zenshina's chimney.
He saw how the cloud and the wind and the rain took care of
the earth. He looked in the window at the sobbing woman.
He would find a woman in America and take care of her as
the wind took care of the crops in the earth. And he would
take care of his mother, too, if she came back.

Just then he heard the sound of heavy, stumbling feet, a
low curse, and a dog snarling. "Out of my way or I'll kick you
again," said Pyotr the peasant. Esheal slipped quietly around
the side of the house. The candle must have burned through
the string. He heard Pyotr's gruff voice and the zenshina's
sharp answer. There would be no more weeping tonight.
Esheal promised himself that no women he loved would ever
come to this. Women had to be protected, and he would
protect them.

Back on his pallet, under his covers, Esheal listened to the rain gain in strength. Every now and then, a flash of lightning lit up the barn, frightened the horses who neighed and the dogs who howled. He got up and went outside to the corral in which the dogs were kept and found Kopatchnik, his favorite dog, snoring with the others under the little lean-to which formed one side of the enclosure. He coaxed the dog into the barn and into lying down on his pallet with him. Terezkov, the peasant, opened his eyes, saw the boy and the dog, muttered something, and fell back asleep.

Esheal knew that the streets of the town were turning to mud, and that tomorrow the mud would be knee-deep. He saw the townspeople walking on the planks between their houses. He heard the slap, slap, slap of their long coats against their high leather boots. With his head on the dog's belly, he saw each of the poor wooden houses, each with its corkscrew of smoke dispersed by the slanting rain. He thought about each house, and how each house and each family was its own complete world, breathing its own air, living in its own light, speaking with the language of the same blood. He wondered where his own family was. But he wanted his own family, his own children. "It will take a very long time," he told Kopatchnik; "first I will have to leave Russia and go to America." He looked at the dog and wished that she could also go to America. The dog lifted her head and growled. He apologized to the dog for disturbing her. He put his head back down on her belly. He felt the dog stretch her body beneath him and he fell asleep thinking that in the morning, he would have to inspect himself for lice and fleas.

Chapter 6

The next day was hot and sultry. Esheal helped the peasants groom the horses and the dogs. He stared dutifully at the onion on the table. He studied his Russian books. The books were insane in their variety. The zenshina gave him whatever books she had and whatever books people brought her. He had read novels, treatises on philosophy, handbooks of chemistry and physics, an eerie work on the transmigration of souls. The heat made the books seem heavy and the words long. The first cool breeze made Esheal yearn for the town. When he arrived, the sun was setting and the eastern windows of the houses blazed red and gold. As he walked down the crooked street toward his house, or the house which had been his, darkness settled on the village. As if the dark were a signal to the people in the houses, doors began to open. The women were carrying out chairs and seating themselves before their front doors in order to gossip and make the most of the sweet, cool air. The men, on their way to the synagogue and evening prayers, greeted each other with a nod or a brief word. Women began getting up from their chairs and drifting to the doorways of nearby houses. They would stand there gossiping, and if the gossip was interesting enough, would return to their own houses, pick up their chairs, and join the women at the other house. Someone flew out of one of the houses and ran off in the direction of the doctor's. All the women observed this and drew their own conclusions, either silently or out loud. No one seemed to notice Esheal as he moved along the planks above the mud.

He thought that he would cross the village and come out into the fields on the other side of it without anyone noticing him when Deborah, the glazier's wife, ran up behind him and seized him by the back of his jacket. "There's a letter for you at the dry-goods store," she said, "from America!" "From America!" he repeated. "And don't forget who told you the news," said Deborah, looking at him meaningfully. Esheal turned around and began walking toward the dry-goods store. He picked up his letter and had not gone fifty feet beyond the store when Sarah, the cobbler's wife, ran up behind him and seized him by the shoulders. "Go to the synagogue!" she gasped. "There's a man sleeping there who's looking for you!" "A man sleeping in the synagogue?" Esheal echoed in astonishment. "A man from Targi," said Sarah, still panting. "He slept in the synagogue last night. Go see what he wants!" Astounded, clutching his unopened letter, Esheal hurried in the direction of the synagogue. The men were just leaving and as he came up to the synagogue door, they all stared at him curiously.

The man from Targi had already curled up on the front bench of the synagogue. He was still chewing some bread when Esheal came up to him. "Sarah, the cobbler's wife, told me you came to see me," he said to the man. The man grunted and sat up. "Are you the Luria boy?" he asked. Esheal said he was. "I have a letter for you," said the man, "and some money. Look how she sealed it up. She didn't trust me." The little package of money bore an elaborate wax seal. "Imagine wasting money on something like that," grumbled the man; "as if I couldn't have opened it and taken it to someone else and gotten them to seal it up again. Women aren't worth much." Esheal tore open the letter.

"It's from your mother," said the man, watching him. "What does she say?" "She says," said Esheal, his voice trembling, "that she wants me to meet her in Stettin, in Germany. I am to go to Riga and take a boat to Stettin and there I will find the shipping company that will take us to America. She says she has sent me four rubles for the trip, but that no one knows she has sent me the money." "When are you supposed to meet her?" the man asked. He was interested, even respectful. "In ten days," said Esheal; "they will wait for me until I get there. The ship's company has barracks they can sleep in until I come. She says to take a good supply of bread, enough to eat until I get to Stettin because it is hard to find kosher food when you are traveling."

The man looked him over. "The men here say you no longer eat kosher food," he said. "What of it?" asked the boy; "she left me here to take care of myself!" "Don't take it wrong, little man," the stranger said. "You should think up some story for your mother, that's all I meant." "I don't need stories," shouted the boy. "Do what you want!" the man shouted back at him; "I've given you the letter and the money. Now I'm going to sleep." He stretched out on the bench and turned his back on the boy.

Esheal walked home, stunned, listening to the cries of the frogs in the distant swamp. He already seemed to be in Stettin, speaking to his mother, looking at his two sisters and, over their shining heads, at the new teacher. Then he would be in America. The wind bore the sweet, damp smell of newly mown grain toward him. All this already seemed alien. As he approached the zenshina's house, he heard Kopatchnik's wail and heard her jumping against the gate, straining at her chain. He would come out and get her later. He hoped that the dog would not keep jumping and rub her neck raw.

"So," said the zenshina when he walked in, "we have a letter." "No," said Esheal; "we have two." The zenshina got up from the bench and sat down in the chair near the window. "And?" she said; "what do the letters say?" He told her what his mother's letter said. "So you will go," she said; "you once said that when a person has only one living relative and she comes to get you, of course you must go." "She didn't come to get me," said Esheal. "This is the same thing," said the zenshina; "what does the other letter say?"

"The other letter!" the boy exclaimed, and began slapping himself all over. He had hidden the letter inside his sleeve. Finally, he heard the sound of crackling paper. "Here it is," he said, and tore it open. "I can't read it," he said; "I can't read the letter."

"Give it to me," said the zenshina. She looked at it briefly. "Of course you can't read it," she said. "It's written in English." She looked at him for a long time. "Now don't you think you should have studied English?" she asked him. She did not wait for an answer, but began reading the letter. "This is from your Aunt Dora," she said, looking sternly at Esheal. "She says she lives in something called Houston Street in something called an apartment and she has four boarders. She says you are her brother's son and she will always have room for you. Next week she will send all the money you need for a ticket." The zenshina looked up and took a deep breath. "That's all very nice," she said, "but you don't have any papers."

In the silence that followed, there was something expectant, quivering, as if the zenshina hoped that the boy would say, well, since I don't have any papers, I will stay where I am. The boy averted his eyes. He listened to Kopatchnik howling and heard her straining at her leash. "Then how am I to get across the border?" he asked. "You will be smuggled across," said the zenshina. The boy sighed. "Do not sigh," said the zenshina; "you have nothing to sigh about." "But," said Esheal, "there have been no smugglers here since the gang of thieves moved to Bytok." "This is a different kind of smuggler," said the zenshina. "Call Terezkov. I will send him for the man who will take you across." "When will he take me?" Esheal asked. The zenshina calculated rapidly. "You should be over the border in two or three days. A man will meet you there and take you to Stettin. Then you can decide where you will go, with your mother to her new house, or to your Aunt Dora's."

"Now that I am going," said Esheal, who had been made both rash and bolder by the unexpected excitement, "may I ask who you were? Before you came here?" The zenshina looked at him. "A rich woman," she said. "What are you now?" the boy asked. This time the zenshina hesitated before she answered. "A rich woman," she said again. "You are not a princess?" the boy asked. "I am no princess," she said; "but I might be a countess." "Are you a countess?" he asked. "Stranger things have happened," said the zenshina. "If you are a countess, what are you doing here?" asked the boy. "Do you still think it makes any difference where one lives?" she asked. She smiled bitterly. Just then Terezkov came in. "Well," she said, "*you* are going to America to become a prince. Go out and get Kopatchnik," she said; "I'll see to the arrival of your escort." "But who will pay him?" asked Esheal. He knew how expensive it was to take someone without papers across the border. "Go out and get Kopatchnik!" shouted the zenshina.

Chapter 7

Two days later, a strange man in a wagon was waiting in front of the zenshina's house. Terezkov shook Esheal out of a deep sleep. The boy picked up his cloth-wrapped bundle and came out of the barn. The morning air was fresh and sweet; the new blue sky was streaked with pink. Never before had Esheal sensed so acutely the essential malevolence of the world, unfolding this beautiful day as if to say that no matter where he went or when, he would never find anything to equal it. A flock of ravens flew overhead cawing loudly. Esheal watched them, astonished. Ravens never flew together in such harmony as he saw them flying now. He knew that the day would not relent, that it would continue to mock him with its variety and its splendor, with the enormity of its dark forests against its pale skies, with the beating of huge, dark ducks' wings against a swiftly traveling cloud, with the colors of wheat, changing from brown to gold as the wind bent the wheat down and then let it go. The day knew that he would not see these sights again and the day would not let him forget it.

He walked into the zenshina's house. "Here," she said, handing him a huge burlap bag. "Food. For your trip. It's a little dry. I left the tray in the oven too long." "It's fine," said Esheal. "It is?" she said; "there's a bread knife in the bag." "Good," he said. "Take this money," she said, handing him an envelope; "when you learn to write English, send me a letter." The boy nodded. He could not speak. "Well," said the zenshina, pointing to the man in the blue soldier's cap, "go with him." Esheal wanted to say something to her, but could think of nothing. "Goodbye," he said; "and thank you." "You are very welcome," she said. "Ask Terezkov to take care of Kopatchnik," he said. She nodded and turned to look out the window. "The horses are ready," she said. "Should I kiss you?" he asked in a small voice. "Why not?" she said, and held out her hand. The boy kissed it and burst into tears. The zenshina shook her head. Then he ran out the door and climbed into the cart.

Chapter 8

In Bytok, Esheal's guide exchanged the wagon for horses. For the next three days they rode toward the border. They progressed so slowly because they wanted to avoid the railroads and the patrols that rode along it. As they traveled, Esheal's guide named each town, told him the names of the people who lived there, what sort of business they were in, and which villages were rendezvous for thieves. They often left the main road and found their way quickly along hidden paths. At times they entered the forest and rode into it so deeply that the only light which reached them filtered down as narrow, milky shafts. But when they came out, the guide always knew where they were. Before two o'clock of the second night, they came up to a tavern. The tavern stood in the middle of wide, empty fields. The smell of a swamp mingled with the smell of wet grass. The voices of frogs mingled with the voices of crickets. "This is a good night to cross the border," said Esheal. "No, it's not a good night," said his guard. "Bad weather makes a good night. The patrols cannot see so well with rain in their eyes."

The two of them went in and sat down at a table. The man behind the bar winked at them. Esheal drank something dark and began to feel very tired. He took a hard cookie from the bag the zenshina had given him and ate it. Just then, he heard the sound of a shot. The man came out from behind the counter, took off his apron, and put on his cap. "The border patrol is gone for the night," he said to the boy; "come with me." Esheal followed the man outside. They walked without speaking, and they walked for a long time. Finally, the man turned around and ordered Esheal to lie down. He lay with one ear pressed against the ground, listening for footsteps, his other ear filling with the song of the crickets. When he heard none, they continued walking. At last, they came to a wide ditch. The man pointed out a hut and told Esheal that was the sentry hut and the blinking light was the sentry light.

"Let's go," the man said. He and Esheal crossed the trench. Just then came the sound of a shot. "Don't worry," said the man; "he has to fire a shot but he's paid to aim at the moon. Well," he said; "you're over." "Where am I?" asked Esheal. "In Poland," said the man; "Kraznowitz will be here in an hour to take you on to Stettin." "Am I supposed to pay you something?" said Esheal, sitting down on the ground to wait for the arrival of the next stranger. "No, you shouldn't pay me anything," said the man. He looked annoyed. "A healthy and prosperous voyage," he said, going back across the ditch. Again, a shot rang out. Esheal watched the man until he disappeared from sight.

The rest of the journey was uneventful, unremarkable, as if even while it was taking place, it was trying to erase itself on the boy's memory. At night, the boy slept in the bottom of the wagon while Kraznowitz drove. Then he seemed to hear the mechanical voices of the people in his village, the quick twitter of the newly dead, the long, slow song of those who had been dead and sleeping for a long time. The zenshina danced and sang to these voices and they sang back to her, while outside, the frogs told stories about those who had long since ceased to exist.

Esheal stood in the entrance to the shipping company's barracks and wondered how he would recognize his mother. At once, he was enveloped by arms, hair, a familiar smell, and his cheeks were wet with someone else's tears. When he could see again, he saw his mother holding his face between her two hands, looking down at him and crying uncontrollably. He felt perfectly happy. She led him over to his sisters and his stepfather. Esheal opened his bag of cookies and offered some to them, but they refused, saying that they had already eaten. He wondered if they knew where and how he had been living. Everyone began talking at once. He told them about the man who had come with the letter and that reminded him of the letter he had gotten from his aunt in America the very same day. "Good," said the new teacher, his stepfather, "then you can live with your aunt. You won't be far from us." Esheal looked at his mother, who started to say something and then changed her mind. He started to cry and, although he felt terribly ashamed, he could not stop. His mother pulled him into her lap and pressed his head into her bosom, and so they sat for the next hour, his mother staring defiantly over his head at her husband.

Several weeks later, the zenshina stood in her courtyard reading a letter. It said, "I have come to America. It is made out of gray stone. That is a good thing. Each street must hold up so many people. From the ship, America looked like a castle. From closer, it looked like a cemetery. I go to school now and soon will go to high school. I learned much English on the boat. The Russian-English dictionary was unfound until most of the cookies in the bag were eaten by me. If I could not say a word, I asked the steward on the ship and he gave me help. I must decide what to be. At night, I shovel coal and paint cellars. All have ideas about what I should be. My stepfather, the new teacher, wants me to shovel coal always—days and nights. You gave me very much money. I give some to my mother. You gave me so much money I can go to school in the day. I live at my aunt's. The new teacher did not want me. There I sleep on the floor. My bed is a door. It was in a stony yard and I carried it up. At night, my mattress is all my clothes on top of the door. My pillow is my jacket. On my way to shovel, I stop to see my mother. My stepfather works in a tailor's shop. He wants to be a teacher again. He says this country steps upon him. Soon I will write again. My cousin Minnie gave me much help in writing this letter."

So, thought the zenshina, crumpling the letter, that is the end of the child. That night, the dead in the cemetery sang to her more loudly and more insistently than ever before.

BOOK TWO

AMERICA

Chapter 9

Esheal: 1949

Once again, I have decided to write down the story of my life. This is the second time I am trying it. Before, I did not get too far and I will probably not get too far now. I want to see if there is anything in it; a life should not be a book full of blank pages.

The first time I tried to tell the story of my life, I saw that I had vividly conveyed a sense of what the woman who raised me was like, while I myself seemed to have remained vague and indefinable, as if I were a cloud that the wind was scattering down the sky even while I talked. For some time I thought the trouble was that a child was cloudy and unformed, and since that was the case, I could naturally give no clear picture of myself.

Now, when I reread the sheets I wrote during the last few months while the pharmacy was empty, I see that I am still cloudy and that the characters who come alive are the women, the women in my family and in my wife's. They are the only figures on the plain, which is hopelessly gray and flat, and they are gigantic, marble figures. Long ago their flesh lost its warmth and its ability to generate warmth in others. They are cold as stone because that is what they are. The light in this scene does not seem to come from the sky, which is gray and flat as the land the women stand on, but from somewhere inside the statues of the women themselves. This may be why, in the landscape I have created of them, they cast no shadows. Where are they standing? What are they standing on? The gray ground, when I look at it carefully, has the same pattern as the tiled floor of this shop, which means that the land they are standing on is mine, although they are insensible of that. They give little thought to whose land they stand on. No one pays much attention to the land beneath his feet.

In one light, the women seem to be huge figures on a chessboard, and then what is strange is the absence of male figures. The women have moved from space to space and, against all laws of probability, have removed all the men. And whenever I attempt to tell the story of my life, this is the landscape I seem to create, and in it, I am nowhere visible. And every so often, women come in and stand near the display in the storefront where I keep the cosmetics and the powders and the pictures illustrating how they could look if only they had that powder, and when they stop moving, I no longer see them as women. My eyes no longer seek out the curves of their bodies; I forget the ways their eyes watch me watching them and against the gray sky darkening outside the window, they too look like marble statues, statues dressed in draperies of sensible black. And when I see the women standing in front of the window as if they were frozen, as if their flesh had frozen, turned to stone, the other women in the other landscape seem to take their places and then I see that those women are like stone carvings in a cemetery and the landscape they inhabit is the landscape of death. Then I am glad to be nowhere about and I am sorry for them and their victory.

But this is not my usual view of the scene. Usually, when I see the women, I feel terribly lonely, as if these women had somehow destroyed the women of flesh and blood and taken their place, as a stone statue in a cemetery takes the place of the living person. But I envy the women because they are happy together. At least that is what their smiles seem to be saying, that they do not need men, that without men they are at peace.

So I have begun the story of my life knowing that I am likely to become the character no one sees, the one who is least vivid. I do this for myself because I hope that perhaps someone who reads this will understand me. Perhaps my granddaughter, Emily, will read this. Even when she speaks, she seems to be listening. There are times when I think I have already come back in that child, which must mean that I feel as if I am already dead, already gone. These are hopes that are better off dead. At any age, life has few happy endings up its sleeve. But at the beginning, my life seemed happy, as everyone's does when life is still all promise.

And from the beginning of my life in this country, my life was hopelessly tangled with the lives of my wife's family, the Romanoffs. I fell in love with Lily's family long before I fell in love with her and in the end, they took her away from me.

Chapter 10

Emily: 1978

When I think about my family, as I now know it to have been, it seems to me as if everyone in it was always in court. My own grandfather was acquitted of a poisoning charge, shot and killed a man, and later was shot and killed himself. My great-aunt, Diana, was twelve when a neighbor took her to court for assault. My great-uncle Dave spent almost ten years in Sing Sing after he was convicted of running a bucket shop. Of course, I know that their lives were not violent lives, and that it is a trick of perspective which makes me see them as if they were. It is like looking at a good, workmanlike piece of cloth, the threads tightly and regularly woven and meant to last, but these threads are not what one sees. Instead, it is the knots that stand out, calling attention, saying look, this is where the hand and the eye failed in their skill.

And it is easy to see these knots which stand out, as events will in a monotonous life, and to think that it is the knots that had importance, marking, as dots do on a map, places of great significance. And then one forgets about the threads which form the great plains of the fabric, the long stretches of plain, expertly woven, sensibly woven fabric, made up from the regular, desperately sensible gray threads. It is easy to ignore the importance of the regular, gray threads, and what it must have meant to lay down one plain gray thread after another plain gray thread into this bleak, sensible, sturdy gray fabric that one knew would last. It is better to look at the knots, and the dramatic shadows they cast on the fabric than to ask if it is worth the effort, weaving a fabric like this, one that will last. And lately, that is what I have been doing, looking at the knots which I never knew existed until most of my family was dead.

When I was younger, my family seemed to be a group of staid, reliable people whose one concern was to see me eat well, and later, to see me safely married. To see me safe. They spent a great deal of time deciding whom I took after, and although my grandmother, Lily, thought I took after her, my mother insisted I was just like my grandfather; she said I looked like him, and as I got older, I sounded just like him. When I began to write, she said I wrote just as he did. She said I was concerned with the same things and that I wrote — about them in the same way. But when I asked her how she knew, she could not tell me. At least, she would not tell me.

I would have been willing to believe that people in my family had bad tempers; I knew they had bad tempers, often violent ones, but not that they had passionate natures. The idea of my grandmother kissing my grandfather would have struck me, even in middle age, as ridiculous. So that now, as I sort through their papers, I am struck by how little of them is left in the world except us, their descendants, and how little we know of them.

And I begin to wonder if they knew it was coming, this wind coming down from the mountains, scouring the brick streets of all traces of their lives, and if they feared this wind and if they regretted leaving this world and leaving so little behind. And at other times I wonder if they have left at all. Because as I hold this faded clipping in my hand and read its headline, SLAIN IN FIGHT FOR MORPHINE, or this one, LITTLE GIRL FOUND NOT GUILTY OF ASSAULT, it seems to me that their voices get louder and louder and it seems that if I would only try hard enough, or in the right way, I could hear each of their words distinctly, and instead of watching the curtains blow shadows across the floor of my room, I could watch them as they moved, nervous, from place to place.

For by now I know where the voices come from. They come from my hands and lips; they are deep beneath my skin. And I think of how long I studied to learn the songs and dances of the flesh, and it is as if I am again looking through a microscope, and I see them all, lined up on both sides of the room as if for an intricate dance. And then the music, which is high and faint and difficult for me to hear, begins, and they hear it and immediately start their dance. And some of them on each side of the room move backward into the shadows and disappear, while the others, in couples, join arms, turn each other about, and return to their positions near the wall. Then others move into the shadows and are gone, and the participants who remain continue their dance, and when the dance ends, the partners are left looking at each other for the rest of their lives. I see each of them dancing in this huge dance which is the dance of the genes, and I am only a new step in the continuing dance.

So in a sense it is true to say that I was there when it all happened. It is true to say that, yet seem to mean less than I do. Much later, after the events and the shadows of events were over, I found out what happened by asking questions of everyone who was left alive. To say it was this way, to say that I found out what happened by asking those who are still alive, to say that I found out more than they could tell me because I was their own flesh and blood and deep in my own cells their genes shone like stars in the living sky of flesh, this is to hide what I really believe—that they are not dead at all, that they chose not to die and leave, but that they speak to me, not as ghosts, but as living people who have refused to go until they have made themselves understood.

Before my grandmother died, she believed she spoke to her mother and her father. She asked her sister, Diana, who was still alive, when her dead mother was coming to visit her. She spoke to the dead all the time and we said she was senile. Perhaps she was. But I know that the longer my life goes on, the more time will add new rooms and courtyards to the small, plain building I have always been, so that now there are open places I never knew of before, and of which no one else knows except the dead, who enter more and more freely. And the more they come, the more I am certain that what my grandfather wanted was to be understood, which is a small enough thing to ask. To be understood and then to be loved for what he was. Just before he died, in the large, white emergency room of the hospital, he said something which would have allowed us to understand him, but it was too late.

And even if he had lived, he would not have been able to retouch the portrait each of us had of him. And we were all in such a hurry to frame his picture, to hang it on a wall, or to paste it onto a sheet in an album. And then the wall was painted and the picture came down. The album was closed and the picture was pressed between the black sheets like a flower.

But the pain of his life is like a wind that will not die down, and for some time, it has been howling around the walls of my house, and on some days I believe that it always howled around the walls of my house but that I have just begun to hear it, and one day, as I watched the sun scrubbing a white wall, I said, such pain must have a home. Take mine. And it did.

Snapshot: The Luria Family Album, 1915

Chapter 11

The pharmacist, Esheal Luria, stood behind the counter and observed the empty store and the empty street. What, he asked himself, was he doing here until twelve o'clock at night? No one would come in. But if he went upstairs, someone would be sure to call him, and then he would have to make excuses to his wife, who would want to know what was so important that it couldn't wait for him to finish his dinner, and he would have to rush downstairs with his napkin still tucked under his stiff, white collar. So he stayed in the store. Then if anyone came in, they came to him. He was not at his customers' beck and call. If a customer called him at home, he no longer felt like the head of the house. He felt like a dog who came wagging his tail when his owner whistled. Absently, he picked up a rag and began to polish the swan neck of the soda-fountain faucet.

He was very proud of his window display, although his daughters had suggested that putting everything he owned into the window was not the most elegant form of window dressing they had ever heard of. But if he did not put everything in the window, how were people to know what he had? His girls were smart enough, but they had no common sense. He looked at the window display and sighed. He changed it once a month, and the month was almost up. He wondered if one of his daughters would come in and help him. When they were younger, they had counted the days until the one for the changing of the window display arrived. Then, after they were finished helping, they would go outside and play their game: "I see an *O*," one of them would say, and the other one would have to guess which particular word on which particular item had the *O* in question. From their expressions, which always gave the girls away, he guessed that they often cheated. Whatever. They enjoyed the game. He peered into the street. There was no sign of anyone. He gave up straining to see into the darkness and watched the cone of light which the streetlight was trying to maintain against the mists which drifted like the haunted down the street. It would be raining within the hour.

The little bell over the heavy wooden door rang. It was Mrs. Murphy and, as usual, Mrs. Murphy was crying. The pharmacist, who usually felt a shudder of fear when he saw someone cry, did not feel fear this time. Instead, he sighed the deep sigh of resignation, the sigh of a victim who knew he was about to be taken advantage of, and who was going to cooperate in his own fleecing. "Someone sick?" he asked Mrs. Murphy. She was crying so he assumed she was sick. She could manage sobs, but not real tears, if her husband or child were sick.

"I have a terrible cough," she said, proceeding to demonstrate the seriousness of the malady. "Cover your mouth," he said. "I'm coughing something terrible," she said. "Mr. Luria, I'm dying. And do I have a penny in the house? No, I don't. Every penny I have is here," she said throwing a twisted handkerchief onto the counter. "Everything on medicine. If I live, I won't have what to live on." "Put your money away," said the pharmacist. Mrs. Murphy's hand flew out, seized the kerchief, and plunged it back into the deep pocket of her black coat. "You have something that can help me?" she asked suspiciously. The druggist sighed again.

This was always the way it was; he gave them the charity they wanted and they thought there was something wrong with his medicine. They went home, looked with an evil eye at his medicine, and told themselves that they got what they paid for. "No," he said, printing the name of the elixir on a label, pasting the label onto the bottle. "It won't help you. It's going to poison you. It's going to put you out of your misery." "What a joke," said the woman, eying him. "I guess I'll take it," she said. "Yes, do me a favor," he said, pushing the bottle across the counter. "I'll pay you back, don't think I won't," Mrs. Murphy said. "Sure," said the pharmacist, "if it doesn't kill you, you'll pay me back."

Mrs. Murphy hesitated as if it had just occurred to her that the druggist, to whom she owed a great deal of money, might indeed be trying to do her in. Then he wouldn't have to give her any more free medicine. "I guess I'll take it," she said again, reaching for the bottle. "Good," said the druggist; "I knew there was a reason I was in the store all night. You made my night worthwhile." "Are you sure this stuff is all right?" she asked, tilting the bottle this way and that. "Tell me, Mrs. Murphy," he said, "what do you learn about that medicine by holding it up to the light? It takes me a long time to decide what's in a pill or a syrup. I have to do all kinds of tests, but look at you." The woman looked him over and started laughing. Her laugh ended in a cough. "Oh, Mr. Luria," she said, "you are a funny one. I see green syrup. It's a pretty color. You look good in that blue suit," she said, leaning over the counter and fingering his lapel. "That's good fabric." "I can afford the best," he said grinning at her; "I have such a hopping practice. Look how busy the store is in the middle of the night."

He liked Mrs. Murphy. She flirted with him and she told her sister, who had told him, that she thought he was a fine figure of a man. He should have sent the sister up to tell that to his wife. "Well, I'll take the medicine," Mrs. Murphy said again; "you should get some sleep, Mr. Luria." "How can I go to sleep," he asked her, "before I know if that medicine works? I'll stay here until twelve just to see if you need another formula." "Get on," she said, pleased. Just then, the bell tinkled and Mrs. Luria walked in. Mrs. Murphy said goodbye, quickly tied her shawl under her chin, and was out the door. He saw her walk through the streetlight's haze and disappear.

"How much money did you give away this time?" his wife asked him. He did not answer her. "Mrs. Murphy this and Mrs. Murphy that," she said; "I ask you to send me some stamps in the country, and you write me and say I should make my money last and you don't send me any. But some Irishman is starving and you give away the family jewels." Mr. Luria sighed and looked at his wife. She was a beautiful woman. "You send them money so they can go and get, and your own family doesn't have anything." "You have everything you need," he said. "When I have to write down each thing I take from the closet? When I have to write down when I take a bar of soap? Does Mrs. Murphy have to write down how much you should get for the medicine? Does Mrs. Murphy have to tell you why she used up two bottles of syrup?"

Esheal's face, as he looked at his wife, was expressionless. He thought about the first time he had gone to Mrs. Murphy's rooms. Everyone in the family had been too sick to come to the store. And what he saw when he got there did not surprise him, because he had long since grown accustomed to the way people in the neighborhood lived. For a while, they would be able to live decently, as long as all of them were well and all were earning a living; then one would get sick, and the loss of income meant no meat for weeks. And by the time whoever it was got better, more relatives from Europe would arrive and set up camp in their rooms, and naturally, they had to feed the newcomers. When he walked into Mrs. Murphy's, he thought he had walked into an unweeded garden where beds grew like weeds. There were iron beds with paint chipped everywhere placed in front of the icebox, and every time someone wanted to open it, the man in the bed had to get up, wait, and then get back in. As he looked around, he saw that those with the beds were the lucky ones. Two children were sleeping on a piano and two more were sleeping under it. A man was asleep on top of the kitchen table and two chairs had been pushed together to form a bed for a young boy. It was a warm night, and the window to the fire escape was open and Esheal heard someone outside coughing. He had never seen such overcrowding, not even in steerage.

"You've got to do something about this," he said to Mrs. Murphy, who was trying to take care of the others. "There's no air in here. Everybody will get tuberculosis." "In a month," she said, "it will be over. They'll all have jobs. Then my husband, bless his soul, he'll be a citizen and the whole family will be citizens, and then he can sell his vote and the boys' and we'll have plenty of money. We'll be rich." "But what are you going to do in the meantime?" said Esheal; "you need money to eat." "Oh," said Mrs. Murphy; "you know how it is. You tell this one a story, and you pay that one a little, and when you wear out your welcome, you pay a little more, and sooner or later, they get paid. It works out." Esheal expressed disbelief. "Well, Doc," she said, "you know what I'm getting at. You don't exactly tell the truth. You say your son's getting a good job, you make the salary a little bigger than it is; you say your uncle's coming and he's rich, and then when he comes, you run in with some money and say he gave it to you and there's more where that's coming from. They believe you. Look, they *want* to believe you. You're a customer. They need customers. It would happen to them, too." Esheal looked around; the rooms were hot as a steambath. He was afraid to move lest he step on someone. "Put me on the list of the men waiting for your rich uncle," he said. And three months later, she came into the pharmacy with the money she owed him. All her relatives, she said, were working. "I'm rich," she said; "until the next boat comes in." And for a long time, that was how it was for all of them.

"Where are the girls?" Esheal asked his wife at last. As if he cared a damn about me, she thought. "They're upstairs, asleep. Where should they be?" She looked around at the empty store, the empty street. "I'm going to bed," she said; "if you want anything to eat, you know where to find it." "Some women would make something hot for their husbands when they finished working at twelve o'clock midnight," he said. "Some wives don't clean the house, have one child after another, cook all the meals and do all the sewing," she said; "I'm tired when the day is over." "Some wives would," he said. "Then you should have married some of them," said his wife, going out the door.

Whenever he saw his wife, he was surprised by how beautiful she was and how lucky he was to have married her. He knew other men sized him up, trying to understand how such a short man, a man who was only five feet four, had managed to capture this tall, statuesque, and willowy woman. He saw them drinking in her heart-shaped face and her beautiful black hair which she parted in the middle and combed back into two wings, one on each side of her face. Her complexion was exquisite. He had bought an entire set of china because its coloring reminded him of his wife's. She never knew why he came home with it. He had done what she always did when she wanted something: he bought it and brought it home and gave it to her, telling her that it was her birthday present. Whenever she wanted a chair, or a new couch, something big, she bought it and told him it was his birthday present, or Chanukah present or anniversary present. So he caught her; she couldn't very well tell him to take her present back.

The Lurias lived on the first floor above the pharmacy, which was on the corner of Chauncey and Howard. Mr. Luria, whom the neighbors called Doc, was forever looking for another good corner for a drugstore. He had been looking for a good corner for years, but he had not found one. There was no reason to move; his wife never tired of pointing that out, but he felt it was time. He was sure that if he stayed, something would happen.

Mr. Luria heard Lily's voice. It was coming down through the dumbwaiter. They left the dumbwaiter open and had rigged up an alarm so that each could ring the other if one needed something. Lily was talking to someone on the phone. Probably she was talking to one of her brothers, but you would never know it from listening to her. "Well, dear," she said, "that's how things go. So did the doctor tell you to stay home? Well, then, put your foot up, dear." She called everyone dear. She called the proverbial iceman "dear." He couldn't stand it. When he heard her call the iceman "dear" he wanted to kill her. "I love you, too, dear," she said. She must have hung up. Silence poured from the open dumbwaiter. He thought about Lily and how difficult it was to talk to her. She was his wife, but he did not feel he possessed her. When she went into a store, he would look through the window to see how she talked to the man.

She talked with the butcher easily, she laughed easily, she leaned over the counter, leaning her chin provocatively on one finger. Everyone loved to see her come in. She found everything funny but him. All an actor had to do was push another actor and she was hysterical. If one actor pushed another actor, and the actor fell down, she would fall back into a chair or against a wall. She would seem to be helpless with laughter.

What mistake could he have made? Her daughter had died, but the child was his daughter, too. Did she blame him for not saving the child? Probably. She blamed him for everything. There were days when she seemed to blame him for the bad weather. On certain days, he would see her in a cold light and she seemed older than he remembered. She always looked worried. There was a perpetual furrow deep between her eyebrows. Did she blame him for having taken her out of the house after Celia died? They had taken the child to the biggest specialists. She had a very bad heart, her head was too large; finally, she had spinal meningitis. Whenever Lily talked about Celia, she blamed the child's fate on herself. She had been so hysterical, laughing so hard at the boys playing baseball, that she hadn't noticed when one of them hit the ball toward her, and the ball hit her in the abdomen. Whenever Lily spoke of Celia, she blamed that ball for her misfortune, although whenever Lily spoke of the child, she stared at her husband as if what she meant to say was, it was your fault; you could have done something.

What could he have done? If his youngest daughter hadn't been burned, if he hadn't been in the shop when his wife called down, if he hadn't had his jugs of linseed oil and limewater, if he hadn't poured their contents over the child, if he hadn't let the clerk run the shop, while he stood over little Fay, whose lips were burned and sealed shut, holding a dropper and dropping one drop after another onto those lips, then the child would have been scarred; the child would have died. Then, after Fay got over the burn, she came down with pneumonia. He had hired a tutor for both his girls because they had missed so much school. And Fay was fine. Lily was fine, and Lucy was fine. Still, it was as if the death of the youngest child had killed Lily's pride in her husband. When he stood with her, she no longer put her arm around his waist. She folded her arms over her stomach now.

And after the assassination of the czar, when he had tried to find the woman who had taken him in after his mother left him, Lily went wild. Spending so much money, and the woman wasn't even a relative! He didn't trust Lily then; he waited outside the store for the mailman. He was afraid that Lily might see a letter from Russia and throw it into the stove in a fit of temper. He doubted that Lily would be jealous of anyone now, not unless her precious "security" was threatened. But then! Then she had been beside herself as he waited for news from the families who had stayed behind in Pobrosk.

Finally, he received a letter from Morris Sikorsky. As far as he knew, Sikorsky said, the zenshina lived as she always had. She still lived twelve versts from town and her peasants still lived with her. The townspeople had come to regard her as something of a prophet and, when the turmoil was at its height, had sent a committee from the synagogue to ask her what was to be done. After the assassination of the czar, there had been many pogroms and they feared there would be many more. "There is always Siberia," she said; "and the Ukraine. The Ukraine is better." "People go there to die!" Mr. Sikorsky cried. "From there," said the zenshina, "they can go to China, and from China they can go anywhere. From Siberia, one can see Alaska. Look at your maps!" she taunted them. "This village is not the whole world!" "She knows no more than anyone else," the townspeople murmured to each other as they trudged home. "She's a meshuggeneh," exclaimed Levy; "Siberia! The Ukraine! Of course if you freeze to death in the snow you have no troubles!"

So, thought the pharmacist, that was what the zenshina would do. She would disappear with her peasants into Siberia, and from there she would cross to Alaska. Or she would appear in China. Or in America. And if she did appear, what would he do? Now that he was older, the zenshina's memory came alive, and he wanted her as he had wanted his wife, as he still wanted his wife who did not want him. He could talk to the zenshina and she would listen to him. He had been so young when he had lived with her that she had seemed much older. How much older could she have been? She was not very old when she had taken him in.

Now, when he remembered watching her dance, he seemed to feel the faint rain drifting through his hair; he heard the larks trilling under the deep blue vault of the sky; he heard the hoarse cry of the frogs. She would never come, he told himself. And then he would ask himself, but if she did? What would he do? He told himself he was despicable for even asking himself such a question. He looked at the picture of his wife which he kept on his counter. No matter what she did or did not do, he could never leave her. It was, he told himself, a preposterous notion to torment himself with, asking himself which woman he would choose, as if it were possible to choose between someone in the present and someone in the past.

He had no way of knowing what life had done to the zenshina. Perhaps she had been disfigured by smallpox. He tried to conjure up the woman's horribly pocked face. It did no good. He wanted to talk to her. And then he thought of the zenshina's hair, which was the color of inky black nights in Russia, and of her skin, which was cool as the night air in Russia. Often, as he nodded over the counter in the pharmacy, he thought of her, and as he fell asleep, he saw her face coming closer, as it did when he was a child and had fallen ill, and her face grew until it seemed to fill the sky, and the larks sang in her hair and the winds played on the strings of her hair and her dress drifted with deep forests and cool grasses, and the moon would shine like a silver birthmark on her pale cheek. Then the wind rose, the clouds shifted, the sky was empty, and when he woke, he saw only the outline of the apartment buildings across the street.

Once, he had tried to talk to Lily and she had become more

and more uneasy. He had been trying to tell her about his life in Russia and how he saw life now. The more he talked, the more she fidgeted. "What's the matter?" he asked at last. She didn't answer. "Men don't talk that way," she said. He felt his cheeks burn; he knew he was as red as a fire engine. "I talk that way," he said. "You should have been a poet," she said; "or a girl."

"You and your rotten brothers!" he shouted at her. "You think to be a man someone has to be like your brothers? Your brothers are perfect? Your brother, the jailbird?" "My brothers *are* perfect," she said, turning and staring at him. She had, he thought, the cold, blank stare of a prostitute. "Perfect?" he cried; "because they're tall? Because they're charming? Because they have good singing voices? Because they can soft-shoe? Then let them support you! They can't even support themselves! You want a perfect man, go marry your brothers! *You* bail Dave out! Don't come to me!" "No one wanted to come to you," Lily said; her skin had gone white with rage. "You mean they had to come to me!" her husband shouted; "they didn't have any choice! They came to me and then they resent me for helping them out. That's your perfect family!"

"A man who can't even father boys!" his wife said in a low voice. He stared at her. Was the woman mad? Didn't she love her daughters? Was that what she had been thinking about when he thought she was thinking about Celia's death? How she didn't have boys?

As if he watched himself from a great distance, as if he were standing outside their window looking in, he saw himself pick up the big white pitcher which sat on the dressing table next to the bed; he saw himself throw it at the mirror behind her. The mirror shattered and Lily screamed. "Something's in my back!" she shrieked. He ran over to her and turned her around. At the sight of his face so close to hers, Lily began crying uncontrollably. Her whole body convulsed with sobs. He saw that the back of her dress was soaked in blood. He took his straight razor from the dresser and cut open the back of her dress. As he pulled it away from her skin, which was sticky with blood, he saw that a splinter of the mirror had lodged in her shoulder. When he had pulled the dress from her shoulder, he had pulled the splinter partway out. He pulled it out gently and laid it on the dresser. The bleeding was not serious; the cut was not deep.

"Come downstairs and I'll bandage this up," he said. He looked down at his hands and saw they were shaking. He looked at Lily and saw her staring at the razor. "I'll bandage it," he said, taking her arm; "come down to the shop." "No," she said. "You can't just let it bleed," he said. "No," she said again. She was still staring at the razor. She thinks I meant to kill her, he thought again, and he felt sobs choking his throat. If he tried hard enough, he could stop himself from crying.

But he began to sob. His wife's eyes narrowed. She watched him standing in the room crying, as if his tears were the final disgrace. He led her down to the shop like a crying child leading his mother. While he was bandaging Lily's shoulder, he looked out the store window and thought he saw the zenshina standing there, watching him. We are still in the same world, he thought; no matter how wide the world is, we are still in it. He cut a piece of adhesive tape from the long roll and finished fastening Lily's bandage to her shoulder. "Don't stand up!" he snapped at her; "you want the whole street to see you in your corset?"

Lily sat down on a stool behind the counter, then held onto the counter with both hands. "Here's your blouse," he said; "I brought it down with me. Put it on." "You don't want anyone to see me in my corset," Lily said slowly, "but you throw a pitcher at me. What if the whole street saw me bleeding to death?" "I lost my temper," he said. Lily started to cry. "What's the matter with you?" he asked; "nothing happened. It was an accident. You started the whole bregus." She didn't answer him. He watched her back shaking, saw her shoulder blades protruding like trapped wings. "What's the matter?" he asked her; "you're frightened of me? A man who's so short? A man who's so much older than you?" She lowered her head onto her hands. Then she straightened up suddenly and reached over her shoulder and placed a hand over her bandage. The cut hurt her, he thought. He thought of all the little mirrors lying on the floor upstairs like a terrible snow. In each of the mirrors, he and Lily were shouting ancient grievances at one another. She would forgive him in time, he thought; everyone forgave everyone else in time.

After Mrs. Murphy left, Mr. Luria thought about his wife, who never listened to him. Lily was still laboring under the delusion that he came from Poland. Her family came from a town in Russia called Teray. When she told him this, he had said there was also a town in Poland called Teray. Moreover, he went on, he thought there was a Polish town named Pobrosk. Isn't it interesting, he had said, how people try to take things with them? Pobrosk was obviously a Russian name for a town, but the people who left it must have missed it terribly and they named their new town after it. Did Lily remember a word of what he had said? No. She had come to the conclusion that, since he said there was a town in Poland called Pobrosk, he came from Poland. "But I come from Russia!" he once said in exasperation. "So you lived in Russia for a while," Lily said, stirring her hot pot of thick green-pea soup. The pot of soup thought more clearly than his wife did.

He ought to, he thought, get on with writing the story of his life. He worked on it at night in the drugstore, and hid the sheets in the opiates section of the pharmacy. Lily would never find it there; she was terrified of the powerful, dangerous medicines and had long ago given up watching him fill the doctors' prescriptions for such things. "But if something should go wrong," she would say, her eyes dilated; "if you should make a mistake." "I don't make mistakes," he said; "I'm a careful man." And it was true. He never had.

But when her brother worked for him, there was nothing but trouble. One woman after another coming in, bringing back huge yellow pills. "Tell me, Dr. Luria, aren't these bigger than the ones I usually get?" Bigger! They were double the dosage. "So?" he would ask, grinning, taking the pills back calmly, controlling himself so that he didn't jump across the counter and snatch the deadly pills out of her hand, "you get two for the price of one. You could have cut them in half and saved a lot of money. I'll get the little ones for you."

Then, as soon as the store was empty, he would corner Lily's brother, Bill, in the back of the shop, grab him by the shirt front and slam him into the wall once, twice, three times. "Murderer!" he shouted at him; "Butcher! Lunatic! You're going to put us in prison! Thank God the stupid women like you! You give those pills to a person with an ounce of brains, we'll be explaining to the judge. Nothing in your head! Your whole family lives in the clouds!" Bill would turn pale. Lily, who had listened to everything through the dumbwaiter, would rush into the shop to save her precious brother from extermination at the hands of the monster she had married.

"Everyone should work like you do?" Lily would cry,

throwing herself against Bill, as if to say that she was ready to die in his place. "Everybody should work like a dog! Leave him alone! He's only a child!" And Esheal Luria would stand there, the murderous pills in his hand, open-mouthed, flabbergasted by the spectacle of treachery before him, his wife's idiotic brother, gaping at him, terrified, while his wife dangled from the idiot's neck, staring at him as if he were the devil himself. So he would try to write the story of his life and he would hide it under the bottles on the bottom shelf of the locked opiates case.

The Romanoffs

Chapter 12

When the Romanoff family came to America in 1885, the men found jobs as tailors and rooms for their family on the Lower East Side, as everyone did in those days. They lived on Delancey Street, right in the middle of all the pushcarts. Mrs. Romanoff thought this was a wonderful thing since the streets, which were really one vast market, reminded her of home. She was an intelligent woman and looked around her once and saw that she could never again hope to see her little fishing village of Teray and that from now on she would have to be contented with the grays and blacks of this new world. She saw people everywhere and assumed that they would keep her occupied and happy.

When she and her husband, Meyer, went for their first walk, through the neighborhood, she saw she had a problem on her hands. When their ship had come close enough to the shores of the new world, all the passengers had rushed to the rail to catch the first possible glimpse of the magic city. And there, still on the broad cheek of the sea, the city had fulfilled their wildest dreams. It stood, with its towers and spires catching the gold lights like an enormous crown on the face of the earth. "It is the crown of the world," breathed Meyer; "it is all they said it would be and more." And so they were completely unprepared for the shock of Castle Garden, where they were lined up like criminals, put in long lines according to the letter of the alphabet with which their name began, and roughly examined by impatient and contemptuous doctors.

But it was not until they had passed inspection and were out on the street, sure that they would not be sent back, that they began to look about. The Romanoffs had befriended a family named Simkoff on board ship, and after they were all out on the street, the Simkoffs, whose relatives had come for them in a carriage, insisted that the Romanoffs ride with them. The heat rose from the asphalt pavements in wide waves which caused the tall gray and black buildings to quiver, as if they were insubstantial and might, any minute, give way to the new world the Romanoffs had hoped to see. But they did not give way. Nor did the heat, which rose as the minutes passed. When Meyer and Sarah Romanoff climbed into the open carriage of the Simkoffs, the leather seats burned through their clothes and set their skin on fire. The wagon drove through the shadows of the high buildings, the heat following them as if it had an old score to settle.

Sarah Romanoff fanned herself with her hand and watched her husband. He had not eaten since his arrival; he had had nothing to drink. He was wearing what he had worn when they left Russia, his galoshes of thick rubber over his heavy shoes, his coat was long and heavy and buttoned, and his black skullcap of thick rep sat heavily above his flushed face. Sarah watched the buildings fly by, fascinated, but to her husband, the hot wind in which the buildings seemed to fly came directly from the caverns of hell. Everywhere, hundreds and thousands of mouths were opening in the walls of the huge buildings, in the stones of the streets, pealing like bells, thundering as trains spun metal against metal, honking like monstrous ducks as carriage after carriage passed, roaring with the voices of enormous waves of people who seemed to occupy every inch of the city's pavements.

And as the noise rose, so did the smells. The odor of tar mingled with the odor of the dust which the wagon's wheels threw into the air; the fish market smelled like the swamps of Russia which were now gone forever; the smell of onions cut through the smell of cheeses, and the smell of the river, like a rotting body, floated over everything. Sarah watched her husband, who seemed incapable of moving. She saw his face redden and purple, and then he fell over. She screamed and the Simkoffs screamed, and the wagon stopped, and the men carried her husband into a luncheonette.

When he came to, Meyer Romanoff felt cold cloths on his head, and saw Sarah peering down at him, her yellow shawl coming loose and freeing some of her hair. "Well, here we are," he said to her, trying to smile. "Yes," said Sarah, "we are here." "And we can never go back," said Meyer. "We can go back," said his wife. "No," said Meyer; "we should go back and feed the czar? We can never go back." They heard the Simkoffs in back of them, impatient. Sarah asked them where they should look for a place to live, and they suggested Pitkin Avenue, and, after Meyer had drunk several cups of téa, they were taken there by the Simkoffs, whom they knew they would never see again. There were some rooms for rent, and they took them.

As Sarah and Meyer walked through the neighborhood for the first time, Sarah feared for her husband's health because the longer they walked and the more he saw, the redder he became. Old, huge buildings crowded together everywhere like huge, long-dead animals. When Meyer insisted that they walk into an alley and see what was behind one of the buildings, they found a clapboard building leaning sadly against the brick building which they had seen from the street. Slightly to the right of that building, another clapboard building was going up and headed for the brick building as if it were a train which wanted to knock the brick building down. In the middle of the two buildings, where the yard should have been, were outhouses which stank like open graves and one stable. "Let's go see the horses," said Sarah nervously; to Meyer, a horse was as strange as an elephant. She did not like the fixed expression on his face. "That such a life should befall an innocent beast," sighed Meyer. Sarah repressed an answering sigh and said nothing.

They went to the stable and pressed their noses against the window. Inside, they saw the outline of the horse's neck and behind the horse, many, many beds and many, many people. "People live there!" Sarah exclaimed, astonished. "They are not people," said Meyer; "they are brutes." "Come," said Sarah; "let's go back." "Let us finish what we started," said her husband. They continued to walk, past the ash barrels, on top of which children sat, past an ash barrel which was decorated with a huge, dead rat, past the curbs heaped with rubbish, past the buildings whose fire escapes groaned with jugs, tubs, trunks, food, and which were festooned with socks, skirts, drying rags, under the endless clotheslines which sailed crazily out of every window, past all the signs in both Yiddish and English, into the yards in which the children played under the dripping clothes, into an alley in which the children rolled huge barrels at each other, trying to knock one another down. Everywhere they went, children with sunken eyes stared at them from stoops, from back porches, from doorways, from windows, from wagons.

"They do not look like children," said Meyer; "they look

like demons." "Do not say that," said Sarah; "whatever they look like, they are still children. One day, our children will look like them." "God forbid," said Meyer; "they should die first!" Sarah spit on the ground. "Do not say such things!" said Sarah. "The children live here. They are used to what they see. It is terrible to us because it is new." "It is terrible to us," said Meyer, "because it is terrible." "Soon," said Sarah, "you will get a job and we will have money. Things will not be terrible long." "And these men?" asked Meyer. "Do they not have jobs?" "I will see to it," said Sarah; "things will not be terrible." "You will see to it," said Meyer, a shiver of a smile appearing on his lips for the first time since they had arrived. "I will see to it," said Sarah. "Fine," said Meyer. "Then I have nothing to worry about." And although he would not admit it, Meyer believed that somehow, Sarah would see to things. He had faith in little in the world, but he had faith in Sarah.

When they reached the building in which they lived, Sarah saw Meyer hesitate in the doorway where the steps were steep and always dirty and no light dared come in. Inside, it was damp and clammy and smelled of cats. The door was not locked and men slept in the halls and the warmth of their bodies kept the halls warm. The Romanoffs lived on the fifth floor, and Mrs. Romanoff said this was a good thing, because the fifth floor was the top floor and let in more light and air. Thus, the children would be healthier.

When Meyer seemed unimpressed by this view of their new situation, saying that they did not yet have their children with them, Sarah said that soon their two boys would be with them, as soon as they earned the money to bring them over, and when they arrived, they would be healthy children, because they would have so much light and air. Sarah made a game of lighting a match to see her way through the halls. If, when she struck a match, she saw a man or a woman asleep in the hall, because there were no locks on the front doors of the buildings in the neighborhood, and if there had been a lock, a tenant would have ripped it from the door and sold it, she would try to imagine his life story. Gradually, her husband found it harder to complain, not because he found his wife's cheerfulness contagious; indeed, he did not believe in it, having found her one night sitting at the kitchen table crying, but because time was passing, and as time passed, their three rooms began to resemble their one-room house in Teray.

Sarah scrubbed the floors until they shone, and Meyer liked to watch the light on the wooden floor and remember how the women had told Sarah that in the new country it was impossible to get floors to shine. Sarah had gone down into the streets, asked questions, and came up three hours later with a large, flat package. "Sandpaper!" she said, triumphant. For weeks after that, Meyer could not speak to his wife face to face. She was always down on the floor, sanding it. "It's no use," Meyer said; "you will never get it clean." But Sarah persisted, sanding small areas at a time, exclaiming with delight when one sanded area met another. Then she would sit back, put her hands on her hips, and say, "Look how much is done! Sit there," she would say to Meyer; "don't help me. You've been working hard all day."

Naturally, both of them were soon on the floor, crawling diligently after their pieces of sandpaper. Their floor became the wonder of the building. Sarah herself took off her shoes before walking on it, and soon everyone who came in did the same thing. When it got colder, and some people hinted that it was not pleasant, putting one's feet down on a cold floor without shoes, Sarah pretended not to understand their complaints, but rapturously explained how much warmer it was inside her rooms now, because the shining floor captured all the heat, reflected it, and sent it into the walls! And before anyone had time to wonder about the sense or senselessness of such an explanation, Sarah would be serving tea and cookies, or seltzer, bread, and beet jelly and, of course, after enough glasses of tea, everyone felt warm.

When they first came, and Meyer watched Sarah mixing rat poison and ground glass with challa dough so that she could set it in the corners of her rooms in hopes of killing the rats who traveled happily about at night, he wondered why he had ever been afraid of wolves and the snarling dogs of the peasants in Russia. He thought of the rats as wolves, but smaller, and hence even more frightful. A wolf could be shot if, God forbid, one had a gun. But a rat! He listened to all the stories about rats that ate children, and he did not dare fall asleep for his first week in his rooms. Even then he only fell asleep when Sarah, who was again worrying about his health, put a huge pot over his face, saying that it was like a suit of armor and that it would protect him. He liked the idea so much that he asked her to put a pot over his toes, too.

He would have had his first good night's sleep that night if he hadn't turned over and sent the pot bouncing and clanging against the floor. Sarah was awakened by the noise of first one pot, then another, and then her husband, who was shouting, "Stop, thief! Stop, thief!" and hopping on one leg because the toes of the other were caught in the pot handle which made a dreadful noise every time it hit the floor. Within minutes, their rooms were filled with people from the building, all half asleep and half dressed, who, when they saw the source of the commotion, shook their heads, laughed, and disappeared. For a quarter of an hour afterward, there were shouts of laughter coming from this room and that. Finally, they heard someone knocking on their wall. "It's me, Mr. Kaminsky," said the voice from the other side of the thin partition; "rats don't like light. Put the gaslight on in the bedroom. Do it for me. I need the sleep." They thanked him, they blessed him, and they lit the gaslight. Whether or not the light did any good, whether or not it was their faith in the old man who spoke through the wall, they slept well after that, probably because, by nightfall, they were exhausted.

And Sarah began her war against bedbugs and cock-roaches. With a feather, she painted the cracks between the floorboards with kerosene. The mattress spent its days on the fire escape airing and sunning, and whenever Sarah finished with her other chores, she would go out on the fire escape and beat the mattress. But there were still bugs. Sarah concluded that they were "coming up" from down below. In return for pencil portraits she drew of new arrivals, who wanted to send them back to relatives in the old country, Sarah had obtained material for curtains, enough material for a new dress for herself, and money to put under a creaking board in the shining floor. In the new country, Sarah saw with satisfaction, every board creaked, and her money would be safe. Only a maniac would tear up a whole floor.

When she found herself pregnant, she knew that the family finances would need fattening, so she went back down into the street and persuaded the used-clothes man to lend her one end of his pushcart. She wanted to put up a sign which said, "Send Your Portrait Home To A Weary Mother And Fa-ther," but the used-clothes man said a sign had to be short; people in the street would not stop to read books. "Write," he told her, "Your Professional Portrait. Ten Cents." "Ten cents!" Sarah gasped. "Say, listen," the man said, "if they want it enough, they'll pay. It's cheaper than the photographer's studio. Tell them you'll draw their house, their horse, their wagon. What photographer is going to come out on the street to take a picture of their horse and wagon? You'll see. You'll have a lot of business, and you can pay me a dollar a week for using my cart." "A dollar!" gasped Sarah, falling backward, clutching her heart; "he wants to steal the life of my unborn child!"

Serious bargaining began. When the man stuck at seventy-five cents, Sarah cursed him. "May your stomach be of wood, and your head of glass, and when your stomach burns, may your head break in pieces." The man was impressed. "I never heard a curse like that," he said, rubbing his stomach nervously; "you must come from a good family." "Fifty cents," said Sarah, seeing the snake hidden in the flattery. "Fifty cents," he said, "but if it is worth it to you to pay me more, I won't argue." "Let's shake hands," said Sarah. "Shake hands with a woman!" the man gasped. "This is not the old country," said Sarah, holding out her hand. The man watched her hand as if it were a cobra. Out of the corner of his eye, he saw someone coming up to the pushcart. He pumped Sarah's arm up and down. "So, good for you," he said; "a woman shaking hands in the street." In the end, Sarah paid him a dollar a week because business was so good that she would have been ashamed to do otherwise, and whenever he had something too poor to sell, he gave it to her. She fixed it up for her husband, cut it up for herself, or put it away for the child who was coming. So, she told herself, she was not really paying him a dollar; if one looked at it in the right way, he was paying her.

One day, she came back to the stand with a young boy. "My assistant," she said to the used-clothes man. "He walks through the street with a sign and one of my pictures and more people come here. Also, he delivers." "Delivers what?" asked the confounded used-clothes man. "My pictures," she said. "The men work seven days a week. When can they come to get them?" "I thought you finished them and gave the pictures to them and that was the end of it," he said. Sarah winked. She began to undo a package. "Ta-tah!" she said, and out came a portrait in color. "It's beautiful!" said the used-clothes man; "it's a work of art! Look at the flesh and blood!" "Don't touch it!" cried Sarah; "you'll smudge the pastels." "Pastels!" he exclaimed; "I never saw colors like that except through a door to the inside of a

church." "One dollar," said Sarah, "and you can have one of
your own." "One dollar," said the used-clothes man; "all
right; I'll think it over. So, anyway, who's this?" "My
assistant's name is Esheal Luria," said Sarah. "Shouldn't he
be in school?" the man asked. "He is," said Sarah; "this is his
Easter vacation. At night, he works shoveling coal for a big
building. He's a strong boy." "He's a little on the short side
for carrying a sign," said the used-clothes man. "I should hire
a giant?" asked Sarah; "then everyone would look at him and
not at the sign."

And so Esheal Luria met the Romanoffs. By the end of
that summer, their first daughter and third child, Lilian,
whom everyone called Lily, had been born, and the Romanoffs had enough money to send for their two sons,
Emmanuel and Shmuel. While Sarah was recovering from the
birth, Esheal would come upstairs to visit her on his way to
work and tell her what people would want their portraits
done when she was ready to begin work again. Esheal looked
at Sarah and looked at the baby and saw no reason why Sarah
should be any different from other women he knew, and
every woman he knew produced one after another of these
little creatures, and when there were enough of them, there
was no money to be found anywhere in the house. So he
thought that Sarah should get back to work at once.

"They could come here," he said; "when you have to nurse
the baby, you can go into another room and say you are doing
something with your chalks." Sarah looked at Esheal, wondered fleetingly what had made him so precocious, and then
marveled at the prospect of earning money without leaving
her child or her room. She looked at the gas meter over the
gas stove which was always so hungry for quarters. "My
husband would never allow it," she said; "a man's home is his
castle after all." "Does he have to know?" asked the boy.
"But strange people!" said Sarah. "Men! In my house." "I
have a sister who could stay with you," Esheal said; "or I
could stay with you after three o'clock. When does your
husband get home?" "Seven," said Sarah, "sometimes eight,
sometimes nine." "What will you do if he finds out?" the boy
asked curiously. "I'll think of something," Sarah said with a
sigh.

During the autumn of that year, Esheal became well
acquainted with the story of the Romanoff family because,
when Sarah was not busy, there was nothing she liked to do

more than talk about the old country and her life there. One day, when Sarah was drawing a picture of a man who wanted to send it back home, she took a deep breath and said, "Oy, marriage. How anyone decides whether to get married! Of course, in my case, it was different. My husband the suicide!" "Your husband committed suicide?" asked Esheal. "He only threatened," said Sarah. "I wasn't ready to marry him. It was an arranged marriage. I was a Kapturak, and the Kapturaks and the Romanoffs had always been very close. Plus his family was a trifle richer than mine. So my parents arranged it. If they had a girl, and the Romanoffs had a boy, or the other way around, they would get married. So I was the girl. I was born three years earlier than Meyer, and I thought when I got older, they wouldn't like that, their boy having an old wife. But no such luck. And to make matters worse, Meyer fell in love with me and he realized I didn't want to get married, so he began threatening to kill himself. First he said he would jump off the roof of his house. So I used to say, let him; if he sprains his ankle, will that be so terrible? Because in our village the roofs weren't so high off the ground, you know. Then he said he would drown himself in the river, so I said he would have a better chance in the river than on the roof. His parents, naturally, were hysterical, and used to come and plead with me. But I couldn't understand it. Why should he be so set on one woman?

"It fascinated me, and naturally, I liked all the attention. So even when I told my mother, if I get married now, I will be unhappy, and unhappy women do not have children or keep the house clean, and I will be a disgrace to you and to all the Kapturaks, I was trying to figure it out, you know, what he liked so much about me. I began to look at myself in the mirror, but there I found no answer, because the mirror was rippled and I looked like I was underwater and had been underwater for some time. So I suppose it was all the attention. You know, it's hard to resist it. He said I carried myself like a queen. Later on, I found out he knew more about me than I did myself. The women used to take baths in the river once a week when it was warm enough, and he used to climb into a warehouse which looked down on the river and there he would watch us. So he always used to say, 'My Sarah is the most beautiful one of them all.' And he knew. Because he saw for himself. He still likes to tell that story, how he watched us taking baths."

"You didn't know that you loved him?" asked Esheal; "not right away?" Sarah hesitated. "No, not right away. My parents couldn't understand me. They asked me what was wrong with him. Wasn't he funny? Wasn't he handsome? Didn't he make me laugh? Didn't he take me for walks in the fields so that I could draw the ravens sitting in the trees? So I used to say that we walk in the fields, but we do not walk together. He walks and I walk. And my mother used to get so angry. 'He walks and I walk!' she used to say. She would be scouring the pots with ashes, and I'd hear her muttering, 'He walks and I walk!' She couldn't get over it. But I was going to defy my parents?

"So I married him. I was twenty-two when I married him, and my parents already called me the spinster. That's how they called me. They wouldn't call me Sarah anymore. He was nineteen. And when I finally said I was ready to get married, they were overjoyed. But all they said was good, you're no spring chicken anymore. When the wedding was over, I found out how excited they were. When I said I would marry him, they were afraid, afraid I would change my mind. So they didn't want to make too much of it, you see. But the night I got married, they got drunk and cried all night. *Both* families got drunk! They stayed outside the door to our room so long, giving me advice, giving him advice, that the rabbi had to drag them away. Anyway, to make a long story short," said Sarah, "here we are. Except for my two boys who haven't gotten here yet."

"What will happen if you don't get enough money to bring them here?" asked Esheal; "would you leave them there?" "Leave them!" said Sarah; "I would go back." "But you left them once," said Esheal. "I didn't leave them," said Sarah; "they are with their grandfathers in their grandfathers' house." "Once," said Esheal, "I heard of a woman who left her son behind in the village because when she got married to a new husband, the man didn't want the child." "Such a woman," said Sarah, "should be fed to the dogs." "But if she had no money," said Esheal. "She could find a way," said Sarah. "But if she could not?" asked Esheal. "Why couldn't she find a way?" asked Sarah; "I know I could find a way." "You are not every woman," said Esheal. "Believe me," said Sarah, holding the portrait away from her, "a mother loves her children more than her husband. And she ought to. A man can have more than one wife but a child has only one mother." "Is that true?" asked Esheal. "It is not written in the Bible, but it is written in here," said Sarah, tapping her breast. "All women do not feel that way," said Esheal. "All women!" Sarah said contemptuously.

She finished the portrait she was working on and set it on the floor next to her chair. "And you?" she said; "well, you are too young to get married. Where do you come from?" "Pobrosk," he said; "in Russia." "And your family? What do they do?" "My father was a teacher," he said. "Was?" asked Sarah. "He died. My mother married the new teacher, and then we came to America." "And that's all you have to say for yourself?" Sarah asked. "In Russia," said Esheal, "my life was like the life of any child." "So?" asked Sarah; "and wasn't that an interesting life?" "Well," said Esheal, "I had a grandmother who was pushed into a stove during a pogrom. She came back to prepare for the Sabbath and the soldiers caught her. She was burned to death. That was interesting." "*That* was interesting?" Sarah said, staring at him. Esheal sighed. He had hoped that story would turn Sarah's interest to something other than himself. "It's not *not* interesting," he said. Sarah shook her head. "If you were older," she told him, "I would suspect you of keeping secrets."

He sensed that she was going to continue questioning him about his life in Russia. "Romanoff," he said, "that's the name of a royal family." "We're not descended from the Romanoffs," Sarah said; "we're descended from the royal house of Liechtenstein." "The royal house of Liechtenstein," said the boy, impressed. "My great-grandfather was married to a Liechtenstein," she said. The boy turned this over. "But if you are descended from a Liechtenstein in the royal house of Liechtenstein," he asked, "how did your family get to be poor and come to live in a poor fishing village?" "Anyone," said Sarah, "can become poor. That's not hard. Then once you begin, you get poorer and poorer and go downhill fast, and soon you live in a little fishing village where all the families live on herring most of the year."

"Yes," said Esheal, "but how did you get to be Jewish? While it's true that anyone can become poor, not everyone can become Jewish." "That is a great mystery," agreed Sarah; "nevertheless, it happened." It astonished Esheal that this sensible woman should believe such a fantastic story. But all women were silly in this way; all women were hopelessly romantic. You thought they were darning socks or

sketching portraits to buy the family milk and bread and tea
and they were thinking about how they were descended from
the royal house of Liechtenstein. If she hadn't believed this
nonsense, thought Esheal, she might have been ready to
marry her husband before her family took to calling her the
spinster. He wondered about her husband, and whether he
asked himself why his wife had taken so long to marry him,
and whether remembering how long it took her to make her
decision ever worried him. But, thought Esheal, here she
was, sketching portraits and rocking their baby. Soon the two
boys she left behind in Russia would be here and they would
get jobs selling papers or sweeping basements and when all of
them pooled their salaries, they would have enough money to
live on without depending on Sarah's portraits.

"What are you going to tell your husband when he finds out
about your sketching at home?" the boy asked. "Aha!" said
Sarah; "I will show him all the money I have and tell him we
can bring his father over. He won't be able to say a word
against it!" "You are going to use up all your money on that?"
Esheal asked. "Of course not," Sarah said; "I'll use some of it
to bring *my* father over. And I'll still have plenty left."

Esheal said it was six o'clock and he would have to go back
to his aunt's house if he wanted any dinner. It was already
dark and no one had come to have his portrait done. He
picked up a package wrapped in brown paper and tied in
string; he carried it like a sick cat. "And what's in that?" she
asked him. "A phonograph," Esheal said; "I found it up on
Fifth Avenue. Someone threw it out because it didn't work.
But I fixed it." "Let me hear it," asked Sarah. "Oh," she
gasped when she saw it; "it looks like a shofar!" "See how it
works," said Esheal, putting a blue wax disc on the cylinder.

Immediately, the room was filled with music. The one disc
Esheal had, which had been thrown out along with the
machine, was a wonderful aria. "Oh!" said Sarah, whose eyes
had opened wide and were filling with tears. "What a
wonderful thing! It's a miracle," she said solemnly. "It is.
That a man's voice should come out of a little box like that!
And so beautiful. And you don't have to pay him every time
he comes to sing!" She stared at the phonograph, stunned by
its powers.

"You keep it," Esheal said abruptly, and when he saw
Sarah collect herself enough to protest, he said that he could
always find another one. The room was filling with people

from other parts of the building who wanted to see the little machine producing the wonderful music. Sarah could not stop thanking him. Now, he thought, her husband would come home, and with the machine would come the story of her sketching, the jig would be up, the two children from Russia would arrive, the husband would be angry at him for helping his wife to betray him, and he would not see Sarah again. And that was exactly what happened.

Chapter 13

The back windows of the Lurias' rooms, like the back windows of the Romanoffs' rooms, opened into a dark court in which children, cats, and rats played amid the barrels, the brooms, the shovels, the crates, and the refuse which the families threw out their windows. When Mr. Romanoff looked out the window of his back bedroom, and when Esheal's new father looked out the window of his back bedroom, it seemed to both of them as if the earth were very far away, as if the rich earth from which living things grew had ceased to exist, as if there were no earth below this concrete which perpetually sprouted only garbage and broken glass. Both men, like all the men who came from Russia, lamented the absence of sun and light, though it seemed to them that the women did not miss it. The women made friends, they saved their money, and within a few weeks, they had already gone to one or two Yiddish shows. They talked happily of candy stores in which one could buy four chocolate-covered almonds for a penny, stores whose clerks put the candies into long, thin paper bags. The women ate the almonds slowly, often sucking the chocolate from them first, so that it seemed as if they were eating two candies instead of one, and they saved the elegant white paper bags to wrap special gifts. After dinner, they stared out the window where the sky's pink glow made the buildings across the street look like black-painted tin cutouts.

Did they miss the sound of the wind in the far trees? What they heard now was the wind rustling the folded papers which fell like ugly leaves into the gutter every evening. Did they miss the harvests, the wagons under their domed loads, moving like so many planets along the ridge of the new, night sky? The women had their markets before; they had their markets now. They tended their children before; they tended their children now. To Esheal, and to all the men, it often seemed as if they had traveled across a universe and gone nowhere. There were more Jews here than there were in the towns from which they had come. Here they spent their days worrying about how to make a living so that their families could live well and happily, which was how they had spent their days in Russia. It was when they sat back in their chairs and looked at their wives, in that brief instant before sleep when they looked out the window and saw other windows, that they had time to think about what they had lost.

And right outside the window was the sign of how far they had come: the fire escape. Everything found its way on to the fire escape in this new country where there was never enough room for anything: mattresses and blankets which needed airing, clothes which the women wanted to freshen in the sun, bottles of milk and seltzer, butter wrapped in wet towels, chairs, cushions, bags of fruits. Eventually, new babies found their way on to the fire escape, where they slept while their mothers cooked, mended, or took care of the sick children inside.

Meyer Romanoff saw his wife watch their new daughter in the carriage with an almost ravenous curiosity. It was as if she expected something more of this child because it had been born in a new place, although she could not have said what it was she expected. But she expected something. She watched the child with an air of expectation. She was outdoors every morning, pushing her child in its white wicker carriage with its high, domed lid. Every morning at ten to nine, Sarah appeared on the street, weaving her way through the push-carts, crossing street after street, until she came to the little park near the river. Then she sat down on a bench, and with one foot rocked the carriage.

Soon other women came to talk to her. Sarah soon became known for her knowledge of what herbs would cure what illnesses, and because the doctors never seemed to scold the women for following Sarah's advice, although they yelled themselves senseless over everyone else's attempts to deal with illnesses, her stock in the community rose higher and higher. Sarah would talk to the neighborhood women until the bell in the high, gray church steeple struck one and then she would start home. She would arrive at her building at two-thirty, not one minute earlier and not one minute later. She did this every day, regardless of the weather. On Sundays, her husband accompanied her on her walks. When she came home, she dragged the wicker carriage, which countless women had told her was impractical, up the first flight of stairs and then she would chain it to a banister with a chain and lock the used-clothes man had got from a construction worker he knew.

She cooked and she sewed and she cleaned, and soon, when people saw her or her husband, they would nod to each other and say, "Isn't she the cleanest thing you ever saw? Look at her dress! Look at all those tucks! She must fall off her feet from cleaning!" When her two boys, Emmanuel and Shmuel, came, Sarah took them down to the local photographer's studio. Both boys still had long curls and wore their hair parted in the middle. They wore fancy, ruffled jackets and white skirts with two rows of velvet buttons down each side. The photographer posed Emmanuel on a curved wicker chair. The backdrop was an elaborate Victorian room filled with ferns, plant stands, Oriental rugs, oil paintings, and boasted a carved marble mantel. Shmuel, the younger, was set upon a tricycle, one foot high on a pedal as if he were about to ride off. His skirts parted uncomfortably over the high iron crossbar, and his leather high-button shoes had been polished until they shone. Sarah had twisted his long hair into corkscrew curls, and because his hair had never been cut, each curl ended in a scraggly wisp of blond hair.

When the photographer assured Sarah that the pictures would certainly turn out, she took the boys home, had them change into little suits she had sewn for them, and took them to the barber's. The day before she had explained to them that, if they were to go to school, they would have to look like the other schoolboys, and now that they had come to America they must look like Americans. Soon, she told them, they would be doctors, engineers, lawyers, locomotive drivers, even Presidents! They would go to shows, they would go on ferryboats, they would play ball with the other boys, they would explore the streets and the alleys and come back to tell her what they had found. By the time she was finished, the boys felt as if their mother had been waiting for them to come, to grow up, and then to protect her against the world, and they were sure they could do it. But first they had to get their hair cut.

So they hopped happily into their chairs and stared curiously at themselves while their hair was cut short. They looked like all the other children they had seen on the streets, but somehow, they looked handsomer. When Sarah brought them home, each holding onto one side of the carriage, women stopped her and told her that she had two beautiful children. "And what's wrong with the third?" she would ask, tilting the hinged roof of the carriage forward so that the women could get a proper look at her nine-month-old daughter.

"A daughter's a daughter," said one woman, "but a son is a son." "A daughter can have sons," said Sarah. "A daughter needs someone's son to marry," said the woman, shaking her head at the child in the carriage. "*This* child will have no trouble," said Sarah; "look how beautiful she is!" "A beautiful woman is a temptation and an expense," said the woman. "It is too late for me to have an ugly child," said Sarah; "perhaps you have been more fortunate." "If I had two boys," said the woman, "I would not have any more children." "You can ask only for male children," said Sarah; "you can decide when children will come. I have no such powers." "A girl," said the woman, "is like a sunny day in a season of drought." Sarah shook her head again.

"You see," she said to her sons when the woman had gone, "women are ignorant, weak, and often silly. You must take care of your sister when she grows up. She will be your first sweetheart. If you learn to treat her properly, you will learn to treat other women properly. And from you, she will learn what to hope for in a man." The boys nodded solemnly but looked dubiously at their sister in the carriage. "I know," said Sarah, "she does not seem to be much now. She does not have much hair and she sits on the floor as if she were a bucket of ashes. But soon she will be beautiful, with red lips, blue eyes, and black hair, and then you will want to bring her with you when you go to shows, and when you bring your friends home, you will be happy to have her with you." The boys still appeared unconvinced. "You will see," said Sarah; "she will be your first sweetheart."

But before the boys had a chance to begin school, a terrible fever swept through the tenement in which the Romanoffs lived, and the two boys and their father came down with the fever. The doctor did not seem to worry about the boys, who were young and strong; instead, he worried about Meyer and about the baby, who, should she catch the fever, would certainly die. But the baby did not catch the fever and Meyer recovered easily. The boys, too, were recovering rapidly, but the morning before Sarah intended to let them sit out on the fire escape, their choking awakened everyone in her family and in the rooms on both sides of theirs as well. Before the doctor could arrive, both of the boys had suffocated.

For six months, Sarah was not to be seen on the street. She sat on the fire escape, holding Lily, singing to her and staring sightlessly into the sun. One day, Lily, who had begun to walk, went over to the railing and began climbing up on a jug trying to get over it. The next day, Sarah was back on the street with her white wicker carriage. When she caught sight of the woman who had said she would not have had more children if she already had two boys, Sarah crossed the street to avoid her. It was not reasonable, she knew, but she blamed her for what had happened.

Chapter 14

Esheal, who was just beginning high school, looked for Sarah every day. He began looking for her as soon as he was out the door. His eyes scanned the women, hoping to catch a glimpse of her. He often caught sight of her in the morning, because then she would be taking the baby for her walk just as he was leaving for school. He happened to have seen her on the first day she brought her two boys on to the street because, that day, his teacher suddenly sat down in his chair, then slapped his hand over his mouth, got up, and ran out of the room, and the children were dismissed early by the principal, who told them their teacher was sick.

Once in the schoolyard, the boys began to laugh, and to shout to one another. The boys began to chase each other, to hit each other with their bookbags which they swung against each other's legs, while the girls stood around the edge of the schoolyard holding their schoolbags in both arms as if they were grocery bags. They watched the boys and laughed. But this interlude did not last long, because most of the children had jobs, or chores to do at home, and soon the schoolyard was empty.

On his way home that day, Esheal had seen Sarah's carriage, and then Sarah and the two boys who were holding onto its sides. He saw that they must be about seven and eight, and anyone could tell by looking at them that they would grow into very handsome boys. Sarah's pride in her children seemed to set her apart from everyone else in the street, as if she were surrounded by her own, special light.

Esheal wanted to go over and say hello to her, in spite of the fact that her husband, Meyer, was openly suspicious of him and referred to him as "that criminal" since, when Sarah confessed to working at home, she naturally had blamed the boy for giving her the idea. And her husband, who could not bear to see his wife unhappy, had been only too happy to absolve her of any blame for improper behavior. He ranted about the boy as if he had been a pimp instead of a valuable assistant.

Once, when Sarah was very tired because the baby had been restless all night, and would wait until the instant her mother fell asleep before she again began howling, her husband had said something about the boy who was a criminal and who had encouraged his wife to work at home at all hours with strange men. Sarah lost her temper and pointed out that Meyer did not object to using the money she had earned by doing her portraits at home, and if it were not for her money, they would not have had enough money to bring their two boys from Russia, much less enough money to now bring over her father and his father, who, since their wives had died, were living miserable bachelor existences together in the Romanoff house in Teray. Mr. Kapturak had sold his own house, intending to use the money to buy himself and Mr. Romanoff a ticket to America, but a pogrom had put an end to their hopes. When the police ransacked the Romanoff house, they confiscated the money. Sarah, who received weekly letters from Teray, read about this with exasperation. If her mother had been alive, or if Meyer's mother had been alive, the police would never have found the money. Women knew how to hide money, she thought, and she beamed at her smooth, creaking floor which told no tales.

When Sarah said that if she had not worked at home, they would not have had enough money, her husband said nothing. He looked at her sadly and went into the back room. Sarah's mother had died before they had enough money to send for her. When they had left Russia, his mother was already dead. It was true; if it were not for Sarah's money, both their fathers would probably be dead before they could hope to send for them.

Sarah tried coaxing him out with his favorite food, split-pea soup, but he would not get up from the bed. Everything about his curved back, everything about the way he had turned to the wall, said that he knew his wife was right and that he was useless and weak and ineffectual. One hour passed, then two, and still he would not come out of the bedroom. The window filled with rose lights, then darkened. From the windows of the front room, Sarah could see the other men from the building begin pouring out into the streets. They formed little groups and began to walk up and down in front of the buildings in the middle of the street. Up and down, in the middle of the street they walked, just as they had done in Teray. Of course, in Teray, Sarah thought, there was good reason for walking in the middle of the street. The sides of the street were always wet and usually muddy. Here, the men walked in the middle of the street because the women and their children sat on chairs they had carried down from the rooms to the sidewalks, and it was as if, by walking in the middle of the street, they once more found themselves walking as men, with men, along a wide, limitless expanse. Whenever a horse and wagon came along and forced them to move back on to the sidewalk, the men muttered among themselves. Meyer loved to walk up and down in front of the buildings, but still he did not come out of the back bedroom.

Sarah thought about men and about how unfair they could be and about how women had to put up with this because, really, men had less sense than women, although they had a finer sense of right and wrong, which only made them helpless when women were not. She thought about Esheal, and how unfair it was for her husband to call him the criminal, when he was responsible for her children coming, for her father coming, for her father-in-law coming. She knew that her husband would forgive her, because he could not do otherwise, but that he would not forgive the child, who was already taking his place in family anecdotes, in which he was never referred to by name, but always by her husband's new name for him: the criminal.

She picked up the sharp knife she used to cut up chickens, looked at the chicken she had just set on the draining board, and put her hand over the zinc sink she had just that morning painted, as she did every Monday morning, since otherwise it was impossible to keep the sink clean and free of rust. She sighed and thought that she would be painting it again in the morning, took the knife firmly in her right hand and pressed it down against the soft flesh between her thumb and forefinger. It was less painful to cut her hand than she had thought. When she let the knife up, blood streamed down her hand onto her wrist, and then dripped onto the floor.

Sarah contemplated this spectacle with satisfaction and then screamed as loudly and terribly as she could. Her husband shot out of the bedroom. "What happened?" he gasped, looking around him; "who's here?" Sarah held up her hand and watched Meyer from behind it. "What happened?" he demanded again, running over to her. He saw the knife in her other hand. "You didn't try to, God forbid . . ." He broke off, silenced by the enormity of the thought. "I was cutting a chicken," Sarah said dully, pointing to the draining board. "You go back to bed and sulk. I hear someone coming. Maybe whoever it is will be good enough to bandage up the hand of a poor, bloody woman."

Meyer was frantically wrapping a towel around Sarah's hand, but the hand was still bleeding, and drops of blood continued to fall onto the floor. Meanwhile, Sarah refused to look at him. "I was roasting a chicken," she said, "so that, should you remember you had a family, you would have something to eat with them." Meyer saw the little pool of dark blood on the floor. "Sarah!" he said, but his wife would not turn her head. "The blood will stain the floor," he said, sure that this danger to the shining boards would cause her to speak to him at last. "What do I care about a floor when I don't have a husband?" Sarah asked him, starting to cry. Meyer too started to cry. "What do you mean you don't have a husband?" he asked; "I'm your husband. Here I am!" "You are a back turned to the room," said Sarah. Meyer fell on his knees and began mopping up the blood. "Don't worry," said Sarah; "it won't stain the floor. There's too much wax." "Forgive me!" the desperate man shouted; "for the sake of the child in the cradle!" "For her sake," said Sarah. And Meyer seized her. He hugged her and kissed her until one of the women from the building who had come to stand in their front room shouted at Meyer, "This is a time for hugging and kissing, when your wife is bleeding to death? Get out of the way!"

She marched over and looked at Sarah's hand. "Some bandage," she said, looking at Meyer with disgust. "Some place for a knife to slip," she said, looking knowingly at Sarah. "So this is what happens," she said to the air, "when a woman with a little baby is so tired from getting up all night, and a man comes home from work and has nothing to do but make his wife miserable. This is what happens. She cuts herself instead of the chicken. Look at that chicken! It looks healthier than she does!"

She began bandaging Sarah's hand and continued to talk, as if one activity were part of the other. "A woman crossed a thousand miles of water to come to a strange country with a man who, God forbid, could be a monster, an invalid, a thief, but she comes with him and he is the whole world to her and she leaves behind her father and her mother and her brothers and her sisters, and he is all she has in this world, and does he think about this? No, he comes home from work and looks at his wife and he thinks to himself, I have nothing to do, I might as well make her miserable. So that's what he does. He says to himself, the boss was mean to me, I'll make my wife miserable so she knows how I feel."

"Enough," said Sarah. The woman stopped bandaging and looked up at Sarah in surprise, as if she had just been awakened from a dream which was going on and on. Sarah saw the expression on the woman's face. "Enough bandaging," said Sarah; "my hand is heavy." "The better to hit your husband on the head with," said the woman, who, on the subject of husbands, was evidently irrepressible.

When the woman left, Meyer was still crying in the back bedroom and Sarah began crying also. They got into bed crying. After that, Meyer never openly blamed Sarah for having worked at home on her portraits. Instead, he told amusing stories about how his wife had fooled him with the help of "that criminal," and how it was a good thing she had done so, because if she had not, her father and the two boys would not have come to the country. But every time Sarah looked at the fine scar between her thumb and forefinger, she thought about Esheal and shook her head, and one day when she met him on the street, she told him what her husband called him and why, and said that, at least until her husband forgot who "that criminal" was, it would be better for her not to talk to him, especially if they were near her house.

After Sarah spoke to Esheal in that way, he never approached her on the street again. His mother noticed that he seemed to have become more protective of his sisters, as if he sensed they were in some danger, although she had no idea of why he would feel such a thing. She thought he worried about his sisters because they were younger and often ill. Because of this, she tried to explain why her new husband had chosen to take his sisters but to leave him. Girls, her new husband had said, could not be left alone to fend for themselves in a town. Anything could happen to them. But a boy could take care of himself. Nothing would happen to his reputation. If he was left on the town, his plans to marry would not be ruined as a girl's would be. People would not look at him and say, oh, he was on the town and lived with many families; he may not marry my daughter. On the contrary. He would have seen something of the world and shown that he could take care of himself. Thus, said his mother, had her new husband argued.

But she did not say why she had listened. His new father was handsome and tall, but he was not that handsome and not that tall. And his mother was a beautiful woman, or at least so she seemed to him, and everyone in the town had always said that she was. Was she afraid that her new husband would leave her if she did not keep her promise and leave her son behind? Why wasn't his new father afraid that she would leave him? Surely, he thought, it was even more of a disgrace to be left by one's wife than to be left by one's husband. A man whose wife left him was a figure of fun. Of course, his mother had been worried about having enough money to feed herself and her daughters, but unless her husband left her, she would have had enough money for all of them. Esheal thought that she should have threatened to leave him. But he knew that she must have seen it as a choice between her son, who was only a child, and who could only earn a few rubles, and a man who was grown and could support her and give her back her place in the town.

Esheal thought about himself, and saw himself as even smaller, paler, and thinner than he was. His new father, however, was tall and strongly built. Gradually, he became convinced that if one were only tall, one could do anything one wanted with a woman. Only when he looked into the mirror and remembered Mrs. Romanoff's voice saying how mischievous was his expression, how comically he grimaced when he was given a compliment, how broad his shoulders were in spite of the fact that he was not tall, did he feel anything but misery as he surveyed his physical charms. If he could only grow taller! How would he ever find a woman to marry him? Mrs. Romanoff had laughed when he asked that and said that a woman would find him; that was always what happened. But he had said no, women were not like that; they were shy and good, and that was the kind of woman he wanted to marry, one who was shy and good. At this, Mrs. Romanoff raised her eyebrows. She said once more that a woman would find him, but when she saw how uncomfortable this idea made the boy, she did not say it again.

Chapter 15

When Esheal heard that Sarah's two boys had died, he wanted to go and speak to her. But now, he no longer spoke to Mrs. Romanoff and rarely even nodded to her on the street, so afraid was he that her husband would see him talking to her and become enraged with him all over again. Yet, as the years went by, he became more and more obsessed with her and with her two daughters. The eldest, Lily, had thick black hair and unusually fine, high coloring, and she seemed tall for her age. Her sister, Diana, never seemed to grow from year to year, and had thick brown-gold hair. In personality, the two girls differed entirely. Lily was quiet, although she was also high-strung and cried easily whenever she thought she was being teased or insulted. Diana was ungovernably mischievous, was never still, was always laughing, and rarely lost her temper or cried. Even though she was three years younger than her sister, Diana always seemed to have the upper hand. Men and women alike took to Diana. Everyone who came near her wanted to play with her hair, to pick her up, to bounce her on his knee, or, as she got older, simply to be with her. She was the general, her sister the troops. Rarely did Lily have an idea of her own. When she was involved in some scheme to revenge herself upon her younger brothers, or to surprise her mother, or her father, or her grandfather, she was obeying her younger sister's orders.

As the two girls grew older, this state of affairs persisted, and Lily began to resent her younger sister, who, having invented the jokes, was almost never the butt of them, and, if she was, she always managed to laugh as if she thought she was pretty funny even though she had been made to look ridiculous. And because she was what their younger brothers called "a good sport," it was not as much fun to tease her as it was to tease Lily. The boys would lie in wait for Lily behind trees, in back of doors, everywhere. When they decided to nail one of their sisters' underskirts to a chair, it was Lily's skirt that they nailed down, and when they saw her struggling to free it, attempting to wriggle into it even though it was still fastened to the chair because she had overslept as usual, and was late again, the hilarity was boundless.

At night, Lily and Diana slept in one bed in the middle, windowless bedroom, but Lily had no rest from her sister's pranks. One night when Lily climbed over Diana, waking her for what seemed like the hundredth time, Diana had an inspiration. As soon as her sister left the room, she crept under the bed and waited. When Lily came back, shivering from the cold, Diana waited until she could see her sister's ankles, and then seized one of them and refused to let go. Lily screamed for help, Diana let go, and, from under the bed, watched her sister run out of the room. By the time Lily came back with the rest of the family, Diana was standing up in the middle of the bed, grinning like a maniac.

Everyone looked at Diana, then at Lily, then at Diana again, and then everyone was convulsed with laughter. "What's so funny?" Lily asked; "what's so funny?" And every time she asked this, the laughter would rise until it slapped against the corners of the room. "Aren't you even going to look?" poor Lily shrieked, beside herself. At this, everyone doubled up. Lily looked at her sister, and although she was beginning to suspect the truth, she was too proud to admit it. Instead, she began to wail that some man had grabbed her by the ankle and no one cared enough to check the closet and the corner and to look behind the curtains. By the time Lily suggested that they look under the bed, the whole family was howling, laughing so hard they began crying.

That night, as on many others, Lily went to bed sure everyone in the world was against her, and when she heard her sister's deep, regular breathing, she glared at her back with hatred. Nevertheless, the two girls were inseparable. Sarah insisted that as soon as Diana was old enough to do so, she was to accompany Lily, and when Diana was invited somewhere by her friends, she had to take Lily with her. In time, they came to assume they would go everywhere together.

Esheal managed to learn almost everything there was to know about the Romanoff family. He knew in which grocery store Mrs. Romanoff shopped, and whenever he went in, managed to turn the conversation upon her family. When, after some time, the storekeeper became suspicious and asked Esheal why he was always asking about the Romanoffs, he said that his grandmother had known the family when they lived in Russia, and since she was still in Russia, she wanted to know anything he could tell her about her old friends. Esheal, whose mother never shopped in the man's store, knew he would not be found out.

At other times, Esheal would manage to read in the same park in which the two Romanoff girls played. Occasionally in the mornings, before he left for school, he would stand in a doorway and watch Sarah hanging her clothes on the fire escape or set off down the street to haggle for the vegetable scraps with which she made gevetch. As he watched, Sarah would sit herself down next to a pushcart and find a lettuce leaf here, a carrot with some dark spots there, a potato which was almost one black eye, the outer leaves of a cabbage which were brown and crumpled and limp, and if she were lucky, the man would feel sorry for her and give her some of the things he was going to throw away anyway, and then she would take them home, add some bones, and steam them for four hours. Esheal's mother always made gevetch, but when he ate it, he thought of Sarah's instead because he always said it was the most wonderful-tasting thing.

So year after year, Esheal watched her, and, while he loved watching the girls grow more and more beautiful, he hated watching Sarah grow older. She still carried herself like a queen, but it seemed to Esheal she moved more slowly. He had befriended their doctor, Dr. Linde, and from him, he learned that Sarah had diabetes and a bad heart; nevertheless, she entertained every blessed Sunday night of the year. Her friends, her sons' and daughters' friends, all of them came to her. From Dr. Linde, who never thought to question his interest in the Romanoffs, he learned why only one old man had been brought over from Russia. Meyer's father had traveled all the way to Germany and, while staying in the shipping company's barracks, caught pneumonia and died. Itzak Kapturak, Sarah's father, buried his friend and came to America alone.

Esheal knew all this, but he never came close to the family itself. When he learned the Romanoffs had decided to move from Delancey Street and the Lower East Side to Herkimer

Street and Brooklyn, Esheal was desolated. How would he keep track of the Romanoffs now? There would be no grocery store man, no nearby park to which he could go when he was not working on weekends. He would have only Dr. Linde.

On the day the peddler's cart drove up in front of the Romanoffs' Cherry Street tenement, Esheal's despair was immeasurable. When he looked around him, it seemed to him as if he were seeing the city for the first time. It was a barren place where no green things grew, whose people's skins soon took on the gray tinge of the concrete below and the gray skies overhead. Everywhere people rushed in all directions, trying to make enough money to stay alive one more day, and during that next day, they would rush about trying to make enough money to keep alive another day.

Esheal remembered the peasants in Pobrosk, and how, in the winter when the river froze, they would jump from chunk of ice to chunk of ice, and how their huge dogs, who had been trained to do so, would jump after them. Once they were on the other side, they would fish or hunt, and there were days when they crossed the river for the sheer excitement of getting across. As they jumped, their cheeks were red and their voices loud. But if they had been forced to do nothing but cross that river, jumping from one flat piece of ice to another! In the spring, the river was not the same river; it thickened and overflowed its banks and when it rained, its currents were wild and the water buried the rocks of the riverbed. On gray days, the river foamed black and white, and was an ebony river where it ran smoothly. In the summer, it was hard to remember that this cheerful blue and green sparkling which swifted over the rocks and which only came up to one's ankles would once again change into that rushing, foaming current. Esheal's eyes filled with tears remembering that river, and he became angrier and angrier at the stony, flinty city which surrounded him.

Once the Romanoffs moved to Herkimer Street, he would have no life. He ought to leave home! But he was finished with high school, and soon he would be finished with pharmacy school, and Dr. Linde had told him that when he graduated he would recommend him to all his patients. He was just fine where he was. And if he went to his mother and told her that he was moving out of his aunt's house and was going to live in a neighborhood far from hers, it would kill her. Her new husband had a bad cough, and Esheal was sure he had tuberculosis. The money he gave his mother allowed her to manage. She had gone bald with worry and now wore a little black wig. To Esheal, she looked more beautiful than ever. She depended on his visits. How could he explain why he wanted to move? It all sounded so senseless. Whenever he tried to imagine appearing at his mother's, telling her he was moving, he went cold with spite and satisfaction. It would serve her right if he left her there alone. But at the thought of his mother crying, when he thought of leaving her alone with a man who had become nothing more than a terrible cough and maybe had tuberculosis, he turned away from this tempting tableau of revenge.

He had asked only to remain near the Romanoffs and fate had turned a deaf ear. He knew that someone would say if he talked about the Romanoff girls, that there were many more fish in the sea; they would remind him of how many mothers had introduced how many girls to him once they found out he was going to pharmacy school. But somehow he had no use for any of them.

He loved his cousin Minnie, and she adored him, but they were first cousins, and he did not think of her in that way. He suspected, at times, that Minnie thought of him in that way. Several years ago, when Dr. Linde had gotten him a job as a streetcar conductor so that he could work at night and go to school during the day, Minnie used to get on the streetcar and ride around with him until all hours. Finally, he had his aunt put a stop to it. "A girl needs sleep," he told his aunt; "it's cold on that car. And if I talk to Minnie, I can't study." The next day, Minnie walked around with red eyes, and when he asked her what was wrong, she said nothing was wrong. When he asked his aunt what was the matter, she said, what should be the matter? She's upset about school. So he paid no attention. Now he was twenty-seven years old. He wanted to marry a decent woman, and none of the women he met appealed to him, although they were certainly decent. And now the Romanoffs were moving, and he was twenty-seven and there was no one he wanted to marry.

For once, chance took a hand. That afternoon, when Esheal came home, his mother was singing and packing things into a cardboard carton. All of the pictures had come down from the walls and were placed in a corner. For an instant,

Esheal thought that someone had died, but his mother was singing and his new father was there smiling. "We're moving!" his mother cried; "we're moving to Chauncey Street! Your new father's boss bought a building on Chauncey Street and he's renting us some rooms. It's just like the country there. There are fields all over. The fresh air will be wonderful for your new father. I heard *crickets*," she whispered, as if she did not believe it herself, as if she were afraid that, should she say it loud enough, everyone would laugh at her. "Crickets!" she whispered again, and then she burst out laughing, ran over to Esheal, and threw her arms around him.

Esheal wanted to hug his mother back but he could not. Often, when he came home, he wanted to kiss his mother, but he could not; he did not know why. Whenever he came home from work, he tried to stop at Woolworth's and buy his mother whatever she needed. If she needed black combs for her wig, he bought them for her. If she needed a new corset, he would tell one of his sisters to find out what kind she needed and what size, and he would give his sister the money and she would buy the corset, and after work, he would give it to his mother. But he could not touch her. He wanted to, but he could not. He had seen the Romanoff family together, and the boys kissed their mother and flirted with her as if she were not their mother at all but a girl they were taking out. They were always hugging and kissing each other. The boys kissed their mother; they kissed their sisters, and the sisters kissed everyone. They were so affectionate. He envied them that.

But to be moving to Chauncey Street! They would be right near Herkimer Street! When he opened his own pharmacy, he would open one near Herkimer Street. His mother was holding him at arm's length, watching him. "So," she said, "nothing surprises you? Not even the crickets? Not even the open fields? It's country!" "I'm surprised," Esheal said. "So," said his mother; "you're going to stay where you are? My sister, she wouldn't know what to do without you, and Minnie, she'll drop dead if you move out. So you'll stay there?" she asked, her voice trembling. "Are there any more rooms in that building on Chauncey?" he asked. "There are!" his mother cried; "there are!" "Then I guess I'll take them," Esheal said; "I earn a pretty good living working in the pharmacy here." "Won't it be a long ride for you?" his new

father asked; "all the way from Chauncey Street back here?"
"I can study on the train," said Esheal. "Nu," said his new
father.

So it was settled. Esheal went over to the building on
Chauncey Street and met his new father's boss, the landlord,
who showed him one room on the third floor. The room was
really part of a larger set of rooms, but it had a separate
entrance and, said the boss, Esheal could keep to himself as
much as he wanted to. But the set of rooms had only one
bathroom and Esheal would have to share it with a family.
Esheal said that was fine as long as the family in the other
rooms was not unreasonable. He paid the man five dollars,
shook hands, and stayed behind when the man went back
down the stairs. It was getting dark, and Esheal sat down on
the floor. His own room. Outside, the sky was putting itself
out, showing off, spreading pinks and purples over the tops of
the trees. Then the crickets began. And somewhere, three
blocks away, the Romanoffs were living.

For the first time in some years, he thought about the
zenshina's onion, and he did not understand why, now that
things looked brighter, now that he was paid so well to work
in the pharmacy at night and on weekends, now that he had
saved so much money he would soon be ready to open a
pharmacy of his own, he wanted to pull the outermost skin of
the onion—the layer in which the zenshina lived, in which the
people of Pobrosk lived and moved—tighter and closer about
him. He remembered the zenshina dancing, and remembered
the peasants, awakened each night by their primitive clock,
and how, when each was awakened, he would get up and go
into the zenshina's house and she would take him to bed. He
remembered his cousin Minnie saying, "Oh, Esheal is so
afraid he won't marry a decent woman." Was that why he
thought so much about the Romanoffs? He looked through
the empty window of the new room. It had filled with
darkness and, because the gaslight was lit, it reflected the
blank wall on the other side of the room.

In the window, the zenshina began dancing, and Esheal
saw himself coming toward her, taking her hand, and beginning to dance with her. Esheal watched himself dancing as if
he were someone else, someone he ought to call back. But he
did not want to call the dancer back. The zenshina was a
decent woman, he told himself, and his eyes burned and his
throat clenched so hard he could not swallow. A decent

woman, what was it? He wished that the zenshina were here now that he was older, now that he was old enough to ask her questions which would be worth answering.

He did not know what she had been before he had known her. A person could be made into someone else, he thought, if he were treated badly enough. He remembered his mother saying that when two heads shared the same pillow, their hair mixed; they became one head. On whose pillow had she lain her head? With whom had her hair mixed? Of what use was blame when there was always another person with whose hair one mixed, who could change you so completely? Did the decent become indecent? When he married, he wanted to marry a woman who would be loyal and fine and who would love him and who would never change. As he thought about this, he thought he saw the zenshina coming closer, as if she wanted to ask him something. If he could marry anyone in the world, he said, he would marry Diana Romanoff. She was so beautiful and so delicate and she was always laughing. But Diana Romanoff was only a child. Still, if he knew she would marry him, he would wait for her. In six years, she would be eighteen. He would be thirty-three. Then he thought about Diana's mother, Sarah Romanoff, and how he had not spoken to her in years. But now, her husband would have forgotten who he was and what he looked like. Probably she did not remember him after all this time.

And then, astonishingly, two weeks after he moved into his room in the building on Chauncey Street, one floor beneath his mother and his sisters, he had an excuse to see her. The neighborhood was buzzing with the news. A Mrs. Pohs was taking Diana to court, and Dr. Linde told him that all the neighbors who knew the Romanoffs were going to the hearing, which the Romanoffs called a trial. "I'm going too," said Dr. Linde; "I wouldn't miss it for the world. It should be quite a circus." Naturally, Esheal said he would come too; he wouldn't miss more than a day of pharmacy school, and he had never been in a court of law before. Dr. Linde said he hoped he would never have to spend time in court again and, when Esheal came to the courtroom with him, it seemed like the most natural thing in the world.

Chapter 16

Diana

When we moved to Herkimer Street, my parents were so pleased with themselves because they had gotten out of the old neighborhood on the Lower East Side, and Mother never got tired of saying what a joy it was to raise her children in a good neighborhood. But it was in the good neighborhood that we had all the trouble. A Jew couldn't walk there without getting into a fight. There was nobody Jewish in that neighborhood. They were all goyim, and my brother Dave, he had just gotten out of the hospital, because what did he have to do, he had to jump off a stoop to show the other boys he could jump faster and farther than they did, and finally he had to jump from the top of a stoop, so he ruptured his appendix and he ended up in the hospital. Eight years old and already he was operated on. So naturally, when he came out of the hospital, I wasn't going to let anyone look at him cross-eyed let alone hit him, and of course I slapped this boy for bothering Dave. And this boy was going to hit Dave for no reason. So he was slapped, but good. And I was going to pick up my geography; years ago, geographies were this big, so I picked it up, and I saw the boy's mother was after me. So I put it down to see what's going to happen here, and I told Dave to go into the house. I wanted him out of the way, nobody should touch him, and if anything's going to happen, let her take care of me. I knew I had two good hands. So she carried on afterward. She took me to court, a child of twelve.

In that neighborhood anyway, you were hit. I once asked a neighbor boy, why did you hit Bill, why do you always hit Bill, why do you always fight with Bill, he don't fight with anybody. Bill was so quiet. He was not at all like Dave. He was an angel, that boy. Dave was in every kind of trouble, but not Bill. So he'd say, he's a Jew, isn't he? That was enough for him. And when I beat him—I beat the life out of that boy in front of his father and his mother in his garden in the front

yard—the mother was on the porch and she was ready to
jump down off the porch to kill me. The father would not let
her go. He said if that little girl can beat him up like that, let
him take his licking. And I told his father why I did it. I said
for no reason he said that he's going to kill Bill every time he
sees him and for no other reason than that he was a Jew. I
asked the father, did he think that was a good reason. He
wouldn't let his wife come down off the porch and I beat that
boy up.

I protected my brothers. They were such Jew-haters there.
She was a tall, skinny mick, that mother on the porch, and she
didn't want her boy touched. After that, he left my brother
alone. I went to his mother before I beat him up; I rang the
bell, and she didn't even bother coming out. She came out
wearing a hat like all   goyim sixty, seventy years ago.
They didn't go to the grocery store without a hat on, so when
I told her about her son and how he was going to kill Bill, she
just turned around and walked away, so I said, I'll fix him
without you. I knew she wasn't going to say anything to him. I
was twelve years old. Bill was three years younger than I was.
He wasn't afraid of me, that boy, although when he saw me
coming, he ran into his house and that's where I got him.
Right in the gate.

But he didn't bother Bill from then on. Because Bill had to
go to Hebrew school, Bill had to go on Shabbes to temple,
Bill brought Grandpa to shul. I brought Grandpa to shul too.
They never bothered Grandpa when I took him, but when
Bill brought Grandpa, they would scratch their chins at
Grandpa, making fur of him Three   them would stand in
the street looking up at Grandpa. We were up on the third
floor, and Grandpa always sat on a narrow windowsill looking
down that side street where we lived, and Grandpa would see
these boys making fun of him, scratching their chins, because
he had a beard, carrying on. It hurt me terribly, but Grandpa
said he's not even bothered. But you see when I was taking
Grandpa to shul, nobody bothered him, nobody bothered
me. But when Bill went, they wanted to kill Bill, they wanted
to kill Grandpa. They threw stones at Grandpa. It was an
ordeal in a goyish neighborhood when Jews moved in.

I stopped them from hitting Grandpa with stones and I
didn't let Bill take Grandpa to shul anymore because me they
didn't hit. It wasn't the thing to do, to hit a girl. So I could go
with Grandpa. And what could I have done to these big

goyim? When I was tallest, I was four feet ten. I don't know
how tall I am now and I don't want to know. I've been
shrinking. I have to keep taking up the hems of my dresses.
They would have pulled at his beard if they'd had the chance.
He was in his late seventies. In a goyish neighborhood, he was
really afraid to walk alone and we wouldn't let him walk alone
and we would buy whatever he wanted.

Grandpa used to eat cottage cheese by the ton, and there
was a Mr. Miller who made butter and his own cream cheese
and cottage cheese, and we bought it for Grandpa. Poppa
used to shlep bottles of wine and certain liquors that Grandpa
drank. And his tobacco that he had. I have his snuffboxes
here.

To get back to the other fight. There were a lot of those
boys and someone put one of the boys up to hitting Dave. So I
pushed the boy aside and he went and told his mother I hit
him. He was ten years old and I was twelve. I didn't hit him. I
pushed him away from Dave and sent Dave upstairs. When I
was going upstairs, the woman came over to me, and she says,
you damn little kite. I thought she said kite, but she said kike.
I didn't know what she was talking about anyway. The
woman was going to slap Dave. I held her hand, she slapped
me, I slapped her back and up the stairs I ran, quick as a flash,
and good, my kitchen door was open, and I said, Grandpa,
this woman's chasing me, she wants to hit me. So my
grandfather says, She'll hit you? And the woman came in and
started to tell him that I had slapped her face. You know I had
to climb up on the steps to hit her back, I was so short and she
was so tall. She was a doctor's wife, so she thought she was a
hell of a lot. So my grandfather shouted at her, even when he
was in his seventies he had the voice of a giant. You'll hit her!
I'll break you in pieces and I'll throw you out the window and
the cats will eat you! She turned around and ran down the
steps, and he was cursing her until she was out on the street.
So she took me to court.

When we got there, the judge called me up, and Mother—
we were so clean and so neat, my mother was the cleanest
person on earth. So we four children were brought up for that
woman to look at, and the woman pointed at me and said I
was the kite that hit her. The judge said to me, Did you slap
that lady on the face? I said yes. Because I did. He said, Why
did you do that? I said she slapped me, so I slapped her back,
that's all. And I said she called me names, she called me a

kite. And he says to me, What does it mean? I said, I don't
know. And I didn't know. Anyway, he questioned me. I was
so short I sat on his lap and Mother sat in the chair, and I
answered his questions and he was very thrilled with me.

Of course, he threw the case out of court, and as we're
walking out, Lily and I both looked at each other and said
nyah nyah nyah to her, because, you know, she didn't win her
case. We walked back to the house and when we came back,
we told Dave that he's not to talk to this boy anymore. And
Mother was so proud, and she was out on the street talking to
some man who used to work in the pharmacy near our old
building on Delancey Street, and they were laughing, and I
was surprised, because I didn't know she knew him. Maybe
that was how Lily met him, through Momma. I forgot all
about old Esheal being there until now.

Anyway, the judge came to visit my mother, and when he
did, he asked her how many children she had, and she said
just these four. He said, Just these four? I haven't even one.
Would you let me have, adopt your daughter, because I'm a
very rich man and I could do a lot for her. My mother would
part with a child! Anyway, he told her she didn't know how
wonderful it would be, a Jewish child to be raised by a
Christian. The combination would be wonderful. So she said
that's very foolish. I never would part with a child. I parted
with two. That's enough. He stayed for a while, he left, he
came again another time, thinking maybe she would change
her mind. He evidently was very fond of what I had said.

And she kept us so neat and so clean. He never saw four
children like that. In the morning, when we went down, we
went down in little wrappers. In the afternoon, it was
starched dresses, and she stood and ironed every dress, with
    ruffles, the things that she made, little tucks with the lace
going down here, everything, and we were the nicest children
on the street and the cleanest. So that was how I was in court
even before Dave was and how I didn't get adopted. I was
lucky. No matter what happened, someone always wanted
me. And I always knew it. So I was lucky.

Chapter 17

Not only the judge was taken with Diana Romanoff. Esheal was hopelessly impressed by the girl. She was so spirited and so pretty, and he saw that she would always be small, always resemble a doll, because she was unusually mature for her age, unusually well-developed, so he knew that she would not suddenly shoot up into a tall, gangly creature. He thought about how wonderful it would be to look down at someone like Diana and see her golden-brown eyes looking up at him. He was now a very good-looking man, if not a handsome man, but he was only five foot four, and his mother told him that his father had been even shorter.

"When we were courting," she said, "and we went out into the fields, I always waited until he was up higher than I was, so I would climb up on a log, and jump down, and then, when he was still standing on the log, I would look up at him and ask for a kiss. He used to laugh at me and say there was something about my bottom hitting a bench that made me want to kiss him. But it wasn't that. When I was sitting, he looked so tall. And he *felt* tall. But there weren't too many tall men in the village then, I don't know why. Here they grow tall. But you were born there, so you'll be short, like your father. But does a woman care if a man is short?

"What do you think a husband and wife do all day, stand back to back checking to see which one is the taller? The attendant at the baths used to say it. 'A man lying down in bed is never short.' So when you walk with your husband, he doesn't tower over you. What does it mean? You notice that only the first few months. Then you notice whether you have with what to cook, with what to sew, whether he leaves the other women alone, whether he beats the children. That's what makes a man tall. To me, your father was a very tall man."

When Esheal saw the Romanoffs at the hearing, he wanted

to be tall; he wanted to be everything. He thought carefully about his prospects and saw that within several years he would be able to run his own pharmacy, and, if he were lucky, he would be able to own his business by the time he was thirty. He would be what the women called a good catch. But what would a woman think of him? He had no idea. After the hearing, he went to the fanciest photographic studio in the neighborhood and sat for his portrait. The photographer, who was bathed in an eerie blue light, was bald, and his head was pointed, and the blue light made a pimple on his nose shine as if it were a small moon that had landed there and decided to stay. If, Esheal thought, he turned out to look like the photographer, he would forget about the Romanoffs. In fact, he would forget about women. It would be the least he could do for them. But this man was married. Esheal knew because his wife was always in the pharmacy pleading for more time to pay her bills. They had six children. Still, thought Esheal, if that was the way you looked, death was the only answer. Well, he had to know how he looked.

"Can you rush the order?" he asked the man. The photographer smiled at him sympathetically. "The bride's family wants to get a good look at you, eh?" he asked. Esheal flushed and said that the picture was for his mother. "For your mother?" said the man; "and you're in such a hurry for a mother? She's on her deathbed, God forbid?" Esheal said his mother was healthy as a horse, but he thought only a man with a pretty rough sense of humor would tell jokes about a man's mother dying. The man apologized and said that, in the old country, he used to work for the burial society and he had gotten into bad habits joking about the dead. "So when do you need the order?" he asked Esheal. "Tomorrow," Esheal said. "So mysterious," said the man; "everyone wants their pictures immediately if not sooner. No one comes in without a wallet full of excuses. Usually, in Russia someone's dying who wants to see the pictures. Or the mother of the girl is on her deathbed, and if she could only have the picture to hold onto, she'd come around. You wouldn't believe it. But you want the picture tomorrow and no reasons. Why should I do it?" "I'll pay you more," said Esheal. "How much more?" asked the man. "Double," said Esheal. "Tomorrow will be no trouble," said the man.

The next day when Esheal picked up his portrait, he was pleasantly surprised. For one thing, he had been seated in a low, beautifully carved chair, and it was impossible to tell by looking at the photograph whether he was tall or short. He was heavier than he thought he was, and he realized that this new state of affairs had been brought about by his having moved into the same building in which his mother lived.

Recently, he had been giving her more money, not because she needed it or because she had asked for it, but because he was so proud of being able to give her more. And his mother was so grateful, so happy to be free of worries about money that she had to celebrate, but how was she to celebrate? Her new husband was almost dead from coughing and he crawled home from the shop more dead than alive. So she thought about it, and she decided that even if she didn't know anything about celebrating, she did know about cooking. So she began to cook for her son, and his mother's idea of a meal was a huge meal. Now his suppers began with a big plate of fried onions, and eggs and liver. Then she served tsmluch, a plate of soup, green-pea or potato soup, and her plates of soup were huge; they reminded Esheal of the bowls his mother had used in Russia, only then what was in the bowl had to feed the whole family. And then she would serve him some meat or some fish, apples or prunes, cake or tea. At first, Esheal could not get past the soup without beginning to gasp for breath, but in no time, he was finishing everything his mother put on his plate.

So the man he saw in the picture looked older, heavier, and more distinguished than Esheal thought he would be. He looked at the picture as if he were looking at a stranger, and asked himself whether he would trust a daughter of his with that man. He saw some suspicious things. His eyes were deep-set and large, but they were hooded and gave him a brooding air. Brooding airs, he thought, were fine for movie-picture stars, but in husbands, they were to be avoided. His nose was slightly hooked but it was almost straight and it was not large. His mouth surprised him. It was the mouth of a sensualist, a wide mouth, a full lower lip, and a finely chiseled and nicely shaped upper lip. His ears were small, and his forehead was high, and his hair, which he had slicked down with water for the occasion, shone. He was proud of his posture. He sat up straight.

He looked at his hands with regret. In the picture, the fingers of one hand were holding onto the thumb of the other and they betrayed his nervousness. But his stiff collar was immaculate, his tie neat and perfectly in place, and his suit was elegant. He was a man with a good square face and a good square jaw, and he would have to learn to think of himself as he now saw himself; he was no longer a thin, sallow-looking boy with a mischievous smile. Suddenly, he missed the mischievous grin which others had often pointed out to him, but when he looked carefully at the picture, it seemed to him that his lips were about to begin to smile. So he was the same person after all.

The next day, Esheal took the picture and, without telling anyone where he was going, went to the pharmacy at the corner of Chauncey and Howard. He had heard that Mr. Sapirstein wanted to sell, and he had looked at his bank account and decided that, if he used the money the zenshina had given him, he could afford to take over the business when he finished pharmacy school that spring. As he was walking to the store, he saw a newspaper boy and decided to let the paper pass because he was in a hurry to look at the store, but then he heard the boy shout, "Read all about it, read all about the Romanoffs in court." So he turned around and bought a copy of the newspaper, and there it was, a long clipping about the hearing on the fifth page. He stood in the middle of the sidewalk reading it, oblivious of everyone else on the street so that people had to push him out of the way to get by and went on their way muttering.

IT IS A NEW TERM OF OPPROBRIUM
JUDGE IN CHILDREN'S COURT
PUZZLED OVER THE WORD "KITE"
USED BY LITTLE GIRL

DIANA ACCUSED OF ASSAULT
MRS. POHS SLAPPED HER FACE
AND SHE SLAPPED BACK

Diana Romanoff, 12 years old, appeared in the Children's Court today to defend herself against a charge of assault brought by Mrs. Sophie Pohs of 1000 Herkimer Street. The little girl didn't look as if she could inflict serious punishment upon an antagonist, especially not upon the complainant, who is a stout, broad-shouldered woman between 30 and 40, but she admitted that she had slapped Mrs. Pohs' face.

"I did it in self-defense," Diana told the court. "Mrs. Pohs called me a dirty little kite and then I called her an old kite. I guess I had a right to do that."

At this point, Justice Fitzgerald interrupted the little girl's story to learn the meaning of the word "kite" when used as a term of opprobrium. Diana, however, was unable to give the definition. Mrs. Pohs couldn't tell, either. Someone else volunteered the information that it was a synonym of "high flier" but the court looked pained and told the girl to proceed with her narrative.

"Well," continued Diana, "when I called Mrs. Pohs a kite she jumped at me and slapped my face three different times, one after another. The third slap was more than I could stand, so I raised myself on my toes, and gave her a slap, too. I guess I had a right to do that, didn't I, Judge?"

The Judge looked gravely at the defendant but made no reply.

"Is that all?" he inquired.

"No," said the little girl, hotly, "it isn't. After I slapped Mrs. Pohs' face, I ran toward home, which is only a few doors away from where Mrs. Pohs lives, and what do you think she did?"

"I can't imagine," said the Judge, with a faint smile.

"Well," Diana went on, after taking a deep breath, "she followed me right up. I ran into the hallway of our house and called as loud as I could for my momma. Just as Momma came into the hall to see what was the matter with me, Mrs. Pohs caught me and again slapped my face right before Momma. Wasn't that terrible?"

Here the little girl almost broke down. "Right before Momma," she kept on repeating, as if to have her face slapped before her mother was an insult that went straight to her heart.

Diana was triumphantly acquitted of the charge of assault, as well as of the charge of using profane language, also brought against her by Mrs. Pohs.

The friends and relatives of both defendant and complainant attended the hearing of the case in unprecedented numbers and listened to the testimony with breathless interest. Some of them got so excited that they couldn't keep their seats and had to be told to keep quiet.

Esheal read the clipping four or five times before he began to hear the noise of the traffic again and realized where he was and what he was doing there. He folded the paper so that it was open to the page on which the article appeared and set off for the drugstore. He noticed with pleasure the arrow-shaped black-and-white tile design which had been set into the sidewalk in front of the pharmacy. Chauncey and Howard was a busy corner, a very good corner. He went into the drugstore and pretended to look for something along the back aisle where Mr. Sapirstein kept the powders and perfumes. He did not want Mr. Sapirstein to know he was looking the place over. The last time he had gone to look at a pharmacy, the owner had caught the scent of a new prospect, and there had been more of his friends and relations walking around in the store than there had been bottles on the shelves, so Esheal had to send a friend in later in the week to look at the store, and of course he reported that not a soul came in.

Mr. Sapirstein had a flair, Esheal could see that. His white-and-black floor, with its geometrically patterned tile flowers, was spotless and shone. Overhead, ceiling fans whirled lazily even though it was cold, and inside, the air was fresh and faintly scented with powder. Esheal was surprised by the number of children who were going in and out of the store. He moved down to the end of the aisle and saw that Mr. Sapirstein had a wonderful display of candies, each kind in its own huge glass jar. And he had an enormous apothecary jar filled with jelly beans and, for a penny, each child got two jelly beans from a smaller jar, and a chance to guess at the number of beans in the large jar, and, if the child guessed correctly, the sign said, he would win ten dollars. What a fortune that was to a child, Esheal thought.

One group of children left and another came in. Suddenly Esheal heard what was unmistakably her voice, full and unaccented and pitched low even for a grown woman. "Well, don't you know I lied?" Diana was saying; "she never slapped my face in front of my mother. Momma wasn't even home." "So why did you say she did?" asked a friend of hers. "Oh, Dinney!" said Lily. "Because you could get into trouble lying in court," Dinney said stubbornly. "I was already in trouble, being in the court," said Diana, "so I thought I'd get out of it that way. Anyway, it worked." "But you could have been sent to jail!" said Dinney. "I wasn't, was I?" asked Diana; "and it's a good thing for that big kite I wasn't, because when I came out, I would have laid for her with stones and I would have gotten her. I would have killed her." "God forbid," said Dinney; "they'd put you in jail and throw away the key." "Well, I ain't in jail, am I?" asked Diana. "You sure aren't," said Lily; "last night, she was at me again. They wouldn't want her in jail. That's what my mother said."

"So why didn't the big kite take your grandfather to court," asked Dinney; "if he cursed her like that." "She was afraid he'd lay for her, that's why," said Diana. "Grandpa laying for someone!" exclaimed Lily. Esheal bent forward to see the three girls. Diana looked at Dinney and the two of them burst out laughing and then Lily started, and soon the three of them were helpless. "Look out for Dinney!" gasped Diana; "she's going to wet herself!" "Get the pail!" shrieked Lily. "Oh, no," said all three of them at once as they saw the yellow pool fattening on the tile floor.

"Come on, Dinney, get out of here," hissed Diana, grabbing Dinney's hand, running with her out the door. Lily ran after them, and Esheal walked toward the door, looked out, and saw the three girls leaning against the window of the pharmacy, helpless with laughter. Then he saw Mr. Sapirstein come out from behind the candy counter holding a mop. "Those girls," said Mr. Sapirstein; "each and every time." "Every time they come in?" Esheal asked in astonishment. "You get used to it," said Mr. Sapirstein, beginning to mop up. Outside, he could hear the girls laughing. The laughter would die down, and then one of them would say something, and that would set the others off.

It was a good store, Esheal thought. A store with children was a good store. He looked around, measuring the pharmacy with his eyes. It would be a perfect store if only it had a soda fountain. Then there would be children in it all the time. Even Mrs. Romanoff and her boys would come. Everyone would come. If he put the soda fountain against the wall to the left of the door, people would be able to see it from the street. He thought about Diana, who was only twelve, and who would be eighteen in such a short time. He thought about how wonderful it would be to be married to a girl like the one Diana would be when she got older. There was nothing she would not be able to handle. And there was so much to her.

He thought about what it would be like to have children, girls—he wanted to have girls—who looked like her and would depend on him and look up to him. He did not know which he liked more, the idea of having Diana for a wife, or having Diana as a child, and he decided he did not know which he preferred, and how lucky her husband would be, because he would not have to decide.

He asked himself why he loved little girls so, any little girls, and he thought that it was their fragility which made him love them, their delicacy, the little curves and swellings and concavities which were so touching and so comical when one thought of the women the little girls would become. The poor little things, he thought, soon enough they would be shut up in kitchens, they would have to beg their husbands for every penny, learn to hoard up pennies from what little they were given so they would not have to beg and crawl. They would have children, lose their teeth, get old before their time. And it was because they did all these things without complaining even though there was no one else to do them that he loved them so. There were hundreds and hundreds of swords hanging above their heads that did not hang above the heads of men. Women were remarkable creatures.

Just as Esheal thought this, and just as he was again telling himself that a soda fountain would be a wonderful thing in the pharmacy, it would be a place where the women could rest and gossip and forget about their rooms and their families, the girls came running back in. "I forgot Grandpa's cinnamon drops!" Diana said, running to the other side of the store. "Say, Diana," Dinney said, "who was that man your mother was talking to after the trial?" "Hearing," Diana corrected her. "So who was he?" asked Dinney. "Momma said he used to help her out when she first got here, when she did her drawings, you know those drawings," Diana said; "she's still drawing everyone who comes in. She said he was a ridiculous little boy, he was so thin and so old in his ways. She said every time she looked at him she used to think of that joke, you know, your socks ought to have a party and invite your pants down." Under his clothes, Esheal's flesh burned.

"So why was she talking to him, if he's so ridiculous?" Dinney asked; "he didn't look ridiculous to me." "Well, that's what she said," Diana answered; "she said look what he's made of himself. Who would have thought it? She said when she first saw him she didn't think he'd last out the year. But he's not so bad-looking now, is he?" "He's terrible short," said Lily. "So what does that mean, short?" asked Dinney. "I want to marry someone tall and handsome," said Lily. "I want to marry someone who loves me," said Dinney. "I want to marry someone who loves me and who I love," said Diana.

"You may have trouble getting anyone to marry you," said Dinney. "Why should I?" asked Diana; "everyone wants me. Even the judge wanted to adopt me." "Your *name*," said Dinney; "Diana's no name for a Jewish girl. That's what my mother said. That's why they used to call you Doris." "They don't anymore," said Diana; "my father said Momma named me, not the neighbors." "You'll see," said Dinney; "you're not going to get married with that name." "*You're* not going to get married so fast," said Diana; "with your big nose and your pop eyes and your shoemaker father!" "Oh, you don't mean it!" Dinney gasped. "I do mean it!" said Diana. "Say you don't mean it!" begged Dinney. "I do mean it!" Diana said again, starting to cry. "Do you mean it, too?" Dinney asked Lily; "do you think she's right?" "She's right," Lily said thoughtfully, looking carefully at Dinney; "you have pop eyes and you have a big nose." Dinney began to wail, and Diana began to cry and Lily began to sniffle, and soon all three girls were crying, and they ran sobbing out of the store. "That's a new one," Mr. Sapirstein said to Esheal when he came over to the counter; "girls. Laughing one minute, crying the next. They're all the same." Esheal nodded and went back to the powders.

Mr. Sapirstein wondered what was taking Esheal so long. He didn't like to go after customers with a hook, but he had been standing in front of those powders for an eternity. "So," said Mr. Sapirstein, "when there are so many things it's hard to decide. An embarrassment of riches." Esheal agreed with him wholeheartedly, and at the same time decided that he had to buy something from Mr. Sapirstein's powder section, not because he had spent such a long time standing there, but because he wanted to pay tribute to the remarkable way Mr. Sapirstein ran his store. So he said he'd like to buy his mother some fancy powder, but he didn't know what kind women liked. "Mothers usually like lavender. Or lilac," said Mr. Sapirstein. He showed Esheal two or three of each.

"What's the best you have in the store?" Esheal asked at last. "Well," said Mr. Sapirstein, setting down a huge oval box covered in peach satin and decorated by a bouquet of tiny purple roses, "this is the best, but it's terribly expensive. It's three dollars." "I'll take it," said Esheal; "can you wrap it up?" "You can bring it back if you change your mind," Mr. Sapirstein said nervously. This was the most expensive cosmetic item he had in the store. He had really bought it to keep it on display. He had never believed anyone would buy it. "Or if your mother doesn't like it, you can always bring it back."

Mr. Sapirstein was both ecstatic to have made such a sale and unhappy to think he would now have to reorder the expensive item which had made his display so elegant, and this time, when he reordered it, he would never sell it again. "A special occasion?" Mr. Sapirstein asked. "Yes," said Esheal, "it is." He grinned at Mr. Sapirstein and pulled out his wallet, and as he did so, he pulled out his portrait, which fell on the druggist's counter. "You're sure this is for your mother?" Mr. Sapirstein asked, seeing the portrait. "It's for my mother," Esheal said; "I wish it wasn't, but it's for my mother." "You know someone else you'd like to give it to?" asked Mr. Sapirstein, hoping the young man would say yes, there was a young woman he would like to give it to, because then he might come back and buy the next peach-colored box.

"I know her," said Esheal; "but she doesn't know me." Mr. Sapirstein laughed. "Keep it that way," he advised. "Once they can say they know you, they think they've got you. Those unmarried girls have big, big eyes and long, long nails. You can ask me. I know." "I wouldn't mind this one's nails," said Esheal. "You're caught," said Mr. Sapirstein; "you're beyond help. Once the bug bites you, you're sick. If this one lets you alone, another one will get you. You'll help her catch you," he said; "mark my words." "I wish one would catch me," said Esheal. "Depend on it," said Mr. Sapirstein. Esheal picked up the package and left feeling very pleased with himself.

Tomorrow he would come back and talk business with Mr. Sapirstein; it was not his nature to do things on impulse. Esheal told himself that this was no impulse, that he had been considering buying this business for some time, but he did not believe in making any decision until he slept on it. So he went home, resolved to come back in the morning, and on the way home, he kept taking out his portrait and looking at it, and hearing Sarah's voice saying why didn't his socks give a party and invite his pants down. People in that family could be cruel, he thought, but then he thought about the pharmacy and the soda fountain and he forgot about everything else.

Chapter 18

Diana: 1960

After my sister Lily died, her daughter called me to tell me
that Lily had been sick for a very long time. Lucy said they
didn't tell me about her earlier because they didn't want to
worry me. She went into the hospital to have a wart removed,
and there was nothing wrong with the wart, but my sister
must have thought there was something wrong with the
breathing tube they put down her throat in case there was any
trouble with the anesthetic, and she decided to take it out
herself. So she yanked out the breathing tube, and she
scratched her throat, and the scratched throat became in-
fected, and the infection became double pneumonia, and
after that, she was never the same. I went to see her in the
home where they put her, and she said to me, do you see
Momma, do you talk to her? I said yes, I saw her; she asked
about you. She's coming next time to see you. What was I
going to say to her? It was terribly sad. Lily started to walk
away from her daughter's house, or she'd go on the streetcar,
she didn't know where. She had to be in a home. Once she
almost set fire to the house. She'd turn on the stove and forget
to put on the pot, or she'd put on the pot and forget to take it
off. One day the wallpaper in the kitchen had actually begun
to burn before her daughter came back and saw it. Believe
me, it was lucky. She just had time to throw some water on
the wall.

The night after the funeral, her daughter told me that Lily
had always been envious of me. Now isn't that a peculiar
thing? I used to envy Lily her figure. She had a beautiful
figure, but I was short and stumpy. So I didn't think she had
anything to be envious about. I never believed that story
about her being in love with my husband. It was bad enough
that *I* was in love with my husband. We were first cousins. At
the time, there was no law against marrying first cousins.

Everyone liked my husband. All the girls were crazy about him. But he only had eyes for me. And then he went off to Nome, Alaska, and left all of us alone. He fixed us. Anyway, I'm sure Lily wasn't in love with him. That's a loose way of talking, you know, to say they were all in love with him. So it was odd because I thought I envied Lily.

My mother used to sew all of our clothes and then she would stand there and iron them, you know, with all their little tucks and gatherings. But when Lily had to have a dress, Momma would send her to the dressmaker, or to our cousin Fannie Romanoff, and she was a wonderful dressmaker. So I would say to my mother, why can't I have a dress made at the dressmaker, and she would say you're not ready to get married, or she's the oldest one, and for the oldest you have to do a little something extra.

And then when I wanted to get married, Momma said no, not until Lily gets married. So I used to say, the very day Lily gets married, I'm getting married. So it almost was. Except that the new law came out saying that you had to sign papers and wait two days, which is why I got married two days later. And my grandfather used to watch me washing the dishes, and I was so short that Momma had to build up a little platform for me to stand on, and my grandpa would come over and say, you know, you're half a head, you have half a head, you stand here cleaning and washing, and she's sitting there, playing the piano.

Then he would start on my mother. The poor thing, she had no rest from him. Because I was his favorite, you see. I was the one who ended up taking him back and forth from shul, because me the boys left alone. Whether it was because I beat up that other boy, or because it wasn't right to hit a girl, I don't know. So we would all be sitting at the table, and my mother would fill up the plates and pass them around, and he would look at my plate, and look at Momma, and then he'd get up and look into Lily's plate, and he'd say to Momma, I don't understand you. I don't know what it is; you give her the smallest portion of anybody at the table. She never gets a portion like Lily gets. Lily you bought a big piano and her you bought a little mandolin. Oh, he was funny. Momma told me later that she used to give me extra big portions just to get some rest from him, but still he thought mine were too small. So is it any wonder I thought I was picked on?

I've been trying to remember how Lily met Esheal. I don't

think I ever knew. But when she met him, it seemed to me that he'd been around all of our lives. Of course, we were used to seeing him and saying good morning and good night to him when we came into the pharmacy. But how Lily ever got on other terms with him I don't know. And I almost missed her wedding. Before old Esheal married her, he seemed nice enough, but then afterward, I saw he was terrible mean and cranky. Nothing pleased him. Nobody pleased him. It's a terrible thing to have such a disposition. Of course, my sister's disposition was not what you'd call perfect, but I think if she had married anyone else, things would have been all right. Sometimes when I went to visit her, I thought she blamed me because she was not happy. So of course I was happy. I married the man I was in love with from the time I was a little child. But when unhappiness came, I got it all in one dose. I hate to think of those times.

So, since I was Grandpa's favorite, he used to tell me all the stories, how the year I was born there was a great snowstorm and my uncle came, my mother's brother, and he died in her house, and the snows were so high Momma used to say you couldn't open the windows, and if you went up to the second floor, you could put your hand out the window and touch the snow, that's how high it was. So when he died, they couldn't bury him because there were no roads. There were just no roads. He died in January and it was February before they could bury him. So all that time he lay in the middle bedroom on ice, because there was nothing they could do about it. And once, the iceman didn't come because there was so much snow and Momma went down herself and cut chunks of ice out of the snow in the street and put the ice over and under the body and after that she was hysterical. She was always afraid of February after that. She feared that month.

But at least she didn't have to worry about food because she had a friend who ran a grocery store out of the basement of the building next door. People were poor in those days, so this one had a laundry in the basement, and that one had a tailor shop, that was the way it was. So they broke through the walls between the two buildings and the woman was absolutely cleaned out just by the people in the two buildings. People needed things. They had children. They had to eat. And he would watch me watching Momma clean the house for Pesach, and he would say, your poor momma is very unhappy, she can't take the ceiling down to clean it and put it back up again. Because she was so clean, you see. But we were Jews, so we were dirty Jews.

I was definitely Grandpa's favorite. He wanted me to sing the old Yiddish songs for him, and they were some sad songs. He used to sing the songs for me, and I sounded them out on the mandolin and I did the writing, so I had the music, and when he wanted me to play that song, I would sing and play that song. It was a Jewish song about a father who hasn't got his home anymore and so he's living with his children. It was the saddest song. Believe me, I could sing it today, I know it so well.

And for some reason, I always wound up taking care of my brothers. Lily never did. I don't think she had it in her, but Grandpa thought she just didn't want to. There was the day Dave decided to steal Aunt Sadie's brass bed. Aunt Sadie had a brass bed, and she decided to get a wooden one. I don't know if she was tired of its squeaking or if she thought it was the modern thing to do. Anyway, she wanted to get rid of the bed and she put it in the basement of our building. So Dave needed things, money for a new ball, for the movies, and in those days you could sell a brass bed and get some money for the metal. So he went down to the basement, but first he took down Mother's clothesline and he and a friend tied up the brass bed and started lugging it off down the street.

And it happened that on that day Sadie was home; she wasn't working that day in the shirtwaist factory. I don't remember what was wrong with her, but anyway, she looked out the window and there was Dave and his friend dragging the bed. So she ran down the stairs half dressed, she had her skirt on, but no blouse, and she ran down the street hollering, bring back that bed, bring back that bed, and they were running as if they were trying to get off this earth. And I had to run after the boys and tell them to drop the bed, and then, so they wouldn't steal the bed again, I had to give each of them ten cents. And I had to talk to Aunt Sadie, because otherwise, Uncle Murray would have given it to them with a strap when he came home.

My husband used to say I had the most wonderful smile. When he was in Nome, Alaska, he wrote me and said, no, my picture, the one I sent him, wasn't frozen, it was in a frame in a very cozy room and my smile kept the room pretty well heated too. Well, Lily didn't smile as much as I did. Of course, she laughed if you did something funny, and it was so much fun to do something funny when she was there, she was the very best audience there ever was, but that was the trouble. She didn't smile unless you gave her something to smile about. I guess her husband didn't give her too much to smile about. Say, listen, not everyone can be a song and dance man. But now that she's dead, I know you shouldn't say things about the dead, she's dead and she's gone, I think she could have been a little better natured if she'd tried. But Lily never had too much patience.

She went to live with Dave for a while, but he couldn't stand it and she couldn't stand it. Once, Dave nearly set fire to the bed because he was smoking. And she used to carry the picture of Emily, her granddaughter, all over the apartment with her. If she got up to do her daughter Lucy's mending, she'd pick up her granddaughter's picture and put it down next to her. So Dave thought she was peculiar. He was a very patient man. He'd say, I should take a mirror off the wall, I should take a picture down from the wall, and dance with it all around the house? He thought she was crazy, and she thought he'd kill her smoking in bed. So the two of them didn't last long together.

Before Dave got married, I told the woman not to do it. I said, don't marry him, it will never work out. Because I knew it would never work out, he was so impossible. He had a temper that was something terrible, and that anyone should think he would stay with one woman and not run around! But she was in love with him. It lasted two months. I think that was a long time. But when Lily got married, did I know what was going on? I was too busy thinking about getting married myself. So maybe if I hadn't been so busy, I would have known something was wrong, and I could have said something.

But at the time, I remember I thought she was lucky, marrying a rich man and all that. He wasn't rich like a Rockefeller, but he was rich enough. When he died, he left his children plenty. *We* thought he was J. P. Morgan because he owned his own store, and he had a clerk, and who owned a car in those days? You were lucky to have five cents for the streetcar. And for a long time, it looked like they were happy. But I didn't see them much, so how could I know? Then I found out that even their children didn't know they were unhappy until the night they separated. My sister was no angel, may she rest in peace. But she had a wonderful death.

She died in her sleep. Isn't that a wonderful thing? I hope I have a death like that. She died in February. It's February next month. When we had the great flu epidemic years ago, almost fifty years ago, all you heard was the clop, clop, clop of horse's hooves, because we lived on Eastern Parkway, and you had to go on Eastern Parkway to get to the cemetery. Every single pregnant woman got it, and they must have brought six boxes out of the one house across the street. So that was in February. Next month is February. I never used to fear that month, but now I do.

Chapter 19

After Esheal Luria bought the pharmacy on the corner of Chauncey and Howard, he began working long hours. He was in his store by eight in the morning, and he did not leave until twelve o'clock at night. But from the beginning, his store did very well. He was an intelligent man and a dedicated man and he had an instinct for business which surprised everyone. If his soda fountain had not brought in all the neighborhood, then his special sales would have. Dr. Linde, who had become a close and trusted friend, collected old coins and ivories. He introduced Esheal to a Japanese company, and before every holiday—Christmas, Easter, New Year's, the High Holy Days—Esheal would put a sign in the window: *Exotic Ivory Figurines. Free With Every Purchase Of Five Dollars Or More.*

Whole families pooled their resources so that they could buy five dollars' worth of supplies at once, and more than one woman asked Doc Luria to put aside their purchases until they could come back to buy another dollar's worth of aspirin, boric acid, rubbing alcohol, or cold cream. If a hot water bottle had to be bought, or an enema bag, it was bought when one of those sales was in progress. One woman whose arm was sore, and whose doctor had prescribed a hot water bottle, preferred to suffer for a week and buy the hot water bottle during the sale rather than waste her money and lose her figurine by buying the item before the sale began. A mother who came in with a prescription would hand the piece of paper to Esheal and say, "Tell me, Doc, when are you having another sale?" And then she would want to know what he was giving away.

"Next time, cups and saucers," said Esheal. "If you buy enough, you can get six, eight, ten, twelve, as many as you need for Passover." "How much do you have to buy?" the woman would ask. "For you, two dollars," said Esheal. "Two dollars!" said the woman; "God forbid I should have such a sickness in the house!" "No one asked you to poison the family," said Esheal. "We have soaps, we have perfumes, we have camphor ice, mothballs, candy. Use your imagination." "I have more imagination than money," said the woman.

"Look," said Esheal, "use your imagination and think what the sales are like for me. I have to hire a clerk, because if I don't have a clerk, I can't fill all the prescriptions, and if *I* don't fill all the prescriptions, I'm sure whoever is doing it is making mistakes and killing half the neighborhood. So when I'm in the back, I know the clerk is robbing me deaf, dumb, and blind. And then you women. You women buy something expensive during the sale and try to return it after the sale once you've got your cup and your figurine or your saucer. How can I make a profit with sharpies like you for customers?" "I should have such troubles," said the woman, who was finally smiling. "Have a soda," said Esheal. "On the house?" asked the woman. "On the house?" asked Esheal; "your last cup and saucer was on the house. You're a great one for returns." "Well," the woman said, "you know how it is. My husband bought a hot water bottle and didn't tell me about it." "He buys a lot of things and doesn't tell you," said Esheal; "the last time I had a sale, he bought an enema bag and hid it away just to surprise you."

There was something about the way Esheal talked to the women which made them feel indulged and understood rather than scolded or disapproved of. Because, in point of fact, he always let them return what they wanted to return, and he never hinted that they ought to bring back their figurines or cups and saucers. Now when he had sales, he marked many items "final sale." He wrote "final sale" on the receipts, and he had a large sign over the cash register which warned customers that without receipts there would be no refunds. After he posted this sign, he was amazed to learn how many of his customers were illiterate, or how many claimed to be illiterate, and hence had not known enough to save their receipts.

His soda fountain, which sparkled and shone, advertised the best quality ice cream money could buy, and Esheal refused to sell any kind of cone for his ice cream other than the biscuit cone. He was very proud of those biscuit cones since even the finest candy stores could not always boast that they had them. And he liked waiting on the women when they came in and listening to them gossip. He knew a great deal about everybody; he knew what their ailments were and, as he watched them buy powders for their bodies or patent medicines for imaginary ailments, he knew both their dreams and what troubled their hearts. Sooner or later, the woman he knew as the bad heart, the asthmatic, the arthritic, would come in for a soda with one of her friends and he would learn about the tiny dots which together created the picture of her life.

Whenever the Romanoffs came in, he was agitated and excited, eager to serve them, eager to listen to them, anxious not to call attention to himself. Whenever the Romanoffs came in, he began to worry about being short, about being clumsy, about being awkward and often shy. The boys, Bill and Dave, were very tall, and what was worse, everyone agreed they were glamorous. They danced and sang and everyone knew them or wanted to know them. Dave, the oldest boy, was known for his strength; he had a vicious right jab.

Meyer Romanoff had gotten so tired of the fights his boys had with the Irish on the street, so tired of seeing the boys come home black and blue, that one night, after dinner, with his favorite cigar stuck firmly in his mouth, he appeared on the street, his pot of a stomach preceding him, and dragged his son along after him. He took Dave to the pool hall. What, everyone wanted to know, could a man like Mr. Romanoff be doing at the pool hall? They saw Mrs. Romanoff pacing nervously back and forth in front of the building. Here, indeed, was a mystery.

An hour and a half later, Dave emerged from the pool hall wearing a pair of boxing gloves, dancing up and down and jabbing playfully at his father. "So you're going to make your son a boxer?" Mrs. Littenberg asked Mr. Romanoff. "Don't worry, I'm not crazy yet," said Mr. Romanoff; "but if a boy has to fight, he should know how." After Dave had spent a few months at the pool hall, he hit the punching bag so hard he ripped it open, and the boxer who was teaching him asked him if he wanted to try to be a boxer, because if he did, he would train him for nothing. But the boy said he had enough fighting to do on the streets.

And he did. One night, he was playing cards and he won a great deal of money, and while he was sleeping, someone came in through his window, and took the money out of his pants pocket where he had left it. As the man was leaving, a noise woke Dave and he started shouting, "Stop thief! Stop thief!" His shouting woke his father, who started running around his room bellowing, "Where are my gatkes? Where are my gatkes?" In the morning, the whole neighborhood knew the story, how Dave lost his money, and how his father was a great help, running around, shouting where are my gatkes? They also knew that, by the next night, Dave had his money back.

No one knew how he found out who had stolen his money, but he did, and he went out, found the man, and beat him up. When he finished with the man, he had five dollars more than the man had taken from him. "That's how much fell out when I shook him," Dave said, and everyone repeated what he said, that was how much fell out when he shook him, with absolute awe.

So in the neighborhood Dave was something of a legend. If he arrived on the scene, and three boys were beating some-one up, the boys would take one look at him and run. And often, he arrived like the cavalry. He would protect anyone in the neighborhood, whether he knew him or not. Everyone knew that Dave did not do this out of love of their sons, but because he loved to fight. He loved to win. And for a Jew in that neighborhood to be able to fight and win! To be feared! So they called him a knight in shining armor. And for them, he was.

And he was also handsome and tall, and as the women said, he charmed the pants off you. The men admired him, but did not want him near their daughters, but the women were not so sure. And when the men saw their wives looking after Dave as he walked down the street like someone who had just that instant stepped out of a silent movie, they felt short and weak and bald and ugly. And Esheal watched Dave in a particular way. He watched the way his sisters, who were older than their brother, treated him as if he were royalty, as if he were their protector against the world. And one day, Dave had another bright idea and decided to teach his sisters how to dance right in the middle of the street. He lugged the old Victrola out and put it down on their stoop, and soon everyone who passed by was taking dancing lessons and everyone was dancing with everyone else and the whole street was turned into a ballroom. Esheal watched the

Romanoff girls dancing with their brothers, and the girls looked as if they were in love with them. Then he saw that they looked as if they were in love with everyone they danced with. They were, he realized, in love with dancing. And he could not dance.

During the second year Esheal worked in the pharmacy, Diana came in with her grandfather. She was fourteen and her eyes were redder than the liquid in the apothecary jars in his front window. "Two black-and-white sodas," said Itzak Kapturak, who did not take his eyes off his granddaughter. "So," he said to her, "du liebst him?" The little girl did not answer. "So maybe someday you'll marry him?" the old man said. Diana looked up from her steady, regular sipping. "Marry him?" she asked; "he's my cousin. He's my *first* cousin." "I know who he is," said her grandfather; "your mother is my daughter. Cousins marry cousins in our family." "I'm too young," Diana said piteously; "I can't marry anybody." "So what are you crying for?" her grandfather asked her; "he's only fifteen. He's not getting married in such a hurry either. You know," he said, "if you cry like this every time he leaves, maybe we shouldn't have him come to visit." Diana glared at him so long that the straw dropped from her mouth. "So when's he coming back?" her grandfather asked; "whenever I turn around, there he is." "Momma said the whole family's coming to us for the summer because of the fresh air." "Nu," said her grandfather; "in six weeks, he'll be back and all of a sudden you're Bertha Kalish? So he'll be back. Have another soda." He ordered another one for her and she drank it straight down. And when Esheal overheard such discussions, he would become miserable, even though he told himself he had forgotten about the Romanoffs, even though he told himself that only an idiot would wait six years for a twelve-year-old girl to grow into an eighteen-year-old girl, especially when the girl in question didn't know who the hell he was.

That afternoon, Mrs. Dundes asked him if he would like to meet her daughter, Bertha. Esheal had seen Bertha and knew that she was very pretty. She was also said to be very intelligent because she had finished high school, and Esheal had heard her mother telling woman after woman, as they sipped their sodas or ate their sundaes, that she would never find a husband, men didn't like women who were too smart, and how could she hide it now that she had gone to high school, and she not only went to high school, she graduated from it, and then she took her diploma and framed it and put it right over the piano in the parlor, so there was no hiding it, everyone knew right away, and naturally, they all ran like horse thieves.

From the beginning, he liked Bertha. She was taller than he was, but then so was almost everyone else in the world. She was blond and her eyes were green and she had gentle ways. He began to take her to the movies and to take her for walks. Every time Mrs. Dundes saw her daughter leave with the pharmacist, she would run into the kitchen where her husband was sitting reading *The Forward* and start to scream, "Oy! Oy! Oy!" at the top of her lungs. She was beside herself with joy. "Sit down, Menya," her husband said; "a walk is nothing to go crazy about." "It's more than a walk!" insisted his wife. "The only walk I'm interested in," said her husband, "is the walk she'll take to the synagogue the day she gets married." "Such an optimist!" complained his wife. "Listen to me," her husband said impatiently; "the man's a good man. He's an honest man. He's a good soul. But he's a twenty-eight-year-old man and he's not married. If he's twenty-eight and he's not married, maybe he's not going to get married. *Probably* he's not going to get married." "Twenty-eight years old is not old," said his wife; "twenty-eight years old is not dead. He comes almost every night to Bertha." "So start calling her Mrs. Luria right away," said her husband. "Don't say that!" exclaimed his wife; "you'll bring down the evil eye." "Enough!" said her husband, going back to his paper. "Maybe," he said, looking up, "he comes to Bertha every night because she's the only one who's stupid enough to wait up for him." "Go back to your paper!" his wife said angrily.

When the weather got warmer, Esheal took Bertha for long walks. They gave each other books, and when they went to Prospect Park and no one was nearby, he would coax her to sing for him. She wanted to know all about his life, and he told her about it as if it had begun the day he entered pharmacy school. He told her about one of his instructors, a man from Germany, who used to walk around the lab with a black feather, and when they were making pills in the pill press, he would sweep their tables with the feather to see if they had lost any of the powder that ought to have gone into the pill. He told her about how he had learned to mix and distill chemicals and then let them gather in a beaker after they had passed, drop by drop, through the filter.

Bertha wanted to see how this was done, and he took her into the pharmacy at ten o'clock at night, put some chemicals in the flask, turned the apparatus down, lit the bunsen burner, watched the gas begin to bubble through the water, travel through the condensing tube, and then drip into the flask placed under the tube at the other end. "It's like magic," Bertha said, and when he looked at it through her eyes, it was. "It's a tremendous responsibility," said Bertha; "if you should make a mistake!" "It's something," he said; "sometimes I lie awake and think about it, the little children, the people with weak hearts. You can't make a mistake. It's not your mistake to make." Bertha put her hand over his.

For some time, Esheal had felt like two people whenever he was with Bertha. One was the man he was used to being; the other was an unknown person who took one look at Bertha and wanted to pounce on her. Esheal could not concentrate and he was jumpy. One night, as they were sitting in the pharmacy, he looked at Bertha's hand on his and could not decide what to do. He put his other hand on hers. Then he looked at their hands in horror, afraid Bertha would now take her right hand and put it on top of his left hand and the two of them would look as if they were playing a children's game. "Let me turn on the ceiling fan," he said suddenly, extracting his hand as he got up. He pulled the string, turned on the fan, and looked back across the shop at Bertha. He was standing in the dark, and she sat far from him in a funnel of light. She looked like an icon. And yet he wanted to jump on her. He decided to tell Bertha how he felt. Women, he thought, knew what to do about everything.

"Bertha," he said when he went back, "when I'm with you, I want to touch you, to kiss you. All the time." He stopped and watched her nervously. "What," he asked, "do you suppose that means?" "I don't know," said Bertha; "do you feel that way about everybody?" "No," he said. "Perhaps," suggested Bertha, "it means that you and I are serious. I mean about each other," she added hastily. "Perhaps that's it," he said. Bertha took a deep breath. She saw how shy he was, how backward, really. This could go on forever, she said to herself. "Perhaps," she said, "it means you want to get married. A bachelor is a very lonely person. And a very jumpy one." "Do you want to get married?" Esheal asked.

"Every girl wants to get married," Bertha said. Esheal sighed to himself. "Do you want to marry me?" he asked. "Oh, yes," said Bertha. "I would be proud to marry you. When you take me home, I'll tell my parents we're engaged." She was sorry she had been so quick to use that word, but Esheal seemed happy to hear it.

"Engaged," said Esheal. He stared at her, leaned over, and kissed her. To his amazement, she kissed him back. He kissed her again. She put her arms around him and, after a moment's hesitation, he put his arms around her. He had never been so happy. He looked out the window and saw his life painted on the wall of the dark building across the street like a splendid, gigantic mural. There he was, and there she was, and there were their children, and their children would never have anything to worry about, and when he thought about the bedroom they would have, and the bed they would share, his whole body shuddered. He was afraid to kiss Bertha again. Her father would know what happened if he brought her home with his shirttail hanging out over his pants. "What's the first thing to do?" he asked Bertha; "first, I should get you a ring." "And then we should set the date," said Bertha. "You'll stop working?" he asked her; "nothing's more important than being a good mother. Believe me, I know." "When we start having children," she said, flushing, "I'll stop working." And suddenly, he wanted to cry, he was so astonishingly happy, and so relieved. He would have a big wedding. It could not be big enough for him. So it was all settled.

And then, a month later, when he came into the Dundeses' apartment, the door was open and he walked in. Mr. Dundes was not there. He heard female voices arguing in the back room and he walked toward that door. "Don't touch anything of mine again!" Bertha was screaming at her mother; "you ruin everything! I told you to leave it alone!" "Let me take it," pleaded her mother; "I'll fix it," and she picked the dress up from the floor. "Here! Take everything!" Bertha shouted, and she picked up a dress from the chair and threw it at her mother. It hit her mother flat in the face, and Mrs. Dundes raised her hands to protect her eyes, and then held the dress in her hand, looking at her daughter and crying. Suddenly, the two women caught sight of Esheal. "I'm sorry, Dr. Luria," said Bertha's mother, her voice trembling; "it's my fault. I'm such a buttinsky. I never saw her act like this before. She's nervous, cranky, about getting married." She looked at his face and began babbling. "She's cranky, that's what she is, she spent so much money on the dress, and I didn't do it right, she's cranky, she's cranky, that's what it is." "Well," said Esheal. Bertha said nothing. She stared at the floor.

"Well," said Esheal again, clearing his throat, "I have to have a talk with your daughter." Bertha's look told him she knew the engagement was over; she looked at him as if she no longer knew him. "Well," he said, when they were out on the street, "I can't get married just now. My stepfather died and I promised my mother I wouldn't get married until my sisters were finished with school. I'm heartbroken," he said. "Your stepfather died last month," Bertha reminded him. "Well," said Esheal. "That's true." "Is it because you saw me with my mother?" she asked. He looked away and said that it was.

"Can I be the one to say I broke it off?" she asked. She would anyway, he thought, and her mother would swear by everything holy that she was telling the truth. "Why will you say you broke it off?" he asked. "I'll say you were too old for me," Bertha said. "No," said Esheal. "I'll say you wanted to wait too long to get married because you had so many responsibilities to your family and I didn't want a long engagement." "All right," said Esheal. And that was the end of Bertha. It was a long time before Mrs. Dundes or her daughter came into his store again.

Chapter 20

Esheal

After I saw Bertha throw something at her mother, I was down in the dumps, although I hadn't broken any records for long engagements. We were engaged for four weeks before I broke it off. I went down and told my mother I wasn't getting married and told her to tell my sisters. Even though we all lived in the same house, my sisters and I were strangers. After all, they had grown up without me when my mother left me behind in Russia, and when I came to America, I lived with my aunt. I felt responsible for them but not close to them. We were like strangers, really. My mother and I were not terribly close either, although I loved her. She tried to make up for what had happened, but there was always a distance between us. Still, she wanted to know why I wasn't getting married, and I told her.

She said I was just like my father. I said I didn't know my father had had a habit of getting engaged and unengaged, but she said that was not what she meant. She must have considered this a serious matter because she spoke only in Yiddish. And before she started talking, she sat me down on a chair in the kitchen at the enameled table, and she lit the samovar and she stood there thinking until the tea was ready. It was never hard to tell what my mother was thinking, because she had a habit of shaking her head almost imperceptibly from side to side, and that was what she was doing then.

When we were both sitting down, she took the jelly glass she kept the sugar in and spilled some of it out on to the table. "So," she said, "I don't want to mix in with you and Bertha, but you should remember we came from a little town. Everybody knew everybody there. Didn't you notice it, how everybody knew everything about everybody else, and half the time they knew what happened to you before you knew it yourself? Well, your father, may he rest in peace, he used to laugh at me. He said I would run all the way to Dubno to hear a good piece of gossip. He said that even if, tomorrow, God in his wisdom should decide to gather all the rabbis in the world to him, Pobrosk would still tick away like a good little clock because everyone in town was so afraid of what everyone else in the town had to say about them.

"He was disgusted with the rabbi we had then, Rabbi Levitsky, do you remember him? He was always excommunicating someone, so your father used to say that 'cherem' was his favorite word and he carried it around in his mouth like a hard candy. You wouldn't remember, but one Friday he pronounced excommunication on Isreal Shadsky because he hired someone to build him a house, and the man he hired was a goy, so he worked on the Sabbath. Rabbi Levitsky said this would be a disgrace to the community, to have building going on in a Jewish town on the Sabbath, and Mr. Shadsky argued that he hadn't broken the law because he only hired the man to build the house and he didn't order the man to build on Saturday. And he was right. All the men said so. Nevertheless, the rabbi excommunicated him.

"So how he became a broken man in one week is the point of this story. Your father said Rabbi Levitsky could have left Mr. Shadsky to the town, because who in town was going to talk to him after he gave his business to a goy and let the man build on the Sabbath? Everyone knew what was going on, and right away, Mr. Shadsky was a black sheep. And who did anything wrong in that town? If anyone did anything wrong, everybody knew who he was. He was a black sheep, an outcast, someone you didn't need to know from. Such people were a burden to the town and they shut them out.

"So in our town there were only black sheep and white sheep. There were were only angels and devils. Did we know anyone who was any other kind of person? You were good or you were bad, and if you were good, you were perfect; if you were good, you were wonderfully good. So it was never a pretty good day. It was a wonderful day or a terrible day. The weather was never all right, good enough, but not so good; it was perfect weather or rotten weather. A man was a giant and, if he was not a giant, he was a dwarf. So this is where it comes in.

"When I was a young girl in that town, did I feel sorry for the black sheep? Did I ever think, maybe the man was changed, maybe we should give him another chance? I was young. It isn't the business of a young girl or a young man to have sympathy. It isn't their business to make excuses. They see a fault and they condemn it and they don't forgive. That's the business of the young. They judge like the merchant who tests a whole field of grain by the first handful, and if he finds one bad grain, he has nothing to do with the whole field, and he does this with field after field, and so he starves to death.

"But when you get older, you get tired; you learn the whole field is sometimes a very good field, maybe the only good field. You learn to look at more and more. It's easy when you get older. It's like walking backward; you see more and more of what you're going away from. Now when I look back I see I didn't speak to this friend again because she didn't keep a promise, and then I think about how many promises I didn't keep, all the time for such good reasons, because if they were my reasons, then they were good reasons. Or I didn't speak to that one again because she didn't keep a secret, and I went right home and told somebody else's secret and I didn't think a thing about it. So your conscience is strong when you're young and you are hard on yourself and so you are hard on everybody. But is that right? A peach may have several dark spots on its skin and still be a very good peach."

"Bertha is no peach," I said.

"So," said my mother, "you are young. The young are like hard soil in the rain. The rain runs off or it sits there in puddles and the soil stays hard. But what grows out of hard soil?"

"Momma," I said, "you weren't there. A daughter who treats her mother like that will expect the same thing from her own children. A daughter like that can never be a good mother."

"I was there and I wasn't there," said my mother. "You think your sisters are any different? Some days I do nothing right. I will never do anything right. With mothers and daughters it's like that. You were no angel when I married your new father. Mothers and daughters can fight, and if they do fight, is it always bad? A daughter who fights with her mother is no angel, but she is no black sheep. Maybe she's already listening to the Bible and forsaking her mother and father and cleaving to her husband. So a girl like that can be a good girl to marry even if she is not such a good daughter."

"I already broke the engagement," I said.

"So what are you telling people?" asked my mother who, in spite of having lived for years in America, still worried about what everyone would think. I told her that Bertha and I would say that she broke it off because she didn't like long engagements, and she would have had a pretty long one because I had promised my mother that I wouldn't marry until my sisters were through with school.

"Oy!" said my mother. "So now when I go out everyone will point at me and say, that's a mother? She ties her son to her so he can't get married? A stone shouldn't have a mother like that! You had to bring me into it?"

I was annoyed. Now my mother was afraid people would not think she was a good mother because she was delaying my wedding plans. What would they think if they knew she had once been so willing to leave me behind in Russia? I had never told anybody. She never asked me to keep it quiet; she knew I would not say anything. I looked at my mother and asked myself why she should care whether anyone thought she was a good mother or not. But my mother was like a cloud. It would not be true to say she had no will of her own, but she did not have much of one. She was perfectly capable of going into apoplexy because she did not have the right dress, and on such days she could tear up the household and make everybody in it miserable. But she did not have real will, a real center. What she most feared was helplessness and loneliness. She did whatever would keep her from them. She was not her own woman and she was at everyone's mercy. If she had not been my mother, I would have despised her. But she was my mother and so I loved her.

I told her that I couldn't think of any other explanation for breaking my engagement to Bertha because I couldn't tell people the truth. Bertha was twenty and her mother was all over the street telling people her daughter would never get married because she was too smart for a man, and if anyone knew I had been the one to break it off, she wouldn't have any chances at all. So it was better that I take the licking. My mother was angrily sweeping the sugar back into the jelly glass with the edge of her hand.

"So I'm so old that what they say about me doesn't count!" she said. I didn't say anything. Every so often my mother would become angry, and when she was angry, she woke up and saw what was going on around her, and she didn't like what she saw. I was in no mood to humor her. "You think I made a mistake," I said. She pushed the jelly glass away from her. "What I think doesn't matter," she said; "I'm not getting married." "Neither am I," I said, smiling. I meant it as a joke. "Good for you," she said. "It's a good thing you were born a male. For a man, it's never too late. God forbid I should have a daughter who wants to pick and choose until she's twenty-eight." I said that anybody could make a mistake. "Yes," she said hotly; "you can make a mistake. A man can make a mistake. But a woman can't! Bertha can't!"

I said I was sure I had done the right thing. And it was true. I was. But that night I had a dream. I was back in the rooms my mother rented the first year we lived in the city. I was staying at my mother's because she was so sick and needed help, and my father was gone during the day, and I was so tired that I had gone to sleep early. It was not storming outside, but it was so cold that the windows had thickly frosted over; they let in no light. And then I woke up and saw a thin, milky light filling the room and I saw that my breath, which had frozen on my bedclothes, now formed a thin sheet of ice. When I got up, the ice cracked, scattered on the rough wooden floor, and melted quickly, leaving little dark spots all over.

When I tried to break the ice in the water jug, there were only a few drops of water left at the bottom. There was not enough to wash with. I dressed quickly as I could and rushed out into the street. There was no snow, but the street was lost in an icy white glare. When I tried to look back at my building, I saw all of the buildings had somehow moved back and formed into one smooth white wall. The street ran between two sheer white cliffs. And whenever I breathed out, my breath took the form of somebody's face. I wanted to know whose face that was and I walked down the street chasing after the faces my breath formed when I breathed out. Suddenly, I saw the face more distinctly, and I walked forward again, and I knew who it was, and when I knew who it was, the whole street was overwhelmed with rain, and the ground turned to mud, and the mud came up higher and higher until it was over the top of my boots, and I knew that it would keep rising until it went over my head. And in the rain, I could hear doors beginning to open and close, and just as the mud was getting too deep to walk through, I saw a building with a door open and I climbed up the steps which led to the door and went in, and the door to the inner hall was locked, and from behind the door, I could hear someone laughing. It was a frightening dream.

When I woke up, I felt as if part of my life were over, and for some reason, I found myself thinking about the beginning of things. I thought about first coming to this country with a terrible accent and starting to go to school and going out to get work, and how I used to follow the trucks on their way to deliver the coal, and when coal dropped from the trucks to the sidewalk, I rang the doorbell and said I would shovel the coal from the sidewalk to the cellar. They paid me fifty cents a ton. Then, having gotten a foot in the door, I would tell the owner of the house that I was a painter, but I had no work, and I would point out that his cellar and hall needed painting.

I didn't even look around before I said that. Almost all cellars and halls need painting. So people felt sorry for me, an out-of-work painter, a young and ambitious man forced to carry coal from the sidewalk to the cellar at fifty cents a ton, and often I got the job. But it was miserable down there in the dark, and it was always damp, and when I didn't have money for lunch, I went to the Bowery Mission and bought my lunch for five cents: bean soup and brown bread. I put every penny I had in the bank. Every penny was one step on the way to pharmacy school.

If I couldn't shovel coal or paint basements, I shoveled snow. Then I went to work in a toy factory operating the steam boiler. The owner taught me how to do it, but the cop put a stop to that. I was too young and I didn't have a license to run the machinery and I could have blown myself and everyone else up. The policeman was an old man and he let me go, but first he told me that there weren't enough angels in all of the heavens to protect an idiot like me from killing himself off.

And, when we came here, and we were waiting for the doctors at Castle Garden to check us, my youngest sister was so frightened that the doctors would send her back alone that she started to cry, and my mother, who knew they might send her back if she acted strangely, put her hand over my sister's mouth so firmly that my sister could not breathe and she began to go limp. We hid her behind the rest of us until she was breathing properly again, and, for a while, she was so terrified of my mother because of this that she was absolutely quiet and docile. We were so worried about being thought sick that we nearly killed each other.

And all I had was five cents. The money the zenshina gave me was secret money. I always said I wouldn't use it unless I was faced with disaster, but if someone had said to me, You never want to use the money, you want to keep it forever because she gave it to you, I couldn't have denied it. It was true. So as far as I was concerned, I only had five cents. When we came out of the Garden, I spent those five cents on a piece of cherry pie. We had cherry pie often enough in Russia, and I suppose I thought that if I ate a piece of cherry pie here, as I had done there, this new city with its thundering noises and strong smells would somehow become a part of me. But the pie was almost all pits. The man in back of me looked me over as I spit out the cherry pits and said, "A real greenhorn. You spend five cents for some cherry pits. But don't worry; you're not really here until you spend everything you have. Now you know you're really here." After that, I went back to the labor office at Castle Garden and they had several men waiting who came in from other states to look for workers to help on their farms. I would have gone. But I had to stay with my family. I got jobs painting rooms.

Thinking about all the work I used to do made me sleepy, although when I was working so hard, nothing seemed too much for me. I was tired and I was sorry for myself and I was in the mood to remember. When I lived at the zenshina's, I used to go with the peasants when they went into the fields and their jobs were my jobs. After the crops were planted, and after the harvest when the grain was taken to the threshing ground, the oxen which had pulled the plow and pulled the wagons were turned loose until they would be called upon to haul in the corn and to plow the fields for autumn planting. But during the summer, the oxen rambled through the fields along with the cows and the peasants had to keep track of them. They taught me how.

During the day, the oxen and the cattle avoided the heat and the flies and lay down under the huge shade trees. But at night it was harder to keep track of them, because at night they were hungry and they wanted to get into the cornfields. The cornfields were crowded at night. Cossacks from nearby barracks would be discovered in the middle of the fields with the girls they brought with them, and, although the zenshina did not object to the cossacks, she did object to the cattle thieves who hid in the fields and waited until some cattle strayed in looking for something to eat. Then the thieves would fall on them, rope them, and lead them away to the far side of Soraybitebsk, where they would keep them hidden in their own cornfields. Worse than the theft was the difficulty the thieves caused peasants when it came time to harvest the crops. So the zenshina ordered the peasants to keep watch day and night. And I said it was impossible to watch them at night, because even by the light of a full moon, who could see where the animals were?

And Tserevsky, who was in charge of the herd, laughed at me and said you saw them by listening to the earth, and when I said I had had enough of their tricks—they had amost drowned me the day before, persuading me to jump into deeper waters than I could swim in, all for the fun of seeing me go under so that they would have an excuse to jump in and rescue me—they looked at me as if I had gone mad. And that night they gave me a demonstration with their long-bladed, long-wooden-handled knives. That night, I watched them sink their knives into the earth, and then put their ears to their handles. "Enough joking," I said; "you can't hear a thing and the zenshina will cut off your heads if you lose the herd."

"Listen," said Tserevsky, who dragged me over to the knife and thumped me down on the ground. Tserevsky was a man of very few words. Another peasant had a wooden hammer and he hit the handle of his knife with it. "So," said Tserevsky, "what do you hear?" "I hear him hitting his knife," I said; "stop the nonsense." Tserevsky grunted with disgust and pressed my head against the ground. "Now listen," he said. This time I heard a sound coming through the ground. "What do you hear?" Tserevsky asked me again. "A sound in the earth," I said. "From where?" he asked; "from how far?" "Who knows?" I said. I was impatient and Tserevsky was hanging over me; he stank of sweat and of the whiskey he carried in a little flask he tucked inside his clothes. "Again," he said. I could see I was in for it. I was going to learn how to listen to the earth. But it was a soft, moist night, and the stars were out in the high black sky and the crickets were singing and the fireflies were flashing off and on and I told myself there were worse places to be. And after a while I knew where the sound came from, and how far away was the man who made that sound, and thereafter, we kept track of the herd by listening to the ground.

The peasants knew that these sounds would not travel through the soft earth of the cornfields, and the thieves could not hear us signaling to each other, so that they had no way of knowing that we could hear every step the animals took. We knew when the oxen got near the fields and we headed them off before they could go in. And on fine, clear nights, when the wind carried the smell of the grain to us, and the air carried the sound of church bells from all the spires of the distant towns, the beasts were perpetually headed for the grain fields and we were always after them, signaling to each other if we needed help, if we saw anyone in the fields, listening to the hooves of the beasts as they beat upon the earth. And I must have fallen asleep while I was thinking about this, because when I woke up, I was surprised at all the noise, the noise from the neighbors' apartments, the noise from the occasional carriages going down the street, and it all seemed so unfamiliar.

When I first learned to listen to the earth, I was still a child, and I thought that if the dead walked, I could listen to them in that way. So one night after the oxen were back plowing, and we did not have to watch them at night, I took my knife with the wooden handle and went down to the cemetery. I knew all about the evil spirits who lived in the graveyard and I had heard all the stories about foolish people who went through the graveyard at night and were found dead and cold in the morning. Nevertheless, I had to find my father's grave and I had to plunge my knife into the ground, and I was sure that was going to be the last thing I ever did. And right away I could hear someone moving toward me. I could hear that through the earth. But I scared myself stiff and I ran toward the village as fast as I could go, and then, when I was almost there, I turned around. I had to go back and find out whether or not I could still hear him. I found my knife just where I left it. But this time when I listened to it, I heard nothing. And I came back many nights after that, but I never heard anything again. Probably what I heard that first time was the sound of my own heart beating.

Marriage

Chapter 21

After Esheal broke his engagement, the days went by, and with them years, and he came to look upon himself as a student of the passing scene. Everyone in the neighborhood knew him and he knew everyone else, yet he did not seem to belong to anyone. And the more unhappy he became, the better his business grew. He was always so busy, and so many people came running in with prescriptions from their doctors, and so many came in for advice from him, even though he insisted that he was not a doctor and that he could not take the responsibility for giving advice. Still, the neighbors would plead with him until he followed them home, and even though his advice was always the same—don't give anyone anything until you call the doctor—they persisted in calling him.

"What do you think it is?" they would whisper to him as he stood in a dark bedroom looking down at a child wheezing in a bed. "She could have a cold, she could have the flu, she could have pneumonia, she could have asthma. You have to call the doctor. He went to school all those years studying to be a doctor. I didn't." And then the man or the woman would ask the inevitable question: "How bad is it?" or, "How serious is it, Doc?" "Do I know what's serious?" Esheal would ask; "all I know is that I've seen worse than this and the patient was right as rain in a couple of days."

And that was what they wanted to hear; then they calmed down. And when they calmed down, Esheal would tell them again that they had to call the doctor. If they did nothing, he would say that on his way home, he would leave a note for the doctor at the doctor's house. And if they still said nothing, he knew they did not have the money to pay the doctor.

Year in and year out, people existed on almost nothing at all. They worked seventy hours a week and at the end of the week, they had no money left. "Times are bad this year," he would say; "a woman over on Leonard Street didn't have the money to pay the doctor, so she didn't call him." Then he would fall silent, shake his head, and look at the floor. Someone was sure to take the bait. "So?" asked the husband —Esheal was surprised at how often the man was the first to give in to his curiosity—"so? what happened?" "It costs more to pay for the burial than it does for the doctor," Esheal would say; "but why talk about such sad things when you have troubles of your own?" Then the woman would start to cry. It was always the woman who started to cry. "Look," Esheal would say; "you're good customers. Do I want you to die when your business keeps me going? I'll pay the doctor and you pay me back when you have it." Thus Esheal wound up in the installment loan business and every customer paid him back sooner or later. He had, as he often said, a loyal clientele. And on days when he asked himself what he was doing in the world, he would go over the list of people who depended on him: the Steins, the Bibilovs, the Cherneyvskys, the Muriachs, the Fruehofers, the Seligmans.

He looked forward only to his lunch hours, when one of the men in the neighborhood would come in and play chess or checkers, and Esheal had just bought himself a checker set whose inlaid wooden lid was double-hinged and folded back into a board. When the store was empty, and when he had no prescriptions to fill, he would take the box into the store and play checkers with the clerk. He was not crazy about his new clerk, but he liked him better than the last one, who was unreliable and did not play. He had been searching for an excuse to get rid of him when the man got sick and had to quit.

He ate dinner at his mother's less and less frequently as time passed, because his mother would suddenly press his hand and look at him with shining eyes, or she would sigh deeply after a long silence and tell him that sooner or later he would find someone. Far worse than loneliness was the sympathy. While he was alone, he could tell himself how well off he was, how much more he had accomplished than he had ever thought to accomplish, how many friends he had, and if he stayed away from his mother and from others who meant well and who, perhaps wanted to know him better, he did not have to look clearly at his life and think about what he was missing.

He had spent many awkward evenings sitting around Seder

tables in the rooms of families who invited him to meet their daughters, and occasionally, he would take one of them out. This one was too stupid to tell the time of day, and all that one cared about was finding a bargain; if you wanted to know where to buy springs for a single bed, she could tell you where to find the three best places in the city, and the day she missed a sale at Woolworth's because her mother was in the hospital, she could not talk about anything but her own misfortune. She went on talking about the sale she had missed until she was in tears. Worse yet, she wanted to know how much anything and everything cost.

If Esheal said something about needing more sulfur because there was an epidemic of ear infections, she wanted to know how much a prescription for fifteen pills cost, and if it was any cheaper to buy thirty pills at a time, and did sulfur pills keep well because she still had four left from the last time the doctor had prescribed them for her, and if she got an ear infection again, she thought she'd just save the money and ask for four less pills. She wanted to know how much he had paid for his checker set, and although he was tempted to tell her, because he was so proud of the box—no one else had ever seen one like it—he was so sick and tired of answering questions about how much everything cost that he did not answer her. So she asked him again. "I don't remember," he said coldly. "You don't remember?" she said, incredulous; "you bought something like that, and you don't remember? It must have cost at least ten fifty." That was, in fact, exactly what the set cost. "I don't remember," he said again. This time he glared at her. "Hmph!" she said. Esheal found the walk home with her unendurable. She was a perambulatory inventory of the material world. She tried to take his arm, but he disengaged it.

Esheal learned that there were apparently infinite forms of incompatibility. Some women were not happy unless there were at least twenty other people in the room; others fell silent if anyone else was present; still others refused to discuss anything in the papers because life was depressing enough without reading about accidents and wars. There were those who would regale him by the hour with tales of marvelous recipes and stories of how they cooked whatever it was they had served up, or stories about their mothers or their fathers or, worse, stories about a man who was a friend of theirs, and as these stories went on and on, Esheal would gradually come to realize that the man about whom the woman was talking was the man she really wanted.

There were women who walked out with him and spent the evening looking as if they were sitting on a tack; others would fall asleep the minute the lights dimmed in the movie theater, and women who complained about the places to which he took them. Some women thought he was cheap, although they did not say so; they criticized the food and the service instead, and others tried to get on his good side by telling him that he shouldn't spend so much money, he worked hard for it, a single man threw out a fortune eating in restaurants. What he really wanted was a home-cooked meal. He had come to feel that he was less lonely when he was by himself than when he was with one of these women.

He began to refuse all dinner invitations. His thoughts were his own and he was familiar with them. After an evening with one of these women, he felt as if there were no place on this earth where he belonged. One woman had appealed to him more than the others, and of course, she asked him why he had become a druggist and he began talking about how marvelous it was, the way the medicine entered the blood and did battle with the germs so that it was as if the pills were little globes full of tiny armies, and while the body went about its business, wars went on under the skin, and there were two armies in the body even before the medicine entered in, the red cells and the white cells; they were like two armies, and then he saw the look on the woman's face and he stopped. "Isn't it interesting?" he asked her nervously, because, of course, he had said much more than he had intended to say. "You have a peculiar way of looking at things," said the woman, fidgeting with a speck of invisible dust on her lap. After that, when women would ask him why he thought this or why he did that, he would say, no special reason, and they seemed pleased with his answer.

And then Diana Romanoff came running into the pharmacy, red in the face, out of breath, and collapsed against the counter with a prescription for nitroglycerin capsules. "Who's sick?" Esheal called out to her from the back. "My grandfather was sick when the doctor left," said Diana, "but now my father's sick and we can't find the doctor again; he went somewhere else, and his wife said he'd be there as soon as he could, but my father's burned all over his leg; I don't know what to do," babbled the girl; "can you come?" "Irving!"

Esheal shouted to his clerk; "take over the store!" He seized
a gallon jug of linseed oil with one hand and a gallon jug of
limewater with another. "Let me help you carry that," Diana
said, and she tried to pull one of the jugs from his hand.
Esheal tried to pull it back, but she tugged at it again, and the
jug crashed to the floor. "So," said Esheal, "now let me get
another one," and when he had them both, he ran out the
door with her. "Slow down!" he shouted at her; "slow down!
The streets are packed! It's raining out. Someone's going to
hit a jar with an umbrella and we'll be back where we
started."

He followed in back of her, threading his way through the
crush of people on the streets. Men were coming home with
their packs, women were leaning out of windows and taking
things that they needed to cook suppers from the window
boxes which were held to the sills by intricate contraptions of
wire, board, and string.

When they came to the entrance hall of her building, he
hesitated because his eyes had not grown used to the dark.
"Come on up!" Diana called. He squinted and saw that she
was already on the second-story landing. "We're on the third
floor," she said running on ahead. "Oh, listen to that," she
called down to him; "I can hear them all the way down here. I
better hurry up," she said, and she flew the rest of the way
up.

When Esheal came panting in after her, the rest of the
Romanoff family was in an uproar. At first, he could make
nothing of it. "Where's your father?" he asked Diana, and
the wall of family and friends parted, stared in astonishment
at the sight of him, and fell silent. "What happened here?" he
asked Diana, catching a glimpse of Mr. Romanoff writhing on
the bed beneath a sheet. "He burned himself with the hot
water bottle!" Sarah cried, rushing over; "who ever poured
boiling hot water into a hot water bottle? The bottle melted
and it burned him all over his leg. Give me that sheet!" she
shouted at her husband, and pulled it back. "This is no time
to hide what you have below the waist there. Everyone who
doesn't want to look can turn his back!" she scolded,
watching Esheal as he bent over the poor man.

Mr. Romanoff had burned the inside of both his thighs and
most of his left leg. His skin was an angry red and huge
blisters filled with liquid were everywhere. "How bad is it?"
Sarah said. "No burn is a good burn," he said, and began

pouring the limewater over the leg. "You're soaking the bed!" Meyer complained; "you're ruining the bed!" Then he began to shiver. "Cold?" Esheal asked him, and Meyer nodded, his teeth chattering. "Cover him from the waist up," Esheal told Sarah; "don't let anything touch the burn." He set to work pouring on the linseed oil. "That should help," he said, standing back and surveying his work with satisfaction. "What can I do?" Sarah asked. Esheal told her to keep him warm, to give him plenty of fluids to drink, and not to let anything touch the burn. He said he was sure her husband would be all right. Sarah heard that and collapsed on a chair.

They suddenly became aware of the riot in progress in one of the back rooms. "Diana," said Sarah, "you stay with your father. Dr. Luria," she said to Esheal, "you're a sensible man. Come talk to my father." Esheal followed her into the middle room. It had no windows and the gas jet was turned down low. "So," said Sarah to the old man on the bed, "have you come to your senses?" "Not at my age!" her father shouted at her in a surprisingly strong voice for a man who had just had a heart attack. "But you have to do it, Grandpa," said a voice which came from a dim figure which had been sobbing at the foot of the bed. "Ganze, me-shuggeneh," said the old man; "get off the floor, Lily. Get off my bed. If I'm sick, let me at least have my bed to myself." "First say you'll do it," Lily insisted. "The child is right," said Sarah; "say you'll do it." "I won't do it and that's the end of it," said the old man, shaking his fist at them.

"What is this?" asked Esheal. "A man with a heart condition is supposed to have quiet, not aggravation." "Tell them, Doctor," said the old man. "I'm not a doctor, I'm the pharmacist," said Esheal. "Tell them," the old man said again; "at last, the wilderness has a voice. They're so afraid I'm going to die and leave them here all by themselves with that crazy crowd in the kitchen, they're trying to scare me to death." At this, Lily threw herself on the bed in a fresh fit of sobs. "Will you get her up off the bed?" the old man asked Sarah. "Come, Lily, get up," said Sarah; "your grandfather doesn't care about you. He doesn't care about his daughter. We should let him die alone, in peace. That I should live to see this day!" she burst out. "Gevalt!" shouted the old man; "get them out of here!" "I think all of you should go out," Esheal suggested mildly. "He may want to die alone," said Sarah grandly, "but he is not going to die alone. I will stay where I am." "Oy!" said the old man. "Doctor," he said, "take pity on a poor creature. Tell them to go."

"What's going on here?" Esheal asked Sarah; "what do you want from him?" "Nothing," said Sarah; "we want him to change his name." Esheal stared, open-mouthed. "Change it to what?" he asked. "To anything," said Sarah; "what's the matter with you? You're a Jewish man. You change a name to fool the angel of death. You go down to the cemetery and get a list of names of people who are already dead and the angel is fooled. He thinks he already came for him." "The angel of death is not going to be fooled," said the old man from his bed; "that is for children whom the angel of death does not know so well. Me he's known for over eighty years." Lily began to wail. "Do it for her," Sarah pleaded with him; "you know the angel of death so well? How do you know what he thinks about names? Maybe he comes around like the immigration people. He has a list. If you change your name, you won't be on his list. What name do you want?" she asked suddenly, hoping to sneak up on him.

"I want my own name!" the old man said; "I was born Itzak and I'm going to die Itzak!" Lily began crying louder. "You want me to help you over to the window so you can lean out and call the angel down here," Sarah said, spitting on the floor to ward off evil spirits; "God forbid you should say that word." "What word?" asked the old man. "The one you just said," Lily answered. "Itzak?" asked the old man. "Itzak is bad enough!" said Sarah; "the other word, what we will call you when you're still not feeling so well." She was not going to say the word and call the spirits' attention to her father.

"Death?" said her father; "a man my age should be afraid of the word death?" Sarah picked up a glass of water and took a sip and spit it out. "Stop with the spitting," said her father; "what will be, will be. You go on with the noise, and the angel will come all the way back from China to get me." "God forbid!" exclaimed Lily. "God forbid!" said Sarah; "change it to anything you want. Change it to William. You like that name. When you are better, you can change it back." "Oh, no," said the old man; "you know I can't change it back. If you change the name, you have to keep the new one. Unless you die you do." "God forbid!" said both Lily and Sarah together. "I'm not changing nothing," said the old man; "I want some quiet. Go change your burned husband's name. Take the red ribbon away from here and put it on his bed. Let it scare the angel away from him. How is he?" the old man asked.

"Waiting for the doctor," said Sarah; "he's not dancing any jigs." "Jigs," sighed the old man. Esheal said once again that he thought what the old man needed was quiet and peace of mind. "Peace of mind, what's that?" asked the old man, opening his eyes wide. Sarah and her daughter looked at each other, looked at Esheal, and withdrew to a corner to confer. "Uncle," said Sarah, "we are going out." "Don't call me Uncle!" shouted Sarah's father; "I won't talk to you." "Get Uncle Fred some coffee," Sarah told her daughter. Lily went out. "You go out too," the old man told Sarah; "I want to talk to the doctor." Sarah looked at her father suspiciously, but Esheal told her that she ought to go. She went, staring back over her shoulder.

"Tell me," the old man said to him, "after these attacks, can people live?" Esheal pointed out that the old man was, after all, still alive. "But for how long?" the old man asked. "It depends," said Esheal. "On what?" asked the old man; "on the angel of death and his bad hearing?" "It depends on a person's constitution. Everyone's different," said Esheal. "I'm tired of all the suspense," said the old man; "sit down, Doctor, and have a glass of tea with me." Esheal sat down. Lily handed him a glass of tea, went back to the kitchen, and came back with another. "Do me a favor," said the old man; "say, 'How are you feeling, Itzak?'" Esheal hesitated. He was as superstitious as anybody else. "How are you feeling, Itzak?" he asked in a small voice. "Much better," said the old man. "Lily," said Itzak, "when Mr. Luria comes to see us this Sunday, you show him how you play on the piano."

Chapter 22

On Wednesday, Esheal was invited to the Romanoffs for the first time, and, although he had been almost giddy with happiness when he heard himself invited, and knew he would be coming that Sunday, the days which succeeded were a misery to him. Time stretched out inexplicably and every task seemed to take an unimaginable length of time. Esheal was reminded of a nightmare he had not thought of in years. In it, he was walking along a street toward his house and the street got longer and longer and the house farther away, and when the street returned to its usual dimensions, he found himself unable to stand up. He would begin crawling along the street, his eyes fixed on his home, and on his family standing before it, and it seemed incomprehensible to him that they could not see him and the superhuman effort he was making to reach them.

And then the dream would change slightly, and he would be walking, when suddenly his legs would refuse to support him, and he would concentrate all his energies on getting up, first straightening one leg, then trying to push himself upright with one hand, which he sometimes placed on his thigh in an attempt to straighten his body. And then at times he would find himself standing and walking toward his family, and his relief was immense. But in his dream, he never reached his family. Although his long, slow progress toward the Romanoff home reminded him of his torturous approach to his own family in this dream, Esheal was annoyed to find himself remembering the dream because the return of the dream seemed an evil omen. He could understand why he suddenly remembered it, but he wished he had not.

And then there was the matter of the cake. Mrs. Bibilov, who had been to the Romanoffs', was consulted and said that, yes, she always brought something, the Romanoffs didn't have much, but the girls and their friends brought so much,

he didn't have to worry. Esheal explained his predicament to
his mother, who said she would bake him a cake, the same
kind of cake she always baked for him when he went to eat
dinner at someone's house. But he had eaten every kind of
cake his mother could bake, and since he had eaten those
cakes without giving much thought to them, even though they
were very good cakes, he could not believe they would be
special enough for this remarkable occasion. So he resolved
to buy a bakery cake. But he could not leave the matter of the
cake until the last minute. The bakery might not have enough
of them on Sunday, or they might not have anything worthy
of the occasion.

He determined to inspect the neighborhood bakeries. The
first bakery he inspected advertised HOME BAKED GOODS. ALL
HOME MADE, and when he looked over its shelves, he saw his
mother's kitchen all over again. He bought a brownie so he
would not insult the woman behind the counter, and went out
munching it, looking for another shop. In the third bakery, he
found what he wanted, a giant, tall, round cake, covered with
pink and green flowers. And then he remembered that the
Romanoffs kept a kosher home. The baker assured Esheal
that his was a kosher bakery, but he asked Esheal what he
wanted the cake for. "It's for a birthday," the man said
without waiting for him to answer; "they always are." When
Esheal said that it wasn't, the man was horrified to think his
cake would not be consumed on a day of great importance.
"It's the best in the store," the man said gloomily.

Esheal said he would take that kind of cake, but he wanted
his cake to be ready late Saturday night because he didn't
want to bring a stale cake with him. "How late are you
open?" he asked the baker. "Ten o'clock," said the baker; "is
that late enough for you?" Esheal said he guessed that would
be all right. "Look, mister," said the baker, "I don't know
what kind of bakers you've bought from before, but my cakes
don't get stale so fast. The trouble is, some shops sell you
things that are stale already. The cakes are older than the
baker. Here you won't have any trouble." He said he would
put the cake in a box, and he would wrap the box in a
newspaper. "Put a lot of that string on it," said Esheal,
pointing at the large cone of red and white string. He had
seen people going by with white baker boxes tied up in that
candy-stripe string, but he had never had such a box himself,
and if he had never had one, he knew the Romanoffs had

never had one. "How much string do you need?" the baker asked; "nobody's going to eat the string." "Put some bows on it," said Esheal. The baker leaned over the counter. "So where is this cake going?" he asked confidentially. "To a house, where else?" asked Esheal. "You're a big spender with your talk," said the baker; "you should try this business. You'd want to know where your cakes were going." "It's going to a party," Esheal said, "but not a birthday party." "So long as it's a party," said the baker. "I'll tell you if it had a good time," said Esheal. "Don't make fun," said the baker.

Carrying the box as if it were made of glass, Esheal set off for the Romanoffs'. Mrs. Bibilov had said that people began arriving at noon, but Esheal dreaded arriving before everyone else, and, at the thought of sitting on a chair in the middle of a room while the entire family stared at him and attempted to make polite conversation, his hands began trembling. So he planned to arrive at two o'clock. When he got to their building, he heard music pouring out of a window like clear blue air pouring out into a gray, gray day. Perhaps that was Lily, playing the piano.

Holding tight to his cake box, Esheal climbed the stairs, hoping he would not meet anyone else who was going up. He did not want anybody to ask him who he was and make him feel even more out of place than he did already. As he climbed flight after flight, the music grew louder, and so did the unfamiliar din of many people talking and laughing together. When he came in, he was surprised by how many people were there, and how happy they all seemed to be with each other. There was no one who looked awkward or out of place. The women leaned gracefully and casually against the piano, against the back of chairs, against each other, even against the men. The room was bathed in an odd gold light whose source he could not immediately identify, and then he saw the light came from the golden floor, which reflected the light of the day as well as the flickering gaslights which had been lit for the occasion.

He looked around the room, and saw that it was threadbare and immaculate, and saw the curtains, which were snowy white and full of little holes where the bleach must have eaten through them. Then some people moved toward the kitchen, and he saw a new sofa and chair, noisy in their newness. He wondered if he was going to stand there forever, holding his cake, feeling like an idiotic delivery boy, and had just told

himself that he could turn around and leave, when Itzak
Kapturak grabbed his arm. "So," said Itzak, "my friend, the
only sane man. Come in here and meet everyone." Esheal
asked him if he ought not to be in bed. "Who can rest with
this racket?" he asked; "who wants to stay in bed? I didn't
change my name and I'm still here. So I thought I'd walk
around." He paused and looked around the room.

"Dave!" he shouted suddenly; "where's your sister Lily?"
Dave lifted his hands to show that he didn't know, and Esheal
was struck again by how graceful he was, how beautiful he
was. But his grandfather was not so impressed with him.
"Dave!" he shouted again, "Lummox! Gangster! If you don't
know where she is, go and find her." Dave disappeared and
reappeared almost immediately. "She is in a place I dare not
name," he said. "Go wait outside the place and bring her
here," said Itzak.

"God gave me nothing for a good reason," he told Esheal;
"if I had money, I'd throw it out on them. You don't take
snuff," he asked Esheal. "So why do I ask? All the people I
know who take snuff are dead. 1906. The twentieth century. I
should have left with the last one." Itzak took a little silver
snuffbox out of his pocket and breathed a pinch of it in and
then sneezed tremendously. "A sneeze like that, it clears you
out," he said. "Sneezing like that isn't good for your heart,"
said Esheal. "What's good for my heart?" the old man asked;
"I'll tell you what's good for it. Death, that's what's good for
it."

"Again?" asked Lily, materializing at Itzak's elbow;
"again?" "Why," asked Itzak; "has anything changed? All of
a sudden, I have a new heart? Dr. Luria," he said, "I want
you to meet my granddaughter. She is a very stupid girl, this
one. You think her sister is any better? I was reading in my
book, and I said to Lily, see where it's written that someday
carriages will fly through the sky like birds, and she looks at
Diana, and Diana looks at her, and Diana says, don't you
know if you drop a dish, it falls to the floor, and they laughed
at me. But it will come to be," said Itzak; "don't you think it
will come to be, Doctor?" "Why not?" said Esheal. "So tell
him why not," Itzak told Lily.

"Because," she said, then broke off. "He knows why as
well as I do," Lily said, glaring at her grandfather. "Isn't she
cute when she's mad?" said her grandfather, pinching her
cheek; "and she's always mad, my Lily. So, Lily, how long

are you going to let him stand here like a statue with a box?"
"Oh!" said Lily. "Look at the box! Come into the kitchen
with me," she said, taking Esheal's arm, as if she had done
that a hundred times before. "We have tea and seltzer and
cookies. Don't you think we should save this cake for last?"
she asked him worriedly; "the box looks so fancy. I can't
imagine what the cake must look like." "A little better than
the box," said Esheal. "Let's save it until after dinner," said
Lily, placing the box carefully on the kitchen table. "You'll
stay for dinner?" she asked.

There was a sudden commotion in the living room and Lily
seized his arm. "Come on," she said; "Dinney's coming. I
want to see this." They pushed through the others in the
room until they were near the door. "Just a minute, Dinney,"
Diana called out. Esheal could not see her; she was so short
that she was hidden by the others standing around her. "What
am I waiting for?" Dinney asked, hovering in the doorway.
Suddenly, someone began playing the wedding march, and
Dave marched solemnly through the room toward the door
carrying a pail. "Your pail, madam!" he said, bowing deeply
and setting the pail down in front of her. Dinney looked at the
pail and then at Dave, and, for an instant, she looked as if she
were about to burst into tears, but then she started to laugh.
"Don't let her in until she stops laughing," Bill called out.

"Can you imagine?" asked Itzak, who had found his way
back to Esheal's side; "some funny they are." "So I won't sit
down," Dinney called to Bill. "You can sit down," Bill called
back; "just be sure to sit on the windowsill." Everyone
started laughing as if they had just heard the best joke of their
lives. "When you stop laughing, Dinney," said Diana, "you
can sing with me." "What do you want to sing?" Dinney
asked her. "Oh, must you sail away, Sonny boy," said Diana;
"let's sing that." "You mean, oh, must you mush away,
Sonny boy," said Dave. "I'll chase you!" exclaimed Diana,
starting after her brother. Everyone in the room was laughing, and Lily, who was gasping for breath, leaned against
Esheal. "Lily!" Diana called; "you can't play the piano from
over there." "She can't play it worse over there than over
here," said Bill. "Come on," said Lily; "ask me nicely."
"Lily," said Dave, "won't you please pound the ivories?"
"Make her take her mittens off first," Bill said. "Why ask for
trouble?" said another male voice. "I have to go play the
piano," Lily told Esheal; "I'll be back soon."

Esheal asked Itzak what that was all about. "What was what about?" asked Itzak, who was watching Lily pretend to push her brothers out of her way, while they, in turn, pretended to struggle with her and keep her from the piano bench. "The pail," said Esheal. "Oh, the pail," said Itzak; "that Dinney, when she laughs, she's a faucet. You see the couch and the chair? Brand new. And how is Sarah buying them? Forty cents a week from Engelbert, the furniture man. Four years she was deciding to get it. So we have the chair, we have the couch, and Diana says, let's have a couch party. Dinney's always here for parties, and Dave got funny, and Dinney's sitting on the chair, and she starts to laugh, and the next thing, the chair is soaking, but soaking. And there's pneumonia in that, so oh is the chair stained. Now Dave meets her at the door with a pail. With Dave, it's anything for a laugh."

"She doesn't seem to mind," said Esheal. "How can she mind?" Itzak asked him; "this is more of a family than her family. She has to take it, and it's because she has to take it that I tell him to stop. He couldn't take it, believe me. If Dave met himself, he'd kill himself. Young people," sighed Itzak, but as he spoke, he looked at Dave and his face spoke of nothing but pride.

"The girls are different," said Esheal. "The girls?" said Itzak; "worse. At least they leave the pigeons in their coops. Dave gets mad, this one won't let him sit on his stoop, that one leans out the window and says, 'Go home already, Dave,' so he goes up on the roof and lets the pigeons out of their coops. They know who to blame. But who sees him? The boys go up on the roof, the pigeons don't belong on the roof of the coop, so when they see the pigeons on the roof of the coop, they know who was there. And Dave swears up and down he didn't do it, he doesn't know from nothing. How he gets away with it! No one wants a fight. Believe me, he can fight. You should take Lily out," Itzak said without warning.

"She doesn't know me," Esheal stammered. "So she'll get to know you," said Itzak. Esheal decided to take a chance. "What about Diana?" he asked. "Diana?" said Itzak; "forget Diana. She's engaged to Murray over there. She'll never marry him. You'll see. She thinks she loves him. She doesn't love him. She loves that meshuggeneh Sidney in Nome, Alaska. If it gets quiet, God forbid, we'll talk to her. She's always in the middle of everything." "She's engaged?"

Esheal repeated. "Engaged to be disengaged," said Itzak; "but she don't see anybody else. Someday, I should live so long, she'll have an engagement party. A couch party, a curtain party, a this party, a that party, but an engagement party she doesn't have." "Why not?" asked Esheal. "Her cousin. Off in Nome, Alaska. Ask her. She'll tell you."

Esheal now saw everything through the haze of his disappointment. The room looked shabbier. He saw the pattern of the lathing through the walls which had not been painted in years. The people seemed noisy and they laughed too easily. Then the singing stopped and Lily was back. "Come see my father," she said; "he wants to thank you for coming over." "Diana," she called; "come with me." "Oh, here you are," said Diana, coming up to him. Esheal stared at her as if he had never seen her before, and probably he had not. At least, he had never before seen her looking at him with interest. Her beautiful wavy hair was parted in the middle, her eyebrows were high and arched, her eyes were deep and brown, her nose straight, and she had the most beautiful smile. And she looked at him as if she were in love with him.

He glanced down at the fat gold locket which rested on her bosom and turned red with embarrassment. Diana saw this, smiled mischievously, seemed to consider for a moment, started to say something, changed her mind, and said, "Would you like to see what's in it?" Esheal turned a deeper scarlet. The locket was resting on her bosom and her bosom was enormous. Did she expect him to pick the locket up? Diana suppressed a smile and lifted the locket and chain over her head, handing it to him.

"You touch that spring," Diana told him. The locket sprang open. "My mother and father in Russia," said Diana, "wasn't she beautiful?" "She still is beautiful," he said. "A man with eyes in his head," said Itzak. "I thought girls kept their fiancés' pictures next to their hearts," Esheal said. "Well," said Diana, as if he had caught her at something; "I guess they do." "But you don't," said Esheal. Her grandfather came to her rescue. "She needs a picture of what she sees every day?" he said; "a face like her fiancé's you can't forget." "I heard that," said a young man, who stood next to her, and put his arm around her. "The fiancé," said Itzak; he sounded ironic and bored. "He doesn't like me, I don't know why," Murray said to Itzak teasingly. "Me you're not marrying," said Itzak. "You wouldn't marry me?" Murray asked

Itzak. "Against doctor's orders," said Itzak; "the wedding night would kill me." Everyone laughed, and Diana said that if they were going to see her father, they ought to see him now, because the boys wanted to start dancing and, otherwise, they'd miss the best of it.

When they went into Meyer's room, Esheal saw that the blanket was resting directly on his burned legs and said that they ought to have a box of some kind over the bed so that nothing would touch the burn. "I could make one now," he said; "if someone could find some wood." Diana and Lily looked at each other as if to say, isn't he peculiar, to want to build a box when everyone's going to start to dance. "The box can wait," said Meyer, but Esheal said he would feel better if he built the box right away, and Lily, who was clearly humoring him, went to find some wood. By the time Esheal finished building his bridge over Meyer's bed and finished draping the blankets over it, he was sure Meyer did not recognize him or connect him in any way with the "criminal" who had once helped his wife work on her portraits at home.

The boys had finished their soft-shoe routines and the dancing was over. "It's too bad you missed it," Lily said with a touch of annoyance; "come sit down for dinner." Just then, Esheal saw Dave come back in and watched him go over to Sarah and slide his hand down through the neck of her dress onto her breast and leave it there. Then he kissed his mother and withdrew his hand. Esheal looked at Lily, expecting to see astonishment, outrage, or disgust, but she was smiling at her mother and her brother as if nothing were wrong.

When Dave came over to them, Esheal could not look him in the eye. "Good to see you, Doc," said Dave; "I thought you were nailed to that drugstore wall." "People get sick at all hours," Esheal said, wishing he could think of something clever to say. "What time do they get sick most?" asked Dave. "The instant I close the store," said Esheal, and everyone laughed, and he was so happy to hear them laughing that for a while he forgot about Dave and how he had slid his hand inside his mother's dress to touch her breast.

The cake was the sensation of the evening. Everyone said that they would rather look at it than eat it, but everyone fell on it like ravens on a field of corn. Esheal was so delighted by how much everyone liked his cake that he did not notice Sarah exchange a significant glance with her daughter Lily, as if to say, see, a man who buys a cake like that is a rich man.

Lily avoided her mother's eye, but as her brother passed her a second piece of cake, she said that she had never tasted anything like this cake and she would never forget it. It was like a cake out of a dream. Esheal beamed, took a bite of his cake, and then asked Lily if she would like to go to a movie some night next week. He could feel himself growing warm and knew he would be red in the face; he did not dare look at Lily. He wanted her to say, yes, she would come, and at the same time, he thought that if she said she would come, he would never be able to see Diana, even if she broke her engagement. But then her grandfather had said she was really in love with someone else who was in Nome, Alaska. Perhaps he was joking. "Oh, yes," said Lily, but she had hesitated just long enough to make Esheal wonder whether she really wanted to go, and if there were not someone else that Lily, like her sister, already cared for.

Chapter 23

The last guests left the Romanoffs', and Diana was cleaning up. Murray Zalman, her fiancé, trailed after her and began to pick up a dish here and a dish there, and just as he began to wander off in the direction of the kitchen, he would bump into Diana, whose arms were filled. "Murray," she said; "get out of the way already. You're slowing me down. Go in and talk to Grandpa. I'll be through in a minute."

He did not have her attention, which was divided between two subjects: whether or not tomorrow's mail would bring a letter from her cousin Sidney in Nome, Alaska, and what Lily thought of Esheal Luria and, as her hand flew over the surfaces covered with cups and saucers and crumpled white napkins, she sensed that her whole family was preoccupied by the same questions. She passed Murray, who was talking to Grandpa about a murder that had taken place down the street, and when she passed again, they were talking about the Gold Rush.

That irritated her. It was as if Murray had no right to talk about Nome, Alaska, because in her mind, Nome, Alaska, belonged to her cousin Sidney. Nevertheless, she rested her hand on Murray's shoulder as she passed him. The next time she came to rest behind him, she put her hands on his shoulders, and stared at her grandfather. Lily, who had finished drying the dishes in the kitchen, looked at her sister and said, "Murray, go home already." Murray looked around at Diana, hurt and surprised. "Lily wants to call a powwow," said the old man; "she didn't mean anything by it, did you, Lily?" "Mean what?" asked Lily. Diana always said, "Murray, go home already, Sam, go home already," and when she said that, they would laugh and smile and put their arms around Diana, and bend down and kiss the top of Diana's head. Sarah was forever saying, go home already, and no one was insulted.

"Mean what?" said Lily; "all I said was, 'Murray, go home already.'" "All right, all right," said her grandfather, who was in no mood for one of Lily's storms. "What did I say?" Lily asked, her voice trembling. "Nothing, nothing," said her grandfather. "I didn't mean anything," said Lily, whose eyes were filling; "I only meant it was time for you to go home so we could talk about something, you know, something in the family. You're not a member of the family yet," Lily went on, knowing she was making things worse with every word she said. "God forbid the poor thing should be in the family so soon," said her grandfather; "after all, he wants to live to a healthy old age." Murray laughed and the tension broke.

But Lily could not understand it. Why couldn't she say things like, "God forbid he should be in the family so soon," without starting a riot? Perhaps she did not understand the trick, which was to take the sting out of what one said to the other person by turning the joke against oneself. She was not as quick as the others, although she wanted to be like them. Her mother was her idol, and when she thought of herself as a married woman, she thought of herself as her mother, the one to whom everyone came, the one who gave the advice to which the others listened, the one whom everyone adored.

And did she want her husband to be like her father? Certainly, she wanted the man she married to adore her as her mother was adored by her father. But she also wanted her husband to be like one of her brothers and, of the two, she had to admit that she preferred Dave. Dave, who wore his clothes as if they were a second skin, as if they had been molded to his body by the most skilled tailor in the world. Who wore his hat as if he were about to tip it, who had once gotten into an argument with the street cleaner who proceeded to pick up his broom and swirl the dust into the air until Dave stood in a cloud of it, one foot forward, one hand on his hip, smiling as if the street cleaner were paying him homage. And when the dust began to settle, Dave stepped out of the cloud and knocked the man out with one blow. He said afterward that he had hit him so that he would fall in the street, out of the way of traffic, and away from the curb. After all, he said, he didn't want to kill him. He only wanted to teach him a lesson. And it did not occur to Lily that Dave was really what Diana said he was: lousy husband material.

The year before, when Dave became engaged to a wealthy young woman, Diana said, "Bring her home; I want to meet her." Everyone had been a little suspicious, because, ordinarily, Dave was only too quick to bring home a girl and introduce her to the family. This time he seemed in no hurry to do so. And Diana wanted to know why. She knew the instant she met the girl. She was a beautiful girl, a gentle girl, and a nice girl, and Diana saw immediately that she did not deserve a husband like Dave. She took Dave aside and said, "I'm going to tell her not to marry you. You'll only ruin her life. You have a terrible temper, you run around with women, the whole thing is impossible." "You're going to tell her not to marry your *own* brother?" he asked; "is that how a loyal sister behaves?"

"It's for your own good," Diana said, bracing herself for a storm. Dave lit a cigarette, looked Diana up and down, turned to the window, and began to blow smoke rings. "Then tell her," he said; "it won't do you any good. She's dying to marry me. What do you think, she's stupid? These rich dames know how to get what they want. She knows if she waits, I'll find someone else. She's the one in a hurry to get married." "You call a woman who wants to marry you a rich dame?" Diana asked, aghast. "That's what she is," said Dave; "she's not a lady like Momma." "No one's a lady like Momma anymore, goddammit," said Diana. "Your language is nothing to brag about," said Dave. "I'm not bragging," said Diana, "but Momma grew up in Russia years ago. She's a different kind of lady, that's all." "Go talk to her," said Dave; "take her out on the fire escape." "That's just what I'm going to do," said Diana.

And she did. She took Louise out on the fire escape and said, "Look. Don't marry my brother. I'm his sister, and I'm telling you this. He has a terrible temper, he runs around, you won't have a moment's peace. Better to break it off now than go through a messy divorce." But Louise married him anyway, and for a while she was very cold to Diana. She thought Diana had tried to break up her marriage plans because she wanted to keep her brother to herself. But three weeks after they were married, Louise knocked at the door. Everyone inside knew it was Louise before the door opened. She was the only person they knew who ever thought to knock. She asked to speak to Diana alone, and the rest of them leaned forward on their living room chairs, trying to overhear the two young women in the middle bedroom, but all they could hear was Diana's low voice and the sound of muffled crying. When they came out, Louise thanked Diana profusely, said goodbye to the others, and left.

"What was that all about?" Lily asked. "I knew it," said Sarah; "I knew it. It was a crime to let him marry a girl like that." "So, Sarah, what kind of girl should he marry?" asked Meyer. "A big lummox with a broom who would give it to him good!" said Sarah. "Maybe things will blow over," said Itzak. "Blow over, my foot," said Sarah. Three months after Dave and Louise were married, they were divorced.

Still, it never occurred to Lily that in wanting a man who would adore her, as her father adored her mother, and in wanting a man like Dave, who was so glamorous and charming, she was asking for something she was not going to get. Although, for some time it did seem as if she had achieved the impossible, just as she always thought she would if she only tried hard enough and refused to compromise. Bill introduced her to a young dentist, who was said to have the beginnings of an excellent practice, and he was handsome and tall and came to the house every Sunday. When he sang with the others, her mother used to close her eyes, clasp her hands, tilt her head up toward the heavens as if to say that the wonderful entertainment she had in her own home was more than any human being could ask for. The whole family had high hopes for the dentist. From the beginning, he appeared to like Lily, and after he took her out, she would sit alone in the living room for hours, smiling at the wall. And the next day, she would talk about nothing else but what she had said to him and what he had said to her. "So you think he really likes me?" she would ask after retelling these conversations by the hour. "Of course he likes you," said Sarah. "Of course he likes you," said Diana.

But six months passed, seven, eight. The dentist was faithful in attendance on Sunday afternoons, and on Saturdays, he took Lily to every new show and then out to restaurants. Sarah was busy every morning at her sewing machine; suddenly Lily needed more and more clothing. She could not, she said, wear the same dress over and over again. Diana wanted to know why she couldn't wear the same dress again and again, since that was what she did, but her mother said that she was already engaged and she had Murray nailed down tight.

However, nothing happened. "I don't know," Diana said one night; "maybe he can't bring himself to ask her. Some men can't." "She can't ask him," said her father. "Louise asked me," said Dave. "And look where it got you," said his mother. "Maybe Bill should talk to him and find out what he's about," suggested Diana, who was beginning to see her own chances of marrying shrinking day by day, since her mother was still determined to marry off her oldest daughter first. "He's his friend." They thought it over carefully; it seemed like a drastic move. "Wait another month," said Sarah. Diana sighed but did not object. Her mother's word was law.

Another month passed, and another, and another, and Diana began to wonder if her mother had forgotten how to use the calendar. Then, one evening at supper while the dentist was out with Lily, Sarah put down her fork and looked up. "Bill," she said, "I want you should talk to your friend." "What am I going to ask him?" said Bill; "when are you going to marry my sister?" "You could say," said Diana, "that there's someone else interested in Lily, and that if he's not serious it's not fair for him to take up so much of her time. If he doesn't have intentions." "That's what you should say," said Sarah. "Lily won't like it," said Bill. "Lily," said Sarah, "does not have to know. She will like it better than being jilted. Or than being an old maid." "Anyway," said Diana, "don't you know that she doesn't talk about him much anymore? She knows something's not right."

So Bill talked to the dentist, who said he was very taken with Lily, but that he was not ready to settle down yet because his practice was just starting and he could not afford to keep a wife. "A wife could work for you in the office," said Bill. "No," said the dentist; "in the beginning, I'll be giving all my attention to improving my work. It would be no kind of life for a woman." Bill pointed out that he was doing that now, but he still found time to take out his sister. "Did Lily say anything to you?" the dentist asked suddenly. "My sister?" Bill said; "she'd kill me if she knew I said anything." "I thought Lily said something," said the dentist. "My sister would never say anything," said Bill; "she thinks she can take care of herself." "Still," said the dentist. "Well, she didn't," Bill said.

But after that, the dentist did not call Lily for three weeks. He had called her a few days before Esheal Luria came to the house for the first time, and Lily hoped that the dentist had made up his mind and brought himself to propose to her. So she was thinking about him, and whether or not he might propose, when Esheal asked her to go out with him. "You should always keep a man jealous," her mother said; "at least until you've got him. And after that even, it's not such a bad idea." Lately, Sarah had been saying that more and more often, and the suggestion appealed to Lily, who liked to think she could control her man. So when Esheal asked her if she would come out with him, she said yes. And that was what the family wanted to talk about now, what she thought of him.

The samovar was lit again, and all of them sat down around the big oval table. "What do you think of him?" asked Sarah. "Who?" asked Lily. "Who, who?" said Itzak; "don't get cute. Dr. Luria, that's who." "He's not a doctor, he's a druggist," said Dave. "Did I ask you?" said Itzak. "So what do you think of him, Lily?" her father asked. "I don't know," said Lily; "what do you think of him?" "I like him well enough," said Diana; "he's something quiet, but ain't he awful old?" "He looks old to me," said Dave. "He's twelve years older than Lily," said Itzak. "How do you know?" asked Sarah. "I asked him," said Itzak.

"Twelve years older is not so much," said Sarah; "how do you like him in other ways?" "He seems nice enough," said Lily, "but he's awful short." "Your father's no taller," said Sarah. "Well," said Dave, who was irrepressible, "Lily doesn't want to feel as if she can set her cup of tea down on her husband's head." "Don't speak for your sister," said Sarah sharply.

"Well, I guess I don't know," said Lily; "I guess if I could draw a picture of a perfect man, it wouldn't look like him." "Twenty-one years old and she still talks about a perfect man," said Itzak. "At her age, she ought to dream," said Sarah. "You still have your eyes on that dentist?" asked Itzak. Lily said she guessed she did. "But does he have his eyes on you?" Dave asked. Lily said she guessed time would tell, and Dave said time was telling, especially in the lines around her eyes. "Enough," said Sarah; "Lily, when you go out with him, you wear your new, canary-yellow dress." "Just don't let your dress carry you away so much you start singing," said Dave; "you're no songbird." "Enough," said Sarah again. "You'll look better than one of his pills," said Dave.

"Say, listen," said Diana, "he's a nice guy, he makes a good living, and his engagement to Bertha Dundes is off, so he's probably ripe for someone." "Like a rotten apple ready to fall off the tree," said Dave. "Dave, leave the table," said Sarah. Dave got up and went out into the street. "He's not easy to talk to," said Bill, "and he is damn short." "He didn't seem so short to me," said Diana. "How could anyone seem short to you?" asked Bill; "what are you now? Four foot ten?" "In her high heels," said Itzak. "I don't know," said Diana; "a man who's too tall, you're always looking up at him, you could get a crick in your neck." "But so short," said Bill; "suppose she should have a son? He'd be a dwarf." "A dwarf!" exclaimed Itzak; "everyone knows boys over here grow up to be giants. Look at yourself. Your father's no taller than Dr. Luria. Where do you think you come from?" "The point is," said Sarah, getting up, "that Lily likes the man well enough to step out with him. And Grandpa likes him, and Poppa likes him, and Diana doesn't see anything wrong with him. Would it kill us to put ourselves out a little? To make him feel at home a little?" Bill collapsed against the back of his chair. The decision was made and there would be no appealing it.

Chapter 24

When Lily finally went out with her dentist, he told her what he had told her brother Bill, that he was not ready to get married and that he did not think it was fair of him to take up so much of her time. Whether he did this because he believed that, if he did not, her brothers would beat him up, or whether he simply had a sense of fair play, no one ever knew. Lily, made confident and courageous by her canary-yellow dress, which showed off her figure to advantage, calmly said that he did not have to worry about wasting her time, because she was seeing someone else. He said he was glad for her, and she said she was glad for herself. She said she hoped his practice would soon be all he wanted it to be and that someday he would find the right woman for him. A bachelor existence, she said, was a terrible thing, but of course a bachelor had fewer worries. She, herself, did not expect to be living with her family much longer.

She was gratified to see that she was upsetting him thoroughly, although when she got home, and he shook her hand goodbye, she closed her door and threw herself down on the new couch and sobbed as if someone had just died. Sarah, throwing a shawl over her shoulders, rushed out of her bedroom. She asked Lily what had happened, but Lily would not pick up her head to answer her. She shook Lily until her daughter propped herself up on one hand. "What happened?" demanded her mother. "I'm not seeing him again," sobbed Lily. "Forget him," said Sarah; "you have to look to the future. Put him behind you." "I can't forget him," said Lily. "Give yourself time," her mother said. "I don't want to give myself time!" said Lily; "I'm sick of having time!" Sarah sat up straight, looked into her daughter's eyes, and slapped her hard.

"You want to die over this?" Sarah asked; "you think this matters? You're healthy, you have a family, you have what to eat, and you want to die over this? So this is how I raised you? This is my daughter I hear saying these things? I am ashamed." "Of me?" Lily asked. "Of myself," said Sarah; "what did I do to make you like this? There's only one man in the world? There's only one thing in the world? A man? A man who doesn't even want you? You have no pride? You have no courage? It's good he didn't want you! Such a baby!" Lily began to cry again, and Sarah put her arms around her and rocked her. "You're the oldest," said Sarah; "you have to set an example." "I'm tired of setting examples!" Lily said, pulling herself free. "Nevertheless," said Sarah; "it is what you must do." Lily sat there staring at the flickering gaslight. "All right, Momma," Lily said at last; "I'm going to bed."

The next morning, Lily walked through the rooms with her head held high, and her lower lip, which she had chewed in her nervousness, was caked with specks of blood. She helped her mother and sister with the cleaning and the cooking, and it seemed to Sarah that she was more efficient than usual. But toward nightfall, Sarah saw that Lily's eyes were unusually bright, and her cheeks flushed. "Let me feel your head," said Sarah, stopping her as she went by. "Not too warm," she said, puzzled. She told herself that Lily was still upset about the dentist and would get over it after a few good nights' sleep. But late that night, Sarah woke up and heard one of the girls coughing in the back room. She got up and went in to look. Lily was sitting on the edge of the bed, half coughing, half choking, trying to get her breath.

"She's like a hot iron," Diana said, frightened. "Wake up Dave," said Sarah; "send him for Dr. Linde." Lily started to say that she did not want the doctor, but was interrupted by a fit of coughing. Diana ran out of the room, and they could hear Dave mumbling through the wall, and then Diana, who had raised her voice. "I'm going," Dave said. Then they heard Dave clattering down the stairs. "He has to wake the whole world," Diana said. "Never mind the whole world," said Sarah; "come on, Lily," she coaxed. "Try to sit up straight. You'll breathe easier, come on, Lily, sit up straighter."

Diana sat down on the bed and helped pull her sister up. Finally Lily got her breath. Her mother felt her head. "She's like a hot stove!" said Diana. The two of them looked toward the door. "What's taking Dave so long?" asked Lily. "He just left, Momma," said Diana. "What's going on in there?"

Meyer shouted from his room, from beneath his wooden structure. "Go talk to your father," said Sarah. "What's the noise?" Itzak said, coming in. "She's sick," said Sarah. "Sick?" said Itzak; "I can hear sick. Dave went for the doctor?" "He'll be back soon," said Sarah, and, just as she turned to the door again, Dave flung himself in. "Dr. Linde's not there," he said; "I left a note. His wife said he'd be here as soon as possible." "She always says that," moaned Sarah; "go and get Dr. Luria." "He's closed up for the night," said Dave. "Go to his house and ring his bell," said Sarah. "What good will it do?" asked Dave. "Go get him," Sarah said. Dave ran back down the stairs. "Going to a fire?" someone called out from the apartment below. "I wish he'd stay there," called out someone else. "So now it's a fire," said Itzak.

Then Dr. Linde walked in. He listened to Lily's chest; he looked at her throat. "What took you so long to call me?" he asked them. "She just this minute got sick," said Diana. "Just a half-hour ago," said Sarah. "She wasn't coughing before?" the doctor asked, tapping Lily's back. "No," Diana said, "she was fine all day." "Well," said Dr. Linde, "she has pneumonia. She's got crackles in her lungs. I'll stop by the druggist's and get the sulfur."

"You don't have to do that," said Esheal from the doorway; "I'll go down and get it. Can I talk to you for a minute?" he asked the doctor. "What about a steam tent?" he asked Dr. Linde; "I could set up a tent made out of sheets." "Where are you going to get the steam?" the doctor asked him. "I'll bring over a bunsen burner. I can attach it to the gas jet. I can fix it so it won't get knocked over, and if they just keep filling the pot with water, I can't see why it won't work." "It's a good idea," said the doctor; "I'll go and explain it to them and you get the pills and the bunsen burner."

Dr. Linde went back in and found Sarah staring at Lily as if she never expected to see her again. The boys were standing at the foot of the bed looking down at their sister as if they were viewing a body. Itzak was pacing up and down, and no one was answering Meyer, who kept shouting from his room, "What's going on, what's going on?" "Come out into the hall, everyone," said the doctor, and they all trooped out after him. "What she needs is rest," he said, "and cheerfulness. You stand around her bed like ravens, you'll scare her to death." "Is she going to live?" Sarah asked the doctor. She had thought of at least twenty people who had died of pneumonia in the short time which had elapsed between his diagnosis of Lily's illness and this conference in her living room. "She's young, she's strong, why shouldn't she live?" said the doctor. "She's very upset," said Sarah without thinking. "About what?" asked the doctor. "About a boy, what else?" Sarah asked. "When did she get upset about the boy?" he asked. "Last night," said Sarah. The doctor looked serious. "Try to keep her cheerful," he said again; "read to her, tell her jokes, but don't make her laugh. See to it that she doesn't move around, help her to the bathroom; don't let her go alone. And leave her in the tent." "What tent?" asked Sarah. Dr. Linde explained that Dr. Luria would come back and help them set up a steam tent. "He's an angel, that man," said Sarah. "He is," said Dr. Linde, who said he would stop by first thing in the morning.

Esheal came back and, with Dave's help, set up a steam tent. They went down to the basement, where there were always plenty of boards, and nailed the boards to the bed, and the sheets to the board, and then they got to work connecting the tube to the gas jet at one end and to the bunsen burner at the other. Esheal had bought a small tripod with a small grill and they started with a small pot of water. In the morning, he said, he would find something larger so that they could use a larger pot. And he refused to go home. He wanted, he told them, to keep an eye on Lily, and this way everyone in the family could get some sleep; they wouldn't be getting much sleep for the next few days. A few hours later, Sarah got up and joined him. "She seems to be breathing a little easier," said Esheal. "She looks so beautiful," said Sarah, sighing. Diana came back from the living room where she had gone to sleep on the couch. "I can't sleep," she said. "Go make Dr. Luria some tea," Sarah told her; "if he won't go home, he doesn't need to die of thirst."

Diana and Esheal sat across the table from each other, staring into their tea. "Well," said Esheal at last, "what's this about Nome, Alaska?" "Who told you?" asked Diana. "Your grandfather," said Esheal. "He never talks about the family to strangers," Diana said; "I'm surprised." "He said something about a Sidney," said Esheal. "I just got a letter from Sidney," Diana said, smiling as if she had just caught a glimpse of the next world. "He said the only whore in town is a Jewish woman. Can you imagine that? How did she get there, I'd like to know?" "The same way he did, I imagine," said Esheal. "Don't you wonder how he knows about her?" "Oh," Diana said, "my Sidney wouldn't be, I mean, he wouldn't know directly, not from experience, you know. Someone told him." "Your Sidney?" asked Esheal.

"He's my first cousin," said Diana. "Weren't you in love with him once?" Esheal asked. "Once!" said Diana; "but he went to Nome, Alaska. He's been in Nome, Alaska, for two years. And you know how often I hear from him? Every six months. That's how long it takes a letter to get here from there. And if I send him a letter, it takes mine six months to get there, and then six months before I get an answer, so a year goes by before I get an answer to a question. And how do I know what's going on out there when I don't hear a word for a whole year? So is it any wonder I found someone else? He said I would and I did."

"What would you do if he came back?" asked Esheal. "What could I do?" asked Diana, fidgeting with her napkin. "I'm engaged to Murray Zalman." "Engagements can be broken," said Esheal. "I wouldn't do that to him," said Diana; "I'd have to have a very good reason." "What kind of reason would that be?" Esheal asked. "Something goddam terrible," said Diana. She saw Esheal looking at her in surprise. "Oh, the way I speak," she said; "I don't have to tell you anymore. My language is something terrible. I've been around my brothers so much I talk like them. I wish Lily wasn't sick, goddammit."

Esheal smiled at her. Dammit, goddam, the words sounded so funny in her mouth. She leaned farther forward against the table and her bosom was so large that it rested on it. "What do you think, Doctor?" she asked; "I think my sister likes you." "She does?" Esheal asked. "I think she does," said Diana; "I think you're swell." Esheal looked at her and thought about Sidney in Nome, Alaska, and Murray Zalman in Brooklyn and how much he would like her to throw both of them out and come to live with him.

"What does this Murray Zalman do for a living?" he asked instead. "He runs a dress factory, and he invented a machine, you know, for putting all those little pleats in the dresses? He makes a terrible lot of money." "That's always a good thing," said Esheal. "I'm surprised he walked out with me twice," said Diana; "the first time he took me out, he came in a carriage. I thought a carriage, who ever went for a ride in a carriage, so I ran up and called Lily and Dinney. And my conversation wasn't with him, it was with the girls in the back. So he was annoyed, and he says to me, next time I come for you, don't bring the girls. I thought, he don't like me, and he don't like Dinney, it can never be. But he kept after me, and after a while, I didn't bring anyone else with me. I guess he had a right to be mad; he spent a lot of money on that cab. But now he says he liked Lily and Dinney so long as they don't come with us in the carriage."

Esheal coaxed Diana into talking on; she made him laugh and he was happy watching her and listening to her. Her voice was like a little animal's. By the time Esheal decided to relieve Sarah, who was watching over Lily in the bedroom, Diana had invited him to her engagement party, and Esheal felt both great happiness and a great sense of loss. At least, he thought, she would be a presence in his life: like the ivories he collected. They did not talk to him but they lent a radiance. Diana, he thought, would do more than add radiance; now that they were friends, there would be some emotion which would join them to each other.

Lily seemed much improved in the morning, although she had a high fever and could sit up only with help. When Dr. Linde came, he was surprised at how much better her cough was, and told the Romanoffs they could blame this fortunate state of affairs on Dr. Luria. Sarah's lips quivered when she thanked him, and Meyer asked to see him so that he could thank him himself. Sarah and Diana kept tripping over each other as they cooked him breakfast, and Itzak insisted on sending Dave out for some special black bread and herring.

For the first time since he had his own store, Esheal opened the pharmacy late. And he was not in the store long before Diana came in and sat down at the soda fountain. "How's Lily?" he asked, coming over. "She's so much better," said Diana, "but the doctor said it would take awhile for her to get back on her feet." "I thought I'd go over to see her at lunchtime," said Esheal, who was pretending to wipe the counter. "She asked for you when she woke up," said Diana. Someone came in with a prescription; Esheal went over and looked at it and told his clerk to take care of it. He went back to the soda fountain. "How about a black-and-white soda?" he asked Diana; "you always used to like them." "I still like them," she said. This time, when Esheal made the soda, he put the ice cream in first so that he could give Diana twice the usual amount; after he added the syrup, there was barely room for the soda water. He stood there watching her drink it.

"Say, listen," said Diana; "we have a problem. Maybe you'll have an idea. I told you about my engagement party? Well, Dinney, she wants to give it, but my parents won't hear about it. Her family has three rooms in back of their store and hardly any windows, and my grandfather, Dinney's family is poison to him. He calls them the shoemakers, because, you know, she's a shoemaker's daughter, and he thinks shoemakers are just the lowest things, but Momma's not so thrilled with our place either. I think it's fine, but for a long time, they've been talking about buying their own house, you know, one of those graystones on Sullivan Street, and they have almost enough money saved up because last month Dave made a killing, we don't know at what, but he made it, except that if we buy the house, we won't have money for the party and so that's a problem. But I think," Diana said, "they should buy the house and I can persuade Murray to pay for the engagement party. He knows we don't have much. What do you think?"

"Whose house are you thinking of buying?" asked Esheal. "Mr. Plinsky's," said Diana. "I think Mr. Sigan is selling his house," said Esheal; "it's not on Sullivan Street, it's on Carroll, but it's a good house, better than Plinsky's and it costs a lot less. Let me look into it." "Buying a different house," said Diana; "I never thought of that. Once my father gets used to an idea, he likes to keep it. He doesn't like change. You know how it is. But if it would work out, it would be wonderful. He would never have to know," considered Diana, "not until he saw the van pull up to a different house. He might not even notice." "I can't promise," said Esheal; "but I'll look into it." "Anyhow," said Diana, "if we do buy Mr. Plinsky's house, and we don't have money left for the party, what do you think I should do? I think a house is more important than a party. You can't live in a party." "Don't worry about it," said Esheal; "it'll work out."

Esheal began stopping by at the Romanoffs' every day during his lunch hour, and it was evident to everyone that Lily waited restlessly for his visits. Whether this was because she responded to his kindness, as everyone in her family did, or because she saw each visit he made as a slap in the dentist's face, she did wait for him, and she seemed to wake up and grow stronger just before noon. Esheal would tell her stories about people in the neighborhood, how Mrs. Rosen had told her husband she had a heart attack so she wouldn't have to clean her own house, but could have a cleaning woman do it instead, and how Dr. Linde had a patient who wasn't getting any better, and he couldn't understand why until he asked to use his bathroom, and on a hunch, he opened up their medicine chest, and there were all the medicines he had prescribed, unopened. He had gone back in and asked the man how he intended to get better if he wouldn't take the medicine he was given, and the man said that he thought medicine was for very sick people. So Dr. Linde told him he was a very sick person, and the man got so frightened that he stayed in his bed for two weeks, and finally, the doctor had to call in a specialist who told the man he was all right and also told him that if he did not get out of bed and start walking around, he would be an invalid the rest of his life.

Lily listened to these stories and would fall back against the pillows trying not to laugh, because whenever she laughed, she began coughing. Meanwhile, Esheal had checked on Mr. Sigan's house, and just as he thought, the old man wanted to sell his house and did not care how much he got for it as long as he got back what he had paid for it. One day, after visiting Lily, he took Diana and Sarah aside and told them about the house on Carroll Street and how much less it cost than the house on Sullivan. And, he said, it was a nicer house and had stained-glass windows at the top of the first flight of stairs and in the living room as well. What's more, Mr. Sigan had worked as an electrician and a plumber, and, as far as he could see, the house was in tiptop shape. Sarah asked Esheal if he would take them over to meet Mr. Sigan, because he had hinted that Mr. Sigan would not sell his house unless he liked the person who was buying it, and Esheal said he would take them over around six or seven, whenever the store was not busy.

That night, the three of them went over to Mr. Sigan's, and Esheal had very little to do. Diana and Sarah ran from room to room exclaiming at how beautiful the house was, and how high the ceilings were, and how nice the moldings were, and how smooth the floors were, and they stood silently and worshipfully in front of the stained-glass window in the living room which was lit by the streetlight.

"You like it?" asked Mr. Sigan, beaming at them. "I never

saw anything like it," said Diana, who never had. "I saw something like it, once," said Sarah; "in Russia when one of my little boys, may he rest in peace, ran into a church, and there was gold everywhere. I thought I was in heaven, but it was the wrong heaven, so I got out of there fast." "A thing from heaven," said Mr. Sigan, looking at the window; "that's what it is." "Tell me, Mr. Sigan," said Sarah; "why do you want to sell a house like this? Where can you go that's better? Such a beautiful place. Sliding doors! Bookcases growing out of the walls!" "Sarah," said Esheal.

"You think I want to sell?" asked Mr. Sigan; "but an old man like me, all alone. I can't clean it. I should go up on the roof now at my age? I should climb up and dust the moldings? A house like this needs a family. You want to buy it, I'll give it to you cheap. Believe me, I'm giving it away." "On one condition," said Sarah. Esheal stifled a groan. "What kind of condition?" asked Mr. Sigan; "either you pay me or you don't." "Listen to the condition," said Sarah; "what will it cost you?" "I'm all ears," said Mr. Sigan.

"If you keep the rooms in the back on the first floor and you let me cook meals for you, we buy it," said Sarah. "That's a condition?" said the old man. "A man like you should be parted from his house?" said Sarah. "I don't fix the roof no more," said the old man. "So don't fix it," said Sarah; "do we have a deal?" "How much are you charging for the room?" Mr. Sigan asked cautiously. "How much? Three dollars? Four?" said Sarah. "Five," said Esheal. "Five it is," said Mr. Sigan. "Let's shake on it," said Sarah. Mr. Sigan gave her an odd look and stuck out his hand. "Look, Doc, I'm not moving," he said, and did an odd little dance in front of the fireplace. "You're in good hands," Esheal said; "she'll get you fat." "I'm already fat," said Mr. Sigan. "I tell you what," he said to Sarah, "before you move in, I'll wash the stained-glass windows with vinegar. Maybe all the windows!" Sarah started to tell him not to bother, that the boys would wash the windows, but Esheal nudged her. "I would be delighted," she said. "Go outside," Esheal told her. When they went out, he asked Mr. Sigan what he wanted for the house. "Four thousand?" he said; "five?" "Five," said Esheal; "you have to live too."

When Meyer Romanoff heard about the new house, how many rooms it had, how much light and air, how it looked like a rich man's house, and finally, how little it cost, he did no mourning for the lost house on Sullivan Street. His only regret was that he could not yet walk and so could not see it. This gave Esheal an idea, and he called on his Japanese friend who provided him with the figurines he gave away at sales time, and asked his advice about buying and using a camera. The two men went out to purchase it, and then went to Mr. Sigan's house, where, to the old man's amazement, they began to photograph the house room by room, Esheal carrying the camera, his Japanese friend following with a large light on a stalk which fastened to the top of a tripod. When the pictures were developed, he took them over to Meyer. For some time after that, the Romanoffs regarded Esheal as their golden savior. Esheal often wondered what Sarah made of his reappearance in her life, but gradually, he understood that what affection she had for him once had faded, although enough of it remained to make a difference in at least one way. He knew what he did and said often annoyed her, but she had more patience with him than she would otherwise have had; he understood that, in some way, Sarah still considered him a child, a child in need of her protection. Yet, to him, Sarah was still as wonderful, as fascinating as she had been when he first saw her.

And Diana's engagement party was postponed until the Romanoffs were settled in the new house. Meanwhile, Esheal continued to visit Lily, and it was clear to everyone that she had come to like him. One day, Esheal asked her what she thought of getting married, and she said she didn't think much about it because no one had asked her. "I'm asking you," he said and turned beet red. "But you don't have to give me an answer right away," he said; "think it over. Wait until you're feeling better," and he would have gone on in that way indefinitely if Lily had not stopped him. "I can give you an answer now," she said; "the answer is yes." "Yes?" Esheal repeated incredulously. "Yes." Lily laughed, and this time she did not cough. Later, Lily said that this would be the best news in the world for Diana, because now she could get married herself.

That night, as if everything were determined to happen at once, a man from the Alaskan shipping company in Nome who knew Sidney stopped by to visit the Romanoffs. When he heard that Lily had just become engaged, he looked surprised, and said something about how Sid would be coming home now, and the Romanoffs looked at each other, because they knew what the man meant. Now that Lily was getting married, Diana could get married, and that was what Sidney had been waiting for, because if and when Lily got married, he could marry Diana. Everyone looked at Diana, who said nothing. "Maybe," Sarah said after the man left, "we should put the engagement party off some more. The house needs so much; there are no curtains; the floors need polishing; there's so much to do." "Don't put the party off," said Diana; "the windows are so fancy, no one's going to miss the curtains." Sarah looked at Meyer, who shrugged his shoulders. "Do you think Sidney is really coming back?" asked Lily, who was now sitting up in a chair. "Without doubt," said Sarah. "How long," Lily asked, "do you think it will take him to get here?" "Sidney?" said Sarah; "how long does it take a train to cross the country? He'll be here in a month, maybe less." They all looked at Diana, who got up and went into the kitchen. "Nu?" said Itzak. Sarah shook her head.

Chapter 25

The engagement party was a beautiful one, and Diana finally had her dress made by a dressmaker. Lily stopped at the drugstore to wait for Esheal, who was wearing the new blue serge suit he had had made for the occasion. The boys had new suits and hats and shoes and none of them had ever looked more elegant or more happy. Esheal's clerk was to bring twenty quarts of ice cream to the party two hours after it began. Dinney and her sister came to the Romanoffs' hours before the party began and helped set out platters of food and bread and cake. There were bottles of seltzer and homemade wine everywhere. The girls came with a bag of balloons which they proceeded to blow up and thumbtack all over the walls. Streamers had been put up the night before, and the huge cake, which said *Congratulations, Murray and Diana*, was kept under wraps in the kitchen.

And people began coming in. Soon the two big front rooms were crowded with people, and the boys had to throw open the windows because it had gotten so hot. One of the young men who always came to the Romanoffs' on Sundays arrived with a box of wax cylinders, put one on the Victrola, and opened the Victrola's doors to make the music as loud as possible. The older people gathered around the edge of the room, and the younger ones began dancing. Lily insisted that Esheal dance with her, although once he agreed and permitted himself to be dragged into the center of the room she knew she was disappointed in his performance. Still, he was determined, and after three or four dances, they managed to look like most of the other couples on the floor; at least they were not forever moving away from each other instead of moving together.

"Say," said Diana, gliding back with Murray, "isn't this some party, Doc?" "It's the best," he said. He felt giddy. He had never felt giddy before. "Hi, there, Doc," said Dave, tapping him on the shoulder, and when Esheal said, "Hello, there," but kept on dancing, Lily told him that Dave wanted to cut in, and when he still looked blank, she said that meant that Dave wanted to dance with her and he ought to dance with Dave's girl. Esheal obediently began dancing with Dave's girl, but he didn't like it; the girl's cool, polished skin and her sophisticated airs frightened him, and he kept his eye on Lily, who was dancing with Dave and looked as if she were in love with him. Then Bill cut in and he wound up with Bill's girl, and still Lily was nowhere in sight. When he finally caught a glimpse of her, she was dancing with the boy who had brought Dinney. Each and every one of the other men he saw danced splendidly.

When Lily was finally returned to him, he felt as if he had three clay feet. "Oh, just one more dance!" begged Lily, who was out of breath, but Esheal still had his eye on the others and how well they danced, and he wondered what they thought about him and what they would say about him afterward. "Not now," he said sharply. Just then, Dave came over, bowed deeply to Lily and held out his hand, and off she went. Esheal was furious, but told himself he would get over it, and just then Diana came up and asked him to dance, and, perhaps because he was annoyed at Lily, who should have known how he felt and should have stayed and talked to him, he let himself imagine that this was *their* engagement party, his and Diana's. When he and Lily had their engagement party, he decided, he would rent a hall. *That* would be a grand affair, he thought, and when Dave brought Lily back and Murray came for Diana, he asked Lily if she wanted to dance. He wondered if he were dancing with her because he felt so guilty about pretending that this party had been his and Diana's engagement party.

And so the evening went on. People began congregating in little groups around the punch bowls, and the women fanned themselves with their little fancy fans, and flirted with the men by fanning them. Everyone's face was hot and flushed and everyone was talking as if this were his last chance to do so. Geysers of laughter rose up from the little groups and bubbled through the smoky air; here and there was the sound of an old man sneezing, and everyone knew someone had just taken his snuff. Then someone began popping balloons and the girls pretended to be frightened by the noise and begged the boys to stop. "Stop!" said Sarah's voice, rising above the others; "leave them up for the party." Meanwhile, Murray kept leaving Diana to talk to one friend after another, and when he returned, he would say worriedly to Diana, "I wonder where my father is?" "Maybe something happened to him," said Lily. "Nothing happened to him," said Diana; "don't say such a thing." But Murray looked worried. Then, just as Mrs. Romanoff and Diana were getting ready to carry in the cake, and the boys were going in front of them throwing confetti at all the guests, the door opened and Murray Zalman's father walked in.

"Did I miss the party?" asked Mr. Zalman, and lurched across the room toward his son. " 'Gratulations!" he shouted to Murray, throwing his arms around him; "the very bestest!" Then he turned to Diana. "The little lovely!" he shouted; "give a kiss to the old man!" Diana, who had never seen anyone drunk before, backed away from him horrified, but Mr. Zalman walked after her. Diana kept backing away, and Mr. Zalman kept walking after her. This pursuit went on until Diana found herself against a table, and, when she realized she could not get away from Mr. Zalman, she burst into tears.

This was more than Murray could stand. "Get away from her, Pop!" he cried, trying to pull his father away, but his father was determined to kiss his son's fiancée. Esheal watched the scene in horror, as if it were taking place somewhere far away, at the wrong end of a telescope, in someone else's life, when Murray finally gave up trying to pull his father away and started shouting at him. But his father was not to be stopped. He was bending over Diana, who swayed from side to side, trying to avoid his mouth. When Murray saw this, the veins at the side of his neck stood out, and he grabbed his father by the collar and hit him square on the jaw. Mr. Zalman fell to the floor and lay there in front of the table laden with food. "Oh, my God!" screamed Diana, and covered her face with her hands.

Esheal and Dr. Linde reached Mr. Zalman at the same time. "He'll be all right," said the doctor, and Esheal stood next to Diana. "For a son to hit his father!" Diana whispered to him. "He's not hurt," said Esheal. "For a son to hit his father!" Diana said again. "Murray thought he was going to hurt you," Esheal said; he stood closer to her, wanting to protect her from the fear making her tremble so. "But for a son to hit his father," Diana said again. She's in shock, Esheal thought, but when he looked at Diana again, he knew this was the end of the engagement.

Chapter 26

Diana

Sidney and I were raised together. He was my first cousin. He was thirteen, I was ten, when he used to come in the summer, because to go from New York to Brooklyn was to go to the country. There were not so many houses and we had all those fields in the back where the orphan asylum was, and we enjoyed ourselves on the hill, and they all came. Even Fannie Romanoff would come in the summer to our house. I remember when Fannie got a sewing needle stuck in her arm, she left it stuck in a cushion, and put her arm down on it, and it went right through the skin and they couldn't remove it, until it finally worked itself out enough for them to get it, so she was at our house for six weeks. We never lacked company. Mother had a terrible time of it. When they came from Europe, they all came to her. Then when we moved to Brooklyn, they all came to her in the summer.

My husband proposed to me when I was sixteen years old. He was going to Nome, Alaska, and he said, if you'll marry me, I won't go to Nome, Alaska. He was taking up book-keeping there. A bookkeeper made twenty-five dollars a week. It was plenty of money seventy-five years ago. But my mother said, no younger sister gets married before her older one. When the older sister is married, then the younger one gets married. So it was out of the question. And everyone said, Diana, it's wrong to marry your cousin. You'll have children, they'll be idiots. And now, the law forbids it, but then it didn't. I waited until I was nineteen years old. He left New York when he was nineteen and he spent three years in Nome, Alaska. By the time I was nineteen, I had two other guys already and it was only two weeks before my wedding to Murray Zalman.

I broke the engagement because Murray's father came to my engagement party drunk. For a Jew to be drunk was a terrible thing and I realized that, and he hit his father, and the

father fell when he hit him, and I saw this. And this turned me
so against him; after that I was afraid to marry him. He was a
big, strapping man, and I just could not marry him for fear he
would kill me. So I said no. And I was terribly in love with
Sidney. Sidney was coming back, and I knew that, and of
Murray I was afraid, so I broke my engagement, gave him
back everything he ever gave me, my diamonds, my furs, my
everything. I was so anxious and so fearful of him. And he
came to Aunt Fannie Romanoff's house to see if she could do
something for him. He asked this one; he asked that one.
Even years after I was married, and he was married to
another woman, he came to Dinney, to her husband's funeral, and after that, he came one evening to Dinney's house.
This was maybe ten years after I broke the engagement and I
already had both of my children, and he asked Dinney, Call
her, tell her you have to talk to her. And Dinney said to him,
How do you expect me to call her and she should come in and
find you? She is no fool. And he said, I just want to look at
her, I just want to say one word to her. I'm still terribly in
love with her.

When I had my first child, I took her out on the street,
walking with the carriage, and a woman in the neighborhood
stopped me in front of old Esheal's store and looked in at her.
Was she a beautiful child! So the woman says to me, Is she an
idiot? And I says to her, Of course she's not an idiot. So what
do you think the woman said to me? If she's not an idiot now,
she will be.

I was married to Sidney for three years before I had a child.
For three years we didn't sleep together because I was so
afraid I'd have an idiot. And then after three years, I got
caught. And Sidney brought me medicine to get rid of it, and
for a while, I pretended I was taking it, but I wasn't. I was
throwing it down the toilet. Because I wanted a child. You
can imagine how fearful I was. And Sidney used to say, don't
you know what could happen? It could ruin our whole lives.
But I was determined. I wanted a child. And when the little
one was about three or four months old, she already knew her
father. When she'd look out the window—we were on the
ground floor—if she saw him, she'd scratch the window
wanting to get out to him. She didn't do that when anyone
else came, so I realized I don't have to worry, she's a normal
child. And when I saw she was normal, I wanted another. So I
had my boy.

Sidney called me all kinds of names when we were children. We were raised together from the time we were little tots. In fact, he and his mother were in the house when I was born, so he called me Diana, or mouse, until we were married. Then he started to call me honey and I called him hon. But when he asked me to marry him, and he said if I married him he wouldn't go to Nome, Alaska, I said no. His mother wanted me to marry him; she was very anxious to see us married, but I told her he would always regret it if he didn't go. He read every book that was ever written about Nome, Alaska, and don't forget, he was only nineteen when he left. And when he got there, and got himself his job as a bookkeeper, he made money and bought a mine that the lawyers took away from him. Then he asked me to marry him and come to Nome, Alaska, with him. To go to Nome, Alaska, in 1904, you know what that meant. And I was only sixteen.

In Alaska, they called him Stan. He couldn't be called Sid there; they'd kill him. He was the only Jew among God knows how many, and the only whore in town was a Jewish woman. In the winter, the ice froze over and you couldn't get a letter through for six months. There was no ship that could get through. Siberia was right across the ocean. He could see Siberia from his shore, and he said if they found gold there, he was going to Siberia. He would have been one of the first; he was already so close. When he wrote letters, he wanted me to know that I'd have to wait for him. He wanted my picture, so I sent my picture. I knew that he loved me. But he said he knew I would meet someone else before he came back; he said he knew me better than I knew myself. And he was right. I did meet someone else. But then Murray hit his father and that was the end of him.

I always knew Sidney was in love with me. He didn't go for any of the other girls *but* me. He came with a friend and his friend fell in love with me, and *I* fell in love with both of them and I didn't know which I really liked best for a long, long time. Did you ever hear of being in love with two people? The one I liked best was his friend. He told Sid that *he* was in love with me and that he was going to ask me to marry him. I didn't know what went on between the two boys. They came up one night for dinner and Bill was at the piano playing quietly in the living room. In the dining room, I was setting the table for supper. Mother was coming in with whatever she's bringing, and this fellow would pull me down on his lap and he would grab my hand and I would say stop, or holler, or murder. I never realized. When Sid came outside, he said, If you don't stop, I'll take my hat and coat and go home. So I just thought he was cranky. Then I realized. He was jealous of the other one. But being a kid, did I know what he was jealous about?

The other one died of some kind of a terrible sickness. And then Sidney went away for three years. If he hadn't gone away, I would have married him in a minute. He was such a gentleman, such a gentle boy. Every girl was in love with him, every cousin was in love with him, and when everybody compared him to the others, he was head and shoulders over everybody, and you know, if you've got a little bit of brains, you realize, quiet, gentle, intelligent, what else do you want? But his mother and mine were sisters, so children, that was a fear that I had.

Then when I saw Murray hit his father—of course, his father came in drunk—right into a beautiful engagement party, but he had no right to do that. And I turned immediately from him. I just figured, I'm hot-tempered, you know, and I should do something, and he would hit me. And the thought of a man hitting a woman was so terrible I couldn't get over it. And he almost died from it. There wasn't one in my family that he didn't talk to. He used to watch when I came out of business, to get me as I came out of work, and I would watch and look, and suddenly find him standing there. He was so tall, you could really see him in the crowd. Then I would go up the stairs and go out another door. Another day, he'd wait on the elevator steps where I had to go up to the office. I would get the Fulton Street elevated. I don't know if that station is there anymore.

And one time, Momma was visiting her cousin, Aunt Fannie, and he came up there and talked to her and pleaded with her. Call her down for five minutes so I can talk to her, he said, my hand should fall off if ever I should lift it to her; I don't know what makes her so frightened. And Momma came upstairs, and she said, she went down and said, she's asleep; I'm not going to wake her. So he said, please go up again. Maybe she's not really asleep. Maybe she's reading. Because I'd read until all hours of the night. He knew. So she came up. She said, he's downstairs waiting. Sit yourself down and talk to him. I said no, Momma, no. So she went down to tell him I'm fast asleep and she can't wake me. Then he went to Lizzie

Romanoff, my cousin who was working in a shirtwaist factory. He invented a machine that put the little pleats in the fancy shirts we used to wear. I never had a figure, but Lily had a beautiful figure. On her, these things looked wonderful. And she had the waistline, which I never had.

I couldn't go back to him, and it took him an awful long time. Jake, who was Dinney's husband and his best friend, said to him, why don't you try to meet another woman? You make wonderful money and your inventing machine makes money. Go and get married and forget her. She don't want you. Why do you want her? He married some other girl, gave her the ring, gave her the mink scarf that I had, and whatever he gave me, I gave everything back. Oh, I was so anxious. It could never be. And many a night before I went to bed, I saw him sitting on the bench under the streetlight in front of our house. It was terrible. There was another man I used to go with, and he had such terrible big hands and feet, I told Momma, how can I marry him, if we should have children, and they should be girls, what will they look like with such big hands and feet? And he was so tall, so I said, Momma, a girl six feet, six feet two, what kind of life would she have? But it wasn't like this with Murray Zalman. Because I was so afraid of him I couldn't be in the same room with him. And then Sidney zipped my dress and that finished it.

Chapter 27

When Esheal's mother heard that he was getting married, she started to cry, and nothing could stop her. It was a snowy day, and big white flakes fell slowly through the air. It was the kind of day that Esheal remembered in Russia, only there, when it snowed like this, the snow would settle on the black coats of the Jewish men of the town, and melt, leaving them the only black things which moved in the scene except for an occasional black bird. When the snow settled on the peasants' clothes, they bore the snow along with them. When they chopped wood, the snow rose and fell on their arms as easily at it rose and fell on the long, black branches in the forest behind the town.

Esheal asked his mother what was wrong, but she did not answer. He wondered what could be upsetting her so, as if her tears now would give him some clue to her behavior in the past. He watched his mother and asked himself, as he had a thousand times before, if she had ever loved him. He knew she depended on him; she always had, but that was not the same thing. Every now and then, she would look out the window at the falling snow, as if hoping for its advice, but she would turn her head, see her son, and begin crying again. "You don't want me to get married?" he asked her, and his mother raised her handkerchief to her eyes and shook her head no. "Why don't you want me to get married?" he asked her. She shook her head more violently than before, looked out the window, and tried to say something in Yiddish. "I don't understand?" asked Esheal. She nodded. "You do want me to get married?" he asked. She nodded.

For the first time in his life, Esheal lost his temper. "Then goddammit, what *is* the matter?" he shouted. His mother stopped crying; in fact, she seemed to have stopped breathing. "Oh, my little son!" she wailed and began crying softly.

"Are you sick?" he demanded; "has the doctor been here?"
"I'm not sick," she said, weeping hopelessly. "Then what's
wrong?" he insisted. "You said you liked the Romanoffs.
You're always asking me when I'm going to get married. All
you talk about is other people's grandchildren and how you'll
be ready to die when you see your son's children, and now I
tell you when I'm getting married and you're acting like an
old Pobrosk woman at a funeral. What's the matter with
you?" He didn't like the sound of his own voice; it was so
rough, but he was at his wit's end.

"It's my head," said his mother, who let her head fall
forward onto her shiny black bosom. "Your head?" asked
Esheal; "you have pains in your head? How many times do I
have to say it? You don't feel well, you tell me, and I'll call
the doctor. I have only one mother. I have God knows how
many sisters, but I have only one mother." "You should pay
more attention to your sisters," said his mother; "they're like
strangers to you." "Whose fault is that?" Esheal shouted at
her. "Never mind my sisters! They have enough money; they
have enough clothes. They'll have husbands soon enough.
They don't need me. What about the pains in your head?" "I
don't have pains in my head," said his mother; "it's here."
And she smote her heart. Esheal stared at her in bewilderment. He needed, he thought, a translator. He knew if he
asked her whether or not she had pains in her chest, she
would say no. "You're making me unhappy," he said at last.
"Well, can't you see for yourself?" she asked him, pointing to
the top of her head. He threw up his hands. "What is it?" he
shouted; "tell me, already!"

"My wig," she said, pointing at it; "I can't go to your
wedding in this wig. I can't go out in this wig. It's small. It's
thin. I'll shame my son at his own wedding!" "For God's
sake," said Esheal; "that's all it is? A wig? You need a new
wig? I'll get you a wig. We'll go shopping together on my
lunch hour."

But his mother began crying again. "What is it now?" he
asked. "To go out on the street looking like this?" she cried.
Esheal started to say something, then looked at his mother,
who was looking mournfully out the window. So that was it.
She was worried about what others would think. She had
always worried about what others would think. If she had not
been so worried about what people would think, she would

not have been in such a hurry to remarry and to leave him behind. For the first time, he realized that she could never have stayed on alone in Pobrosk after his father died; she would never have been able to stand it, the pathetic way in which the other women would have seen her: another poor widow on the town, another poor woman out to take one of their husbands from them. He looked at his mother and sighed. She had, he thought, a certain wisdom, but she was spineless. A spineless woman, he thought, should never have children.

Now that he thought about it, he realized that his mother seldom left the house anymore. His sisters did whatever shopping needed to be done. He gave her money for the week and the girls made her clothes. What friends she had came to see her. She appeared to be so perfectly happy in the house that he had not noticed how infrequently she left it. "All right; Momma," he said, "I'll get someone to come by with some wigs and you can pick one out right here. How about that?" His mother sniffled and blew her nose. "All right," she said. "So forget about the wig," said Esheal; "what about my getting married? What do you think?" "What do I think?" she cried; "who cares what I think! It's wonderful; it's more than wonderful!" Esheal went over to her and bent down to kiss her, but she got up, grabbed him around the neck, and hung on. "It's the most wonderful thing," she kept saying.

"We'll have the wedding here?" his mother asked him when they were sitting in the kitchen over their glasses of tea; "the place is fixed up so nice. You give the money. Your sisters are busy with the sewing machine. I wake up some mornings and wonder where I am. You know, some mornings I wake up early, and everything's still blurry, and you'll laugh at me, I think I'm in the little house in Pobrosk and I even start to get up to light the fire for your father's breakfast. Then I fall back in bed because I don't have what to do or where to go. Your new father died last year, and I hardly ever think about him. I never think I have to get up and make his breakfast. But I think I have to get up and make your father's.

"But you remember," she asked excitedly, "the way the light used to come in under the door in Pobrosk like jagged teeth? Whoever had a door that went straight across? Do you remember it?" she asked. "I remember," he said. "And the old table, where it turned gray from so much soup spilling on it? And the ash barrel from the stove, and how you used to spread the ashes out on the snow? You remember?" "Of course I remember," said Esheal. "You always had a good memory," said his mother; "mine is no good and every day it gets worse."

"A good memory is no blessing," said her son. His mother looked down at her hands. Was he reproaching her? She felt he was. "Things over are better forgotten," said Esheal. "Before a wedding," said his mother, "is no time to sit and remember old things." "Better before than after," said Esheal. "A person should remember from where he came," said his mother. "I remember," he said. "Anyhow," he said, getting up, "tomorrow night Lily and I are talking about wedding plans with her family. I told Lily I wanted a big wedding, but her family doesn't have much, so I'll pay for it. But they're proud. It's a problem." "It is," said his mother. "Isn't the little one getting married too?" "Diana?" said Esheal; "maybe before we do. If her cousin Sidney gets back in time."

"Can you imagine that?" asked his mother; "marrying a cousin? It's something peculiar. You said they grew up together. Your cousin Minnie, she would have been so happy to marry you." "She was like a sister to me," said Esheal; "we lived in the same house for years." "But a cousin?" said his mother; "I don't think they should do it." "I think Lily's parents are cousins," said Esheal; "it runs in the family." "That's something to run in a family," said his mother; "maybe they're a little peculiar." "I don't think so," said Esheal, who was getting annoyed.

"Listen, Momma," he said, "when you meet Mrs. Romanoff ask her to draw a picture of Lily for you. She's always flattered when someone asks her for a picture." "She still draws pictures?" asked his mother. "I'll see you in the morning," said Esheal, putting on his hat and coat, wrapping his muffler around his neck, and tucking one end under his coat lapel. As he did so, he was surprised to find himself thinking about Bill and Dave, and how they would be walking around without mufflers and gloves as if nothing were falling through the air.

That evening, Lily came into the store to discuss wedding plans with Esheal, and as soon as the store was empty, he took her into the back where she sat watching him grind yellow substances with his mortar and pestle and where she nervously watched the gas bubbling through the long tubes overhead. Each time Lily came into the store, Esheal felt the same satisfaction and excitement and pride. He liked to look up from his work and see her, a beautiful young woman, sitting on the stool near the zinc counter, her long, magnificent legs crossed at the ankles. Tonight, she was wearing a black suit with red silk lapels. Time after time, he had to remind himself that he was marrying this woman, that she was going to belong to him and no one else. Occasionally, he would feel a chill, as if to be so lucky was to invite the attention of the evil angels.

He was, he thought, used to dealing with unhappiness; he was not sure how one dealt with contentment. As he looked up at Lily, he thought he would enjoy learning that discipline. Every task he performed in her presence was transformed, and Lily seemed fascinated by his least movement. Why did the doctor order one kind of medicine rather than another? Why did people, fat and thin, get the same amount of medicine? Esheal thought her questions reflected a penetrating mind; it had never occurred to him to wonder about her intelligence, partially because he did not believe that women needed intelligence, and partially because he assumed if Diana was so bright, then her sister was also.

Esheal tapped the pill press, counted the pills and put them into a white envelope which he had already labeled. "I've been thinking," said Esheal, "what about Alexander Hall?" "For the wedding?" gasped Lily; "we couldn't! That's a huge place!" "It's supposed to be the best in Brooklyn," said Esheal. "Well, yes," said Lily, "but my family could never afford it." "I want to pay for it," Esheal said; "your family could make the mazel tov at your house." "I don't know," said Lily. "That's how my mother wants it," said Esheal. "Oh," said Lily, who had met his mother only once and had been made nervous by her silence; "your mother." Esheal watched her think things over and realized that she thought only in terms of her own family. But he did not think much of his own himself, and his was not very big; she would manage to find room for his mother and his sisters.

In the front of the shop, the clerk, who was put out because Esheal now spent all his time with Lily, so that he no longer had his lunchtime partner at checkers, was thumping boxes about noisily. "We'll talk to them tomorrow night," said Lily; "I'll explain it to them. They might be upset. Poppa has to make a wedding for Diana, too, and I don't know how much money Momma has under the floor, but it's not enough for two weddings. I don't think they'll like it, letting the groom's family pay for the wedding." "How much can they dislike it?" asked Esheal. Lily said nothing. "Maybe," said Esheal, "we should wait until that Sidney your sister always talks about comes back. A double wedding doesn't cost any more than a single one." "A double wedding?" asked Lily. "It would kill two birds with one stone," said Esheal; "don't you think it's a good idea?" "No," said Lily, "I don't think it's a good idea." Esheal looked at her, surprised.

"For once," Lily burst out, "for once, I'd like to be the center of attention!" Lily saw the expression on his face and began to cry. "A person only gets married once," she said; "why can't I have my own wedding to myself? Why do we have to share it with Diana?" Esheal was flattered by her possessiveness and was happy to let the question of a double wedding drop. After all, he was not anxious to share the spotlight either. "Well, tomorrow night, we'll talk about it with your parents," he said, "and after that, all we'll need is the rabbi." "And someplace to live," said Lily, who was having trouble imagining herself all alone with Esheal. She had always wanted to be married, but somehow she had expected to marry and still live with her family. "Don't worry about that," he said. "Why not?" said Lily; "it never hurts to worry." "Does it help?" he asked. "Of course it helps," said Lily; "if you don't worry, you can't see what might go wrong and you can't do anything to prevent it." "You can't prevent much," said Esheal. "Of course you can!" said Lily, annoyed, wondering whether Esheal might have a spineless streak like her cousin Stanford, a man who was forever letting things happen to him, a man who could not see to it that things happened the way he wanted them to.

The next night, everyone was unusually quiet and restrained, as if they had met to sign a contract rather than to discuss wedding plans. Esheal told them that his mother wanted him to get married in Alexander Hall, and since he was her only son, and she hadn't been too well in recent years, he hated to disappoint her. Sarah looked at Meyer, but neither of them said anything. Esheal guessed that Lily had already told them about his plans. He had spent the day thinking about how best to bring up the question of who was to pay for the wedding, but here he was, sitting in the middle of the family, and he still had not thought of anything. Out of the corner of his eye, he saw Diana, who looked angry. And no wonder, he thought. She probably thought this meant the end of her own plans to marry. Now she would have to get married at City Hall. Partly because Esheal did not know how to say that he would be paying for the wedding, and partly because he could not bear to see Diana look at him in that way, he blurted out the surprise he had been saving up for the end of the evening. "And Lily and I," he said, "will be living in the apartment over the pharmacy. I just bought the building!"

The Romanoffs gasped, but there was not quite the commotion he had expected. "That way," he said, trying to hide from the silence which greeted his announcement, "Lily can call down to me through the dumbwaiter if there's anything she needs, and if she wants to come down to the store at night, she can. Without going out on the street." "And if you have a baby," said Dave, clearing his throat and taking care not to look at the others, "you can send it down in the dumbwaiter, and when it wets itself, you can send it back up to Lily." "Lily can go up and down in the dumbwaiter," said Bill, taking his cue from his brother.

What was the matter with them? Esheal wondered. Sarah was staring at her hands and Meyer was looking at Diana, who would not look up. "You're going to marry a pretty big man, Lily," said Dave, forcing a smile. "So important," murmured Sarah. "It's a wonderful thing," said Itzak, thumping the table; "a man should have a home." He glared at the others. "It's better to sit under a leak in your own roof than sit high and dry under someone else's," he said. "But there are six apartments in that building," said Diana; "what are you going to do with them?" "Let them out," said Esheal; "that way the building will pay for itself. It will even make money." "We're very happy for you," said Sarah in a formal voice. "And my mother said to tell you she wants you to come over for dinner, and she wants to help bake for the mazel tov." "I can't wait," said Sarah in a flat voice. "Well," said Esheal, getting up, "I have to get back to the shop." He waited, expecting them to persuade him to stay longer, but no one did. "Mazel tov," said the old man. In back of him, the family echoed him. "So I'll leave you with Lily," said Itzak.

"What's the matter with them?" Esheal asked Lily. "With them? Nothing," she said. "They don't seem too happy about the building," he said. "Oh, they are!" said Lily; "how could they not be?" Nevertheless, Esheal was troubled by the way they had greeted his news. That night when he got home, he went into his mother's apartment and banged the teakettle about until his mother came out. "How did they like their surprise?" she asked, rubbing her eyes with her tight little fists. Esheal told her what happened. "I can't understand it," he said. His mother sat down at the table, looking up at him. "You made them feel small," she said.

"Small?" cried Esheal; "what does my buying a building have to do with them?" "A lot," said his mother; "they don't go around buying buildings." "They bought their house," Esheal pointed out. "A house is not a big building," Sarah said; "a man who's thirty-three is not a man who's sixty. Meyer didn't do it himself. All the children put their money in. So you made them feel small." "All of a sudden it's my fault that I have money?" he asked. "Don't start," said his mother; "they'll get over it." "What do they have to get over?" he asked. "Lily didn't think they were upset." "Before she gets married, a woman is blind to trouble," said his mother; "we'll all have dinner together. Things will get back to normal. Don't hang around there for a while."

Three weeks later, whatever the trouble was had been forgotten in the wake of excitement caused by Sidney's arrival. He was staying with his Aunt Sarah, and the whole family talked about nothing but him. He came home with a small bag of gold nuggets, and he gave one to this one and one to that one, and soon he had none left. "Look at the millionaire!" said Sarah; "I thought you'd come back a maharajah." "I'm no maharajah," said Sidney, "but I have enough money to go to dental school." "Dental school!" exclaimed Sarah; "when did you decide to become a dentist?" "When I got a toothache and there was no one to fix it. Look," he said, pulling back his lip with his finger; "see that hole? I did it myself." "Look at that," said Meyer, impressed; "so tell us, what was it like there?"

"You got my letters," said Sidney. "No one got your letters," said Meyer; "the mouse took them to her room and nobody could see them but her." "What was it like there?" asked Dave; "did you have to fight a lot?" "No," Sidney said, "it was the same as here. I fought once and beat the guy up and then they left me alone. I never felt better in my life." Sarah, who had gone out to get some cake, stopped in the doorway. "Don't tell any stories until I come back," she said. "Wait," said Meyer; "let me go to the toilet." "What did you do every day?" Lily asked. "Oh, I had quite a schedule," said Sidney; "I used to get up at seven, get to the office at seven forty-five, and then I'd work for a couple of hours and then I'd go out collecting until eleven-thirty. Then I went to dinner. From three to five, I went out collecting again." "It doesn't sound so interesting," said Bill; "it sounds like an accountant's job here." "It was interesting," said Sidney; "rounds were interesting, talking to all the prominent men out there; I visited the ladies at their pink tea affairs, I had a drink with the saloonkeeper when I came for his rent. It was fun. At night, I did all kinds of things, skating, going to a vaudeville or a moving picture show. On Sundays, I took long walks. I took mushes, trips by dogsleds, that's what a mush is, to the mine, and the mine was twenty miles away, and wherever I went, of course I took Diana's picture with me, so she was pretty warm. And it got pretty hot out there when she wrote and told me she was getting married." "He wrote and asked me if I ever cared for him, or was he one of my playthings like the rest of the boys!" exclaimed Diana. "Some plaything!" said Sarah.

"How did you know if you had a strike?" Dave asked, and Sidney started to explain about sample pans, and how the sample ones netted three hundred and fifty dollars each in gold dust, but it didn't stay that way, and if each pan had only averaged out to five cents a pan, he would have made some money, but if it fell far below that; well, what could he expect, he asked them. Life was a gamble, after all, so what was the difference if his ship came in loaded or not. Anyway, a dental student didn't need a fortune. He needed peace of mind and when he got out, he needed a good wife, and he said he guessed he knew where he could find what he needed now that he was back.

Esheal felt thoroughly eclipsed by Sidney, but he would not have minded the family's turning their attention to him had he not sensed how much they preferred Sidney to him. Of course, he told himself, Sid was a member of the family, and he was not, and Sid had been gone for a long time, and he was right around the corner, and they were all so happy that Diana would be marrying him after all, and not that lummox Murray Zalman, which was how they now referred to her ex-fiancé, as if they had never liked him. He could understand it. Nevertheless, he resented it.

Chapter 28

Outside the pharmacy windows, rain was falling in soft, slanted lines as if an artist were quickly embellishing the pale gray scene. There was little traffic on the street and, for some time, the only sound would be the sound of the rain, and then the occasional swoosh of a passing car. The door to the pharmacy had not opened for over an hour. Esheal had moved his Hood's ice cream sign inside so that it would not rust, and he alternately stared at the Lipton Tea sign that filled the bricked-up window in the building across the street and the National Biscuit Company advertisement painted on the building's lower level. While he looked at these two signs, he thought of how the Romanoffs had reacted to his announcement that he had bought the building, and how they had lost their minds with joy when they heard Sid was back, and back as broke as he ever was. The picture of Lily, sitting in the worn brown chair, with its bald spots where the back of heads and arms rested, gazing up at Sidney adoringly, was vivid before him. And yet Esheal liked the man himself. Sid was easygoing, he was charming; he was what men and women called a mensh.

But so was he a mensh, and no one gazed up at him out of chairs with cow eyes. The closer the wedding came, the greater Esheal's passion for Lily grew, as if the thought of possessing her added value to the woman herself. That she was beautiful he had known before, but now, when he thought of her as his wife, she became the most beautiful woman in the world. Now when he compared her with Diana, he saw that it was true: Diana was too short, her bosom was too large for a person her size, not that he did not like it, but it was an imperfection, and her charm, her warmth, which had drawn him to her, would they not be hazardous in a married woman? Anyone who married her, he thought, would have his hands full swatting away the many moths circling around that flame.

But Lily had a magnificent figure; it was an hourglass, and he was not the only one to appreciate it. When he walked with her on the street, or when she was in the store, he would see men turn to follow her with their eyes. And she had a beautiful face, an unusual one. It was saved from roundness by the heart shape her slightly pointed chin caused it to form, and her teeth were tiny and white and regular, like a baby's. She parted her thick black hair in the middle and pinned the rest of it to the back of her head, and fought an unending battle against the heavy hair, which was always trying to free itself and wind down her back.

Her most common gesture, which he loved, was raising one hand to the back of her head, where she pressed it against the hair which she had pinned up into a circle shaped like a snail. If she detected a loose pin, she would push the pin back into place, and before she lowered her hand, she would shake her head slightly, as if she knew the hair would get the better of her soon. And that was how he saw her when she was not there, one arm raised to secure her hair so that she seemed to be resting her head on her hand, and when she did that, she looked like all the pictures of seductresses he had seen. And when she raised her arm in that way, the outline of her breast was firm and lovely and her elbow was bent and her arm took the shape of a wing. He thought over an exchange he had overheard between Lily and Diana the day before. "His collars are awful stiff," Diana said, and Lily said, "What do you mean? All men wear collars that way." Sometimes he thought he had too much time to think things over, but he did not have a chance to think this over, because a man with an odd air about him was making straight for him with a large envelope in his outstretched hand.

"Are you Dr. Luria?" the man asked him. "I'm Dr. Luria," said Esheal; "what can I do for you?" "Take this," said the man, thrusting the envelope into his hand. "What is it?" Esheal asked. He did not like the look of the envelope, grease-stained by the man's large, flat fingers. "It's a summons," said the man. "A summons for what?" asked Esheal. "You've got the wrong man." "Listen, Doc," said the man, "I've got the right man. You want to know what it's about, read it," and he turned around and started to walk out.

"Wait!" shouted Esheal; "let me check and see who it's for." The man shrugged his shoulders and, standing in the doorway, pinched the lapels of his coat together, and went out into the rain. Esheal, who had gotten halfway across the store trying to stop him, went back to the counter and opened the long envelope.

Long envelopes, like telegrams, frightened him. They were unusual, and anything unusual meant disaster. Inside was a summons, and Esheal had to read the document three times before he began to understand what it meant. Mary Bailey had charged him with poisoning her child! That he should poison a child! He knew the child had been ill; he remembered Dr. Herriman, who was Mary Bailey's doctor, saying that the child was gravely ill. And he remembered that so well because Dr. Linde never said the child was gravely ill, or critically ill, or anything of the sort. He would say, the child is very sick, and that was the end of it.

As Esheal stared at the paper, the meaning of the words "gravely ill" struck him for the first time, and he was stunned by his vision of the little baby, who had been in his pharmacy countless times, lying gray and waxy in a deep, dark place. In the cold. Like a stuck needle on a record, his mind kept up that refrain: in the cold, in the cold.

"What now, Doc?" said his assistant, who had been stacking things in the back of the store. "Who did you poison?" said the assistant. "Mary Bailey's baby girl," he said, his eyes still on the paper. "Will they send you to jail?" asked the assistant; "because if they send you to jail, I won't have a job." Esheal looked up from the paper, and, as he looked at his assistant, a mist seemed to rise and clear off. "I didn't poison anybody, you idiot!" he shouted; "why should they send me to jail? They asked for some limewater, I sent them limewater." "Don't tell me," said the assistant; "you better get a lawyer. You know any lawyers? God, I don't want to look for another job!"

A lawyer! Esheal stared at the clerk and all of his rage and bewilderment focused on him. "You want to be out of a job?" shouted Esheal; "you're out of a job! This is America! You don't convict a person because you point a finger!" "I'm fired?" asked the astonished clerk. "You're not fired!" shouted Esheal; "get back to work! I've got to find a lawyer." "My brother's a lawyer," suggested the clerk. "You want I should go to jail and they should throw away the key?" Esheal shrieked; "your brother! I want the best lawyer in the city!" "He's not the best lawyer in the city," said the clerk meekly. "Go run out and leave a message for Dr. Linde," said Esheal, banging his fist on the counter. "What should I tell him?" asked the clerk. "What should I tell him?" mimicked Esheal in a falsetto; "tell him I'm dying!" And the clerk ran out of the store, just as he was, without his hat and coat and before Esheal had a chance to alter his message. When Dr. Linde came puffing into the store ten minutes later, Esheal was embarrassed and ashamed.

Without a word, he handed Dr. Linde the summons. The doctor, who was not accused of anything, had little trouble understanding the meaning of the document. "So," he said, looking at Esheal, "you're in the habit of substituting acetic acid for limewater?" "I could fill a prescription for either one of them in my sleep!" said Esheal. "Herriman's trying to cover up," said Dr. Linde. "To cover me up!" shouted Esheal; "to cover me with six feet of dirt!" "You should get Everett Caldwell," said Dr. Linde; "he did a fine job for me when I was charged with letting a woman bleed to death. They said I didn't put in the sutures right. He did a fine job," Dr. Linde said again, remembering. "He's the ex-assistant district attorney. Believe me, he knows the ropes."

"That's what I want," said Esheal; "a man who knows the ropes." "We'll send for him," said Dr. Linde; "stop worrying. Hundreds of people know what a careful man you are. Caldwell will get a witness no one can argue with and it will all come to nothing. You've got to calm down. The way you're shaking, you *look* like a murderer!" "That I should poison a little girl!" said the pharmacist. "Mistakes are made," said the doctor; then he saw Esheal's face. "But if you didn't make a mistake, you shouldn't pay for it. Don't worry about it; you won't pay for it. I'll get in touch with Caldwell." "Caldwell. Not a Jewish man," said Esheal. "Since when are you worried about whether he's a Jewish man?" asked the doctor; "you with your Japanese friend?" "I don't know," Esheal said. "Being the ex-assistant district attorney is better than being Jewish," said the doctor.

Esheal watched the rain all afternoon. It had given him great pleasure to think that Lily and her mother were spending the day shopping for Lily's trousseau, and that they had the money to do this because he had found them the house on Carroll Street, which had been so much cheaper than the one they had found by themselves. Now he was pained at the thought of Lily, pausing at counters, picking up this peach-colored gown and that, dropping one lazily back onto the heap, holding another up against her body, turning this way and that in front of the long, silvery mirrors while Sarah, her arms folded at the waist of her black dress, smiled her approval. Now it was poison to think of the two women in the store, under the bright lights, moving among the still plaster figures modeling the store's best clothing. When he went to the Romanoffs' tonight for dinner, he would have to tell them. He could not stand it. He could see Dave and Bill winking at each other, grinning maliciously, he could see them looking at Sidney as if to say, see, we knew no one could compare to you; we knew he was no good. And that would be the end of everything he had hoped for.

As the hand of the clock inched along toward six, Esheal became more and more despondent. He seemed to hear sounds as if they came from a great distance, and he was so slow to respond to what his customers said to him, more than one woman asked him if he was all right. It was a superhuman effort to hit the lever on the cash register and a superhuman effort to push the drawer closed again. At six o'clock, Esheal told the clerk which medicines would be picked up early, and where he could find the new powders if someone asked to see something unusual, and left for the Romanoffs' like a man walking to his own execution. And as if life were cooperating with his evil dreams, he found them around the dining room table, listening raptly to Sidney, who was telling them another of his apparently inexhaustible Alaska stories, this time some nonsense about how every night he had to go out and look for his partner for fear he might have fallen asleep in the snow and started freezing to death.

He stood in their doorway without making a sound. He felt like a ghost who had come back to haunt his favorite place, and, like a ghost, who could no longer hope to enter into the warmth there, he felt cold and lost. He tried to think of how he would tell them about the summons, about how he had been accused of killing a little child, and his mind was grayer and emptier than the day had been. He went in and sat down at the table. He saw Lily beaming at him, and he felt her excitement, and he knew what she was excited about; she was so proud of whatever it was she had bought, proud to be the center of attention, proud to become the wife of what her family and the entire neighborhood thought of as a rich man. He sensed that, somehow, in marrying him, Lily was getting her revenge on her family. He had known for some time that she believed they did not value her enough. Now they would have to. She would be the one with the money; they would have to come to her. As the wedding drew closer, he could feel Lily allying herself with him and pulling away from them. It was a slow, torturous movement, barely perceptible to him, certainly not to her, and as he watched Lily come to think of herself as his wife, not their daughter, the slow, painful nature of the change reminded him of nothing so much as pulling an adhesive bandage away from a wound. Now all that would be over. He looked around the table hopelessly, reluctant to sign his own death warrant.

"What happened to you?" said Sarah; "you look like you saw a ghost." "I did," said Esheal; "mine." "You're sick?" said Sarah, starting to get up. "I'm not sick," he said. "Then what can it be?" asked Sarah; "you look something awful." Esheal was painfully aware of what a plain man he was. He came right out with it. "Today I got a summons," he told them; "they're accusing me of poisoning a child." "Who's accusing him?" asked Itzak; "who dares to accuse him? I'll knock him down," shouted the tiny old man. "Mary Bailey's accusing me," he said. "A mick! I knew it!" said Meyer; "they don't have any money, they sue the doctor. Tell me, did she owe you money?" "Yes," said Esheal.

"That's it," said Meyer, hitting the table so the plates jumped; "that's what they do. First they run up a bill and then they sue. They ain't going to get one penny!" Esheal sat there, stunned. He was afraid to move or to say a word lest he break the spell. Finally, he looked at Lily. "I'll claw her rotten eyes out!" Lily said with such venom he felt a chill. "Well, there'll be a hearing," Esheal said; "in the Court of Special Sessions." He thought if he mentioned the name of the court, the reality of the charge would come clear; he was sure they had not yet grasped what was happening to him.

"Just tell us when it is," said Sarah, "and we'll come. I'd like to see anyone stay home." Esheal cleared his throat. "You don't think we should postpone the wedding," he asked; "in case something should go wrong?" "Nothing's going to go wrong," said Sarah; "postpone the wedding? For what? For a crazy woman who doesn't want to pay her bills? Who wants to sue you so she'll have money for a stone for her baby? She should live so long!" Sarah looked at Esheal's face and saw him swallow hard. "Lily," she said, "take Esheal into your room and show him what's in the packages."

"Nu?" said Meyer, after the two of them left. "It's been a day and a half," sighed Sarah. "You don't think there's anything to it?" asked Dave. "Bite your tongue!" snapped Sarah; "that your sister's chassen should murder a child!" "I just thought," said Dave. "You should think about something useful for a change," said his father.

Because Esheal had retained ex-Assistant District Attorney Everett Caldwell, the hearing was scheduled to take place within a month, which meant that the wedding would take place two weeks later. The Romanoffs refused to hear a word about delaying the wedding, and insisted that they would come to the court with Esheal. By this time, Dave had fallen in with the spirit of things, and hinted repeatedly that it would not go well for the Bailey family if Doc was not acquitted. Bill kept after Esheal, telling him a drink before the hearing would be just the thing. He would be more relaxed; he would be more confident; he'd make a better impression on the court. At this, Esheal came to the conclusion that Bill did not have a brain in his head. Terrified as he was by the prospect of appearing in court, he did not think it wise to drown that terror in whiskey and lurch about the witness stand like a refugee from the Mission Soup Kitchen.

When the night of the trial finally arrived, Esheal was thankful that he and Everett had gone over their strategy so often, because the Romanoffs insisted on escorting him to the room, and they surrounded him completely and efficiently. As they walked to the court, Esheal wondered what they looked like to others on the street. He imagined that he looked like a victim surrounded by a friendly lynch mob.

The actual hearing proved to be a cut-and-dried affair. Ex-Assistant District Attorney Everett Caldwell called only one witness, Dr. G. A. Ferguson, who was a member of the state board of pharmacy, and he testified that an ounce and a half of acetic acid, which was what Esheal was said to have substituted for the limewater, would curdle six ounces of milk, and if the milk was curdled, then it could not pass through the nipple of the child's bottle, and obviously, if the liquid could not pass through the nipple, the child could not possibly have drunk it.

When he was cross-examined by the prosecution, he said that the odor of acetic acid was so strong that the mother could not have avoided noticing that the wrong liquid was in the bottle the instant the bottle was opened. "But if she did not notice?" asked the prosecution; "if she had a cold?" "Then," said Dr. Ferguson, "the baby would not have drunk the liquid. Nothing would have induced it to do so. The taste would have been so bad that after the first taste, the baby's throat would have contracted so that it could not possibly have taken four ounces of the mixture." At that point, Mrs. Bailey let out a loud wail and pointed at Esheal. "Murderer!" she shouted and began to sob. "I'll claw her eyes out!" shrieked Lily, whereupon the judge banged his gavel, and threatened to clear the court. At this, the Romanoffs sat back simultaneously, the same vindicated look on all their faces.

Then the defense called Dr. Herriman, the doctor who had been attending the child when it died, and, upon cross-examination, he admitted that the child had a diphtheric condition for several days before it died and admitted that he had given diphtheria as the cause of death on the certificate on file in the Department of Health. The Romanoffs listened with indrawn breath to Mr. Caldwell's summation.

Mr. Caldwell was saying that, of course, it was always a tragic thing for a child to die, and that nothing could ever compensate the parent for its loss and, although, to the bereaved parent, revenge against the child's killer might seem to lessen the pain of the child's departure, it was not right to seek revenge against an innocent man who had done nothing but try to help her child.

Had not they called upon him in the middle of the night, at three in the morning, to be precise, and had not he come down without asking any questions, to give them the lime-water Dr. Herriman had prescribed? And was it not obvious that limewater would not cure a child with diphtheria, nor could limewater cause its throat to constrict, but diphtheria could kill a child and cause its throat to constrict, and Dr. Herriman himself had said the child suffered from diphtheria, for which, alas, there was as yet no cure, and diphtheria did kill, and had not it killed this very child, and was it not unworthy of the poor, confused mother to try and ruin an innocent man? Had they told the druggist that the child had diphtheria? Had they not withheld this information out of fear that the druggist would not want to come with them and give them the medicine lest he contract the disease? And did not all the evidence point to the disease as the murderer, not the pharmacist? And at each question, the Romanoffs nodded their collective heads as if they were listening to a sermon, and the judge, who was listening to the summation, was distracted by Itzak Romanoff, who out of habit had begun swaying back and forth in his seat as he did in synagogue, while praying.

When the judge gave his verdict, pronouncing the pharmacist not guilty, the Romanoffs began swarming over Esheal, squealing, shouting, thumping him on the back, turning around to glare at Mrs. Bailey, whose attorney was talking to her earnestly, and at Dr. Herriman, who stood uncomfortably behind the two of them. When Mrs. Bailey and her attorney got up, Dave could restrain himself no longer, and shouted "Quack! Quack!" at the other doctor. Lily took up the cry and at a signal from the judge, who looked amused, the court attendants began to push them all out of the room.

Once out on the street, the cries of "Quack! Quack!" got louder and louder, and only Sarah, who grabbed this one and that one, telling them to leave the poor woman alone—after all, she had lost a child, and who even knew if she was in her right mind—prevented them from trailing after Mrs. Bailey. The boys were so distracted by their pursuit of Dr. Herriman that for a minute they left Esheal alone. He looked up at the sky, which was clear and blue and studded with a few bright blue stars. It was over, but he could not believe it. He asked himself why he always believed in bad news immediately, and why good news seemed so unreal for so long, so that, by the time it came to seem real, bad news had already arrived and replaced it. Just then, Lily took his arm and pressed it against her side. "I told you so," she said, triumphant. "Acquitted of murder, convicted of marriage," Dave called back to them. Everyone laughed. "Two weeks to the wedding," Lily said, jubilant. "Such a long time," said Esheal, but it passed quickly. His mother was in and out of the house, making lists with the Romanoffs, consulting over the menu, going shopping together for dresses. Esheal had never seen them so happy, and he was proud to be the source of their happiness. Even his sisters, whom he hardly saw any longer, stopped to kiss him as they flew in and out of the house on their way to school or work. It was an enchanted time.

Chapter 29

The day of the wedding arrived. Esheal's mother began weeping as soon as she opened her eyes. Then she would stop to straighten something up, or to check on one of the girls' hems, and at the sight of her son, she would begin again. By four o'clock, his mother was still not ready, although his sisters had been ready for hours, and continually walked up and down the stairs to see what was holding their mother up. Finally, Esheal had his mother dressed; he had pinned a huge cameo to the neck of her dress while she protested that on one's wedding day one got presents. One did not give them. Nevertheless, she was pleased as she could be with it. She kept returning to the mirror to gaze at the cameo. "If I only looked like that," she sighed, looking at the carved woman's face. "You look better," Esheal told her. "And you look, you look . . ." She stopped, at a loss for words. "Like a stuffed corpse," Esheal prompted her. "Like a corpse!" said his mother, spitting on the floor in horror. "You look, you look *grand!*" she said, and she began crying again. "You'll have something to cry about," said Esheal, "if we're late for the mazel tov." "Do you think they like my cakes?" asked his mother. "They said they did," said Esheal. "Of course they said they did," said his mother, exasperated; "what would they say? They wanted to bury them in the yard?" "All I know," said Esheal, "is that Dave caught it for stealing some icing on the layer cake you made." "He did?" said his mother, standing up straighter. "He did, and Diana thought maybe they ought to save the pineapple cake for the family and not waste it on the party." "She said that?" asked his mother. "So what are we waiting for? Let's go." Esheal looked out the window and saw that the carriage was waiting. "Let's go," he said, taking his mother's arm.

Esheal was in such suspense about the wedding that the

mazel-tov party passed in a blur, and later, when he asked
Lily about it, she said she did not remember a thing about it
either. The wedding itself stood out, a sequence of brilliant
pictures, like so many scenes set in glass globes. Outside the
Romanoff house, so many horse-drawn carriages lined up to
take the guests to Alexander Hall that the entire block was
encircled by them, and although the Romanoffs lived only six
blocks from the hall, the carriages were there to take the
guests. The carriages were the astonishment of the neighborhood and all the children for blocks around came and stood
on the sidewalk across the street from the Romanoff house
trying to catch a glimpse of the wedding party when it came
out.

The carriages went twice around Carroll Street, turned the
corner of Chauncey, went around Chauncey, then down
Howard, and finally down Eastern Parkway to Alexander
Hall. They took this circuitous route so that the people in the
carriages would have plenty of time to marvel at them and, by
the time the carriages drew up at Alexander Hall, they felt
they had gone a long, long way. Dinney, who was in the third
carriage, hung out of it, marveling at the length of the
procession and saw that crowds of people were following on
foot after the slowly moving people.

When the carriages drew up to the hall, Esheal went off
with one party and Lily with another. Everyone else congregated under a huge crystal chandelier in a room paneled with
dark wood and red velvet. At one end of the room was a
beautiful canopy heavily embroidered with gold threads
almost as thick as rope, and thick gold fringes hung down on
all its sides. Then the bride and groom were brought in and a
hush fell over the audience. When the bride and groom stood
under the canopy, the rabbi addressed the bride and then the
groom and began to sing. Then he took Lily's arm and guided
her around the groom three times. When the rabbi lifted
Lily's veil, she was white as a sheet, and when the rabbi held
the glass of wine out to her, it seemed, to those who were
close enough, as if he wanted to revive her. Lily's lips brushed
the edge of the tall, shiny glass and then he offered the glass
to Esheal, who sipped the dark red liquid. Then Esheal
placed a gold ring on Lily's finger and as he did so, Lily
shivered. The rabbi began to wrap the wine glass in a large
white napkin, and the guests began to murmur. He set the

glass in its napkin down near Esheal's foot and Esheal stamped on it. At the sound of the breaking glass, everyone went wild, rushed up to Esheal and Lily shouting Mazel tov! Mazel tov! while in back of them, the four-piece band broke into an uproarious melody.

This was the signal everyone recognized, and Esheal and Lily danced down the long lines of guests who pressed in from each wall of the huge room. Everyone was clapping, everyone was singing, everyone was trying to reach the newly married couple, who, having finished their dance, now sat like a king and a queen upon their tall, carved chairs at one end of the room. One by one, the guests came up to them to offer their congratulations, and often, to press an envelope into either Esheal's or Lily's hand. Dave and Bill had made a game of keeping Dinney away from Lily; whenever she was about to approach her friend, the boys pulled her back by her waist and did not let go of her until two or three people had gotten ahead of her. Dr. Linde took up a permanent position near Esheal's chair; Lily was occupied with the many friends of the family who kept pushing each other aside to talk to her or to whisper to her, and whenever anyone whispered anything in her ear, she laughed, blushed, looked quickly around toward Esheal as if she were afraid that he had heard what was said.

A drumroll like gathering thunder filled the room, and the master of ceremonies climbed on a chair and shouted, "Supper is ready! Gentlemen, escort your ladies!" Laughing, people parted from those they were talking to and returned to their husbands or children or boyfriends, and then all eyes turned to Esheal and Lily, whom they would follow downstairs to the bridal banquet. Esheal was staring straight ahead, as if he were seeing someone invisible to everyone else, but in fact he was concentrating on walking carefully so that he would not trip and fall in front of this enormous throng. He had gone over the guest list, but he had not imagined how large a crowd that list would summon up. Lily stood beside him, clenching his hand, appearing to be equally terrified. But then the grand march struck up, and the two of them went off quickly across the great room followed by the long procession of guests. Sarah, who was standing next to Esheal's mother, marveled at the grandeur of the procession, but just as she was about to say something about it, some of the children rushed forward and thundered down the stairs. Instantly, others followed suit and soon everyone was rushing down the stairs trying to seat himself near the bridal table.

The master of ceremonies pushed people aside, tugging Lily, who held firmly to Esheal, until they reached the sanctuary of the bridal table. Then began the process of evicting those who were in the wrong seats and sending them to the tables where they belonged. Some of the guests thus evicted glared at the master of ceremonies, and then at Esheal and Lily and Sarah. Sarah saw Esheal looking at her questioningly and shrugged her shoulders; she knew that for years after this, members of the family would not be speaking to her because they would be "offended" at how far from the bridal table she had seated them, and some would never forgive her for whom she had seated some of them with. But that was the way it was at all weddings worthy of the name. She was not going to let it spoil her fun.

And then the procession of entrees, the main course, half a baked chicken for everyone! Desserts, noodle soup, the courses were endless. Everyone was toasting everyone else at the bridal table, and Esheal listened to these toasts in a daze, miserable, knowing that his toast would never come up to one of the Romanoffs'. "A Lily a day, keeps the doctor away. But not the druggist!" roared Dave, and everybody nearby shouted with laughter. And then everyone began clapping for Esheal. "To my wife," he said, holding up his glass, and sitting down in such a hurry he splashed some wine on the clean white tablecloth in front of him. He was relieved when the master of ceremonies brought in a basket of telegrams, and attention was diverted from him. Some of the telegrams must have been funny, but Esheal did not hear them. Occasionally, he heard the name and the telegram when the master of ceremonies boomed out: from Aunt Bertie and Uncle Isaac in Boston.

When the meal was finally over, and the endless telegrams were read, and the dancing that followed the meal had wound down, Esheal became more and more nervous. Mothers had gone down to the cloakroom to retrieve their coats and their children, most of whom had fallen asleep and had been placed by their parents atop the huge piles of coats. "Time to go home," said Meyer at last, winking at Esheal. The room was empty of everyone but the bride and groom and their immediate families. "Let's go to Mother's house for a few minutes," said Lily. "Lily!" exclaimed her mother. "Yes, let's go," said Esheal. Meyer looked at him in astonishment, but did not protest. They all left together.

Chapter 30

Diana

I almost missed my sister's wedding. When Sid came back, Lily was getting married, and Lily had a beautiful big wedding and my father didn't have the money to make anything for me. But Esheal and his family wanted a big Yiddish wedding, so they made him a big wedding. They didn't pay for the wedding, my family, but they paid for the mazel tov; you know, before you have a wedding, you have a party with all sorts of cakes, and that was the mazel tov, and after that they didn't have any money anymore. And we all got lovely clothes and I had a dress made up by the Romanoffs, so Fannie made me a rose-colored silk gown, and at that time, ladies wore something like a feather boa, so she made me one of them too. And it was the first time in my life that I wore silk stockings and I had my hair done up. Lily was twenty-two, so I was nineteen.

We went to City Hall. When Lily got married, they were signing the papers, and when you sign the papers, you have a mazel tov, a cake and wine and nuts and candy all spread out on the table in the living room. The bride and everybody else left, and I was all alone in the house. How could I leave a table of food like that and go away? To me, everything had to be back in place. By the time I had everything in place, I realized I'm going to miss the wedding ceremony, and I called down. My sister-in-law lived downstairs, she was my cousin then, and I said, "Sadie, don't go and leave me. I'm still up here alone and I need somebody to zip my dress up. I just got through cleaning up."

And she sends Sid up to zip my dress. When he zipped my dress, he turned me around and asked me would I marry him, and after all those years I said, Let's see if we can get married tonight. But just before that, they passed a law so that you had to go to court to get some kind of paper; you had to get blood tests, and that was all something new. So we couldn't get married Sunday; we got married Tuesday, two days after Lily. When Sid zipped up my dress, that did it. But I almost wasn't to the wedding. I had to clean up. I couldn't leave things there. And all of our friends were at that wedding. All the boys and girls who came on Sundays were there. And I came in last. And of course they were all standing at the top of the stairs. There was this big ballroom, and the bride, my sister, was sitting there, and all the family. Sadie was still downstairs because she had six little children, and until she got somebody to stay with them, she was late too. And until she got dressed and until I got dressed, we came in at the end. And we should have been there. I was the maid of honor. They were waiting for me and as I came up the stairs, all of the boys that were always in the house, you know, singing and playing the piano and the guitar Sunday after Sunday for years, all of them turned and said to Sidney, "Jesus, Romy, isn't she something?" And of course Sid had a brother Ike who was in love with me. So of course, you're pretty when you're dressed up for a ball. And I was wearing Dinney's hat. I never bought my own hats. I never had to go shopping for a hat. When Dinney went and bought a hat, I'd go down and buy it from her. So I looked wonderful in my hat and dress and I wore that hat and that dress to City Hall, and Lily and old Esheal, they would have come too, but they already left on their honeymoon. I know Lily thought I came in late just to take the attention away from her, but I didn't. Momma was so clean and I was so clean and I couldn't let the things stand there. So that's how it happened.

Chapter 31

The morning of Esheal Luria's wedding, countless arguments broke out in the homes of the guests. Itzak Kapturak remembered that his grandmother, who was Lily's great-great-grandmother, used to say that once she got older, she understood why everyone spent the morning of a wedding having a fight. The new couple took a look at one another, and all of a sudden, they were like two cats tied in a sack, and when they saw the rabbi getting ready to sew the sack shut for good, they started to claw each other. That was why, she said, the bride and groom were not supposed to see each other on the day of the wedding. "A man takes getting used to," she used to tell her grandson, Itzak, "and a child takes getting used to. You think it doesn't? You have it, and you're happy to have it, but you find out it's staying for good and didn't just come for dinner, but for all its meals, maybe for all its life." And she said she knew why people cried at weddings; if the bride and groom knew what was in store for them, they'd cry too. Not because what was coming was bad, but because there was so much of it.

Itzak was not surprised when Esheal and Lily wanted to pay one last visit to the Romanoffs' before going to their new apartment as married people. But it was beyond the boys. "Jesus!" Dave said to Itzak, as they were riding back in the carriage; "if I got married, I'd be in some hurry!" "If you got married," said Itzak, "you should be in a hurry. The woman should stay long enough for you to get to know her!" "Come on, Grandpa," said Dave; "I'm not so bad." "No?" said Itzak; "let me tell you, you're not so good either. Don't let me hear you rib your sister about going home." "Oh, come on, Grandpa!" said Dave; "it's half the fun." "Make your own fun for a while," said Itzak; "leave other people out of it." Dave turned away from his grandfather, who was glaring at him, and began whispering to Bill. The two boys began laughing together. "What's so funny?" asked Itzak, but they did not answer him. "I'm watching you!" Itzak threatened.

Esheal and Lily did not stay long at the Romanoffs'; a crowd had gathered around Diana and Sidney and everyone was congratulating them and kissing them, and Dave was saying Diana had better not put any wedding cake under her pillow because she'd never get it combed out of her hair in time for the wedding, and everyone was laughing and teasing her and teasing Sidney, and Lily could see all too plainly that her turn would come next.

What she had wanted was to sit quietly around the table and look at her mother and father and grandfather, and then, sure they would be there and that nothing had changed because she had become Mrs. Luria, she would go home. Now she was sorry she came, because everything seemed to have changed already. Diana was talking about Sidney, and how he would go to dental school in Boston, but she would stay with her parents, because she did not want to distract him, and the boys were asking him how he would like a weekend bride and he said he would like it a lot better than no bride at all.

"First Nome, Alaska, for three years," Sarah sighed; "now three years in Boston, Massachusetts, for dental school." "Instead of having children, they'll have grandchildren," said Dave, and everyone began to laugh again. "What do you think?" Sarah asked the air; "am I ever getting grandchildren?" "They're temporarily out of stock," said Bill. "But they'll be on sale soon," said Dave. Esheal stood up suddenly and said he and Lily had better be going home, and he braced himself for what Dave would have to say, but Itzak had his eye on Dave, and he kept quiet. Lily looked at Diana and Diana looked at her sister. "Sid," Diana said, "let's walk them home." "Sit down," Itzak said to Diana. "No, we'll walk them home," said Diana, and when her grandfather saw her lower lip stuck out, he said nothing more.

The two couples walked home slowly. The air was cold and felt like cold glass against the skin. No one said a word. When they got to the pharmacy, Diana looked up at the building and saw the lights burning in the first-floor apartment. "It's all painted?" she asked. "All painted," said Esheal. "So they got finished on time," said Sid awkwardly. "You've got something to sleep on?" Diana asked. "We've got a big carved bed," said Lily, who looked bashfully at Esheal. "No more sister lying under the bed grabbing your ankle," said Diana. "Why do you think I got married?" Lily said. They all laughed nervously. "Well," said Esheal; "good night." "Good night," said Diana and Sid. Diana ran over to Lily and threw her arms around her. "Now we're old ladies," Diana whispered to her. Lily wished she were an old lady, because if she were, all the frightening things would be over, sharing a man's bed, having a man's children. She started to cry. "Oh, Lily," her sister said; "you were always such a great crier." Lily wiped her eyes and smiled at her. "Good night," Lily said, following Esheal up the stairs.

"Are you hungry?" Esheal asked her, as he helped her off with her coat. "I'm stuffed," said Lily. "So am I," said Esheal; "how about a cup of coffee?" "It will keep us up," said Lily. "That's true," he said. He looked at the yawning door of the bedroom and wondered how to get himself and Lily through it. "I didn't carry you over the threshold," he said; "let me carry you into the bedroom." Lily started to protest but changed her mind.

When Esheal set her down in the middle of the bed, she looked up at him as if he had just left her in a basket on the steps of a church. "I'll go into the bathroom and get undressed," Esheal said. Lily looked down at her wedding dress and slowly unbuttoned the top button. "Let me help you," Esheal said. "No, no, that's all right," said Lily; "I'm used to the dress," she said hurriedly, seeing his expression. "I've tried it on so many times." "Well, I'll go to the bathroom," Esheal said again, and when he came out, dressed in blue-and-white-striped pajamas, he saw Lily standing in the center of the room, her wedding gown unbuttoned to her waist and her nightgown already slipped over her head. She began to unbutton the skirt of the gown, and as it dropped, the nightgown dropped down over it. She was getting undressed under the nightgown. When she was finished, she picked up the gown and folded it neatly on the back of a chair. Then she turned her back to him and began to extract her underwear from beneath the gown. Now that he was sitting on the bed, she was standing in the middle of the room.

Lily came over and sat down on the bed next to him. "Should I turn out the light?" he asked. "Let's talk first," she said. "About what?" asked Esheal. "About our honeymoon. What time is the train leaving tomorrow?" "Nine-thirty," said Esheal. "Maybe while we're there," said Lily, "someone will go over the Falls in a barrel." "I hope not," said Esheal; "what a way to get yourself killed." "Dave always wanted to go over the Falls in a barrel." "Sometimes," he said, "I think he already went over in a barrel." "He's wild," said Lily, "but he's a good boy." "He loves his family," said Esheal, and Lily seemed to take that for agreement. "Should I turn out the light now?" said Esheal again. "Turn it out," said Lily. Esheal turned out the light and for a while they sat in the dark. "Would you like to lie down?" he asked her. "Which side do you sleep on?" Lily asked. "I'd better sleep on the side away from the wall," he said; "so in case anyone calls me, I can get out fast." "I like to sleep near the wall," said Lily, lying down on her back, folding her hands across her breasts and staring at the ceiling. Next to her, Esheal assumed the same pose. "Your mother wants grandchildren," he said. Lily said she did. Esheal said his mother did also. They continued to lie there staring at the ceiling. "I'm afraid," Lily said at last. He was afraid also, afraid that they would spend every night of their married life lying like two Egyptian mummies, staring at the ceiling. "Well," he said, trying to adopt the joking tone of one of her brothers, "don't you want to get it over with?" "Oh, yes," said Lily fervently; "I do."

So he began, and for a while, he could not understand why Lily always seemed to move away when he moved toward her, and finally he realized that she was trying to protect her new nightgown, but when he suggested she take it off, she said no, she would just pull it up around her neck. So Esheal climbed gingerly upon her, but in the light which came in through the window, he could see that Lily's eyes were screwed shut, and he knew she wanted him to get things over with, which he did. Afterward, when he switched on the light, he saw that there had been no bleeding. "No blood," he said to Lily; "it's a good thing this isn't a small town where they hang out the sheets." "What do you mean?" Lily asked him; "women don't always bleed." "In Pobrosk," said Esheal, "they kept a chicken in the house, and if there was no blood, they chopped off his head and then there was a lot of blood." "So if they kept a chicken in the house," said Lily, who had her nightgown settled neatly about her, "a lot of women must not have done any bleeding." "The chicken was just in case," said Esheal. "In case what?" she asked. "In case the woman had some kind of accident and already did her bleeding."

"What kind of accident?" asked Lily; "what kind of accident could I have had?" "A fall," said Esheal uneasily. "Maybe when I fell down the flight of steps," Lily said; "Diana pushed me. She said she didn't, but she did." "She pushed you?" Esheal asked. "She didn't know I was so close to the steps," said Lily.

Esheal could not get his mind away from the subject, perhaps because Lily's blue-white face, with its eyes squeezed shut, was still vivid to him. "Let's go to sleep," said Lily; "I think it's lucky I didn't bleed. Now I don't have to change the sheets." "It could have waited until the morning," said Esheal. "Do you think," Lily said, turning toward him, "if we got up very early, I could go over to Momma's house and say goodbye before we left?" "You said goodbye to them a couple of hours ago," said Esheal. "Still," said Lily, "it wouldn't feel right going away without saying goodbye to them." "All right, we'll get up early," he said. "After you say goodbye to them, I can stop back here for a minute and see how things are going in the store." "They'll be going fine," said Lily; "Mr. Greenspan's been a pharmacist all his life." "He's retired; maybe he's out of practice." "He's only been retired for five months," Lily said. "Let's go to sleep," said Esheal; "if we have to say goodbye to your family, we have to get up at six." "Don't you want to say goodbye to your mother?" asked Lily. "What for?" asked Esheal.

The next morning, Lily put on a kelly-green suit trimmed with a brown mink collar and Esheal could not believe this was the woman he had married. When she put on her black coat, with its deep fur collar, he stared at her. "What's the matter?" asked Lily; "is a button loose? Did I leave on a tag?" "You look wonderful," he said. She stared at him, as if puzzled by his admiration. "Do you still want to stop at your parents'?" he asked her. "Of course," said Lily, and off they went through the gray-blue light. "It's still last night," Esheal said, putting his arm around her waist. "No, it's not," said Lily; "it's a quarter of seven in the morning." She corrected him as she might have corrected a child. He thought, as he had many times before, that she would make an excellent mother. She had Sarah as an example, and Sarah would not let her get away with anything. After last night, he thought, he did not believe Sarah would have to keep after her. She was so thorough in everything she did, so proper. Nevertheless, he was disappointed that she had not bled. He had looked forward to it; he was sure *he* had done nothing wrong, and he was sure she had done nothing wrong before he met her. He imagined what it would have been like, the blood sealing the contract of the marriage bed as the red wax sealed the official scrolls which the peasants brought to the zenshina, comforting his wife, who would have been frightened. But it was a small thing after all.

When they arrived at the Romanoffs', it was seven o'clock and everyone was up. Lily hugged them all and everyone fussed over him, offering him a cup of tea, some cake, anything, and, just as he was about to sit down, he caught sight of Lily and Diana. The two of them were standing in the doorway of Lily's old bedroom and whispering together. Lily told Diana something which seemed to astonish her. He knew they were talking about what had happened the night before, and he was infuriated and hurt. He got up and pretended to walk over to the painting which hung on the far wall, and he heard Diana say, "Well, *she* said if she never had it again, that would be just fine with her," but then the two women caught sight of him and fell silent. Thank God, thought Esheal, that they were going to Niagara Falls. He could see it now: every morning, before breakfast, Lily would rush home to talk to her mother and sister. After a week of that, he would not have the nerve to get into the same bed with her. Still, she was so young. He was thirty-four, but she was only twenty-two. He had to remember to make allowances.

Chapter 32

In the vaudeville shows which the Lurias and the Romanoffs habitually frequented, the funniest thing was often the backdrop which descended and ascended in the craziest ways, half of the mountain ranges wrinkling and hitching up the right corner of the stage, revealing part of a tenement scene, while the rest of the dark city silhouette remained hidden by the other half of the mountain range the ropes were struggling to bring up. And it seemed to Esheal that the curtain which dropped on his life for one week was like that canvas backdrop and kept everything else veiled, so that for a short time, he and Lily and the noise of Niagara Falls were all that existed in the world. Afterward, he often wondered what would have happened if the canvas curtain could have stayed down, separating his wife and himself from the rest of the world. Of course, he knew as well as anyone else that honeymoons did not last forever, but often, when watching the scenery change at the shows, he thought about how the background was so much a part of the story that it might be said to determine it, and one night, when a particularly romantic Swiss mountain scene refused to lift, and an old couple acted out their despair over their poverty and illnesses, the theater could barely contain its hilarity, while, on any other night, the sketch would have reduced the audience to a mob of sobbing, wet handkerchiefs. And when Esheal thought about that performance, and why it was so funny, he thought it was because what had happened so perfectly portrayed what had happened in his own life, and in almost everyone else's in the theater. There they all were, doing whatever they were accustomed to be doing, when suddenly outside, the scenery changed ludicrously, and, as long as they did not look out the window, they could pretend everything was just as it ought to be.

When Lily and Esheal returned from their honeymoon,

they were happy with each other, happier than they had expected to be. Lily, who had always been a wonderful listener, was spellbound by Esheal's tales of doctors and patients, by his views of real estate, politics, and the stock market. If Lily was not enthralled by their evenings in bed, and if she managed to get into bed and pull the covers up under her chin before he could turn around, she was not doing anything unexpected. On the third night of their honeymoon, tipsy from champagne, Esheal was plagued by a suspicion that Lily had noticed during dinner how his hair was thinning, and this suspicion made him angrier and angrier. Who was she, he asked himself, to be so critical? After all, her family had nothing; she had nothing before she met him. Why should she feel so superior? His clerk, who was an idiot in most things, had broken off with a girl, because, as he said, some of them were only looking for meal tickets. And how did he know that Lily did not look at him in that way? Why did he always feel that she was aware of his hair only where it was thinning at the temples, although it was thick everywhere else? And why did she so often comment on how well he spoke English, without a trace of an accent, as if she were amazed that he could speak the language as well as he did.

That night, when he saw Lily shrouded in her sheet, he foresaw hundreds and thousands of nights during which Lily would lie in her bed like a body frozen in the snow, and how, when it got colder, the drifts would get deeper and deeper, and he was already familiar with her passion for pirinis, huge quilts filled with goosedown, eight of which now filled two closets in their new apartment, and that night, he tried to imagine how he was going to find Lily under all eight of the quilts, and then, once he had found her, how either of them would be able to move beneath the weight of the bedding.

Fortified by his champagne and his anger, he came up to the side of the bed and stood looking down at Lily. "What are you standing there for?" asked Lily; "you'll catch cold." "I don't catch colds," said Esheal; and it was true. He could not remember when he had last been sick. "Even if you don't catch cold," Lily said, "that's no reason to stand there all night." "I want to look at you," Esheal said. "What?" said Lily. "I want to look at you," Esheal said again. "You are looking at me," said Lily. "I'm looking at the sheet," said Esheal. Lily stared up at him, her brow furrowing. "Let me look at you," Esheal said; "take off the sheet." "Take off the sheet!" exclaimed Lily; "I'll freeze." "You won't freeze," he said.

"What's so important about looking at me without a sheet?" asked Lily. "So that later I can identify the body," said Esheal; "birthmarks, scars, a husband is supposed to know about those things." "God forbid!" said Lily. It occurred to Esheal that she did not have a sense of humor. "That's not how they identify bodies anyway," said Lily. "No?" said Esheal; "how do they do it?" "The relatives do it," said Lily; "they don't have to know about birthmarks." "What about people who get killed in fires?" Esheal asked; "or run over. If you can't see their faces, then what do you do?" "I don't want to talk about it," said Lily; "it is not a cheerful subject." And as she said this, she pulled the sheet up higher and clamped it down with her chin.

"What would you do," said Esheal, "if I just yanked this sheet up in the air?" Lily looked terrified. "Lily," he said, "you have to take off the sheet. Suppose, when we get home, your brothers should make some kind of joke about a birthmark, and I didn't know whether they were telling the truth or not, how would it look?" "How would it look?" said Lily; "it would look like hell for my brothers to make jokes like that." Esheal sighed. "Well, my brothers," Lily said thinking it over. "Your brothers," said Esheal, nodding solemnly. "Well, could you turn off the light?" Lily asked. "If I turn out the light," Esheal said, "how will I see anything? I married a proper woman," said Esheal. "Well, what did you expect?" asked Lily indignantly. "Can't I see what kind of a proper woman I'm getting?" he asked. "Well!" said Lily, insulted; "to say it like that! As if you want to see if you're getting your money's worth." "That's not what I meant," said Esheal. "Here!" said Lily, throwing aside the sheet, pulling up her nightgown, and glaring up at him.

Esheal stared at her so long that her anger began to turn into confusion. "What's wrong?" Lily asked, but Esheal did not answer. Now that Esheal had finally convinced Lily to remove the sheet, the sight of her hourglass body, her full breasts, the curve of her hips, the slender ankles which, of course, Lily had crossed, filled him with fear as well as desire. "You look," he said finally, "like a painting I once saw in a book." "You must read some kind of books," said Lily, avoiding his eyes. "An art book," said Esheal; "in the book, the woman had her arms clasped in back of her head." "I'm staying just the way I am," said Lily; "I'm not going to get even colder sticking my arms up in the air."

"You look perfect," said Esheal. "I do?" said Lily. She watched him carefully and, impressed with the reflection of herself she saw in his eyes, she softened. "Get in bed," she said, patting the place next to her. "You can leave the light on," she said, looking at him. "No," her husband said hastily; "I think I'll turn it off." That night, they lay awake and discussed plans for children, how it would be best to have them right away, since Esheal was thirty-four and he would be fifty-four by the time they were twenty, assuming they came that very year, and what Lily would do with her spare time until she had children, since her husband had to work such long hours; although he would take every other Sunday off, he couldn't take off more time than that, because he had been in his pharmacy for over eight years and everyone was used to his hours. And Lily said that there was always plenty to do in a house, and if there wasn't enough to do in her own house, her mother, who was having more and more trouble getting about, could always use help in her own. She and Diana, she said, had promised each other that after they got married, they would keep their mother's house running so that she would never have to feel as if she owed her place in the world to a child.

During this conversation, Esheal thought more than once of how the boys would slip their hands into their mother's bosom, and hold her breast, and each time, the thought disturbed him. Finally, he asked Lily. "Why do they do that?" he said. "They've always done it," said Lily, as if that were an answer. "Why does she let them do it?" he asked. "Why not?" she asked; "it's like a kiss, that's all it is." "I thought," said Esheal, "I once saw Dave do that to Diana." "Diana doesn't mind it," said Lily; "they don't do it to me. I don't like it. One minute you're buttoned up and neat and the next minute you're all wrinkles. Dave tore Momma's dress once. She wasn't paying too much attention, and she turned around to get to the kitchen in a hurry, a pot was boiling over or something, and her dress tore, right down the front where no one could fix it."

"But if you weren't worried about getting your dress torn, you wouldn't mind?" he asked. "I'd mind," said Lily; "I told Diana I thought it was peculiar, but she said I was an old maid, so I didn't mention it anymore. It's an old family custom. Every family has its ways." "You have a close family," Esheal said. "That's how families are supposed to be," said Lily. Esheal thought about his mother, who had left him alone in Pobrosk so many years ago, and he thought about telling his wife what had happened. But he was ashamed to tell her. He did not like to think about that time. In this country, no one but his sisters and his mother knew what had happened, and none of them was likely to talk about it, and because no one knew, it all seemed like a dream, something that had never really existed: his mother in the back of the cart, leaning toward him as if to pick him up, but instead beating his hands with a wooden spoon, the cloud of dust rising around their cart and swallowing it up, the people walking by looking at him with pity; it had not really happened. If he told his wife about it now, all of it would come alive again; it would all begin happening again, as if it had never stopped. Already he could taste the bitter yellow dust as it thickened his tongue and tickled his nose.

He would tell her about it later. She had a right to know about his life. It had been easier, he thought, to tell everyone he had been accused of poisoning that child. He did what people often do when faced with a similar dilemma; instead of telling his wife what he wanted to tell her because that was too difficult, he told himself that he would make up for his lack of courage by bringing up another forbidden subject, but one which was, by comparison, a pleasure to discuss. "Lily," he said, "I never came out and asked you how you feel about it, my being so much older than you." "Feel about it," said Lily; "how should I feel about it? It's nothing you can change." "What I mean is," said Esheal, "are you sorry I'm not younger?" "Naturally," she said; "if you were younger, you'd have longer to live."

"I have a feeling," Esheal said without thinking, "I'll live plenty long enough." "I can't live long enough," said his wife. "You can live too long," said Esheal; "everyone can." "Oh, if you're sick or something like that," Lily said impatiently. "There are other reasons," said Esheal. "Well, I can't imagine what they are," answered Lily; "my mother could never live long enough for me. Or my father. Or my grandfather." "Your grandfather seems a little tired to me," said Esheal. "Well, he has every reason to be," said Lily; "he's almost ninety." "But wouldn't you have been happier with a younger man?" Esheal persisted. "I don't think so," said Lily. "Look at my brothers. They're wonderful, but they're not dependable. An older man is someone you can count on." Esheal wondered how often in the last few months Lily had heard that from her mother. "Still," said Esheal, determined to know the worst.

"Well," said his wife, "you're not *old* old. All this nonsense with the sheet! I don't get into bed and fall asleep the way some of my friends say they do, and they're married to younger men and I'm not." Esheal propped himself up in bed and looked at Lily. "Tomorrow," he said, "let's go to that shop you were looking at and buy that hat, the brown one with the feathers. And a dress, the best dress they've got." "Buy a dress here!" exclaimed Lily; "everything here costs double what it should. When we go back, I'll get a dress made up. There's no point in throwing out money." "But I want you to get the dress," Esheal said; "then when you wear it, it will remind us of Niagara Falls." "A senseless waste of money," said his wife. "I want you to buy the dress," said Esheal, surprised at himself and the hardness of his tone. Was Lily afraid of looking ridiculous, a young, beautiful woman, dressed to kill by her old husband? Was she afraid that people would laugh at him behind his back because he had nothing better to do with his money than dress his wife in the most expensive clothes he could find? Did she think other people would look at her and see her clothes and say, oh, that's why she married him, to get all that money, look at the clothes she's got, the jewelry, that's some meal ticket she's got there? In the dark, he felt his cheeks burn.

"Lily," he said, "why don't you want the dress?" "Because," she said, "I can describe it to my cousin Fannie and she can make it. If you want to spend money, there are better things to spend it on." "Like what?" he asked. "I'm not hinting," Lily said, "but there are better things." "Your friend Bertie has a mink stole," he said. "I don't have my head in the clouds," said Lily; "what do I need with a mink stole? I have two good coats." It occurred to Esheal that Lily might be worried about being so much younger, about seeming foolish and impractical, a wife who was unable to manage her husband's money. "I know you don't have your head in the clouds," he told her; "I know you'll be able to manage a house. Your mother is a wonderful housekeeper." "She taught *me,*" Lily said proudly; "I'll be as good at it as she is. Maybe better. I've always known how to save my money." When Esheal heard that, he sighed, thinking of the loose floorboard in his old home in Pobrosk.

But that was it, he thought, relieved. She didn't want the dress because she didn't want to seem extravagant. He decided to forget about the dress, and when he got back, he would get her a mink stole for her birthday. He would give it to her early, he thought, since her birthday was in August and no one wore mink stoles in August. If he was going to get his wife something like that, he wanted her to wear it.

"Lily," he said, "get the hat. I want you to get the hat. We'll get our pictures taken later." "A hat like that," Lily started to say, "if I get caught in the rain," but Esheal interrupted her. "Lily," he said, "get the hat." "All right," she said; "if you want me to get the hat, I'll get the hat. I don't know what's so important about a hat." She started to get up to retrieve her nightgown which had fallen to the floor. "Leave it there," said Esheal; "I'll pull up the extra blanket. It's warm enough."

Lily heard Esheal fall asleep and concentrated on his deep, regular breathing hoping it would prove hypnotic and put her to sleep as well, but all she could think about was how she was lying in bed naked and what would happen if the cleaning woman or the maid came in by mistake. When she was absolutely sure her husband was asleep, she crept out of bed, found her nightgown, and put it on. When she finally got back into bed, carefully, without waking her husband, she lay staring at the ceiling, listening to the sound of her pounding heart.

Men, she thought, were unreasonable. This was something new, getting married. Before no one was interested in whether her nightgown was on or off, only in whether she was warm enough. Before she was married, the dressmaker had been the only one interested in her body, in how long-waisted it was, in how full-breasted she was, and that was because the dressmaker saw all bodies as adversaries which were determined to make her creations look as terrible as possible. It was from the dressmaker that Lily had learned what was right and wrong with Diana's body and from the dressmaker that she had gotten a sense of her own. But her body as a naked body! She would have to look it over, Lily thought, and blushed in the dark.

In the morning, Esheal got up first, and the first thing he saw was his wife, who had turned on her side, in her clean, blue-and-white-flowered nightgown, neatly buttoned. Her hair was loose and one cheek rested on her black hair as if on a thin layer of the night sky. Lily opened one eye and saw him staring at her. She sat bolt upright, frantically pushing her hair back, running her fingers through it, and pulled it all over one shoulder. "Leave it like that," he said; "it looks beautiful down." "Hair should look like hair," said Lily, "not straw. I always braid it at night. From now on, I'll do that first."

Man and Wife

Chapter 33

Esheal

Before Lily and I were married, I began taking stock of myself, which, I think, is a usual thing for a man to do under the circumstances. First, I considered all of my assets. That I was steady and reliable I had proven long ago, even to myself. That I could support a family I had known for years, since for years I had helped support my mother and my sisters. But what kind of person I was, that was another story. I really didn't know. I knew I was very patient with children, and in the neighborhood it was well known that mothers, after a visit from the doctor, would arrive in my drugstore with their child in tow to ask me to give him medicine.

More than one mother had to bring her child in four times a day every day for two weeks if that was how long the child had to take his medicine. There was one woman whose child was too sick to come in and for three weeks, *I* had to go to her house, climb six flights of steps, and give the child her medicine. She had tried everything. She had ground it up in applesauce, and the result was that the child refused both the medicine and the applesauce. By the time I got to her house, she had tried everything and was shouting at the child, cursing her up and down. "You should get the cholera! You should get the first cholera! Come over here so I can kill you!"

Who could blame her? She was at her wit's end. When I came, I brought three ice cream cones with me, and I broke them down to just the tip, so that they were like tiny little cones, and then I put the medicine in. You could smell it halfway across the room. In those days, medicine smelled and tasted like medicine. It was terrible stuff. But the little cones fascinated the child, and she had to eat them. That was how I got her to take it. Even if I didn't bring cones, I knew she would take it. I always had a way with children. I still do. I could never forgive anyone for hurting a child. My wife's

brothers used to love to see children cry, and once, they
pinched Diana's daughter, Gloria, because they said the child
never cried, and they kept at it until they saw four or five tears
drop out of the child's eyes. When I saw that, I wanted to kill
them. But I didn't have to do anything. Gloria hauled off and
slapped her Uncle Dave in the face. She was sitting on his lap.

For years afterward, they told that story, how when Gloria
was only five, she slapped her Uncle Dave in the face because
he pinched her. They didn't pinch her after that. I don't know
if that was because Gloria hit back, or because Diana saw
what they were up to, and came over and pinched both boys
so hard they had black-and-blue marks on their arms for days
afterward. But Diana was one thing. My wife was another.
She would have let her brothers pinch our children black and
blue all over, because they were her brothers, and whatever
they did was always all right with her. Unless they did
something which cost us money. Then she wasn't so sympathetic.

So I knew I was good with children. In fact, my mother said
she never knew a man who wanted to have children as much
as I did. She had seen women in Pobrosk rocking back and
forth crying because they were barren, and she said she
wouldn't be surprised if one day she found me rocking back
and forth because I didn't have anything in a cradle. Then she
reminded me that a man had to have a wife if he wanted to
have children. As if I'd forgotten. Of course I hadn't forgotten. It's one thing to be good with children and good to one's
family and another thing to be a good husband. I was always
afraid I wouldn't be a good husband. I don't know why, but I
was.

When I lived at my aunt's, my cousin Minnie used to say,
"Oh, Esheal, you're so afraid you won't marry a good
woman." But that wasn't it. I was afraid I wouldn't be a good
husband. What did I know about how husbands and wives
behaved? By the time I was old enough to pay attention to my
father, he was dying. Then I lived with the zenshina and then
I lived with my aunt.

Before I got married, I felt very lonely, as if I were
completely alone in the world, as if I didn't have a friend on
earth, as if I were the only man on earth. And I couldn't
understand it, because I had never known so many people,
and a lot of them were real friends, like Dr. Linde. I could
talk to him about anything, although usually we didn't talk

much. We sat and played chess. Afterward, I felt as if I had talked to him, or as if we had been talking the whole time.

And I was marrying into the Romanoff family, and I had been crazy about Sarah Romanoff for years, and if there was one thing of which I was certain, it was that Lily would be a good mother. They were all crazy mothers in that family. And she was young and healthy and I was sure I would soon have children. So it was beyond me why, before my wedding, I felt as if I had been left alone in the middle of nowhere.

And my mother particularly annoyed me with her fussing and her hovering. She wasn't the one I wanted. I wanted the zenshina. I wanted to talk to her. Since that was impossible, I sat down and wrote about seven letters to different families in Pobrosk, promising them a reward if they could deliver the letter I was enclosing for the zenshina. I copied out the letter seven times. I don't think anyone was anxious to deliver it. They were probably still as afraid of her as ever. But it turned out that the Kuratniks were going through a bad period. The husband was dead, and the boys were having a hard time bringing in enough money, so one of the boys went out there and gave her the letter.

Of course, I didn't get an answer until I had been married for over six months. She congratulated me and told me to watch out for my temper, which was the first I knew I had one worth mentioning. I suppose she couldn't send money through the mail, because she sent me a small packet of stamps for a present, and I didn't think much of them until I showed them to Dr. Linde, who said he thought they must be worth at least a couple of thousand dollars and told me to put them in my safe in the drugstore. She said on some days that spring, the mists had been so thick and so long that they had wrapped the ground like shrouds and she knew that both of us were still together. She said she still had her onion, although of course it was not the identical one into which I had stared. She said that she was quite sure we would meet again in this life, because, long ago, when she had read my hand and her hand, she had seen some line or other cross. When I read that, I felt as if I saw her standing in front of me all over again.

I don't understand women and their faith in fortune-tellers and omens of all kinds. Before our wedding, Lily and Dinney went to see the Great Ukrainian Silver Oracle, who told Lily that she was going to get married soon, that her husband would be wealthy, and that she would suffer a severe illness. For days, Lily walked around as if she were under a sentence of death. No one knew what was the matter with her. I, naturally, thought she had changed her mind and wanted a better-looking man. Sarah, who had more experience with her daughter than I did, knew it was something else, something stupid: that was what she told me. We took turns prevailing on Lily to tell us what was wrong, and finally, when we were riding through the park in a carriage, Lily burst into tears and said she didn't have long to live.

She scared the hell out of me. I thought she had been to the doctor, but where had she been? To the Great Ukrainian Silver Oracle. I don't think the woman even knew where the Ukraine was. She liked the sound of the word, that's all. I told Lily that fortune-tellers always said someone was due for a serious illness, because sooner or later, everyone was. Then she asked me how the oracle knew she was getting married and I asked her what she and Dinney had been talking about when they came in. She said they had been talking about their dresses, so I said that was how the woman knew, and anyway, it was always safe to tell a young, beautiful woman she was getting married soon, because even if she wasn't when she came in, she would be soon enough. It took a long time for Lily to calm down. I had no idea she was so superstitious, so irrational, and later, I wished I had kept that more firmly in mind.

Then, on our honeymoon, Lily asked me when I was born. She still had the Great Ukrainian Silver Oracle on her mind, and the oracle was full of astrological theories. When Lily asked me, I realized that I really didn't know. I had asked my mother often enough, and she said I was born around February sixth, but she couldn't be sure. That was the date I decided on, because I couldn't write born on or about February sixth on all the forms I had to fill out. I knew in what year I was born, but that was only because I was born the same year the Russian Army held maneuvers near Pobrosk, and during the year of my birth, their cannon fire broke every window and every mirror in the village.

I've often wondered if there is anything to superstitions, and, if it's true that a broken mirror brings seven years' bad luck, how many years' bad luck come from a whole town full of broken windows and mirrors. Mother also said that mirrors jumped from the walls when the cannon fired, and even though she thought she had taken down all the breakable things, there was a mirror in the corner which had gotten hidden behind the coats, and even though that was a small mirror, when it fell, it sounded like the sharp crack of a gun which had gone off in the house. So if anyone had a right to go around feeling doomed it was me.

But Lily took everything so literally. I remember, when I first came to this country and was learning the language, how astonished I was by what people said because I thought they said what they meant. I remember when Dr. Linde took me to see a friend of his and said, "He throws a wet blanket over everything," and I stared at the man outrageously wondering what kind of a lunatic would do such a thing. Then Dr. Linde said, "He turns everything to ashes," and I couldn't wait to get out of the man's house. I thought he was a maniac. Don't ask what I made out of "his head is in the clouds," and "he has two left feet," or "my stomach's on fire." But when I learned the language, I knew better. If someone said, "He's a loaded gun," I didn't try to jump out of the way. But if the Great Ukrainian Silver Oracle told Lily, "I see a cat in your palm," she would stare at her hand as if she expected to see the tiny animal walking around. So later I should have known better than to threaten Lily with things I didn't intend to do.

And one night, on our honeymoon, I asked Lily why her brothers put their hands inside their mother's dress, and she said her family was very close and that was how families were supposed to be, that blood was thicker than water, and that her grandfather said that a family was like a bank, and you got out of it what you put into it, and that no matter what happened, you could always count on your flesh and blood and that the rest of the world might turn away from you, but your own family, never. I don't know what got into me. I said to Lily, a husband isn't flesh and blood. So how does he get into the family? If he isn't flesh and blood, then he's not really a blood member of the family.

"Not a *blood* member," said my wife, "but he marries into it." "That's not the same thing as being born into it," I said. "Of course not," said my wife; "only children can be born into a family." "So how does the husband get to be a part of it?" I asked; "doesn't he have to wait until he and his wife have children before they turn into a family, and even after they have children, the husband and wife aren't blood relations, so between them, blood isn't thicker than water."

My wife tugged at her eternal sheet. "I don't know what you're driving at," she said; "you get married, the husband and wife, and that's what they are. Husband and wife. And when they have children, that's the family." "So I'm your family," I said. "Of course," said Lily.

But I was thinking about Diana and Sidney, and how Diana was marrying a blood relation and how much luckier Sidney was than I was. So I said something about Sidney and how he was already a blood relation and a husband, while I was only a husband, and Lily lost her temper and said if I wanted to be a husband and a blood relation, I should have married my cousin Minnie, who wanted to marry me anyway; she could tell that by looking at her.

And that was the first I knew that Minnie was in love with me, although now that I was married, it didn't make any difference, and I was so happy to see that Lily was jealous I forgot all about Lily's family and why I had been asking her so many questions about them. They would be there when we left Niagara Falls and went back, and it struck me funny that now, after years of wanting to be closer to them and having married into their family, and having married Sarah's daughter, I was afraid of their being so close to me. In fact, I dreaded it.

Chapter 34

It soon seemed to Esheal as if his wedding had been a signal for which life was waiting, and that, as soon as he and Lily returned to Brooklyn, all manner of things were set in motion. They had not been back two days, when one of his sisters arrived at his store, frantic, and said that his mother was very sick; she was lying in bed because she did not have the strength to get up and she was very hot and what was strangest of all, she was bright yellow. Esheal asked his sister when his mother had turned yellow, and she said the day before, but she had not been very yellow, and so they had not called the doctor until that morning. "She's asking for you," his sister said.

Esheal took one look at his sister, who had rushed out with his mother's old black shawl over her head, and knew that his mother was seriously ill. Otherwise, his sister would never have gone out wearing something like that. When they got to his mother's house, she was bright yellow and bloated almost beyond recognition. "When did this start?" Esheal asked his mother, but she stared through him as if she did not see him. "She's like that since yesterday," said his sister; "she only seems to be awake. She's really sleeping." "I think it's more than that," said Esheal. She wasn't awake, but she did not appear to be sleeping in the usual sense of the word. "Has she been complaining about anything?" he asked his sister.

"Well, she's been going on about a terrible backache for a long time," she said. "And you didn't send for the doctor?" Esheal asked. "We called a doctor," his sister said; "he told Momma it was normal for a woman who had children to have backaches at her age, and when a woman her age did nothing but sit in a chair and sew or look out the window, of course she would have a backache." "What doctor was that?" asked Esheal. "Dr. Herriman," said his sister. "Dr. Herriman's a

quack!" shouted Esheal. "All of you know that. I told all of
you about the trial." "She didn't want to go to Dr. Linde,"
said his sister; "she was afraid he'd tell you and you'd worry
about her and not go on your honeymoon." "She picked a
fine time to worry about me," said Esheal. He looked at his
sister. "You should have had more sense," he said. "All it
was was a backache," she said.

"All it was was a backache," he repeated; "look at her.
Does everyone turn yellow from a backache? What else was
the matter with her?" "Yesterday," said his sister, avoiding
his gaze, "she said she had trouble going to the bathroom.
She said it burned her to go to the bathroom." "You mean
when she urinated?" said Esheal. His sister turned red.
"Yes," she said. "And how long was that going on?" he
asked. "For a long time, I think," said his sister; "she didn't
think it was something a nice woman ought to talk about."
"And now she can't talk at all," Esheal said bitterly. "She'll
get better, won't she?" his sister asked; "you'll just give her
some of that sulfur, won't you?" "Not this time," Esheal said.
His sister sank down onto a kitchen chair and began crying.

Esheal sat down on the chair next to his mother's bed. She
opened her eyes. "My little boy," she said; "you were always
my favorite. My little boy." Esheal stared down at the yellow,
bloated woman who bore no resemblance to the woman he
had known all his life. "If anything happens to your father,
you'll take care of me?" she asked. "I'll take care of you," he
said. He realized that his mother was no longer conscious of
what was going on around her. He also knew that his mother
had never thought of him as a child; he had been the boy, the
one who was to have taken care of her.

When Dr. Linde came in, he found Esheal placing wet
compresses on his mother's head. "It won't help," he told
him. "What is this?" Esheal asked; "it has to do with her
kidneys, doesn't it?" "Kidney failure," the doctor said;
"she'll be gone in a day or two." She was dead the next
morning. Sarah and Lily helped Esheal make arrangements
for the funeral; they came over and helped clean the house
and supervised the women who washed the body. When
Esheal saw his mother placed in her coffin, he felt nothing,
and then he felt anger. He looked at the dead woman and told
himself he was looking at his mother, but he did not believe
it; he felt as if he were looking into an empty box. He told
himself it was wrong to be angry with the dead, but he was

angry, and when he heard the earth hit the coffin where his mother had been buried next to his new father, he felt only bitterness. He asked himself why he was angry with his mother now, when she was no longer alive and he did not know why. He knew only that he was.

And two days after the funeral, Sarah arrived at the shop and disappeared into the back room with her daughter for almost half an hour. Esheal, who assumed someone else had died, tried to eavesdrop in the hall, but all he could hear was Sarah's voice, Lily's exclamations, and the sound of one or the other crying. By the time the two women came back to the living room, Esheal was furious with them. He had been sitting looking down the street, watching the street cleaner take his broom from his cart and sweep up and turn out of sight, watching some children collect around the organ grinder and his monkey, and he could not enjoy his supper or his time off because he was so worried about what had reduced Mrs. Romanoff to such hysteria. Hadn't he had enough in the last few days? Now he felt like a relative waiting for the doctor to come out and tell him whether someone was or was not going to live. And he had to sit there like that without knowing the name of the patient.

Apparently, both women had been crying. Lily came up to him and stopped to wipe a tear from her cheek. Sarah, afraid of bursting into tears again, kept silent. Esheal looked at his wife and felt no sympathy. There was something in her helpless look that he did not like, something in her air of entreaty which made him feel hard and cold. He told himself he felt so unsympathetic, so remote, because the women had excluded him and left him to worry alone. "Did someone die?" he asked. He wanted to know the worst immediately. Sarah shook her head no. "Is anyone sick?" he asked. Lily said no one was sick. "Then why is everyone crying?" he asked; "what can be so bad that your mother has to come all the way over here herself?" He knew Sarah's heart was bad; the whole family knew that. "You couldn't have sent someone else?" he asked Sarah. Sarah looked helplessly at Lily. Esheal knew he was not going to like what the women were getting ready to tell him.

"Dave's in jail," said Lily. "He finally killed someone," said Esheal; "who did he kill?" "He didn't kill anyone," Lily said indignantly; "he was arrested for fighting." "So he almost killed someone," said Esheal; "who was he fighting

with?" "A policeman," said Lily. "A policeman?" Esheal
said, incredulous. "The policeman was trying to take them in
for gambling," Lily said, "so he started a fight with the
policeman so the others could get away." "A matter of
honor," Esheal said. "Come on," said Lily; "all he did was
get into a fight. He's been in fights before. You know that."
"Look," said Esheal, who was starving to death, but knew
better than to mention such a thing in the middle of what the
woman evidently regarded as a great family crisis, "let me
have it all. I don't want to drag it out of you like a broken
tooth. He's been in fights before. So what's everyone crying
about?" "We don't have bail money," said Sarah, who looked
at him as if it were his fault that she did not have bail money,
that her son had gotten into a fight. "How much is bail?"
asked Esheal. "One hundred dollars," said Sarah. "One
hundred dollars!" he exclaimed, but he looked at Sarah and
felt smaller. She had stopped crying and now stood in the
middle of his room like a queen who had come to visit one of
her humble subjects.

"I can't get the money until tomorrow morning," he said;
"as soon as the bank opens, I'll bring it over." "It won't hurt
Dave to spend the night in jail," Sarah said; "what trouble
can he get up to in there?" She smiled at Esheal. "But," he
said, "when he comes out, I want to talk to him. He can't
make a life out of slugging cops. One of these days, he'll kill
someone." "Then talk to him," Sarah said. Her voice was
cold. He understood that, aside from providing Dave's bail
money, he had no rights in any matter which concerned her
son. And, because he was hurt and angry, he did not let the
matter drop.

"A hundred dollars," he said to Sarah; "you know how
much money that is? When we were in Russia, if we had a cup
a person, we had a lot. If something happened to a tin cup,
you took it to the tinker's to fix it. A hundred dollars?
Because someone got into a fight?" "You'll get the money
back after the trial," said Lily, "once they sentence him. They
only don't give the money back if someone runs away and
doesn't come to the trial." "Someday something will happen
he'll have to run away from," said Esheal. "He's just
high-spirited," said Lily; "boys are like that." "When I was a
boy," said Esheal, "I wasn't like that. You don't have to make
it so easy for him. When I was a boy . . ." "When you were a
boy, you fixed tin cups!" Lily interrupted sarcastically; "what

do tin cups have to do with anything? Dave's in jail. He's behind bars." "I have to get back to the shop," Esheal said; "in the morning, you can bring the money over to your mother." "What about dinner?" asked Lily. "Send it down in the dumbwaiter after you take your mother home," he said, and he went out the door.

The two women stood staring after him. "He's angry," said Lily. "He has a right," said Sarah; "we come in, we ask for his money, but we tell him it's none of his business." "It's not," said her daughter; "Dave's my brother, not his." "He's his brother-in-law," said Sarah. "It's not the same," Lily said. "He's your husband," said Sarah; "you can't fight over everything." "I wasn't fighting," Lily said, surprised; "he was the one who said he wanted to talk to Dave. A lot of good that will do." "Better to fight than to ridicule," said Sarah. "I *wasn't* ridiculing," Lily said. "You shouldn't mock him when he talks about tin cups," said Sarah. "What's so important about tin cups?" asked Lily. "We weren't talking about tin cups," said Sarah; "we were talking about Dave. Stick to what you're talking about. You want to wind up fighting about the whole world?" "You were mad at him," Lily said hotly; "I know you were. You didn't think it was any of his business to talk to Dave." "You don't have to fight my battles," said her mother. "He's not my husband. Did I ever take anyone's side against your father? He's probably still upset about his mother's dying." "He didn't seem upset to me," said Lily. "You were at the funeral. Did he seem upset?" "Some people don't show everything on the outside," said Sarah. Lily started to cry.

"What are you crying about?" asked her mother; "Dave will be out tomorrow and he won't have to stay in long; it was only a fight. What are you crying about?" Lily did not answer her, and the truth was she did not know what she was crying about. She was angry at her husband, but her mother said she ought not to be and now she was angry at her mother as well. Most of all she was angry at Dave, who had gotten into one of his ridiculous fights, and started this whole bregus and now her mother was angry with her and her husband had gone downstairs without his supper. "Your father will be worried," Sarah said, getting up.

"I'll walk you home," said Lily. It was still early enough for the children to be out; they were playing hopscotch and stoop ball. One after another, windows opened and mothers leaned out to call their children in to supper, and the children, with their heads tilted way back, called to their mothers asking for just one more minute or promising that they would be in as soon as they finished the game. The women who were leaning out the windows began throwing down little white packets to the children on the street, and the children would unwrap the little packets, take the keys out of the paper they were wrapped in, and let themselves into their houses. Lily watched all this as if she had never seen it before. "Remember when you used to do that?" she asked her mother; "throw me down a key?" "And a cent," said Sarah; "you used to stand in the street and yell, throw down a tent, throw down a tent. And Mrs. Berkowitz next door used to say, come on in, I'll give you a cup of toffee. Soon you'll have one of your own." "I hope I have a boy," said Lily. "Why a boy?" asked her mother. "A boy can take care of you," said Lily. Sarah shook her head. "You'll be happy with whatever you get," she said; "listen, Lily, when Esheal's in a good mood, ask him to talk to Dave in the store, not in our house. I don't want your father to hear it." "All I want," said Lily, "is peace and quiet." "You have it," said Sarah; "this is nothing." "I'll come in and say hello," Lily said. "No," said her mother; "go home and make it up."

At a quarter of twelve that night, Lily put on her Niagara Falls hat and went down to the pharmacy. "You need something for the house?" her husband asked her. "No, I don't need anything," she said; "I wanted to go out for a walk in my hat. It's not raining for a change." "I'll get my coat," said Esheal, and as usual, Lily slipped her arm around his waist as they went out the door.

Three months later, Diana flew into the pharmacy and began running through the aisles looking for Dr. Luria. The clerk, who was new, had seen crazy women before, slipped behind the back counter to warn Esheal and tell him to get his gun. The last woman who ran in with her hair wet and tangled had turned violent and torn down two shelves and then threatened both of them with a broken bottle. Esheal and the clerk crouched down and peered out into the store. Suddenly, Esheal stood up, and the clerk, who was terrified, tried to push him back down again. "Let go," Esheal said impatiently; "that's my sister-in-law. Diana!" he called out. "Not so fast," whispered the clerk, "even if she is your sister-in-law, she could still be crazy." "She's not crazy," said Esheal, still trying to free himself from the clerk's grip. "Sometimes I think she's the only one in the family who isn't."

"Where are you?" Diana called. She was standing in the middle of the perfume and powder section, bawling like a little child. "I'm right here," he said, and Diana jumped as if she had heard a gun go off next to her ear. "What am I going to do?" wailed Diana; "what am I going to do?" "Where's your husband?" asked Esheal. "He's in Boston. In dental school." Esheal sighed with relief. "Is anyone dead?" he asked. It seemed to him that he was forever asking the Romanoffs, who were all very emotional, that question, and that the answer always was no. "Yes," said Diana. "Grandpa's dead. He's lying in the street. Well, he's not lying there anymore. I mean they took him to the morgue. Someone's got to identify the body." "Who?" asked Esheal. "Well," sobbed Diana, "don't you think I should go? Momma's not too well, and Poppa can't walk right since he burned himself, and the boys aren't home, they're working at something, don't you think I should go?" Diana asked again. Esheal blushed.

"I'll go," he said. "It has to be someone from the family," she said. "Please stop crying," he said, taking his handkerchief from his pocket and wiping her face; "can't you stop crying?" "I don't think so," she said. He wondered why Diana's tears did not annoy him as Lily's almost always did. Diana looked terrible, as if she were staring into an empty space which she was fighting not to see, but which she knew she would see again and again. Yet she did not seem helpless. She never seemed helpless. When Lily cried, she was helpless, a beautiful fish a few inches from the water who did not have the will to move, even if staying where she was would mean the end of everything. "When do you want to go?" he asked her; "I'll go with you. Let's get it over with. Do you know how to get there?" "You take the Tompkins Avenue car," said Diana.

"What happened?" he asked; they were standing on the corner of Eastern Parkway waiting for the streetcar, and although it was only four in the afternoon, the rain clouds had so darkened the sky that the streetlights were on, and the rain was falling in fat silver drops. "He got run over," said Diana, and started crying again. Esheal poked in his coat pocket, looking for a fresh handkerchief. Ever since he had gotten involved with the Romanoffs, he stuffed his suits and coats with them, and it amused him to listen to Lily's complaints about how many of them she had to iron. She could not imagine, she said, what he needed with twenty handkerchiefs a week. She went through three of them every time she went to the movies. "Isn't that a stupid way to die?" Diana asked; "you'd think a truck could think of something better to do than chase down an intelligent human being."

"How did you find out?" Esheal asked. "Well," said Diana, "I was sweeping off the stoop, and I was already starting to worry, because you know Grandpa, he's so regular, he always goes to shul at the same time, and then he brings home rolls for the boys, and he was late, so where could he be? I was just getting ready to go and look for him, when one of his cronies comes up to me from the shul, and says he's laying there in the middle of the street. And I ran right off but they'd already taken him away. They swept him up in the horse cart, that's what someone said. They took him in the same wagon they use for dead horses." "I don't believe it," he said. "I do," she said; "they don't know who he was or what he was or where he came from." "Diana," said Esheal, "dead is dead. At least he didn't suffer."

"You know," said Diana, "soon Momma will die, and Poppa will die, and we'll all be alone. Won't it be funny to be the old ones?" "That's how it's supposed to be," Esheal said. "Maybe they'll have good deaths," she said. "Don't think about it so much," he said, leaning forward to peer down the tracks. "I don't think anything's coming. We're going to be soaked." Diana started crying again, and Esheal, who knew what she was crying about, said nothing to her. "To run over an intelligent human being and leave him lying in the rain," said Diana. "Maybe they skidded because of the rain," he said. "What difference does it make?" Diana said; "you're going to miss him, aren't you? He always liked you. He took to you before everybody else did. He said you were like he used to be. But Momma said that when he was a young man, he was wild, so I don't know why he thought that." "I see the car," said Esheal.

Chapter 35

Esheal

The Romanoffs decided to celebrate my wedding by getting themselves thrown in jail and dying and my mother fell right in with the spirit of things and was dead three days after we got back from our honeymoon. At least that's how it seemed to me at the time. I don't think I was in a normal frame of mind for some time after I was married. I was used to being by myself. I wasn't used to noise. Not that my wife was noisy, but the nature of the noise in the house changed once there was someone else there with me. It was as if I were constantly hearing a new sound or listening to something which had not yet been said. I was, I realized, an expert on silences. When Dave got himself in jail for assault and battery, the noise was unfriendly, and it got more so after I gave him a talking to. He must have told my wife that I gave him a scolding. Anyway, the whole family knew what I had said, and that I had threatened him and told him that I wouldn't help him out if he did the same thing again. He didn't do the same thing again. He thought of other things. He must have had a dictionary of troubles, and he was going through them from A to Z.

His brother Bill wasn't much better, but he was too stupid to get into real trouble. I could see the writing on the wall for my wife's family. Sarah had a bad heart and diabetes and terribly high blood pressure and Meyer could barely get to work on his burned leg, and if the boys didn't find some way to make money, Sarah and Meyer would have to be supported by their daughters, and I couldn't see Sarah Romanoff putting up with that. One afternoon, I got hold of Bill and asked him how he intended to keep his parents from starving to death, and of course, he didn't know what I meant, since they weren't starving that very minute. So I painted a pretty nasty picture for him. I scared him out of the one wit he had.

He was a handsome man, even better looking than Dave, so I thought he could sell anything to a woman if he was the one behind the counter. How much do you make from selling drugs in a pharmacy? You make money selling sodas and powders, and I'd watched Bill for years. He could have sold a woman the wall. Once, when he worked for me, he actually sold someone one of our ceiling fans, because he thought it wouldn't be any trouble to get a new one, and in the meantime, we would have the money. We would also have died of heat prostration, but that didn't seem to occur to him.

Anyway, I asked him if he had finished public school, and he said he had. Apparently, Sarah and Lily and Diana took turns tutoring him. He was not a brilliant man. I told him he ought to go to pharmacy school, because if he could only graduate, I could put him to work in my shop and that way he could earn a living until he could open up a shop of his own. He said he would do it. I told him not to say anything about our conversation, just to go home and tell everybody he had decided to go to pharmacy school because he thought that was a nice, easy way to make a living. That was what his family thought in any case. But he went home and told them it was my idea, so naturally they tried to talk him out of it. Or Dave did. The others thought it over and decided it was a good idea, because after all, what could he do? They didn't want their beloved son shoveling coal or working in a coat factory, so they did me a favor and let me put him through pharmacy school. I never thought he'd go through with it, but he wasn't too industrious and the other alternatives weren't so attractive. And I guess he thought if he worked for me, he'd have someone to cover for him, and he knew I wasn't going to give him much responsibility. I didn't see much point in bothering about Dave. He was looking for the easy way out and one day he was going to find it. It's a rotten kind of character to have, but there was nothing I could do about it.

And after I got married, it seemed as if everything made an enormous impression on me. I don't know why. I always had plenty of time to think in the store before I got married, and none of that changed afterward. In fact, I had less time to think, or I should have, because I rigged up a bell system so that Lily and I could call each other through the dumbwaiter, and she would call to ask me if I wanted a cup of coffee or a piece of cake, and if she had company, and I couldn't come up, she would have everyone say hello to me through the dumbwaiter, and then she would send down a portion of whatever it was everyone was eating.

One of the things I thought about constantly was the child who died, the one they said I poisoned. I had seen the Bailey child at least a hundred times. If her mother had to go out, she took the child with her, and the child was never well, so she was in and out of my pharmacy with her all the time. Right after the trial, I didn't think about the child much; there was so much excitement over the wedding. But afterward, that was all I seemed to think about. And I always thought about the child in the same way. First she would be there in front of me, and I would be looking at her, and then she was gone. It was as if she were part of a conjuror's trick, as if she were nothing more than a coin which the magician made disappear. And everything went on just as it had before, and there I was, looking out the pharmacy window at the Hood's ice cream sign and the Lipton Tea sign across the street, and all that was the same. Except that there was one less person to see it. I couldn't keep the child in my mind's eye; that was what bothered me. First she was here, and then she wasn't. That was all I could find to say about her life. I was haunted by the child's face. It was like a moon. It sailed out from behind the clouds and then went back into them again. Then one day I couldn't remember the child's face at all. After that, I wasn't myself. I walked around feeling like hell. If I had been a woman, I would have walked around crying.

One day it was raining and Diana ran into the store; one of the old men from the shul told her her grandfather was run over and I went with her to the morgue. Itzak was killed on his way to shul, and I thought about how he died, and how he would have found it funny. The family was always worrying him about the way he ate; he wasn't supposed to eat anything fatty, and he loved gribbonis and liver and onions, and he smoked like a chimney, and of course none of that killed him. A truck did. I missed the old man, but they didn't want to hear that from me. He belonged to them. So I kept quiet. It was my job to hand out handkerchiefs.

He was almost ninety. He was run over crossing the street. I can imagine the whole thing. Itzak crossed streets as if he wanted to get to the other side by the end of next month; if he heard a car approaching, he'd hold up his hand like a traffic cop. It never occurred to him to get out of the way or to hurry up, but at his age he couldn't really hurry. So when he crossed the street, he knew he was doing something dangerous. But he wanted to get to the other side and he took his chances. And on the day he died, it rained as if the heavens were trying to scour the earth, and the roads were slippery. When we got to the morgue, Mr. Raskovich, one of Itzak's friends, was sitting outside, praying. When he saw us, he said some boys were driving a truck and they saw Itzak but they didn't slow down. And after the truck hit him, Mr. Raskovich and his friend went to look at the body where it was lying in the street, and the muddy tracks of the tires were all over his white shirt, and they said to each other, "See where the man was killed there?" And his watch was crushed and parts of it were scattered all over the street.

Sarah was fine unless she happened to think about the watch. Itzak had gotten the watch from his father, and he always said that when he died, he was going to give it to Meyer. When the watch was crushed, that was impossible. Sarah took that as an evil sign. She kept insisting that Meyer wasn't going to live long, and that was why the watch had been crushed. Of course, she didn't say that in front of her husband. For a while, Sarah was very bitter. She said she didn't see why people went to shul if God was going to run them over on their way there. She got over it. She had her husband and her children.

When Diana and I came back from the morgue, we decided to tell Lily what happened, and then the three of us would go over and tell the rest of the family. I don't know how many times we started to tell Lily and changed the subject. Diana finally faced up to it. "Look," she said to Lily, "Grandpa got himself run over." My wife didn't understand right away. "He got run over and he's dead," Diana said; "we have to go home and tell Ma and Pa." Lily looked at her sister, turned around, ran down the hall into the bathroom and threw up. I thought I was getting off easily. I thought she would do more than throw up. I thought I'd be back down in the shop getting sedatives. While I was waiting for Lily to come back, I asked Diana if my wife always threw up when she got upset, and Diana said that as far as she knew, Lily never threw up. When Lily came out of the bathroom, her sister asked her if she'd been throwing up lately, and she said she had, but it was only an upset stomach. Diana asked her when she threw up, and she said every morning, but that was because she had an empty stomach.

So that was how I found out Lily was pregnant. We had been married four months. And at first, Sarah didn't take the news too well because her father's death had shaken her, and she was sure that if Lily was bringing a new soul into the world, it meant that another soul was going out of it, and she knew that when Lily's child was born, her husband was going to die. But Diana said that Itzak's soul had gone out of the world just when we found out about Lily's child, so that score was even, and this piece of reasoning seemed to satisfy Sarah.

So it seemed to me that all I thought about was death. When I began thinking about Mrs. Bailey's child, I thought, well, this is happening because I'm a married man now, and I'm responsible for someone, and I worry what would happen to her if anything happened to me. And then Itzak died, and when Lily got pregnant, I was sure she was going to die. When I wasn't sure she was going to die, I was sure I was. I've always been an exceptionally healthy man and I never worried about my health before I married. But the fear that I was going to die, or that my wife would, haunted me. I think I had a premonition of approaching disaster, although, as is usually the case with human beings, I was staring off to the east while disaster crept up on me from the west. If I had known what was coming, I might have been able to do something about it. But I doubt it. We grow into our destinies as we grow into our bodies. Even if we could see a picture of ourselves as we will look at thirty or forty or fifty, we could do nothing to change the way we would turn out. That's what I think today, that I could have done nothing to change the outcome of things, although on other days I think just the opposite. Neither way of thinking about my life makes me happy.

Chapter 36

A remarkable calm descended on the Luria house, and that calm seemed to swell with the size of Lily's stomach. There were no more arguments about whose family they would visit on Esheal's Sundays off; they visited his sisters or his aunt and his cousin Minnie. Lily's family was constantly at Esheal's house. At dinner time, Esheal would look out the pharmacy window, and as if Sarah were part of a gigantic clockwork, he would see her slowly walking down the street, assisted by Diana or one of the boys. Sometimes she came with Dinney, who came to visit at least three times a week. Esheal had grown very fond of Dinney, who was not an attractive woman, and whose pop eyes made her look like a fish in the Fulton Street Market, but there was something about her; she made everyone laugh. There was nothing she would not do to cheer someone up, and if she came into the pharmacy and saw Esheal moping behind the counter, she refused to leave until some story or other of hers made him smile. In return, he refused to charge her for any medications she needed for her children. Whenever anyone said anything unpleasant about Esheal, she refused to listen. "He's swell," she said, and she would go on saying it until the subject was changed.

Esheal liked to see the three girls together in his house, Diana and Lily and Dinney, and whenever he saw them there, he thought of the day he had first come to the pharmacy and listened to the three of them talk about getting married. Dinney was the least attractive of the three, and at times she was downright ugly, but she had been the first of the girls to get married, and she had twin boys. Her husband did not make much money, and Diana used to say that she got a nosebleed climbing up to Dinney's apartment, it was so close to the sky, but Dinney was perfectly happy there. When her husband, Jake Rudler, did not earn enough money, she went from door to door selling silverware. She would leave the children in a double carriage at the foot of the steep stairs leading up to the graystones and climb up to ring the doorbell trying to sell silverware to her "customers." In time, she added coffee to her inventory. She became a familiar sight in the neighborhood; everyone knew her and her twin boys, Arnie and Ben. And everyone in the neighborhood told Arnie and Ben stories.

When Esheal saw Dinney coming, he took a deep breath, sat down on his high stool, smiled, and got to work. When he saw Sarah coming down the street, he felt as if his temperature had gone up three degrees. He would never have believed he would learn to dread her visits. She was a different woman now that her daughter was pregnant. She was possessed by a strong belief in Lily's frailty, and she appeared to be afraid to trust her to her husband. Whenever he came up to the apartment, Sarah would trot out all Lily's childhood illnesses and impress upon him how very serious had been her bouts with scarlet fever, whooping cough, and the flu. If Lily got up to take her cup and saucer, Sarah would get out of her chair, panting from the effort, and take the cup and saucer away from her and put them in the sink. Esheal saw that Sarah was frightening his wife, and he spoke to Dr. Linde, who took Lily aside and assured her that she was in wonderful health; he wished, he said, he was as healthy as she was.

But once Lily began to worry, she did not stop. As her stomach grew fuller, her face grew thinner. She walked through the rooms of their house like a woman locked in a cell. Esheal tried talking sense to her but got nowhere. He had Dr. Linde talk to Sarah, and the doctor did more than Esheal had asked him to do. He forbade any further mention of Lily's childhood illnesses as well as any speculations concerning Lily's weakened constitution. The cure was worse than the disease. Sarah, who would never dream of disobeying a doctor's order, now sat silently and stared at her daughter, shaking her head. Whenever he could, Esheal left the pharmacy in the hands of his clerk and attempted to dilute the effect of Sarah's visits, but often he was unable to go up, and by the time he did, he would find his wife walking through the house, weeping.

He begged Dinney to come over every afternoon, but Dinney had her coffee and silverware to sell, and she could not always find someone to stay with Arnie and Ben. But when she was there he had nothing to worry about. He came in one afternoon and found Dinney teaching his wife to make beet jelly, but it turned out that Dinney thought Lily was teaching her, and they soon had a mess on their hands. Two burned pots were resting crazily in the kitchen sink. Lily was collapsed against the wall, laughing. "Oh, will you look at that," Dinney said; "will you look at that lump? Anyone who ate that would have two Adam's apples." Lily came over, looked into the pot, and started screaming with laughter. "So, tell me, Lily," Dinney said, raising her wooden spoon in the air, "where did we get that lump? We started out with a nice, clear liquid. Your pot laid an egg and it's not even Easter." Lily was laughing so hard that she had to sit down on a chair. "We should serve this to your mother," Dinney said; "they'd go to the synagogue and say the prayer for the dead. Maybe we could switch this for hers. You know what she'd do? She'd chase Dave around the kitchen. She'd think he dropped something in it." When she looked into the pot, her eyes seemed to pop out of her head, and that was all Lily had to see. She could not stop laughing.

Esheal never could understand what was so funny about their conversations, but it was clear enough that the two women had only to look at each other and they were off in cloud-cuckoo-land. When Diana was there, they were even worse. Their hilarious episodes always ended with flights to the bathroom, and Dinney was always allowed in first, even though Lily argued that now that she was pregnant, she ought to be given that privilege. So whenever Dinney came, Esheal would push the clerk in back of the register and run out to the bakery to buy something special, hoping that Dinney would stay longer.

He and his cake box would usually arrive in the middle of one of Dinney's twin stories, and Esheal would sit down in a chair and listen to her as if he were hearing a siren song. "So yesterday," Dinney was saying, "they wanted to go to the movies, and I didn't have any money, and they started to cry, they wanted to go to the movies, they wanted to go to the movies, and I didn't know what to do anymore. Do you know what I did? I lay down on the kitchen floor and I made believe I fainted. And what do you think Arnie did? He went to the sink and got a glass of water to revive me and they splashed it all over me, and they were so busy waiting to see if I was coming to, they stopped their crying. But I was mad. I was soaking wet." "Did you spank them?" asked Lily. "How could I spank them?" asked Dinney; "they were so funny.

"Last weekend, they were even worse. I had to go out to the store, and I couldn't find anyone to stay with them, so I locked them in, and they promised, they swore by everything holy, they were going to sit there and leave the ice tray alone in the icebox, and leave the stove alone, and not look for the matches, and what do you think happens? I come home and I see them sitting on the windowsill, you know, with their legs hanging out, and there I am, six stories down and they're sitting there, six stories up. I started to shout at them, they should go back in. But why should they go back in? They were having such a wonderful time. And just then Jake came home, and he went upstairs while I stood there like a lamppost, screaming don't move, wait for your father, and until he got them in, I was half dead from fright. Jake said next time I have to go out without them, I should tie them to the beds.

"He put a lock on the piano. Did you know that? They got gum all over the felt hammers in the piano. I don't know how they could even lift the lid. So you see what you're in for," Dinney said; "but maybe you'll have girls. Girls are easier." "I don't want a girl," said Lily. "Why not?" asked Esheal, surprised; "I always wanted girls." "Most men want boys," said his wife. "I'm not most men," he said. "You're swell," said Dinney, and when she said that, he felt that he was, and later, he got angry when he heard Lily's brothers calling her Old Pop Eyes when she was not there to hear them.

The day Lily gave birth, the Luria house was so crowded that the doctor had trouble getting into the bedroom. "What do you make of this mob?" Dr. Linde asked Esheal. Esheal said he wanted company, but he had not wanted Grand Central Station. He said that Sarah had set up shop in the bedroom from the minute Lily complained of her first pain, and that the rest of the family did not take too much longer to get there. For a while, he said, he thought *they* thought he was having some kind of party. He asked the doctor to tell him the truth; was Lily in any danger because of her old illnesses, and would it have been better if she had waited longer to have children. "What for?" asked Dr. Linde; "it's better for a woman to have them when she's young and strong." Esheal said he felt responsible; after all, it was his baby, and Dr. Linde said that he was worrying about nothing. Of course he felt responsible, since Lily was his wife, but having his baby wasn't a crime or all the husbands in the world would be in jail. He said if he were in Esheal's place, he'd be nervous enough after watching his wife walk around looking like her own ghost for six months. It had always been easy to frighten Lily, he said. She was just like a child.

But no reassurance could hide the fact that Lily was having a hard time of it. After two hours, Dr. Linde told Esheal that he was sending Sarah and Diana home. Sarah's heart was not up to it, and he did not want to frighten Diana out of having children altogether. Esheal did not think that they would go, but when Dr. Linde asked them to leave, they got up, put on their coats, and went home. Dinney, who stayed behind, said that she would come over and tell them what happened as soon as everything was over.

Just before morning, Lily gave birth to a baby girl. By that time, she was too tired to look at her, and she fell asleep immediately. But Esheal was wide awake and could not be torn away from the fat little baby who arrived with a thick mop of black hair and wide, china-blue eyes. "I didn't think they opened their eyes so early," Esheal said, staring at her, and Dr. Linde said that this one was in a hurry all right; she wanted to see everything. "There's nothing wrong with her?" Esheal asked; "look at those purple marks all over her face." "Squashed," said the doctor; "they'll be gone in a few days." "She has such a big head," Esheal said worriedly. "She looks like you," said Dr. Linde; "you have a big head." "I do?" said Esheal; "then it's not so bad." "Plenty of room for brains," said the doctor. He went in to look at Lily. When he came back, he asked Esheal if he was going to hold the child all night, because if that was what he wanted to do, he ought to think again. He would fall asleep and drop the baby. Dinney patted Esheal on the shoulder, took the child, and set her down in the cradle and then went to get the baby nurse, who had been installed in the back bedroom since early afternoon. On her way home, Dinney said, she would stop at the Romanoffs' and let them know everything was all right.

Left alone, Esheal went in, looked at Lily, who was sleeping peacefully, and carried his small pile of bedding out to the living room couch. He could not believe that it was over, that he still had a wife, and, what was more incredible, he had a child. When he had married Lily, he thought he would want at least twelve children; now he thought he would settle for just this one. He did not think he could live through another of Lily's pregnancies. When he asked Dr. Linde about Lily, and why she had had such a hard time, the doctor said that sometimes first pregnancies were like that. There was nothing wrong with her, he said; she could have a hundred children. Esheal was exhausted and fell asleep immediately, but a few hours later, he was awakened by a strange, new noise. For a minute, he thought a cat had gotten in the house and then he realized he was hearing his baby cry. He fell back asleep at once, but a short while later, he was shaken awake by the nurse, who told him his wife was asking for him.

The instant he saw her, he knew something was wrong. Her eyes were glazed and wide, her cheeks unnaturally flushed. As soon as she saw him, Lily began babbling about whooping cough and how the baby had to be kept away from her because otherwise the child might catch it, and she kept pressing her palm to her head, saying that her head hurt her terribly. When Esheal felt her forehead, it was burning, and he sent the nurse for Dr. Linde. "It looks like blood poisoning," Dr. Linde said. "What's going to happen?" Esheal asked. "I don't know," he said. "Will she pull through?" Esheal asked. "I don't know," the doctor said, turning his words over carefully; "the chances are better that she won't. She has a temperature of a hundred and four. If it doesn't come down, it could affect her brain."

"The chances are better that she won't?" Esheal said. "Much better," said the doctor; "I think we ought to send the child to the Romanoffs'. This isn't going to be a good atmosphere for her." "She's too small to know what's going on," Esheal protested; he felt as if the doctor were trying to take everyone away from him at once. One minute he had a family. Now he had nothing. He thought of the poisoned Bailey child and started to cry. "Come on, Esheal," said the doctor, slapping him on the shoulder; "it's only until Lily gets better. There are always miracles." "Miracles," said Esheal, "are for someone else. Not for me." "You have to wait and see," said the doctor; "go down and fill this prescription for sulfur." "Didn't Mrs. Kaminsky get a prescription for this last week?" he asked. "She did," said the doctor. "She's still alive," said Esheal. "It wasn't such a bad case," said the doctor; "we just have to wait and see. I don't want to give you false hope."

"What should I tell the Romanoffs," Esheal asked him. "Don't tell them anything until we see how things are in the morning," he said. "The morning's here," said Esheal. "Until we see how things are in the afternoon," the doctor said wearily. As Esheal looked at the prescription, he realized that, by the next afternoon, Lily might not be there for him to worry about. He went down to the store, made up the pills, gave them to the nurse, told Dr. Linde he had some work to do in the pharmacy that would keep his mind off things, and went downstairs, sat down behind his workbench, and cried like a lost child. He fell asleep with his head on the counter, and the clerk found him there when he came in to open the store.

The vigil which began the next day resembled nothing so much as a funeral. It was impossible to look at Lily and believe that she was alive or that she was going to live. Her temperature had dropped early in the morning, but she had lapsed into unconsciousness and lay motionless on her back. Every now and then, one of her hands would twitch, and everyone in the room would bend forward, but Lily did not move again. Esheal, who usually sat near the head of the bed, felt as if he had been turned to something cold and hard, something inhuman. If, he thought, we lit a candle and put it in back of her body, the picture would be complete. Occasionally, one of the women left and another took her place. The newcomer would take one look at Lily, sit down, and begin crying quietly. When Dr. Linde came in everyone looked expectantly at him, but when he said nothing, or only shook his head, the women would shake theirs and begin crying again.

"Why won't she wake up?" Sarah asked Esheal again and again. "She's going to die. Call another doctor." But Dr. Linde had already called in three specialists, and the four doctors met in Esheal's living room. After they conferred, they told Esheal that it was a good thing Lily's fever had come down, and she had probably gone into a coma because she had lost so much blood, but that all they could do now was wait. When Esheal let them out, he turned around to see Sarah sitting on the living room chair, crying uncontrollably, and Meyer awkwardly patting his wife on the head.

At last, Dr. Linde looked around him and said that he didn't like it. He had attended coma cases before, and when they woke up, they often swore that they had heard everything that had gone on around them. If Lily could hear them, he said, they were scaring her to death. He told Esheal to bring the baby into her room and describe her to Lily as if she were wide awake and he told everyone else to talk to Lily as if there were nothing wrong. At first, Sarah found this impossible, but when she realized that she would be barred from the sickroom if she could not control herself, she began telling the unconscious Lily tales of other people's children, and, the longer she talked, the more she concentrated on how bright other people's children were, and how long they were outside in the fresh air when their mothers took them for walks, and how much each child resembled his mother. It seemed to Dr. Linde as if this was having an effect and that Lily's hand moved more and more often on the coverlet.

Esheal brought the baby in and talked to her. He had been adamant about keeping the baby at home, and after Dr. Linde saw him with the child, he withdrew his objections to keeping the infant in the Luria house. Days passed, and then a week, and the second week began. Esheal was giving the baby her bottle, and like everyone else who came into the room, he had gotten into the habit of speaking out loud, and now he was speaking aloud to the baby. "You can't go on much longer without a name," he said to the child; "can you?" "No, she can't," said Sarah. "I think," said Esheal, "I'm going to name her Edna." "Don't name her Edna," said Lily. "Why not?" said Esheal; "she has to be named after somebody." "Lily said that!" Sarah said, pushing herself up out of her chair. "Lily?" Esheal asked; "Lily said something?"

The two of them bent over the figure on the bed. Lily's eyes were wide open, and for an instant, Esheal thought that nothing had happened, that now she would lie there for days on end staring at the ceiling without so much as blinking. "Well, don't you think you should ask me before you go and name my daughter?" asked Lily. A loud sob burst from Sarah and she sank down on the chair next to the bed. "Momma!" said Lily; "stop crying. Everything's fine. We'll find a name you like." Sarah, stunned, stared wildly at her daughter. "Let me hold her," Lily said, reaching up. "No, no," said Esheal hastily; "you're too weak. I'll hold her and you look at her." "She's a beautiful baby," Lily said; "I knew she'd be a beautiful baby. Look at those big blue eyes! I guess they'll change color." "I don't think so," Esheal said; "you have blue eyes and I have blue eyes." "Their eyes always change color," said Lily, but Esheal was in no mood to argue. "Why are you giving her a bottle?" Lily asked; "I want to nurse her." "Well, Lily," said her husband, "you couldn't nurse her. You've been in a coma for eight days. We couldn't let the baby go for eight days without eating." "Stop your kidding," said Lily; "a coma! Eight days! This is nothing to joke about. Momma! Why are you letting him give her a bottle?" "He told you," said Sarah; "you've been in a coma a long time."

"What day is it?" Lily asked suspiciously. "Sunday," said Esheal. "Saturday," said Lily, "is when I had the baby. So this is the next day." "No, it isn't," Esheal said; "it's the next week." "I want to talk to Dr. Linde," said his wife, and clamped her lips shut. She was not about to talk to either of them until they told her the truth. "What do we do now?" Esheal asked Sarah. "What can we do?" Sarah said; "send someone for the doctor. Oh, is she stubborn, God bless her." "Lily, what do you want to name her?" asked Esheal, but his wife would not answer him. He wanted to kill her. After eight days of waiting for her to say a word, she came to and refused to speak. In that case, he thought, she could lie there, silent.

Dr. Linde came in and told Lily that she had been seriously ill, and for eight days she had lain in her bed without moving or speaking, and that now she would get better quickly, but she would be weak for some time. "I had the strangest dreams," Lily told him; "I dreamt that everyone was crying, and that I was dead, but no one seemed to know it, and everyone said they had to do something, but no one did." "It wasn't a dream," said the doctor, "and we did everything we could do." "I heard someone saying that I wasn't going to live," she said. "That's right," he said; "that's what we all thought."

And Lily began to complain. She did not like a strange woman taking care of her own child; she would rather have her mother and sister take the baby, but her mother, Esheal told her, was not strong enough, and she knew her sister had taken a job in her husband's absence. The nurse, Lily said, did not keep the child outside long enough and neither did Esheal. She needed more fresh air. When the child was on her way out, Lily would insist on inspecting her, and either she had too little clothing or too much. When the baby woke up at night, and Lily walked slowly into the back room, she could not hold the baby for very long, and what was more,

the baby did not seem to like her. She fussed when Lily held
her, and then, if she did not return her to the nurse, she began
crying. Lily was bored and tired of lying in bed, and she did
not like the books anyone brought her. If people came with
cake and cookies, she said that they ought not do it, because if
she ate, she would gain weight. But if they brought nothing,
she wanted to know what was wrong with them, how did they
expect her to entertain them and serve them when she was
flat on her back?

It surprised them all that she did not worry about herself,
but Esheal soon realized that she had focused all her fears on
the infant, who was, fortunately, a strong and healthy baby.
She seemed to grow every day, and everyone who came in
and saw her lying on her back trying to reach the toy which
dangled over her from the roof of the cradle said what a
bright little thing she was. Over everyone's protests, they
named the baby Lucia. Lily wanted a romantic name for the
child, and Lucia was what Esheal thought of, and to his
amazement, Lily liked it.

But, she said, they couldn't call a child Lucia, at least not
when she was so small. Lucy, she said, would be a nice
nickname for her. So they settled on that name. "And if we
have another girl," said Lily, "let's name it Fay." "Why
Fay?" asked Esheal. "It's the name of a princess in a book I
had," she said, and of course Esheal agreed that if they had
another girl, they would call it Fay, because he never dreamed
that they would have another child. He thought that after
Lily's experience producing this child, he and his wife would
want to spend the rest of their lives living as brother and
sister. But he had underestimated his wife's desire to have
children. Every time she went to the park and saw mothers
with two, three, or four children, she looked around her
house as if something were missing.

Before he knew it, Esheal and his wife were arguing over
the sheet, and it would have seemed as if nothing had
changed had it not been for Lily's fear that the child would
hear them, and somehow, even at its age, know what was
going on. But if Esheal suggested closing their door, Lily
feared not hearing the child, and he was constantly hopping in
and out of bed, closing the door, opening it, until one night he
slammed the door, shouted, "Goddam the door!" and insisted on proceeding without regard to the child's well-being.
The next day, he sawed a hole between their room and the

child's, and fitted it out with a little door, so that, even when they were asleep, they could hear the child. But he insisted on closing the door to the room when he and his wife made love. The baby had a set of lungs made of cast iron, and you could hear her out on the street when she started in. When Lily asked him to put a chain lock on the child's door because she didn't want the child getting out when no one was looking, he put on the lock and said nothing about how unlikely it was that a six-month-old child would break out of her crib and room and somehow make her way out to the street. Women with children, he decided, were completely irrational.

Although Esheal adored his daughter, and spent every minute he did not have to be in the store with her, he seemed to feel lonelier from the minute she arrived. Of course, Lily had the same complaint. She said that he came up to eat and see the baby and would not notice whether or not she was there unless either the meal or the baby was missing. Lily began taking Lucy over to her mother's house for daily visits, and then the trouble began.

Chapter 37

The Romanoffs adored Lucy, and afterward Lucy would say that to them she was a little tin god because she was the first grandchild. On Fridays, when Sarah baked, she baked a special little challa for Lucy, and once, when Dave took a bite out of it, Sarah got her ruler and slapped him across the hand, old as he was. On Fridays, Sarah always made her noodles, and she would roll out the noodle dough until it covered the huge oval table, and then she would slice the noodles into wide and narrow strips, and from the beginning, those noodles were a terrible temptation to Lucy, who would hide under the table until everyone was out of the room and then begin cracking them into splinters. And when Lily saw what her daughter was up to, she would chase the child through the rooms trying to catch her and give her the good spanking she deserved. But by the time Lucy was nine months old, she knew that her grandmother was her greatest protector, and, when she saw Lily coming after her, she would head straight for Sarah. By the time Lucy was one and could talk, she would run through the halls of her grandmother's house screaming, "Help! Help! Save me!" and Sarah would fold the child in her voluminous skirts and refuse to let Lily touch her.

But when all the Lurias came to visit, life was not always so pleasant. As soon as Esheal and Lily came in, Lucy was taken from them to be shown off. She was shown off for her tiny ears, for her big blue eyes, for the way she giggled when they tickled her, for the funny things she said. When the Romanoffs knew the Lurias were coming, they left the round light in the center of the living room off, and before Lily could remove Lucy's coat, they would plug the light in, point at it, and ask Lucy what it was and the child would always say it was Grandma's moon. Esheal tried to correct the child, telling her that it was not a moon; it was a lamp. He did not

see, he said, what point there was in teaching a child all the
wrong things when she would just have to learn them over
again, but they either paid no attention to him or brushed his
objections aside, saying that she would learn what the moon
was and that it lived in the sky, not the living room, soon
enough.

They constantly debated about where the child got her
looks. They admitted that Lucy got her eyes from her father,
because, although Lily's eyes were also blue, they were not as
big as Esheal's or the child's. But all the rest of her, they
insisted, was Romanoff. She was a Romanoff through and
through, except, perhaps for her nose, which they thought
was a bit long. "You don't think that nose will get any
longer?" Diana said every time she saw the child; "if it gets
any longer, it's going to cast a shadow on her chin. She gets
her nose from the Lurias," Diana would say, oblivious of the
effect she was producing on Esheal, who knew that they
thought his nose was too long, and that there could be no
worse fate awaiting a girl than to take after a father who
looked like him. And Lily never spoke up for him; in fact, she
seemed to be unaware of what was going on.

One day, when Lucy was almost two, Esheal asked Lily to
tell the Romanoffs what had happened when she took the
baby out walking that week, and Lily said, oh, that was a
funny story. She had been out walking with Lucy, and it was
wet out, so she put her in the carriage, and tied her in with
rope, because otherwise the child would fling herself out, and
when she was walking along, a woman she had seen before
stopped her and said that the child looked familiar, and she
kept on staring at the child, and she said, you know, it's the
most amazing thing, but that child looks exactly like the
pharmacist on the corner, and she had said, that's a good
thing, because the pharmacist on the corner is her father.
And the woman said, oh, you don't say, and she looked at the
baby once again and at Lily once again, and walked off,
shaking her head. Lily said she thought the woman looked
disappointed; she probably thought she'd gotten her hands on
something. Everyone who heard that story thought it was
funny, but the Romanoffs did not. "Well, couldn't the woman
see she looks like Lily?" asked Diana, and Dave said the
woman needed a pair of glasses, maybe two pair.

Soon relations between Esheal and his wife's family were
strained. He no longer arrived with Lily when she visited her

family on Sunday, but instead came toward supper time, bringing several quarts of ice cream with him from the pharmacy. When the others asked him where he had been, he said he had been over at his sisters'; there was always something going wrong in the house, and by the time he was finished fixing things, it was time for lunch. Whenever Esheal mentioned his sisters, Lily's lips would tighten; she did not like their dependence on him, nor did she like the amount of money he contributed to their support.

Now, when Esheal arrived, he was just in time for the entertainment, which consisted of the family singing along with the Victrola, Diana's imitations of everyone they knew, and the boys' comic routines. And when he tried to sing along, they would say, "Oh, Esheal, don't sing. Let someone who can carry a tune do it." He did not like Diana's imitations; they were so deadly and so cruel, and he knew that when he was not there, she imitated him. And when he did not laugh as the others did, someone was sure to say, "Oh, well, Esheal doesn't think that's funny; he's too serious." So he knew they thought of him as a humorless prig.

And he could not help noticing how happy Lily was with her brothers, who made so much of her, and flirted with her as if she were their sweetheart and not their sister, and how their friends all followed the boys' example. And because business had never been better, he had less and less time free during the day. Naturally, he did not want to lock his wife up in the house, but when he thought about her at her parents' house, surrounded by her brothers and her friends, he was worried about what she must think, and he was sure she compared him with her brothers and their friends, and that she compared him with them unfavorably. Then, one Sunday, he saw Lily conferring with one of the boys' friends in a corner, and they seemed to be discussing something important to both of them.

When they got home, he wanted to know who Lily had been talking to, and Lily asked him who he meant, and that convinced him that Lily had something to hide. He brought it up again an hour later. "You were talking to someone in the corner," he said; "he was wearing a blue suit." "Everyone was wearing a blue suit," said his wife; "you were wearing a blue suit." "You were talking to him in the corner near the window," said Esheal; "the corner with the little table and the lamp on it." "So I was talking to someone," Lily said impatiently; "so I don't remember who it was. What difference does it make?" "It seemed to be something important," Esheal said; "you were talking for a long time." Lily looked at him as if he had taken leave of his senses. "Do you mean Ike?" she asked; "a tall man with a mustache?" Esheal said that sounded like him. "He was talking to me about some girl he met. He doesn't know whether or not he wants to get married." "What's stopping him?" asked Esheal.

Lily, who was gratified to find her husband interested in one of her friends, said that he was worried about how he could marry and still support his mother and father, and it was a terrible problem because the girl wasn't going to wait around forever. "So what's he doing now?" asked Esheal; "looking for someone else to take her place in case she doesn't wait?" "What are you talking about?" asked Lily. "He seemed to like you well enough," said Esheal. "He should," said his wife; "we've been friends since I was a child." "Why didn't you marry him?" asked Esheal. "Marry him?" Lily asked astonished; "why should I marry him? We were friends. He always had a girl. I was just a kid." "You're not a kid now," said Esheal. "Now I'm married," Lily said comfortably. "You better make sure he knows that," he said.

In the beginning, Lily was flattered by his jealousy. Then she ceased to notice it. It became a nuisance to answer so many questions about whom she had talked to and what she had talked about, and what she had found to do at her mother's house for so many hours, but Lily answered all the questions as if doing so were one of her tasks. And if it seemed to her that this particular task never came to an end, that made it all the more unremarkable. Her dishwashing and her sweeping never came to an end either.

When Lucy was slightly over two years old, Lily found herself pregnant again. But this time the Romanoffs were not much in evidence at the Luria house. Dr. Linde had ordered Lily to exercise, and every day she would dress the child and go over to her mother's, where she usually fell asleep in a chair. Sarah would wake her up in time to go home and make her husband's dinner. If she did not go to her mother's, she stayed at home and slept. One afternoon, Esheal came upstairs and found his wife standing in front of the stove, a pot boiling over. "Turn down the fire, Lily," he said, but his wife did not answer him, and, when he walked over to her, he realized that she had fallen asleep standing up.

He took Lily by the arm and led her over to an armchair and settled her in it, and when he went into the dining room, there was Lucy, sitting on the floor next to the silver chest which she had pulled down from the sideboard. She had opened the window, and after she looked at each knife, or fork, or spoon, she would drop it out. "Look, Daddy!" she said, holding up a fork, and she threw it out the window. "All gone!" she said, holding up her hands. "Come over here!" said Esheal, and he picked up Lucy, and stared from the floor littered with the remains of what used to be their service for eight, to his wife, Lily, who was sleeping, dead to the world in the dining room chair. "You come down with me," he told the child. "Lily," he said, "I'm taking her down with me," but Lily did not hear him. She was sound asleep. That afternoon, Esheal hired a housekeeper after he talked to Dr. Linde. Lily, the doctor told him, was pregnant again. The housekeeper was to stay until after Lily had the baby.

And of course, Dr. Linde said there was nothing to worry about, and that some women literally slept through the nine months of their pregnancies. "But she's a zombie!" Esheal said; "I took her for a walk yesterday and she fell asleep on her feet." "It's normal," said Dr. Linde. "Normal? To fall asleep while she's walking? If she hadn't started walking slower and slower, I wouldn't have noticed. She could have been killed." "Now you know about it," said the doctor; "there's nothing to worry about. Sit back and enjoy it; you may like it. How often does a woman keep quiet?" "Go over and tell the Romanoffs I'm not poisoning their daughter," Esheal said. "They'll come over to see for themselves," said the doctor. "You think they'll just come over?" asked Esheal; "they'll move in." "Once they see there's no one to talk to and nothing to worry about, they'll go home," said the doctor. "Sarah will want to stay here and cook," Esheal said. "Tell her the housekeeper's cooking; tell her that if she's here, Lily will worry about her and won't be able to sleep." "That's going to persuade her to stay home?" asked Esheal; "even a blind person can see Lily's getting too much sleep. It's like living with Sleeping Beauty."

"Sleeping Beauty wasn't so bad," said the doctor. "No one tried to live with her before she woke up," said Esheal. "Look," said Dr. Linde; "you want to get rid of the Romanoffs? Send Lucy over there. You don't see her much during the day anyway. By the time they bring her home at night, they'll be too exhausted to visit." "I don't want her over there every day," said Esheal. "What harm could it do?" asked the doctor; "they'd never let any harm come to a child. All they can do is stuff her to death." "That's not all they can do," said Esheal, who knew that if Lucy went over to his in-laws, he would soon be hearing about his long nose, his terrible singing voice, how short he was, from his own daughter. But, he thought, it was a small price to pay for having his wife and his house to himself.

The Lurias' second child was born easily, and arrived a few minutes after the doctor. Lily demanded the child right away and lay back against the pillows with her, receiving visitors like a newly crowned queen. She was absorbed in everything the child did, and it was almost impossible to take the child from her. She was nursing the baby, and she was sure the child had not yet finished, but had only dropped off for a second and would soon wake up and want more to eat. Esheal's relief was immense, and for some time, nothing disturbed him.

But six weeks after the child was born, he came upstairs and heard shouting coming from Lily's bedroom. Lily was nursing the baby, Fay, who was, as usual, gazing up adoringly at her mother out of her huge, brown eyes, while Lucy was standing at the foot of the bed, her chin raised to the heavens, screaming as if someone were twisting her arm. "You're going right now!" Lily screamed; "now! I don't want to hear any more about it. You're going!" "I'm not," sobbed Lucy; "I won't! Try and make me!" "Mrs. O'Connoll will make you," said Lily, "and if you don't quiet down, I'll tell her to give you a beating with your father's strap!" Lucy threw herself down on the floor and was trying to squirm under her mother's bed when Esheal walked into the room.

"What's going on here?" he asked his wife. "The brat!" exclaimed Lily; "will you look at her hair! No one can get a comb through it. I don't have time to comb her hair and take care of the baby! She's got to have it cut!" "Cut?" asked Esheal; "you're going to cut her hair?" "And above her ears!" Lily screamed to the child under the bed; "I'm not spending seventy cents for nothing." "I don't want her hair cut," said Esheal. "You don't want her hair cut?" shrieked Lily, beside herself; "*you* don't want it cut? Who's the child's mother? I'm her mother! I'll decide when she gets her hair cut!" "I don't want it cut," Esheal said again; "I'll comb her hair." "She gets it cut today," insisted Lily, at which her mattress suddenly began bouncing up and down beneath her. "Come out of there, Lucy," said her mother; "it will be worse for you if I have to come and get you." "You can't get me," said the voice from under the bed; "I put my arms and legs through the slats."

"Come out," said her father; "nobody's going to cut your hair." Lucy began sliding out on her back. "Do you promise?" she asked her father. He nodded. "Swear to God?" "Get out from under that bed!" shrieked Lily; "you'll listen to me the first time! What are you trying to do?" she asked Esheal; "you'll spoil her rotten." "Lucy," said Esheal, "get out from under that bed. Go out and play. It's a nice day." Lucy flew out of the room and they heard her clattering down the stairs. "Esheal," said Lily, "I want you to leave that store and take that child to get her hair cut."

Esheal pulled a chair up to Lily's bed and looked at her and the new baby. "I want her hair cut today," Lily said, glaring at him. "She is not getting her hair cut," Esheal said. Lily stared at him as if he had lost his mind. The children were her domain; she made the decisions. He never interfered. "And what business is it of yours?" she asked. "She's my daughter." "We all know she's your daughter," said Lily, "but I'm her mother. I decide when she gets her hair cut." "Not this time," said her husband.

When Lily was truly outraged, she stared in front of her and refused to speak; she did that now. "Look, Lily," said Esheal, "before you had that baby, you had plenty of time to comb Lucy's hair." "What do you want me to do with the baby?" asked Lily; "give it back?" "No, I don't want you to give it back," said Esheal; "but you can't just forget about the other child. She was here first." "I know she was here first," said Lily; "what do you think I am, an idiot?" "You're behaving as if she's not here," said Esheal. "She is impossible since this baby was born," Lily burst out; "this morning, do you know what she did? She took the doll Dr. Linde gave her and threw it out the window!" "The porcelain doll?" asked Esheal. "That's right, the porcelain doll. It's smashed to pieces. It cost a fortune! I told her she wasn't getting any more dolls and she said she didn't want any more and she was going to throw the rest of them out of the window when I wasn't looking." Esheal sighed. "Why does she have to get her hair cut?" he asked. "I told you," said Lily; "I don't have time to bother combing it. She screams like a wild Indian when I try to take a tangle out. I can't comb her hair when I'm feeding the baby, and when she starts to cry, she wakes the baby up. I'm no magician; I can't do everything at once." "I'll comb her hair," said Esheal; "Lily, I don't want that child's hair cut." "All right," said Lily; "when she doesn't listen to you, when she runs wild, don't blame me." "Don't touch that child's hair," said Esheal.

Every day after that, Esheal would call Lily up and ask her to send Lucy down to get her hair combed. The child looked forward to this so that Lily would threaten her with no hair combing if she did not finish what was on her plate, and when she did, Lucy would say, "I'll tell Daddy what you said." But she was so afraid that Lily would not let her go down and get her hair combed that she ate whatever was in front of her and said nothing to her father. She sat on the high stool in front of the workbench, and, for the time she was there, Esheal did everything but close the store. If anything important came up, the clerk took care of it. Lucy's hair combing was interrupted only for emergencies.

The child had thick, tight black ringlets and Esheal would comb them gently, separating the larger tangles with his fingers, then prying them apart with a long-handled instrument. If a tangle would not yield to this treatment, he would wet the hair, put a drop of baby oil on it, and comb it out slowly, holding to the roots of the hair with one hand so that Lucy would not feel it when he pulled it. Lucy, young as she was, knew how her father hated to hurt her, and when she got up in the morning, she took a comb she had stolen from her mother's dressing table, and before she heard her mother coming, began combing out the worst tangles herself. She was unmerciful. She would yank out hunks of hair so that her father would not have to suffer through the process later. But no matter how well she combed her hair in the morning, by lunchtime it would be full of tangles, and when Lily saw her, she would say, "You have to get your hair cut. You can't walk around looking like you slept in a haystack." This would frighten the child, who would say that her father said that she didn't have to have her hair cut, and she was not going to cut it, and to this, Lily would always say the same thing: "We'll see about that."

When Fay was over a year old, her blond hair was still thin and no matter how Lily combed it, her pink scalp showed through. She did not talk and she showed no signs of wanting to walk. And her sister lorded it over her, telling her that she was only a baby while she, Lucy, was three, and that she had thick hair, while Fay was bald as an eagle, and when Lily heard her, she would catch her and whack her across the bottom with her wooden hairbrush. Diana, who had just gotten pregnant, stopped working and frequently came over to "borrow" the baby, saying that taking care of Fay for a while would give her the practice she needed. Usually, Diana and her mother came together, and Diana would leave for the playground with Fay, leaving Sarah and Lily alone with Lucy.

"Let's take her out to the park," Sarah said one afternoon; "it's a beautiful day. It's a shame to coop her up inside." "She can't go out looking like this," said Lily; "look at her hair." "So comb it," said Sarah; "why don't you braid it?" "If I braid it," said Lily, "I can't get the braid out, and she gets the rubber band stuck in that jungle there, and she screams bloody murder when I try to get it out. Nothing does any good." "I'll comb it," said Sarah. "No, I'll do it," said Lily, but when she began combing Lucy's hair, the child began screaming and clutching her head, saying she wanted her father to do it. "Well, your father's not here today," Lily said; "he had to go and see his sister. Someone's sick." "Don't pull so hard," said Sarah. "If I don't pull, the comb won't go through," said Lily; "she breaks all the teeth in the comb. Look." And Lily held up the frame of a comb with one large tooth remaining at each end.

Sarah watched the performance of the wriggling, screaming child, and saw her daughter's temper rising until it made her red in the face. "Why don't you just cut it?" Sarah said. "No," screamed Lucy; "don't cut it!" "Do you think I should?" Lily asked. "Why not?" said Sarah; "if it causes so much trouble. I think you should cut it." "Let's go," Lily ordered the child. Lucy tried to run away, but Lily's fingers dug into her arm. "Let's *go,*" she hissed at the child; "afterward, I'll get you a charlotte russe and you can go play in the park." Lucy began screaming at the top of her lungs, and when she began to scream, "Help, police!" Lily smacked her face. "To call the police on her own mother!" Lily said indignantly. "Lily," said Sarah, "if it's so important to her, let it go." "She's not getting her own way all the time," said Lily; "let's go. It's only across the street."

They crossed the street and went into the little barbershop, and Lily held Lucy's shoulders while the barber cut her hair, but Lucy kept squirming, and more than once, Sarah exclaimed, "Be careful, you'll kill her!" "Above the ears," commanded Lily. Lucy began screaming, "No, no, Daddy," and "police," but the barber was used to these scenes and finished cutting her hair. "Should I thin it?" he asked Lily; "it makes it much easier to comb." "Thin it," said Lily.

When it was over, they could not stop the child from crying. When they sat in the playground, she sat on the end of the bench, as far away from them as she could get, with her hands over her eyes as if she were afraid that she might accidentally catch a glimpse of herself with her short hair. Her hands and her face were glistening with tears, and her shoulders shook. "If it was so important to her," Sarah said, looking reproachfully at her daughter. "You have to win, Mother," said Lily; "they have to know who's boss."

After a while, Sarah moved down the bench toward the child and whispered to Lucy that her hair would grow back, but for the first time in her life, Lucy wanted nothing to do with her grandmother. She turned so that her back was to them and went on crying. Lily looked at her mother and could see that she disapproved. "Esheal won't be too happy about this, either," she said; "he hates to see the child cry. At least he won't get home before she goes to bed. There'll be time enough for him to see her in the morning."

But Esheal was home when Lily got back. He was standing at the door when they walked in, and he started to ask Lily what Lucy was crying about, when he caught sight of the child. "Go into the bedroom," he told his wife. "What do you mean, go into the bedroom?" she said; "I have to make supper." "I'll make supper," he said. "She hasn't eaten," said Lily. "I'll give her something to eat; go into the bedroom," he said. Something in his manner frightened Lily, and she went into the bedroom and shut the door behind her. She could hear Esheal talking to Lucy, but even when she opened the small door Esheal had cut between their walls, she could not hear what he was saying, his voice was so low. Through it all, Lucy was crying steadily and softly. Finally, the child stopped. Lily sat on the bed watching the window darken, flare with roses which died into purple waves, and darken again. The streetlights streamed into the darkness. What was Esheal doing? She could not hear him in the kitchen, although his dinner hour was long over. Then she heard the creak of bedsprings, and footsteps, and the door opened.

"Why did you cut her hair?" Esheal asked. He stood in the doorway but did not come in. "Because I wanted to take her out and it was too much trouble to comb it," Lily said. "I told you not to cut her hair," said Esheal; "how many times do I have to tell you something?" "Well, my mother thought I should get it cut," said his wife. "Do you mean to say you cut our daughter's hair because your mother told you to?" asked Esheal. "Yes," said Lily; "she knows what's right about things like this." "Lucy is not her daughter," said Esheal. "She's her granddaughter," said Lily; "I'm her mother. It's a mother's business to decide these things." Esheal looked at her, and then went to the window and looked out. Men were coming home from work and were slowly climbing the steep flights of steps up to their front doors. Everywhere, windows were lighting.

"Lily," he said, "I told you not to cut it. I think it's time you went on a vacation. I want you to go to Lakehurst for a week. You can take Fay with you. Lucy will stay here with me." "What do I need a vacation for?" asked his wife; "I'm happy where I am." "You're going to Lakehurst," said Esheal; "I want you to think things over." "What things?" said Lily. "I want you to think about who you're married to, me or your mother." "I know who I'm married to!" said Lily. "Then think about a wife's duties to her husband." "I don't know what you're talking about," said Lily. Esheal looked at her and thought it was about time that she realized she depended on him and not on the rest of her family. "Your mother can go with you if she can afford it," Esheal said. "If she can afford it," exclaimed Lily; "you know she can't afford it!" "Then she can't go," said her husband; "I'm sorry." "I'm not going to Lakehurst," said Lily. "Then I'll move out," said Esheal. Lily stared at him in disbelief. All this over having a child's hair cut! The man was crazy.

"Go talk it over with your mother," Esheal said coldly; "ask her whether she thinks you should go to Lakehurst or whether I should move out." "You wouldn't move out!" said Lily. "I'll be gone by morning," he said. "Where would you go?" she asked. "To my sisters', where else?" "Well," said Lily, "I don't see what you're so high and mighty about; you're always visiting your sisters." "They don't tell me what to do," said Esheal. "So why don't you ask your sisters if you should move out?" Lily asked; "they'd tell you to stay home and that it was my business to have my own child's hair cut."

"I don't care what my sisters have to say," Esheal retorted; "I said not to cut it. If my mother's ghost came in here and told me to cut her hair, I wouldn't cut it. You wouldn't be so busy cutting hair if you had enough to do. I'm letting the cleaning lady go. If your mother wants a cleaning lady, let her pay for one. You stay home and clean your own house and let her clean hers." Lily started to argue, saying that before she and her sister had married, they promised to keep up their mother's house for her because she was not strong enough to do it, but Esheal would not listen. "No more," he said; "I'm sorry. You'll stay here and clean your own house. Are you going to Lakehurst?"

Lily wanted to say no, she wasn't, let him move out and see where that got him, but just yesterday, she had begun throwing up and she was sure she was pregnant again, and she already had two small children, a four-year-old and a one-year-old. She was in no position to let her husband walk out. "I'll go to Lakehurst," Lily said; "but it's not going to prove anything; it's not going to do any good." "It had better do some good," said Esheal.

Chapter 38

Esheal

When I sent Lily to the country to think things over, she went because she was afraid not to. I knew I could never make her understand why I was so angry. As far as she was concerned, she had done nothing more than cut our child's hair. When I saw Lucy with her hair chopped off like that, I wanted to hit Lily, but I was afraid that if I hit her, I would never stop. And if she had not been a woman, I probably would have hit her anyway. I have never hit a woman and cannot imagine doing it.

If we had still been living in Pobrosk, I would have known what to do with her. I would have grabbed her by the arm and dragged her out into the street, and yanked her this way and that, and I wouldn't have stopped until all the men and women in their black clothes appeared out of nowhere like so many black mushrooms. If there is anything a woman like my wife would have dreaded, it would have been a scene. She would have done anything to avoid another scene, and if we had been in Pobrosk, and if I had dragged her out into the street, I would have known what she was doing with her time; she would have been going from house to house, explaining to each and every woman in the town that what had happened had no real importance, that it was a little thing, someone had not paid me when I ought to have been paid, and she would not have rested until the town believed I was at fault. But what was I going to do with her here? If I had beaten her up, I would have been arrested, and after I got out of court, her brothers would have beaten me to a pulp.

There was nothing I could do to make Lily understand the utter treachery with which she had treated her daughter, the abysmal nature of the betrayal. Lily thought all she had done was cut some hair; I knew she had cut more than that. Before Fay was born, Lucy was my wife's whole life. The sun rose and set around the child's health; there was not one morning when Lily failed to drag out a bentwood chair, put the baby scale on it, put Lucy in it, and record the child's weight in a little book. I don't know how many photographs I have of Lily holding the child sitting in the scale, smiling as if she had just seen an angel coming toward her, absolutely beatified by the scale which confirmed her hopes. In most of the pictures, she was holding Lucy with one hand and pointing at the needle of the scale with the other. When Lucy caught her first cold, Lily refused to let her out of the house until the weather was warm, and then, when Lucy appeared on the street, she was wearing every sweater she possessed, my muffler, and my wife's fur hat. It was seventy degrees. That was what my wife called putting the child out in the fresh air.

When Fay came, she forgot about Lucy. We had a nurse, a nice Irishwoman, Mrs. O'Connoll, who had stayed with us the whole time Lily was pregnant, and Lily turned Lucy over to her. Lucy was a very bright child and she knew what was happening. She always had a bad habit of throwing things out of the window; I think she liked making people look up at her, because when they did look up, she didn't try to hide; she would want them to talk to her. She used to throw out pretty valuable things. She threw out Itzak's silver snuffbox, a candlestick, a silver picture frame. I don't remember her ever throwing out anything that broke. But we never lost anything she threw out, because whenever anyone was coming into the store and saw something lying on the sidewalk, he knew it was thrown out by the pharmacist's child and he brought it in to me.

Once Fay was born, Lucy began throwing out her dolls. She threw them out one after another. The first time I saw one lying on the sidewalk, I was heartbroken. I knew how much she loved those dolls. She couldn't go to sleep without lining them up on her pillow, and she always lined them up in the same way. She would leave just enough room on her pillow for her own head. Each of her dolls was named after someone in the family. There was a Lily doll, and an Esheal doll, and a Sarah doll and so on. God forbid one should be missing at bedtime; she would have stayed up all night. After I saw what was happening, I always bought two of any dolls she wanted, so that, if one broke, I could replace it without driving myself crazy. She called them the Doll Family.

I only found one of the dolls myself; the rest of them were brought in by people coming in off the street. Each and every one of them carried in the doll as if he were carrying in a corpse. Of course, almost everyone I knew had children, so they had some idea of what a broken doll meant. But when Lily saw the broken dolls, what did she think about? How much they cost. Then she said she was throwing out Lucy's doll carriage because she didn't use it anymore and there was no point in keeping it around to collect dust. Of course she didn't use it anymore; she didn't have any more dolls to put in it. I tried getting Lucy more dolls but she wouldn't touch them. She'd say, "Give them to Fay," and make a face.

And when she went to the country, I had time to think. People used to come in and say, "I talked to Lily, and she said her brother was going into the importing business." No one ever told me Dave was going into the importing business. No one ever told me Lily knew all these men she talked to. One of them came in and said he'd seen Lily a few days before, and when he left he said, "Give your wife a kiss for me." So I realized she hadn't been telling me everything, and when she came back I knew I was going to have to keep an eye on her. And I thought about all the times Lucy had come back and told me about the nice man who had given her some ice cream, or who pushed her on the swings, and all of those times I thought Lily was at her mother's house. And it occurred to me that perhaps she was at Sarah's, but what did that mean? Her brothers and all their friends were there also. I couldn't understand the way she treated me, the way she disregarded my wishes, the way she would drop everything and run over to her family's house if anyone so much as stubbed a toe. She wouldn't have made such a fuss over me unless someone shot me down in front of her.

I began to think that she showed so little interest in me because she was interested in someone else. Naturally, this disturbed me greatly. When I talked to Dr. Linde about it, he said I was out of my mind. Lily wasn't the type to run around. I said, Why not? She's a beautiful woman. She's a beautiful woman, he said, but she's a prude. Or a prig. Anyway, she's the prim and proper type. He said that type never ran around, and if they did, he couldn't imagine it himself. He said that I was letting my imagination run away with me. But I said I wouldn't be jealous if I didn't have a reason, and he said once jealousy got started, there didn't have to be a reason. I said I had plenty of reason to be jealous. He told me to calm down and take things slowly.

He said he didn't mean to say anything insulting about my wife, but she was no genius, and if I wanted her to understand something, I would have to first break it down so that she could understand it. I said I thought I had done that, and he said that he was sure I hadn't, because, like most people who are more intelligent than their mates, I had trouble believing that the other one was really as dense as she appeared to be. "Lily's not stupid," I said; "she has brains if she wants to use them." "When Lily was in school," he said, "she used to have to study until one or two o'clock in the morning, and even then, her grades were never as good as Diana's, even though Diana did no work at all. She couldn't bear to make mistakes. So if you scold her, and don't make her understand what you're driving at, she'll be angry. She'll go ahead and keep doing things her own way." I said all that had nothing to do with why she went to her family's house so often, and why she spent so much time with her brothers and their friends. He asked me what I expected Lily to do with her time; after all, I worked long hours and what was she supposed to do with herself? I said she could invite people to the house; there was no reason she couldn't entertain company at home, and he said that everyone was going over to Sarah's house. After all, she was the center of that maypole, and had been for years. Her husband's friends used to sneak out of the synagogue early and come home to talk to Sarah before her husband got there. He asked me if I ever heard the rumor that someone had fallen in love with Sarah not too long after she came over here, but because she couldn't imagine breaking up a family, the whole thing came to nothing.

I hadn't heard anything about it before, but I certainly thought about it now. I thought about all the times I had heard Sarah say what Meyer didn't know wouldn't hurt him, and how easily she had fallen in with my suggestion that she sketch men at home without letting her husband in on it. "He doesn't have to know," was always on the tip of all their tongues. And the more I thought about it, the less I liked it. Look at Diana and that engagement to Murray Zalman. As soon as she heard that Sidney was coming back, she broke it off. The others didn't say a word to her about it. God only knows what went on with Sarah and that other man. How charming could a woman be? There must have been some reason she was always surrounded by men. So if she wasn't up to anything, she was probably leading them on. And after

Lily had been gone for a week, I began to worry about what she was up to herself, and I decided to go up and check on her. But I wasn't going to tell her first. I'd go up and say I'd wanted to surprise her.

While she was gone, I thought about her second pregnancy, and the one time she had managed to wake up during it. It was the second time I got a summons. The same man who brought the first one brought this one. I said, "Take it away. I know this one isn't for me," and he said, "Do me a favor, I'm falling off my feet. Take it and let me go home." I took it, and sure enough, Mrs. Reilly was accusing me of having given her caffeine tablets instead of nitroglycerin capsules. This time I wasn't upset, because when I looked in the prescription file, I saw I had none for her, so I knew she had the wrong pharmacy and the wrong pharmacist.

But I went up and told Lily about it, and before I had time to tell her that the lady had the wrong man, she got hysterical and started crying, telling me that I had to be more careful, we had a baby and we were going to have another any minute, and what was she going to do if I was always being put in jail. Sarah was there and told her to keep quiet, but she was so terrified that nothing would shut her up. "You've got to watch what you're doing!" Lily shouted at me; "you can't just throw anything into a bottle! We're going to end up in the poorhouse!" The only thing she didn't say was that she was sorry she'd ever married me. I was so disgusted that I never told her the end of the story; as far as I was concerned, she could go on thinking that I was poisoning the whole world and that sooner or later the city would put me behind bars for life.

But Sarah came down to make things up, and no matter how fed up I was with her, I never could resist her. She said that Lily wasn't herself, and when I said that she seemed very much herself, Sarah said that no woman was herself when she was pregnant, especially if she'd been through a pregnancy like Lily's last. Everyone, she said, knew what a wonderful pharmacist I was, and Lily did too. It was just that she couldn't stand the idea of any trouble. Hadn't she started to cry the day before because the city cut down a branch from the elm tree in front of our house? I said she wasn't married to the tree and that she seemed to care more about the tree than she did about me. But by the time Sarah was finished working me over, I felt good and guilty, as if I had committed a sin by telling Lily about the summons in the first place.

While I was in the pharmacy that week, Sarah brought
Lucy back for lunch and dropped off a photograph of Diana
and Lily standing on the front porch of their house. When I
first looked at it, I thought I had never seen a picture of two
more beautiful women. But the more I looked at it, the less I
liked it. Diana was standing up straight, her elbow resting on
the porch railing, and she was grinning from ear to ear. Lily
was standing in back of her, one hand on her hip, her head
back, laughing into the camera. They were both wearing
white dresses; Diana's had little black bows, but Lily's was
trimmed with a black belt that called attention to that tiny
waist of hers, and Lily was wearing black gloves that emphasized the length of her long, thin hands. Lily laughing with her
head thrown back, Diana leering into the camera—if I didn't
know who they were and where they were, I would have
thought they were two whores giving the come-on to everyone on the street.

Chapter 39

In the pharmacy, the days passed so slowly they seemed to go by dragging their leaden weights. Esheal counted the hours between meals, because when he left the store, he would go up and eat with Lucy and then stay awhile and play with her. He missed Lily, although he told himself he ought not to, because he hardly ever saw her when she was home. Many times, he thought of telegraphing his wife and telling her to come home, but the sight of his child's short hair would change his mind.

After his wife had been gone a few days, it was too quiet in the apartment, and Esheal went to look for his daughter. She was standing on the closed lid of the toilet seat, trying to twist around so that she could see her back, and she was tugging at her hair and tilting her head back to make it seem longer. Esheal told the child her hair would grow back before she knew it, and then he went out and telegraphed Lily, telling her to plan on staying another two weeks.

When Lily got the telegram, she trembled all over. She had spent a great deal of time throwing up, and comforting herself with the effect she would produce when she, the exiled and badly treated wife, announced that she had been sent away by her evil husband in her condition. But she was not throwing up any longer, and she was beginning to suspect that nothing was going to soften her husband's attitude toward her. Certainly, nothing she could do would help.

And she began to worry about what would happen if the marriage broke up. No one she knew had a bad marriage, and if they did, no one she knew talked about it. No wife she knew lived separately from her husband. It would be a disgrace. And, having gotten this far in thinking about the unmentionable, she began to think about what it would be like to live with her mother and her own three children. Where would the money come from? Lily knew other mothers got jobs, but that she should deprive her children of her presence! And what could she do? She had once held a job working for Martinson's coffee, but she had long ago forgotten how to type and her spelling had never been very good, and now she remembered how everyone was always yelling at her, and how she always left the office crying.

It began to occur to her that her husband had the upper hand. Of course, like every other Jewish woman she knew, she had managed to put away several hundred dollars in a secret bank account, but how long could she live on that? Four months, maybe five. Whereas her husband would have plenty of money, and she thought about how she would have to ask him for everything, and while she did that now, he never asked questions; he always gave her more money than she asked for. But if they were not living in the same house, he might not give her anything. She might have to beg him for every penny.

Lily had plenty of time to think. Esheal had sent her to a huge farm which took in paying guests, but it was autumn and the leaves were beginning to turn, and with the first chill in the air the guests had begun to leave. After Labor Day, she and an old lady were the only women left rocking on the porch. Lily began talking to her. She reminded Lily of the women who used to wait for their husbands at Itzak's shul. "Well, I don't see how he's such a terrible husband, dearie," the old woman said; "does he hit you? does he beat you?" Lily said he didn't, but that was nothing to brag about.

"*My* husband," said the old woman, "used to beat me on the first of every month. And I used to say, 'So what did I do?' And he'd say, 'Now you won't do anything.' See this?" the old woman asked, pointing to a dark space between two teeth; "he knocked that out one day. It was the first of Adar. This knob on my knee? The first of Elul. On this body there's a whole calendar." "Why did you stay there?" asked Lily. "Why?" asked the old woman; "he was a good husband, my husband. A man has his faults. Unless it was the first of the month, he never laid a finger on me. I always knew what to expect. And he never picked up anything to take to me. He hit me with his hand. Not even his fist. What did I have to complain about? We weren't starving." "But to live with a man like that!" said Lily; "how could you look at him?"

"Look at him?" said the old woman; "I loved him. When he died, that's when I hit him. I gave it to him, right across the face, that he should go off and leave me there. The other women pulled me off, I shouldn't scratch his eyes out while they were sewing his shroud." "I can't see it," said Lily; "I can't see how he was a good husband." "Listen, dearie," said the old woman gruffly, "he stuck to *me*. He loved *me*. You love a man when he loves you. So what's the matter? Doesn't your husband love you?" "He says so," said Lily; "but I should believe him? He sent me up here alone because I cut my child's hair." "Out of a clear blue sky," asked the old lady, "he sends you up here because you cut a child's hair? That's not the whole story." Lily told her the rest of it.

"He should beat you," the old woman said at last; "a woman who disobeys her husband! He works all day and all night to feed you and the children, and you can't even listen about a child's hair? For this, my husband would have beaten me in the middle of the month!" "I can't see how it's so important," said Lily; "I can't see what's so important about some hair." "She can't see what's so important about some hair," the old woman mimicked; "if it's important to him, it's enough. If he says, 'Go set fire to the child,' then you have something to argue about. If he says, 'Don't pull her back in the window,' then you have something. But some hair! So what's the matter?" the old woman asked her; "you don't have any faults?"

"Of course I have faults," said Lily. "What are they?" asked the old lady. "Well, I don't know," Lily said; "I guess I'm too clean. And I don't have a lot of patience." "Some faults," said the old woman; "the man's living with a saint." "What *should* be the matter with me?" Lily asked.

"I knew what was the matter with me," said the old woman; "I loved to get his goat. Oh, he was afraid of curses. When he was out of the house and I was cooking, I stood there thinking them up. 'May your teeth grow up instead of down and come out of the top of your head like tombstones.' Who do you think he blamed when his tooth hurt? When his foot hurt, I said, 'May your toenails grow so long they stab your worst enemy in the heel, and when he turns around, he stabs you in the heart.' And as a mother, I wasn't so hot. If it was him or the children, I'd pick him. Some days he'd come home in the middle of the day and they'd be running around undressed. What was I doing? I was cooking his supper. I was afraid of losing him, you see. He said I couldn't lose him if I wanted to lose him; he'd set Nikita the peasant's dogs on me.

"But I feared it. So the house wasn't always the way it should be, and the children weren't always the way they ought to be, and I was cursed with jealousy that was like a fire in a stove. He was a tinker, and one day, he comes home and says he went to Mrs. Kazinsky's house, she had so many pots, and I said that was where you were all day, and when he said yes, that was where he was, I picked up a pot and swung it at him, and half of his face was scalded. For the rest of his life, it was angry like a baby's face. And then I find out Mr. Kazinsky was laying there in bed the whole time he was fixing pots."

Lily said that her husband was jealous; he was always asking her who she talked to, what they said, what she did; there was no end to it. "The poor man," said her companion, rocking faster. She looked at Fay, asleep in the little rocking cradle. "Doesn't anything wake that child up?" she asked. "She's a perfect baby," said Lily; "she's always sleeping. Good as gold." "A nebech," said the old woman; "give me a noisy child." "My other child is a noisy child," said Lily with a sigh.

"Your poor husband," said the old woman; "it's a torment to be married to a beautiful woman. It's a torment to be married to a handsome man. I know. Everyone says something. 'I know your husband, Mrs. Berchinsky. A wonderful man, a handsome man, a kind man.' To everyone but you, he's wonderful and kind. So you wonder what's going on. And every time he walks out on the street, someone stops him, and they laugh and talk. He can't get five feet down the street without stopping. And then you come out, and they say, 'Good morning, Mrs. Berchinsky,' or they don't say anything at all, and they look at you as if they're thinking, so what did she do to trap a man like that? Or your good friend, it's always a good friend, she drops in to cause some trouble on a clear day, and she says, 'You know Mrs. Cahan, the tailor's wife? She said your husband was such a sweet man, she never saw such a sweet man, before he married you.'

"What did I do to him? I told him he had to make a living. He didn't want to study. Without me, he'd be sleeping in the synagogue. But he was such a sweet man until I poured in the vinegar. So you wonder. And if you're smart, you don't give the jealous one too much to be jealous about. When I got older, I was better; he was old, too, so I relaxed a little, not too much, believe me. But before that, you should have seen it, the way he used to go down the street, as if he were afraid of the women; he'd go through such dances to stay away from them; he'd go through mud puddles. The poor man's feet were always wet; they were sore and cracked. See, other men could walk near the house where it was dry, but he couldn't. Your husband is a gorgeous man?" she asked Lily.

"No," said Lily; "he's no matinee idol. He's not bad looking; he's not gorgeous, that's all. And he's terrible short." "A short man and a jealous man," said the old woman; "a beautiful wife and a tall wife. You should walk in puddles. You give him cause to worry, he worries you. You should make him feel important." "How do I do that?" Lily asked; "he wanted children. I have one child after another. He wanted his own house, you can eat off the floor. How do I make him feel important?" "You didn't have a mother?" the old woman asked her. "Of course I had a mother," said Lily; "I still have a mother. She's a wonderful woman. Everyone loves her." "You should love your husband as much as you love your mother," the woman said. "Why do you say that?" Lily asked. "Just look at your face," said the old woman. "If your mother was so wonderful," she said, "you should know how to make a man feel important." "Tell me how," said Lily, but the old woman had settled back against her pillow and fallen asleep.

Chapter 40

Esheal was tying one of the huge white bows all the little girls wore and was about to pin it into Lucy's hair, when the door opened, and a gust of air heavy with the smelling leaves blew through the shop. Esheal stopped what he was doing and stood still as if he were listening to an old tune. "How would you like to go see Mommy in the country?" he asked Lucy, catching her up in his arms. Lucy started to run upstairs, and when Esheal asked her where she was going, she said she was going to get her coat. "In a few days, we'll go," said Esheal. "When?" Lucy asked; "when?" "Sunday," said her father. "Today!" Lucy insisted. "Out and play," said Esheal, tugging at the bow to make sure it was securely fastened.

Just then Dr. Linde came in leading a short man with a sewing machine strapped to his back. As the man came through the door, he seemed to change his mind, and tried to pull back, but Dr. Linde had a good grip on him and pulled him forward. Esheal watched their peculiar procession toward him with amusement; two steps forward and one step back. When they got to the counter, Dr. Linde took the hand of the strange man, held it down on the counter, and sighed with relief. He did not let go.

"Chasing customers again?" Esheal asked him. The man muttered something unintelligible. "Stay!" the doctor ordered the man loudly. "Why don't you let go of him?" asked Esheal. "Because he'll run out the door. He's sick," said the doctor. "He's smart enough to try running away from you," said Esheal.

The little man with the sewing machine on his back looked from one to the other, as if, by sheer effort of will, he would be able to decipher what they were saying. "How did you get hold of him?" asked Esheal. "He was sleeping in the basement apartment of my house," said the doctor; "one of the boarders. And when Mrs. Kamen found out he was sick, she called me, and I said he was very sick, so she threw him out. I came here to get him some medicine, but I don't know how to get him to take it. He doesn't speak Hungarian and I don't speak Yiddish anymore. See if you can talk to him."

"What's your name?" Esheal asked him in Yiddish. The man looked at him as if he were a dangerous animal. His mouth began moving rustily. "Berghoff," said the man. "Where are you from?" Esheal asked in Russian. "Oh," said the man, starting to laugh; "from Dubno. I came here to be a tailor. I was sitting in the park in Hester Street, and some man hired me, and I work for him every day from six in the morning until ten at night and I got sick, they're all sick there, and the landlady threw me out because this man said something." The little man turned and glared at Dr. Linde.

"What did he say?" asked the doctor. "He said the landlady threw him out because you told her to." "I did not!" expostulated the doctor; "tell him all I said was that he was sick and needed some medicine." Esheal turned to Mr. Berghoff, who was still glowering at the doctor, and told him that the doctor told the landlady he was sick and needed medicine, and that the landlady was the one who wanted to throw him out, and that the doctor had dragged him all the way over here so that he could get his prescription filled and get better and keep on going. "Nu?" said Mr. Berghoff, who looked at the doctor, and abruptly stuck out his hand. The doctor shook it.

Esheal told the men to sit down at the soda fountain and he gave them both a dish of ice cream. Mr. Berghoff devoured his, and Esheal gave him a second, then a third, then a fourth. "When did you last eat?" he asked in Russian. "Yesterday, maybe the day before," the man said.

"What's wrong with him?" Esheal asked Dr. Linde. "I don't know. Some kind of infection. I can't talk to him, so how do I know what his symptoms are." "Tell me what to ask and I'll ask him," said Esheal. "You know what to ask him," said the doctor. "He says he has a pain in his back," said Esheal. "Ask him if it bothers him to urinate," said the doctor. "He says of course it bothers him to go to the bathroom, it's so filthy." "Ask him if when he urinates there's any burning; ask if he uses the toilet more than usual." "He says yes to both," said Esheal. "What are we going to do with him?" asked the doctor.

"We?" asked Esheal. "We can't throw a man with a kidney

infection out on the street," said the doctor. "Again, sulfur," said Esheal, looking at the prescription; "you know, if there's anything I hate, it's the smell of sulfur. It reminds me of all those years at my aunt's when every egg in the world decided to rot under my bedroom window." Mr. Berghoff looked at him questioningly.

"All right," Esheal said to the doctor, "he can sit in the back of the store today, and I'll ask everyone who comes in if they know anybody who has a room." "I'll stop by later," said the doctor. "Don't forget," Esheal said. "You're sure it's a kidney infection? It's not catching?" "It's not catching," said the doctor.

Esheal took the little man into the back with him. "I'm making your pills," Esheal said; "they don't taste so good, they smell to high heaven, but they do the trick. Take the machine off your back. What do you think the floor is for?" Mr. Berghoff sighed and unstrapped the machine. "Heavy," he said in Russian. "What's your first name?" Esheal asked him. "Jacob. Everyone calls me Jake." "You have a family?" Esheal asked, putting a little gold weight on one side of his scale; the scales did not balance. He added some yellow powder to the other side. The two sides quivered and came to rest. "I used to operate the city scales in Dubno," said Jacob; "you want me to do it for you?" "Do you have a family?" Esheal asked again. "In Dubno," said Jacob; "maybe they're in England by now. I sent them money. My wife and my son and my daughter." Esheal looked at him; the man's eyes were beginning to close.

When Esheal looked over at Jake again, he was wide awake and sitting in front of the chessboard, moving the pieces about the board. He went over to watch. Jake had set the pieces up on both sides and was playing against himself. He was completely unaware of Esheal's presence. "You like to play chess?" Esheal asked. "I love it, but who has the time?" Jake asked. "You want to play a game?" asked Esheal. "Why not?" said Jake. When the game ended in checkmate, Esheal stared at his opponent, amazed. He had never played with anyone who gave him such a run for his money; even when he played with Dr. Linde, he won more easily.

"So why don't you live here for a while?" said Esheal; "I have a little room on the first floor. It's not much. It's really a storage closet, but I could put a bed in it. You wouldn't have to pay me." "I have to pay," said Jake. "Ten cents a week," said Esheal. The men shook hands on it. Lily was going to love this, thought Esheal; a man who didn't speak English, who still smelled of the ship, who reeked of snuff, who wasn't used to taking baths. He could hear her, going on about how he was lowering himself, a rich man (he always became a rich man in these arguments) shouldn't be seen with men like that. "Why did you come to this country?" Esheal asked him. "To make a lot of money," Jake said; "is there any other reason?" Oh, Lily was going to love this, Esheal thought, but when he saw Jake expertly moving the pieces about the board, he forgot about his wife. There were some things a woman had to put up with, and this was one of them.

"Do you want to play another game?" Esheal asked him; "maybe you want to go to sleep?" "I can go to sleep later," said Mr. Berghoff. "I never saw that opening before," Esheal said, as Mr. Berghoff began playing. "It's my own strategy," Jake said; "look at that world there. All black and white. Everything goes by rules. You know what to expect from everything. The smartest one wins. No earthquakes, no pogroms. A wonderful game." "There was a time," said Esheal, "when I thought the real world was like that." "You should live so long," said Jacob. Esheal studied the board and thought about the zenshina and her peasants and all the people who had come there asking for help and how, no matter how unlikely it seemed, she had been able to help them. While he lived with her, he felt like a very small part of a very large and very important game whose meaning he did not yet know. But whether he knew what it meant did not matter. The zenshina knew; that was what mattered. When he looked down at the chessboard between himself and Jacob, it became that world, the world of the zenshina. When they finished, again in checkmate, he put the pieces away and closed the board with regret. "Good night," he said to Jacob. "No night's a good night in America," said Jacob.

In the morning, after Esheal was sure Mrs. O'Connoll understood that, in his absence, she was to provide breakfasts and cold suppers for Mr. Berghoff, he took Lucy off to help him buy a car. He had wanted to buy a car for some time, and he had learned to drive using Dr. Linde's, and although he knew what he wanted, a gray Westcott, he had put off buying it; he had been too angry at Lily to give her something to be happy about. Now that he was going to see her, he thought he might as well appear in a car.

When the salesman saw him coming, he sighed. For two weeks, he had the gray Westcott ready to drive out of the garage but nothing happened. He cheered up when he saw the pharmacist coming with the child. Children have no patience with delays. If the man had a normal child, she would not take no for an answer, and the car would be out of the garage in no time. Before Esheal had a chance to say anything to her, Lucy began jumping up and down and pulling him over to the gray car. "Oh, get this one, Daddy!" she pleaded; "it matches!" "Matches what?" he asked. "Your coat!" said Lucy. "Do you really want it?" Esheal asked, and when she said she did, he went into the man's office with her, and carefully unfolded the bills, one after another, and placed them on the man's desk. Lucy watched, fascinated, while the man picked up the bills and solemnly repeated the process. "Can we have it now?" Lucy asked him. "Get in," Esheal said; "we're going home to get the suitcases."

It was cold when they started off, and Esheal had to stop continually and pull Lucy back into the car because she was perpetually dangling out of the window. He began to think that he would never get there. And the farther out of the city they drove, the more slowly Esheal drove. When the last traces of the city fell away and the road began to wind along cliffs and through trees, he would slow down to look at the cows, to smell the cut grass and the hay and each time he did this, Lucy would ask impatiently, Are we there yet? An hour before they reached the farm, the light turned green and gold; haystacks glowed against the horizon. The black and white cows shone against the grass like brilliant maps of unknown worlds; the apple trees were heavy with gold apples, and the birds were flying wildly into the orchards, pecking at the fruit. "Do you see those birds?" he asked Lucy; "do you see how silly they are, chasing each other? They're drunk." Lucy said a bird could not be drunk. "They can if they take a drink," said her father; "when the apples are there long enough, they turn into wine apples and when the birds eat them, they get drunk." "Wine apples," Lucy repeated. "Daddy!" she screamed. "Look at that tree full of balls."

Esheal's eyes followed the child's finger and when he saw what she saw, he stopped the car. On the horizon, a great, gnarled apple tree, its leaves gone, was laden down with golden balls, and the sun was behind the tree so that rays of light seemed to stream through each branch. A silence surrounded the tree; no bird flew the air near it. Esheal turned his head, expecting to see the horizon stretch out to the deep black forest, and just where the forest formed a right angle with the road leading to the swamp, the zenshina's house. "I used to sleep under a tree like that," he told Lucy; "when we were out in the fields watching the oxen. We slept under the tree all night." "You slept under a tree?" Lucy asked; "when you had your own bed to sleep in? Can I sleep under a tree tonight?" "No," said Esheal; "you cannot sleep under a tree. Let's go find your mother."

Lily was sitting on the porch. Fay had been staying awake longer and longer, and as soon as the child woke up, the old woman, Mrs. Berchinsky, closed her eyes and fell asleep. She had less and less to say to Lily, and Lily felt that the old woman did not really approve of her. She knew the story of the old woman's life, and now that the old lady had told her about it, she seemed to have nothing more to say. She sat on the porch, rocked, looked at Lily, and sighed. "This is the way to end a life?" the old woman asked her, opening her eyes. "Rocking on a porch? My grandchildren have children. They don't let me carry the babies for fear I might drop them. They all pay money to send me into the fresh air. What do I need with fresh air?" Lily started to say something, but the old woman closed her eyes again, and Lily knew she would not answer her. Just then, a beautiful gray car drove up in front of the farmhouse door and came to a stop. Lily got up to see who was coming. She knew no one was coming to see the old woman; it had to be a new guest.

She did not recognize her husband immediately, because she could not believe her husband was emerging from such a grand car. But when she saw Lucy, who was running around the car and shouting for her mother, Lily looked again and there he was. What was he going to say to her? What was he going to do now? She stood on the porch, watching him walk toward her. "Well, Lily," he said, "we came up for a visit. Do you think they'll have enough supper for us?" "I'll go ask," Lily said, fleeing.

When she returned to say Mrs. Steiner had plenty of room for them, she had almost stopped trembling. Lily said she was sharing a room with Fay, but she was sure they could make other arrangements. "Let's leave things the way they are for tonight," he said. "But what about Lucy?" asked his wife; "where is she going to sleep?" "She'll sleep in my room," said

Esheal. "Ha, ha, ha, ha," Lucy said to Fay; "I'm going to
sleep with Daddy." "That's enough," he said. "You borrowed Dr. Linde's car?" Lily asked him. "It's my car," her
husband said. "I didn't know you could drive," she said.
"Well," he said, "I can." "It's a beautiful car," said Lily. "It
matches my coat," said Esheal. "Don't tell me that's why you
bought the car!" Lily exclaimed. Esheal gave her a look.
"Well, of course that's not why you bought the car," Lily
said; "I know that." Esheal was still watching her out of
narrowed eyes.

"I have something else to tell you," he said, "but it can wait
until morning." Lily decided that she was in no hurry to know
what he had to tell her. "How long are we staying?" she
asked. "I can stay for a week," he said; "I got old Dr.
Mandelbaum. He and the clerk will do all right." "I hope you
brought some warm clothes," said Lily; "it gets cold here at
night." "I know what the country's like," said Esheal. "How
should you know?" said Lily; "you've never been in the
country." "Don't worry about it," said Esheal; "I've got
warm clothes, Lucy's got warm clothes." "Well, you must be
hungry," she said; she looked at the gold watch she wore on a
lavaliere on her jacket lapel. "It's time for dinner," she said;
"let's go in."

She waited for her husband to take her arm, but he walked
in beside her. "So," said a voice at his elbow, "you're Mr.
Luria. I've heard so much about you," said the old lady.
"Could I take supper with you, maybe?" "Come along," said
Esheal, taking the old woman's arm. Lily flushed, held her
head higher, and walked along holding Lucy's hand. She was
silently praying that the old woman would keep her mouth
shut about what she had told her and that she would not take
it into her head to tell Esheal why she thought Lily was such
an unreasonable wife.

Lucy carried on until she was seated next to her mother,
and her husband sat on her other side. Before Esheal had a
chance to put Fay's high chair on the other side of his wife,
the old lady plopped herself down into a chair and offered to
feed the child. "Such an opportunity, you don't know what it
means," she said. Esheal and Lily looked at each other briefly
and then looked away. "So what's for supper?" said the old
woman; "Sunday. Roast beef. Maybe this time she won't
burn it to a crisp." "Does she usually burn the food?" Esheal
asked. Lily shrugged, but the old woman erupted in a Yiddish

invective directed against Mrs. Steiner, the rotten cook. Esheal looked over at Fay. She looked plump enough. The food, he decided, could not be that bad.

Mrs. Steiner brought in a huge tureen of soup. "Chicken soup with matzoh balls," she said proudly, setting it down. "How did you learn to make matzoh balls?" asked Mrs. Berchinsky. "From a book," said Mrs. Steiner. "Matzoh balls from a book," said the old woman; "oy." She waited until everyone was served, and the instant Esheal raised a spoon to his lips, she asked him a question. "So what line of work are you in, Mr. Luria," she said. "I'm a pharmacist," he said. "So you were born here?" asked the old lady. "No," said Esheal, swallowing his soup as quickly as he could; "I was born in Russia." "In Russia!" said the old lady; "a man with some brain! Someone born in Russia should be a pharmacist!" "It's a good job," said Esheal. "A good job!" said Mrs. Berchinsky; "it's something wonderful! It's next to a doctor." "Not close enough," he said. "Don't tear yourself down," she said; "it's a horrible trait."

Mrs. Berchinsky soon had Esheal telling her the story of his life. Lily, who was busy with the two children, caught only snatches of talk. She thought she heard something about his having slept in a stable with a dog, but she knew that Jews never kept dogs, so that was impossible. Still, it annoyed her that Esheal was talking and laughing happily with the old woman. When she looked up, she saw the old woman put down her fork and poke her husband in the ribs. "Oh, you never did it!" the old woman said; "you never listened to music in the ground." Lily stared at Mrs. Berchinsky, and could not stop staring; the old woman was getting younger before her eyes. Her dark eyes, which Lily had always thought of as dried raisins, sparkled like onyx, and Lily was astonished to see that her hair was black, and that the old woman had fewer gray hairs than she did.

Then she heard Mrs. Berchinsky say something about Lucy's hair. "Why, it's so curly," the old lady said; "I bet it snaps back when you pull it." "It does," said Lucy proudly; "and you should have seen them bounce before my mother cut it." "Oh, but now," said the old woman, "you look like that little girl on the stage. You're a little sun with black clouds all around. I hear a raven in that hair. Listen. You hear it," she asked Lucy, and she whistled without moving her lips. Lucy clapped her hands to her head in delight. Esheal looked at his daughter and smiled. The child smiled back. Lily stared down at her plate. "You know," said Mrs. Berchinsky, "when I was a child, I had the longest hair of any girl in my village. I sat on it, and when I sat on it, it was so long it tickled the back of my knees. And then I got this big cut on my head, and there was so much blood, and they couldn't fix it, so they shaved my whole head. I didn't have one single hair. I looked like a chicken egg. I used to look at girls like you and cry. And when my hair grew in! Like needles. They called me porcupine. It grew straight up in the air. I bet your hair is soft."

"It is," said Lucy; "can I get up and show her, Momma?" "When you're finished eating," said Lily. Lily looked at Esheal out of the corner of her eye, and saw that he was looking at her. She smiled at him and he smiled back. She looked up to see Mrs. Berchinsky watching her shrewdly. "Do you suppose," she asked Esheal, "Fay is old enough to sleep with Lucy?" "That depends on Lucy," said Esheal; "are you old enough to keep an eye on your sister?" "I'll stay up all night," Lucy promised. "That's not necessary," said Lily. "No," said Esheal; "if anything goes wrong, you just come in and wake us up." "Oh," said Lucy. She sounded disappointed. Mrs. Berchinsky was staring at Lily as if to say the rest was up to her.

After dinner, Lily took Mrs. Steiner into the parlor and asked her if she would be able to watch the girls in the morning, and Mrs. Steiner said she would love to do it; she'd keep them in the kitchen with her.

When Lily woke up in the morning, Esheal was gone. She ran over to the window, and through the curtains, saw that the gray car was still there. Gasping with relief, she put on her best black dress, although she looked longingly at the red-and-white gingham dress she had had made for the country because it was so much more practical. She woke up the girls and took them down to the kitchen and left them, half buttoned, their shoes in their hands, with Mrs. Steiner. Esheal was not on the porch. Lily stood, shading her eyes, looking for any sign of movement. She sighed and went down to investigate. He was nowhere near the house. The chickens were fighting over their grains of corn, and here and there, a bird cried out from a tree. Lily saw drops of water gathering on her shiny leather boots.

"Over here!" Esheal shouted, but Lily could not see him. Esheal watched her turning in circles, and called out again.

"Over here!" he said; "by the stables." By the stables! thought Lily; had he come up here to get himself killed? She pushed some branches out of her way and hurried down the path. What she saw stopped her in her tracks. Her husband, the man she was used to seeing in the store, the very same man, was leading a horse around the small corral next to the stable. "What are you doing?" Lily screamed at him; "are you out of your mind! He'll kill you." "It's a mare," said Esheal; "a she." "I don't care what it is," Lily said; "look at its feet." "Hooves," said Esheal. He murmured something to the horse and the horse stopped. "Put it back!" screamed Lily. "Why should I put her back," said Esheal; "I want to ride her." "Ride her?" asked Lily; "this isn't a movie! That's a real horse." "I know all about horses," said Esheal, leaving Lily leaning against the corral fence. She was afraid to let go of the smooth wood lest she fall to the ground.

"I don't know if she jumps," said Esheal. "Jumps!" Lily wailed. "She can jump anything you can put in front of her," said Mrs. Steiner proudly. "Did you show her?" Esheal asked. "Sure I showed her; she won ribbons every year," said Mrs. Steiner; "it kills me to hitch her up to a wagon. But I have to live and so does she." Esheal began riding the horse around the corral. "That man can ride a horse," said Mrs. Steiner; "are you going to jump her, Doc?" "Jump her?" said Esheal; "I can stay on a horse if it jumps, but I never learned the fancy stuff." "You could try her," said Mrs. Steiner; "she's been sulking since I stopped jumping. Too much arthritis." "Yours or the horse's?" asked Esheal. "Oh, go on," laughed Mrs. Steiner.

"I bet she could jump this fence if the yard was a little longer," Esheal said. "Oh!" moaned Lily. "Don't worry," he said; "I'm not going to try it." "That's why we made the yard smaller," Mrs. Steiner said; "she used to go right over the fence. You get awful tired of looking for a horse. She used to go clear over to the next farm and she'd jump the fence there to get in with the stallion." Esheal leaned down and opened the gate and rode down the path. "Oh, won't you stop him?" Lily pleaded. "Stop him?" said Mrs. Steiner; "why? It's a pleasure to see a man who knows his horse. Come and watch him jump." "I can't," said Lily. "Well, then, go sit down and rest yourself," said Mrs. Steiner.

By the time Esheal rode back, Lily was half dead with worry. "I'll be right there," he called to Lily; "I have to groom the horse." She could not believe that her husband could go into the stable twice and twice come out alive. "What a horse!" Esheal said to Mrs. Steiner, kissing her on the cheek. "What a rider," said Mrs. Steiner; "take her out whenever you want to. She doesn't get enough exercise anymore. Well," she said, looking down at Lily, who was sitting like a statue on the grass, "I have to get back to the kitchen and start lunch. Your little girls are there with my daughter. It's a pity they couldn't see their father ride."

Esheal sat down on the ground next to his wife. "Why don't you try it?" he asked her; "she's a gentle horse. I'll show you how." Lily stiffened. The country was entirely alien to her. When the wind stirred the heavy, leafed branches, she was afraid that one of them might fall on her. If it began to rain, she was sure lightning would strike her dead in the middle of a field. She looked askance at each and every rock, because who knew what it might conceal? Strange animals came out of the woods at night and wailed under her window. Mrs. Steiner said there were black bears in the hills, and that if she saw one, just to turn around slowly, and on no account should she attempt to befriend its cub. The darkness in the country was something alive and savage; it was solid and filled with living things. Odd clots of blackness flew out of the trees chittering like mice, and Mrs. Steiner said those were bats, and Lily knew that bats tried to entangle themselves in women's hair. Dogs ran mad during country nights. And when she went into her room, and turned on her gasoline lantern, the whole screen was alive with ugly, bumping things which thudded nastily as if demanding she let them in. And no matter how tightly she closed the screen, some things would get through and begin circling the chimney of her lamp.

At night, she lit the lamp just long enough to see that Fay was securely tucked in bed and that her clothes were neatly folded. Then she blew the light out and practiced walking about the dark room as if she were a blind woman. She was afraid to let Fay bring a cracker into the room lest she attract mice, or worse, rats. Not long ago, she had looked out her window and seen a masked animal patrolling up and down in front of the house, and she knew it was something unearthly. When she told Mrs. Steiner about it, she laughed at Lily and said that all she had seen was a raccoon and that the mask was only the pattern in which its fur grew. There was no one to call out to for help. Lily knew that the woods were full of strange, strong creatures waiting to pounce on anything that stumbled and fell.

And a horse! A horse was all the country together in one skin, its murderous hooves, its high, arching neck, its enormous body not like a body at all but an enormous building constructed to resemble a monstrous animal. "I'm afraid of horses," Lily said in a small voice. "There's nothing to be afraid of," said her husband. "Don't make me ride on it," Lily pleaded almost inaudibly. "Of course I won't make you," Esheal said, astonished. Out of the corner of her eye, Lily saw Mrs. Berchinsky approaching.

"How did you learn about horses?" Lily asked quickly. "I used to drive the teams when I was a child," said Esheal; "once the Russian soldiers were stationed near where I lived. So many of them deserted they didn't have enough men to take care of the horses. When they found out I knew how, they took me along to the front with them. Every time we came into a village, the dogs screamed like they were being killed. When they were through with me, they dropped me off at home. I drove the ammunition wagons. One rock and I'd have gone hunting up in the sky with the geese. I wasn't even in the Army, but I knew how to handle a horse. So when I wasn't driving the wagons, they taught me to ride the thoroughbreds. The officers had them. Anyway, they weren't near Pobrosk long. I was only a little kid when I drove those wagons, maybe eight, nine. Shmuel the driver taught me. I wonder if he's still alive."

Esheal toyed with a piece of grass, and then parted the grass as if he were parting hair. "Look at those ants," he said; "ants are remarkable things." Lily shuddered, but bent over to look at the ants. They were huge, black ants, not like the small ones which sometimes invaded her kitchen. "Why are they remarkable?" asked Lily, and Esheal explained why. "Look at that one," he said; "it's carrying a stick bigger than it is." He lay back in the grass and stared up at the sun through the flickering leaves. "It's beautiful in the country," he said; "the city's like a casket. A big stone casket." "I didn't know you didn't like it," said Lily. "Who has a choice?" said Esheal; "a man can't make a living in the country. Someday," he said. "Someday what?" asked Lily. "Someday maybe one of the girls will live out here," he said. "They'll be city girls," said Lily; "like I am." "You never know," said her husband.

"No," said Lily. "Lily?" Esheal said. "What?" "I brought my camera. Why don't we get the girls and take some pictures?"

After lunch, the Luria family walked about the farm while Esheal photographed them. After he had taken pictures of Lily standing on a bench, reaching up over her head to hold on to some branches; Lily appearing to push the two children in a wheelbarrow; sitting with them in the hammock suspended under one trellis of the grape arbor; feeding the chickens; lying in a hammock; looking up at the two girls, whom Esheal had set down in the crook of a great elm tree; leaning against a haystack, he went to find Mrs. Berchinsky so that she could take some pictures of him together with his wife. Mrs. Berchinsky fussed endlessly over the camera, and finally, Esheal set all the dials for her, and then ran back to his place, so that all she had to do was press the button. She followed the Luria family around happily, taking pictures of Esheal and Lily, who seemed to be stepping out of a tree; the whole family sitting in the horse cart while Esheal pretended to pull it; all of the girls, standing next to the horses hitched to the wagon; Esheal, lying back in a field full of daisies, while the two girls threw more daisies at him; Esheal flanked by both girls who gazed up at him adoringly; Lily flanked by both girls; and picture after picture of Esheal holding the reins of the horses who pulled the wagon.

The sun was going down when they all trooped back to the squarish, red frame house and sank onto the porch chairs. Mrs. Steiner suggested that they eat their dinner outdoors because the mosquitoes weren't too bad, and Lily was about to say no when she saw Esheal's face. The Luria family and Mrs. Berchinsky chattered happily and laughed about nothing. As the sun shrank to a thin line on the horizon, Fay fell asleep against her mother, and Lucy, whose head was resting against her father's shirt, began rubbing her eyes. Finally, her head fell forward. "It's peaceful here," Lily said, surprised; "look at those streaks in the sky. Doesn't a red sky mean it's going to rain?" "No," said Esheal, "look at the mountains. There's no mist. It should be beautiful tomorrow."

"You should have seen my husband ride a horse," Mrs. Berchinsky marveled; "my two sons, God bless them, scream if they see a cat. If there's ever a pogrom in the city, he could take care of you out here. A man who knows animals is a wonderful man." Lily beamed at Esheal. "There won't be any pogroms in the city," he said. "Still," said Mrs. Berchinsky. "Still," said Lily. "Lucy's asleep," said Esheal; "let's carry them up to bed." "We'll have to wake them up to undress them," said Lily. "Why bother?" asked Esheal; "let them sleep. They can change their clothes in the morning." Lily nodded and they all went up together.

That night Lily told her husband that she was pregnant, and he said that the next day they would drive into the town and he would get her something to celebrate. After lunch, they drove through the trees which arched over both sides of the dirt road. The leaves had all turned color and glowed rose and gold; it was like driving through pane after pane of softly flowing stained glass. Esheal said he felt like someone in a painting and Lily said she felt the same way, and Esheal said that this picture was wonderful because it had no frame and you could go in and out of it whenever you wanted to.

When they got into town, Lily saw nothing she wanted. They went from shop to shop, and finally Lily said she wanted a handbag because Esheal obviously wanted to buy her something, and Lily did not want to disappoint him. Then they began the drive back. When they drove by the schoolyard, some boys had struck up a baseball game, and Lily said she would like to watch them; she always used to watch her brothers when they played in the schoolyard at home. She and Esheal stood under a tree, listening to the boys' shouts, laughing at their arguments, watching them kick the dry leaves up into the air, and watching their breath beginning to cloud in the chill air.

One of the boys was up at bat and Lily said she bet he was going to miss, but he hit the ball and the next thing she knew, the ball had struck her in the abdomen. The boy ran over to get the ball, and, when he heard what had happened, he apologized over and over again. Esheal told him not to worry; no harm had been done. "But the baby!" Lily gasped when the boy ran away; "maybe it hurt the baby." Esheal told her not to worry; he had heard of plenty of women who had gone through train wrecks and had given birth to perfectly healthy babies, and in any case, he said, the ball didn't hit her hard enough to hurt her.

On the day they were to leave, Lily let Esheal lead her over to the horse, and he even persuaded his wife to lay a hand on the animal's side, but when Lucy pleaded to sit in the saddle, his wife absolutely refused. They got into the car smiling and waving, and Lily kept turning around to wave one last time to

Mrs. Berchinsky and Mrs. Steiner, both of whom stood on the wide porch until the car was well out of sight. "A happy family," said Mrs. Steiner. "You have a crystal ball?" Mrs. Berchinsky asked her. "I don't need a crystal ball," said Mrs. Steiner. "She doesn't need a crystal ball," mocked Mrs. Berchinsky; "some people know everything."

Chapter 41

The long ride home was punctuated by all the usual nuisances. Lucy and Fay quarreled in the back seat; there were incessant demands that Esheal stop the car to find a bathroom for Lucy, frantic rummagings in Lily's large, string bag for bottles or crackers or juice, lollipops or toys, anything to keep the girls quiet. By the time the two children had fallen asleep in the back of the car, blue and lavender shadows were flowing by like billowing chiffon robes.

And by that time, Lily herself had grown accustomed to the car, and to her husband driving it, so that she was no longer grabbing his arm to get his attention before he hit an imaginary rock or fell into an imaginary ditch. Esheal drove along happily, watching the mountains blue and darken, and pointing out the clouds which, with the sun behind them, suddenly shone like heavenly things, edged in silver and gold. Whenever Lily saw something she liked, she pulled on his arm, and the car swerved, and Esheal told her not to do that, just to call his name and he would be sure to pay attention. She nodded and sat back contented.

"A car," said Lily after a long silence, "a car is a marvelous thing. It takes you just where you want to go. Not like the streetcars and the ferries, and you have to walk so far to get to them and they're never on time. And when the girls get ready to go to school, we can go get them if the weather is bad, and we can take them on picnics on the weekend and to the beach." Without thinking, she patted the dashboard. "I should get a car coat," said Lily; "and a car hat." "Not much blows in the windows," said Esheal. "I'll make them," said Lily; "it won't cost much." The idea of his wife in a car coat appealed to Esheal. "A car coat would be stylish," he said.

"Yes, wouldn't it?" said Lily; "but I don't know. They're usually white with black embroidery. White is awfully hard to keep clean." "I'm sure you'll manage to keep it clean," said her husband. "The linings are black," Lily went on; "you'd think it would be the other way around. Maybe I should make car coats for the children." "They never stay clean anyhow," said Esheal; "you'd just have one more thing to wash." "But they'd look so cute in them," said Lily; "you could pick us up at the synagogue with the car and Poppa could really show them off."

Esheal always had mixed feelings about taking his daughters over to his wife's family, but he loved coming for the girls when Meyer took them to the synagogue. Everyone there said they were the brightest, the prettiest, the cleanest, the nicest girls they had ever seen, and the more complimentary they waxed, the wider grew Lucy's eyes, and then the fighting began over who would hold the child on his lap. The old men would do anything to surprise Lucy, because when she was taken unawares, her huge, sparkling eyes would open wide and stay open without blinking. With those eyes and her black, curly hair she looked unearthly, a little icon. And the men paid her homage. And of course, when Esheal brought her home, she was impossible for the rest of the day, utterly spoiled.

Esheal wondered whether she had learned not to blink because she knew her wide-open eyes made such an impression on everyone, or if she blinked so infrequently because she was so determined to take everything in. He could list Lucy's traits: she was temperamental, sensitive, generous, impulsive, but there was something about the child he did not understand, some softness he sensed in her, some desire to give up the little scepter she wielded so successfully in her little kingdom. While Fay, small as she was, quiet as she was, struck him as a small lump of determination. And there was a clarity to her; he was sure she would know what she wanted and sure that she would get it. Lucy, he thought, was the one to worry about. His musings were broken into by the sound of Lily's hand patting the dashboard. He looked over at her and smiled. "I can't get over it," Lily said; "and the way it lights up the road. A car is a very clever thing."

This, thought Esheal, would be a good time to tell Lily about the man living in their house. He thought about Jake in his little room, with his sulfur pills and his orders to drink gallons of water, and wondered how the little man was doing. "Lily," he said, "I have something to tell you." "What?" asked Lily comfortably. "While you were gone, I took in a boarder. He's living in the supply closet." "What!" exclaimed Lily; "a boarder! Why do we need a boarder?" "We don't need a boarder," explained Esheal; "he needed a place to stay. Dr. Linde brought him by, and he was sick and had no place to go."

"What do you know about this man?" asked Lily. "He works in the garment district," Esheal said. "How do you know?" asked Lily; "he could be a murderer! He could be a thief! The whole house could be gone when we got back." "He's no murderer," said Esheal; "he's an operator in the garment district with a kidney infection." "So the whole family has to catch it," Lily said, folding her arms over her breast. "It's not catching," said Esheal; "Dr. Linde said it wasn't." "He has to go," said Lily, "I'll be afraid to sleep at night." "He's not going," said Esheal. Lily refused to look at him. They drove along in silence.

"What kind of man is he?" asked Lily. "He plays a good game of chess," said Esheal. "That's a recommendation?" cried Lily; "he plays a good game of chess?" Esheal concentrated on the road. "What is he like?" Lily asked; "I want to know it all at once." "He's very short," said Esheal, "and he doesn't speak a word of English." "He doesn't speak English!" Lily gasped; "how are we supposed to talk to him?" "In Yiddish," said Esheal; "or in Russian. He'll learn fast. He's a smart man. He's got to bring over his family, so he wants to make a lot of money." "He's probably making it now," said Lily; "stealing from us." "I told you," said her husband, "the man is no thief." "Of course not," said Lily; "a man who plays a good game of chess could never be a thief."

"He stays until he finds another place," said Esheal. His wife recognized that tone; her husband had sounded just that way when he told her she was going to the country. She took a deep breath. "And the girls?" she said. "What is Fay going to think when she sees him wandering around in his underwear?" "He can use the bathroom in the pharmacy," said Esheal. "But the only bathtub is in the house," said his wife; "what about that?" "He can take a bath after everyone's asleep," said Esheal; "the man has children of his own. He's not going to do anything wrong."

Lily had played her last card; if Esheal was not worried about the man's effect on the girls, he would not worry about anything. Nevertheless, she tried again. "How do you know he has a job?" she asked. "He said he went to work for some man or other and he's been doing so much extra work the man wanted to take him in as a partner. That's how he got sick; he didn't dare stay home from work." "These greenhorns always talk big," said Lily; "that a man should take in a penniless person for a partner! Does it make sense to you?" "No," said Esheal; "but these things happen. He said he was very fast, maybe the fastest in the business." "My father," said Lily, "worked in my uncle's shop for thirty years and no one offered to make him a partner." "Maybe he should have worked for someone else," said Esheal. "The whole family worked there," she added irrelevantly.

"Try to make the best of it," he said. "Should I try to make the worst of it?" asked his wife; "I can't imagine what it will be like, a perfect stranger watching every move I make." "Especially since," said Esheal, ignoring her answer, "you probably won't like him. He's a little rough. He's got ears like an elephant and an accent you can cut with a knife, and I know what your family thinks about people with accents. I won't have him insulted in my own house." "When did I ever insult anyone who came to the house?" asked Lily. "I didn't say that," he answered.

But Esheal knew what the Romanoffs would be talking about, and imitating and ridiculing once Lily came with her report. Not that they would say anything in front of the man. Diana would come, take a look, go home and push out her ears with her index fingers, and it would be nothing but Jacob Berghoff for the next two months. "When is Diana's baby due?" he asked Lily. "The same time as mine," said Lily. Esheal was more excited about Diana's baby than he was about his own. Diana needed something other than her sister and her sister's husband to keep her busy. She would be a hysterical mother, thought Esheal, and once she was again running into his store for medicine and advice, she might let him alone, and leave Lily alone with her imitations of him. He did not have to be there to know what went on.

Chapter 42

Esheal

When we came back from the country, I was happy to have Lily back and she was happy to be back. One night when she couldn't sleep, she came down to the pharmacy and said something about how now we were getting a new start and everything would be better. Of course, I agreed with her. But I did not want a new start. I wanted things to be just as they were before Lily forgot she was married to me. I knew now that my wife was not the most rational woman in the world, and that I ought to keep a tighter rein on her. The trouble was, I did not like keeping a tight rein on her. It wasn't in my nature.

When Jacob stayed with us, I had an easier time with Lily. Every time she looked at him, she remembered how I had sent her away to the country and how I was likely to do the same thing again, if not something worse, should she do something I considered disloyal. But I could not keep it up on my own. I loved her and I wanted her to be happy. I did not want to buy my own happiness at her expense. It was not part of my nature to threaten and tyrannize and frighten for no reason. If I had something to rant and rave about, I would have been as good at it as the next man. But there was nothing specific, a feeling of treachery in the air, something like that. And if I had tried to make Lily understand what I meant, where would I have gotten? A feeling of treachery in the air? That phrase would have meant nothing to her. She would not have known what I was talking about. So when things once more became peaceful and quiet, I was out of my mind with relief, even though I felt myself moving further and further from the center of that peaceful existence, as if, the happier my family became, the less I was part of it. And that was all I had ever wanted from life, a family of my own in which I would live happily.

One night, Jacob came home early and we were both too

tired to play chess, so we sat down and talked. And he said, did you ever hear the story about the Jewish man and the Turkish man standing on the corner? I said I didn't know; all stories start with two men standing on the corner. He said this story was about whether or not there was a God, and what kind of God it was, and I said no, I hadn't heard that one.

Well, he said, the Turkish man asked the Jewish man, what kind of God do you have? And the Jewish man, he was a Chasidic Jew, said, I have a very busy God. In heaven, he arranges which men and which women will get together on earth, but sometimes, when the people get to earth, mistakes are made and the wrong people get together. Then God runs around making sure that all the mistakes get taken care of and all the right people get together again. And the Turkish man snorted and said, for that you need a God? I have a whole harem and many slaves, and I can match them up myself. Your God is not worth much. Then, said the Jewish man, go and match up your women and your slaves and you will be just like a God. I didn't know it was so easy, said the Turkish man; I will go home and match them up and when I am finished, I will tell you about how easy it was and how silly is your God. The next week the Jewish man and the Turkish man met on the same street corner. The Turkish man looked as if he had aged twenty years. So, asked the Jewish man, how did it go? How did it go? asked the Turkish man, tearing his hair. Now I see why your God is so busy!

I said that God must have his hands full with me and I wondered if he would undo the mistakes made between myself and Lily before we were six feet underground. Jake said that he didn't know when God was going to get around to him, because he was busy enough with his own family, half of which was in England, but that didn't matter; his wife knew how to torment him through the mail. "What's the trouble there?" I asked; "does she run around?" "Run around?" asked Jacob; "I should be so lucky. She's so unfriendly, she wouldn't have who to run around with. She moved over a little and made room for me, but she still doesn't like it, my being there. We go out to eat somewhere, if someone tries to eat with us, she tells me we have to get up and go to another table. She won't have another person near her. So much trouble for her to talk. Except to me. There she has plenty to talk about. Everything I do is wrong. She sticks to me like glue. There's no rest from her."

"That," I said, "does not sound bad to me. I think I would like a woman like that. I *know* I'd be happy with a woman like that." "Call God," said Jacob, "and tell him to change them around. But my wife, she loves to go on vacations. She likes to look at the sea." "I wouldn't like that," I said; "I'd worry about what she was up to." "My wife? She's up to eating, that's what she's up to," said Jacob; "when she's not working, she's cooking or eating or staring. You could send her to China and she'd eat and stare. With her you wouldn't have to worry. Who worries? I don't worry. I worry she'll be the same woman thirty, forty, fifty years from now. I'll come home, seventy years old, eighty years old, and she'll be staring into the sun and rocking. Maybe rocking and eating and complaining."

"You know," I said, "I think a harpy would be a wonderful thing to marry; a gorgon would be a wonderful thing to marry if only you could be sure they wouldn't change." "A gorgon?" asked Jacob; "a harpy?" I explained. "Listen," Jacob said, "you marry a harpy, and she finds out you don't want her to change, and the first thing she does, she starts changing. With women, you can't win. You should leave them alone. Let them wear themselves out. That's what they want. Why get mixed in? In a fight with shadows, you have to stop in? Stay in the store where you belong." "It doesn't have to be like that," I said; "some husbands and wives are happy." "Nah," said Jacob. "They are," I said; "Dinney and her husband, they're happy." Jacob stood up abruptly. "So they're happy and we're not happy," he said; "what else is new?" "Do you think our busy God will get to us?" I asked. "What do you think?" asked Jacob; "be smart. Pray for peace and quiet." "That's not enough for me," I said. "It's not enough for him," said Jacob; "for him, the clouds are blowing the wrong way. Tell me," he asked, "who has what's enough? So, God," he said, as if talking to the ceiling, "hurry up. This man's not satisfied." He turned to me and said he was going to bed.

Chapter 43

In spite of the boarder, life in the Luria house bubbled along pleasantly. Lily loathed Jacob Berghoff from the minute she saw him, but as her pregnancy advanced, she grew sleepier and sleepier, and it was a relief to her to know that Berghoff was living on the first floor, and would either give the alarm if anyone broke into the house, or would himself be the victim of any intruder. Jacob rarely saw Lily in the morning, since he left the house so early, but when he came back from work at night, he would look her over, nod solemnly, and say something which she could not understand. She was determined to ignore him, but her curiosity got the best of her, and she gave in and asked her husband what the boarder was saying. Esheal asked Jacob, and came back to tell Lily that he was either saying "very good" or "couldn't be better," and Lily, who was all too familiar with her husband's jealousy, could not understand why he took the boarder's assessment of her physical charms so calmly. Indeed, every time Jacob looked at Lily and said, "Very good," or "Couldn't be better," Esheal puffed up like a toad. "What does he mean?" she asked at last. "Didn't I tell you," Esheal said; "his mother was a midwife. He says he can smell trouble a mile away." "With that nose," said Lily, "it's not impossible." Nevertheless, when Jacob nodded at her, and said his incomprehensible two words, she nodded back and smiled.

Then, one morning, Jacob came in, looked at Lily, and did not say the magic words. Instead, he asked for Esheal. By this time, he knew some English, since he and Esheal spent one hour every night playing chess, and the next hour, from eleven to twelve, Esheal taught him English. They had hit upon this arrangement because Jacob was determined to read and write the new language, and if he had to give up chess to do it, he was prepared to do so. This way both men got what they wanted. "Get husband, please," said Jake, and Lily, unreasonably frightened, went into the kitchen and told Esheal to leave his supper and talk to the boarder. "Get doctor, please," Jacob told Esheal, and when Esheal asked him why, he said that Lily was going to have her baby that night, and if he sent for the doctor now, he would get there in time.

Esheal translated what he said to Lily, who protested that she felt fine; she had not felt a twinge. "Get doctor, please," Jacob stubbornly repeated. "All right," said Esheal; "I'll send the clerk." "To get the doctor out of his bed for nothing!" Lily expostulated, but by the time the doctor got there, Lily was biting down on her husband's razor strap and could not get her breath long enough to talk. The children had been bundled off, sleepy and bewildered, to Sarah's. "Trouble," said Jake to Dr. Linde.

The doctor, who was used to all manner of comments from the women relatives, looked surprised, shrugged off his coat, washed his hands, and went straight in. "Trouble," he said to Esheal when he came back out; "a breech baby. Unless it turns, we have to take her to the hospital." Just then Jacob came running out of the room and tugged at the doctor's sleeve. Esheal went in after them. "It turned," the doctor said; "but the child has a big head. It's going to be a forceps baby." He told Esheal not to worry, that Lily would not know what was happening. She was out like a light. And within minutes, there was the familiar, thin outraged wail of an infant. "Another girl," said Dr. Linde. "Good," said Esheal. "Good?" said Jacob; "meshuggeneh." He looked at the baby and shook his head. "I'm going to bed," he told Esheal, who did not notice him leave.

Dr. Linde took him into a corner of the room. "Before the others get here," he said, "I want to tell you something. The baby's head is too big." "All the girls had big heads," said Esheal. "This is different," said the doctor; "this is a mild hydrocephalus. She may have fluid on the brain. And her heart's enlarged. Look at her chest. Doesn't it seem too big?" "She'll grow out of it," said Esheal.

"She's never going to be a healthy child," said Dr. Linde. "Never?" echoed Esheal. He looked at his wife, sleeping on the bed. "What am I going to tell Lily?" he asked. "It's up to you," said Dr. Linde; "how would she take the truth?" "I don't know," Esheal said; "if they get a cold, she tears their clothes. Maybe I should wait until she's a little stronger." "I don't know," said the doctor; "it's up to you." Esheal thought about Sarah and Diana and how they would fuss and worry over the child, and he foresaw a life of invalidism for the baby, misery and dread for the other two girls. "I'll tell her later," he said.

And for some time, he had no reason to regret his decision, although he was uncomfortable lying to Lily; now he found himself lying to her a hundred times a day. "But what about her head?" Lily would say; "doesn't it seem awfully large?" "Some children have large heads," Esheal said. "But hers is so large she can't hold it up," Lily said, looking worriedly at the child. "The doctor said that's because her neck muscles are weak," he lied. After the child, whom they named Cecilia and called Celia, managed to keep her head up, Lily stopped worrying about the size of the child's head, but every now and then she would look at her daughter and say to the air that she didn't know, it didn't look right. And if there was any germ to catch, Celia caught it, and as soon as she caught it, she passed it right on to Fay. Even with Mrs. O'Connoll, Lily was always busy with the three children.

Lucy spent more and more of her time at the pharmacy, and when she was not with her father or playing in front of the store, she was at Sarah's house. One day she came home, and Esheal noticed that no matter where he worked, Lucy insisted on sitting so that she faced him. He told her to come sit next to him; how could she see what he was doing otherwise? She refused. "Aunt Diana says I should always sit like this," said Lucy. "Well," said her father, "if you'll turn sideways, I'll show you how I make these paper dolls." "I can't sit sideways anymore," said Lucy; "if I do, everyone will see what kind of nose I have." Esheal went straight upstairs, and Lily promised she would speak to Diana the minute she saw her. Now that Diana had a boy of her own, they saw her less and less, although often enough, apparently, for her to cause them trouble.

The constant worry about the children seemed to draw the Lurias closer together, and Esheal often thought that his family had been blessed with catastrophe, since it seemed to thrive so on it, while in peaceful times, everything went wrong. When Lucy started school, her mother breathed a sigh of relief and turned her attention to Fay, who was just getting over her second bout with pneumonia, and to Celia, who had such a dreadful cold that Esheal had to come up

every hour and use his little suction machine to clear her
nostrils. But the children were getting better, and aside from
the many notes Lucy brought home from her teacher, all of
which complained about the child's behavior, Lily felt she
could see, as she often said, the light at the end of the tunnel.
And she was in such a happy mood that she decided to make
Esheal his favorite soup, split-pea soup, and she set a huge
kettle of it to boil on the stove while she went in to take care
of Celia.

Fay, who was now two, was left alone in the kitchen and
watched the lid jumping up and down and up and down, and
the little white bubbles were coming out of the top of the pot,
and the lid was rising up on them and then settling back again,
and she was so fascinated by this lively-looking pot that she
dragged over a kitchen stool to get a better look. When she
got to the top of the stool, she pulled the pot toward her, and
the pot fell from the stove and the hot split-pea soup spilled
over her face and chest and shoulders. When Lily heard the
child's scream, she knew what had happened. She screamed
down the dumbwaiter for Esheal, sobbing that the child was
burned, and her husband rushed up with limewater and
linseed oil. While he was working over the child, Lily kept
sobbing, "She's going to die, she's going to die," and finally,
Esheal turned around and hit her. "Stop it, she can hear you,
what's the matter with you?" he asked her. "She's going to
die," said Lily. "Get out of the room," Esheal thundered;
"go get the doctor. Stay out of here!"

From the day Fay pulled down the pot of soup and burned
herself with it a new regime began in the house. Lily moved
Celia into her sister's room so that she could watch both of
them at once. Because Fay's lips were burned shut, Esheal
would spend hours with an eye dropper, letting fall drop after
tiny drop onto the child's burned lips so that some would go
between the lips and the child would get some liquid. After a
month, it was clear that Fay was getting stronger, but she still
could not open her mouth. And Celia simply refused to eat;
as a result, her head looked even larger upon her thin body.
Her father dreamed up a hundred ways to get her to eat, but
although she grew, she did not fatten. Lily was less worried
about Fay than about the baby. "It's not normal for a child to
eat like that," said Lily time after time; "normal children
have appetites. She doesn't have any. You can't live unless
you eat. There's something wrong with her. Something

happened when she was born. Something happened to her head. I know it!" And she would burst into tears.

Esheal thought it might be better to tell her the truth; it was hard to know what to do with a woman like Lily. She calmed down quickly after she saw what needed to be done for Celia, and Fay, lying there, looked monstrous, an animal which had been roasted alive. True, Lily sometimes went into the bathroom and locked the door and cried for an hour at a time, but when she came out, she sat down next to the baby's bed, and between dropping liquids onto Fay's lips, she read to Celia in a cheerful, animated voice. And when Lucy came home with a note saying that her teacher wanted to see her, she called Mrs. O'Connoll, left her in charge of Fay, put on her best dress and stole, pinned on her pocket watch, and set off for the public school.

She listened to Mrs. Brienan, who did not have one good word to say about her daughter. "So what is it really?" Lily asked the teacher; "I cannot see how she is so bad. What does she really do?" "Everything is funny to her," said Mrs. Brienan; "if I write on the board and make a mistake and pick up the eraser, she's hysterical. If another child makes a mistake, she starts giggling. If a bow flops over another girl's eye, she's laughing again. It's an interruption. You can't concentrate." She looked at Mrs. Luria and waited for her to begin apologizing for her child. Later, she thought, Mrs. Luria would give the child the beating she deserved.

"My child laughs?" Lily asked her; "is that the trouble?" She stood up and rested her hand on the teacher's desk. Suddenly, Mrs. Brienan felt thin and pale and shabbily dressed, a spinster who had no husband or children of her own and so punished other people's children. "Look, Mrs. Brienan," Lily said, "I would rather hear that my child is a happy, laughing child than hear she is a sad, quiet child. I'm happy to hear she laughs. I don't call that bad." "Well, I do," said the teacher. "And don't let me hear you're taking it out on her," said Lily, "or I'll come back here and raise such cain you'll regret the day you were born." She put on her mink stole, stared severely at the teacher, and left. Then she went home to care for Fay and Celia.

And then one day, Fay's lips parted by themselves and she was able to drink through a curved, glass straw and swallow mashed bananas. The doctor told the Lurias that she could eat anything but that she was afraid to swallow. And when the

Lurias saw her eating, they both began to cry, and they cried as if they would never stop. Lily did not stop. Every time she looked at Fay, she would start to cry helplessly, and this went on for so long that Lucy learned to ignore her mother's tears and to ask for a nickel for some hot chestnuts, or if she could go to her friend's house, as if nothing unusual were happening.

"I don't think," said Esheal, "that this is the time to tell her about Celia." "Maybe it is," said the doctor; "maybe we should get it all over with at once. Then when she came out of it, she'd be through." "You think so?" asked Esheal. "I do," said the doctor; "one blow after another is sometimes worse than all of them at once." Esheal thought about his wife, and how she seemed peculiarly on edge, as if she suspected something, but had no idea what it was. Lately, she was given to examining the simplest sentences as if they had more complex meanings than she could possibly divine. She would shake Esheal's utterances as if somewhere in them was a hidden coin which would explain everything. Often, he felt her eyes upon him, following him around the room, and when he turned to look at her, she stared at him intently, questioning, almost pleading. If this went on, Esheal thought, she might come to distrust him.

"I'll tell her," he said; "I'll tell her tonight when I come in, and if she's not up tonight, I'll tell her in the morning." After making this decision, Esheal felt as if he had been given back the ability to breathe. Jacob had moved out months ago but still came to play chess, and for the first time since Fay burned herself, he found himself looking forward to his game. Jacob, he thought, was a remarkable man. He worked sixteen hours a day and then came to the pharmacy for his one hour of chess and his one hour of English lessons. None of that mattered to Lily. When Esheal said that soon Jacob would be able to bring his family over, she said that she could not believe there were more Berghoffs, but if there were, she wanted nothing to do with them. Esheal decided to argue about the Berghoffs when the time came.

"Write 'the pen is on the table,'" he told Jacob, who was now learning to write. "Not 'the table is on the pen,'" Esheal said; "'the pen is on the table.'" He sat back while Jacob tried again. It was snowing and the large, flat flakes were framing the window, leaving irregular-shaped centers through which he looked out. "You want to know what my brother-in-law is up to now?" asked Esheal rhetorically; "he went into the importing business. He was going to import olives from Greece, and he and a friend took a boat to Greece, and last week they came back and all the Romanoffs were standing there on the dock screaming and waving, and the next thing everyone knew Dave and his friend weren't coming down so fast. Some good friend called the customs' officer and said they were smuggling in diamonds, so they slashed open all the barrels and that was the end of the import business." "Some group," said Jacob; "what did your wife say about the olives?" "Oh, if you listen to her, it's a tragedy, he would have been a millionaire if some gangster hadn't been so vindictive." "Some family," Jacob said again, watching Esheal going over his work.

Esheal paused and looked out the window. He thought he saw Bill Romanoff in one of them and blinked his eyes. He wouldn't be out on a night like this. But the door opened and the wind blew Bill in. He stood there a minute, gasping, and brushing the snow from his coat. Esheal remembered how, one Passover at the Romanoffs', they had opened the door so that the angel could come in and drink some wine, and when they opened the door, there stood Dave. Whenever either of the boys appeared in the store doorway, he remembered that night and asked himself why he was forever haunted by appearances of the wrong angels.

"Poppa's dead," Bill said. "Meyer?" asked Esheal; "what happened to him? He wasn't sick. I just saw him this morning." "He went out for a walk," said Bill, "and some woman was putting something out on the windowsill, and a brick was loose and it fell down and hit him on the head. No one knew who he was, so they took him to the morgue. So when he didn't come home, Diana said I should go over and just look, just in case, and the man there said they brought someone in who looked like Pa, did I want to see him. That's how I found him. We just brought him home." "Not to the funeral parlor?" asked Esheal. "Momma wouldn't hear of it," he said.

"How is Sarah?" Esheal asked. "If she lives through this," said Bill, "she'll live forever." "She'll live," said Esheal; "she's going to die while Lily has two sick children and Diana has a new baby? I'm not worried about her. I'm worried about Lily." "Lily," Bill said, as if he had just remembered who she was; "Lily's in tough shape, is she?" "She cries all of the time," said Esheal; "I don't know what's going to happen." "I'm going home," Jacob said; "you have enough here." After he left the two men went upstairs to tell Lily.

Lily did not appear to understand what they were saying. At least, she did not react. "So my father is dead," she said; "when is the funeral?" Bill said it was tomorrow afternoon. "I have a black dress," said Lily. "Mrs. O'Connoll can watch the children." She went back to feeding Fay, and got ready for bed. Bill and Esheal sat in the living room, staring at the closed bedroom door. "What does this mean?" asked Esheal. "Ask Momma," said Bill. "Your mother's in no condition to be bothered." "If it's one of the girls, she's in condition," he said. So Esheal woke up Mrs. O'Connoll and left her sitting outside the bedroom door and went back to the Romanoff house with Bill.

Sarah listened to what Esheal had to say about Lily, and said that as soon as the sitting shivah was over, Lily ought to go away. She needed quiet. "Where can she go," Esheal asked her, "in the middle of the winter?" "Where can she go," Sarah repeated. "Listen," Esheal said, "Lily has her hands full. Why don't you take the apartment in back of us? Then you'd be there to help her."

"I was thinking of going to Diana," said Sarah. Bill said that since he would soon be working for Esheal, they would all be together at Lily's. "And what about Dave?" asked Sarah. "He can keep the house," said Bill; "we'll all contribute something." "I'll sit shivah here," said Sarah, "and then I'll come."

Perhaps, thought Esheal, once Sarah moved into their building, he would tell his wife about Celia. And then Fay, who was beginning to sit up and walk around, caught double pneumonia. And so it happened that ten days after Meyer's death, Sarah and Bill moved into the apartment across the landing from the Lurias, but Esheal did not tell Lily about Celia.

For Lucy, this was a wonderful time. Her parents told her that Fay would be fine, and she believed them. When she had first seen her sister's burned face, she had become so frantic the doctor had to give her a sedative, and afterward, she kept patting her own cheek and looking at her own face in the mirror. But as time passed, she became absorbed in her homework and her friends, and before she knew it, it seemed as if her sister were back to normal. Fay healed with only two small scars, one just below her armpit and the other just behind her right ear. When Fay began eating and filling out, Lucy thought a great deal of fuss had been made over nothing. When Fay caught double pneumonia, which Dr. Linde said was due to her long period of inactivity, Lucy thought nothing of it. Fay was having another "time of it," and that time would soon be over. But she was angry at being deprived of her sister, at having to sleep alone in the big back room at night, at only being allowed in to see her sister at definite times during the day.

Lily and Sarah were fanatical in their operation of the steam tent which surrounded Fay's bed, so fanatical that the paint began to peel from the ceiling and the walls in the shape of continents which fell to the floor at startling times, and the curtains hung limply. The walls were perpetually damp, as if covered by an eternal, clammy morning dew, and the steam was so thick that Lily and Sarah moved through the room like two wraiths; their motions were hazy, as if they were tending to something underwater.

This, Esheal thought, whenever he entered the room, must be what the land of the newly dead looked like. And he saw the same aversion to the room in his daughter, Lucy, so he forbade her to enter, saying that Fay was too excited whenever anyone other than her mother and grandmother came in. Lucy sighed with relief and did not disobey.

Lily went about her duties and said nothing, and whenever Esheal saw her, he felt like a man who had seen the lightning and now waited for the thunder. But nothing happened, and Fay was not well enough to go outside until late in June.

Fay was due to begin school in the fall, and Lily was terrified that she would not be able to go; all of them conferred and decided that the child needed more strengthening, and Esheal said that the sea air was excellent for respiratory conditions. It was decided that he would rent a house for them in Rockaway, and they would all stay there for the summer. He would come and visit them every Sunday.

So it was done. The first Sunday he came, he found the women on the beach. They had rented red-and-white striped canvas chairs under whose awnings they sat chatting with other women and shouting to the children not to go into the water. Lily had a hamper of food and enough towels and blankets for an army. "How are you going to drag that back when I'm not here?" he asked. "We pay the boy a quarter a week," said Lily proudly. Esheal saw Fay chasing Lucy, trying to get her doll back, and the two of them collapsed in the sand, laughing. He felt irrelevant, out of place. "Is she getting enough to eat?" he asked his wife. "Is she getting enough to eat?" laughed Sarah; "you should hear her complain. 'If I turn this way, *she* pours cream in my milk. If I turn that way, *she* pours cream in.' She says she's going to get fat." "Let her get fat," said Esheal, who was staring at Lily in her black bathing costume. Three children and she still had that wonderful body. He did not know why, but he had not expected to find many men on the beach; he was surprised to see how many there were. Sarah sat on her chair; her black skirt pulled up over her knees, her black sleeves rolled up to her shoulders. It was preposterous of him to want his wife to dress as Sarah did, he thought; but he didn't like it, Lily showing herself off in that way.

Celia was sitting back on her fat legs, digging in the sand with two other little girls. "You won't be in any hurry to come back," Esheal said to Lily. "Oh, yes, I will," she said; "the house must be filthy by now." "It's not filthy," said Esheal. "How is Bill doing in the store?" Sarah asked him. "Fine," he said. If Bill were only a little bit slower, he could earn a good living as a department store dummy. "I bet business is booming since you took him in," said Sarah. "Booming," he said, "but he can't play a game of chess."

"Did I tell you," he asked his wife, "Jacob's brought his family over? I told him we'd invite them over as soon as you got back from the beach." "I may stay here forever," she said. "It won't kill you to make cake and coffee for them," Esheal said. "No, it won't kill me," said Lily, who was watching Celia, and, as she watched the child, her face gradually assumed its habitual expression of worry, suspicion, and panic. I should tell her, Esheal thought, but the women looked so happy, and the children looked so healthy, he hated to spoil it. "She'll never live to be five," said Lily, softly; "she'll never live to go to school." She stared up at Esheal, as if waiting for his confirmation. "Don't be silly," Esheal said; "don't say that. What if the others should hear you?" But it made him think. The truth was, he realized, that he, not Lily, was the one who could not face the child's death. But he believed it was coming, and so kept a distance between himself and the child, which Lily, who was the child's mother and who spent most of her day caring for her, could not do.

A week before they were to come back to the city, Celia began to run a high fever, and Fay came running into her parents' room to wake them up. When they came back, they found Lucy sound asleep in her bed, and Celia talking frantically to someone invisible. She was talking about angels. "Look, Momma," she said, "at the angels. Look, they're sitting on the posts of my bed. Look, they're flying in the windows. Don't close the windows. The angels can't get in through the glass. Open the windows! Open them!" she kept insisting, and in spite of the child's high fever, they thought it best to open the windows and quiet her. Lily and Esheal sat on either side of her bed, applying cloths soaked in alcohol; gradually, the fever began to come down.

"It's an omen," said Lily; "it really is. It's an evil omen. The child sees her own death. It sometimes happens. I used to hear Momma talk about things like this when her friends came to visit her." The child stirred in her sleep and whispered something about angels. Esheal looked over at Fay and Lucy and saw they were both asleep. "Lily," he said, "it *is* a premonition. Dr. Linde said she would never be a healthy child." "When did he say that?" asked Lily. "The night she was born." "You should have told me," said his wife. "He said he thought there was some fluid on the brain and her heart was enlarged." "My God," said Lily; "I knew it. Did he say she was going to die?"

"No," said her husband; "he said she would never be healthy." "But he didn't say she was going to die?" Lily asked, leaning forward over the child. "No. He didn't. I swear he didn't." Lily sank back in her chair. "You should have told me," she said again. "What good would it have done?" he asked; "I thought you'd only worry more." "What good would it have done!" Lily cried; "do you know what it's like to think there's something wrong but no one else can see it? And every time she got sick, I thought it was my fault. Then if I said I thought something was the matter, everyone laughed at me, and I knew I was right, but everyone said I was nervous. I felt like I was losing my mind." Lily began crying softly. "I'm sorry," said Esheal. "No one would listen to me," Lily cried.

And then Celia recovered, and then the summer was over. With regret, the women returned their red-and-white chairs for the last time, and told each other in unconvincing tones what a relief it would be not to have to shake the sand out of everything. The children were fat and round and brown as Indians. That fall, both Fay and Lucy went to school, and except for the fact that Dave was finally sent to jail, the Luria family remembered that year happily for the rest of their lives.

Fay took to school immediately and, to everyone's surprise, she was faster than her sister and, since she was also quiet, she soon became one of the teacher's favorites. The two girls began going places together, and when Lily saw them go out, she no longer worried about them. "You take Fay or you can't go," she would tell Lucy, and Lucy would take her sister and drag her off. As soon as she got around the corner, she would grab Fay by the ear and say, "Come on. Hurry up."

When Esheal came up for dinner, he would find Lily singing to the children in her flat monotone, and the song she liked to sing best was "Yarma Man" because it frightened the girls so that they would come running to her. They began to help their father dress the window, and when they had product maps to make for their classes, they would come down to the pharmacy, and Esheal would take out his large, clear capsules, into which they would put the "products" of their state, and then he would paste them on.

After school, the two girls would come down to the pharmacy with a big book and a pile of pictures they had cut from magazines and play a new game they invented. Each picture was given a certain number of points, and then the pictures were hidden between the pages of a book, which they then closed, and each girl had a pin which she poked into the closed book, and then she opened the book to see what picture she had found. The one who had the highest number of points won. And when Fay finished playing, she would always say the same thing: "Isn't this the most wonderful game?"

After school, Esheal would come up to help the girls with their homework, and the porcelain kitchen table became their blackboard. They worked out their arithmetic problems on its surface, and Esheal wrote out words with their crayons for them to read. When they were finished, he would wipe the table clean with a damp cloth. When Lucy had fractions, Esheal took a plate or a pot cover and would draw lines dividing it up to explain the idea to her. And the girls were so proud of his book covers. His were so tight and so perfect;

they had the best book covers in the school and the teacher always complimented them on them.

And he began paying the girls a dollar for every A they got on their cards. Both girls got A's in all their subjects, but in deportment Lucy got C's, and when she saw how much less money she was getting, she would resolve to behave or to steal her sister's money, she could never decide which. And now when Lucy wanted protection from her mother, all she had to do was run across the hall to her grandmother, and on Fridays after school, she would go into Sarah's apartment to watch her bake challa and roll out her noodle dough. They went with Sarah when she bought chickens, and they watched the chicken flicker clean the bird.

Neither Lily nor Sarah had the slightest idea of what the two girls found so hilarious about the man who flicked the chickens, but when they reprimanded the girls, saying that he was only a person who sat there and flicked your chicken, and how much money could he make when he only got five cents for a chicken, the girls would laugh until they cried. And when their mother started in, saying she wanted a full-breasted chicken, and that the chicken the man was trying to foist off on her was a chicken "as old as myself," the girls had to run out on the street because the other mothers in the store were already grumbling about their outrageous behavior.

And the wilder they got, the happier their parents were, because it meant they were healthy. Lily had a friend she called Raisie Malkie who came over every Sunday, and every Sunday, the two girls would be forced to sit on the couch and listen to Raisie, with her hands clasped in front of her, and her bust thrust out, while she sang, "Springtime, oh, sweet springtime," and invariably, the two girls would fall off the couch, screaming with laughter. "Lily!" said Raisie every Sunday. "You are bringing up two very unnatural children!"

And they lay in wait for Lily's cousin, Sadie. She was a very particular woman, and wherever she went, she carried her own white washcloth with her. And the two girls found it, and wet it, and when cousin Sadie found it wet, she raised the roof, but the two girls swore they had nothing to do with it, and when Lily asked Celia if she had seen anything, she shook her head and opened her brown eyes even wider than usual.

"No one is ever going to come see me again!" Lily would plead with the girls, but then Lucy would begin mimicking Raisie Malkie singing, "Springtime, oh, sweet springtime," and their mother would be as helpless with laughter as they were.

And the girls would come home and tell their parents about all their adventures. If the story was a good one, Lucy would practice telling it in front of her father, and then go up and tell it again to her mother, and then go next door and tell it to her grandmother, and by that time, the story had a very high gloss indeed.

And it seemed as if life were conspiring to keep them all amused. Lily took the three girls on the Flatbush Avenue trolley on their way to have their pictures taken, and all three of them had had their hair done; the car was packed, so that they were all pressed together, when one woman began to complain about the young man behind her. "What's she carrying on about?" asked Lily; "he's not doing anything. He's not bothering her." Then the woman, who was enormously fat, began to shout, "Leave me alone! You're trying to get fresh!" "What's he supposed to do with his hands?" Lily called out; "his hands are there," and the woman looked around wildly, trying to see who had spoken up. And they laughed all the way to the photographer's studio, and through the entire session, until the photographer said, "Really, I have never seen such silly, idiotic young women as you two," and Lily tried to say, "you don't mean *my* daughters," but she collapsed against them. "This is an example for a mother to set?" the photographer asked her, and that finished them altogether.

Esheal took them to see the troupe of Singer Midgets who came to the RKO Brunswick once a year, and the girls waited all year for them and their midget castle which they set up every time they came. Sarah took them to movies endlessly, and when she took them, she would buy twenty-five cents' worth of chocolate-covered almonds, seventy-five almonds altogether, and the girls could have all they wanted, something their parents would never have permitted, and each time they went with Sarah, they took vows of silence, which, for once, they were not tempted to break. That was also the year that Esheal came to understand why his children looked like such sacks in their clothes; Lily bought clothes for them to grow into, and when they were finished with the clothes, they had still not grown into them. One day Esheal took Lucy and Fay to get spring coats. Lucy bought a bright orange coat with a double row of buttons going down and the coat had a

little velvet collar, and Fay got the same thing, but her coat
was bright blue. When Lily came home and saw the coats,
Esheal thought he would have to hold her up. She said they
looked like Italians. Nevertheless, she let them wear their
coats.

Then Lucy developed dandruff, and cousin Sadie was
called in. Cousin Sadie fought against dandruff as if God
himself had called her, and when Lucy protested, she was
ordered to submit to cousin Sadie's ministrations. Every
Thursday, cousin Sadie came over with a bottle of olive oil
and poured it all over Lucy's head. Lucy's head was then
stuck in a paper bag, whereupon she proceeded to complain
about the smell. Then her hair was washed three or four times
with a foul-smelling tar soap, and through it all, Fay, who sat
on a stool watching, would moan, "Oh, Lucy," until her
mother could stand no more of it and sent her out of the
room. And when cousin Sadie was finished washing Lucy's
hair, she attacked her head with a mechanical gadget that she
fastened to her hand. It was the size of a cake of soap and
covered with little rubber teeth which vibrated, and with this,
cousin Sadie massaged her scalp. Whenever Lucy tried to
straighten up, cousin Sadie would push her head back down
under the faucet, and if Lucy picked her head up again, she
would slap it back down.

If it was raining, the girls would sit outside the pharmacy
and play in the car. They sat in the gray car and did their
homework. On weekends, if the weather was good, Esheal
would drive the whole family to Highland Park and leave
them there with a picnic lunch, and about four, he would
come to get them with a quart of ice cream and a couple of
spoons, and when they were finished, he would take them
back home. On Saturdays, they went to the temple with
Sarah, who would display them to Meyer's old friends.

Friends came over for coffee and cake, or for supper, two
or three times a week. Even the meeting with the Berghoffs
went well. To Esheal's astonishment, Mrs. Berghoff complimented his wife profusely on her wonderful coffee. Lily
would cook, but she was known in the neighborhood for her
poisonous brown liquid. "You should taste my coffee,"
bragged Mrs. Berghoff; "I make it from chicory. The trick is
to cook it all day."

Esheal looked at Jake, who raised his eyebrows to heaven
and clutched his stomach. When he and Lily returned the

visit, Lily went on and on about Mrs. Berghoff's wonderful coffee, and asked her for the recipe. The two women went into the kitchen, and Jake and Esheal stared after them. "So what do you think of that?" Jake asked him; "the two of them make the worst coffee in the world." "I didn't think my wife had a rival," said Esheal.

"Still, too much in common they don't have," said Jake. Esheal understood him. "Let's leave the women out of it," he said; "we can keep the game going." "Sure, the game goes on," said Jake, although both men knew that now that they both had families, they would be less and less likely to see each other. And Esheal did not blame Lily; if Lily did not like Mrs. Berghoff, it was also clear enough that Mrs. Berghoff did not like her. But in the pharmacy, Esheal kept track of the Berghoff family through the neighbors, and in time, he found himself especially interested in tales of Jake's only son, Sam, who first distinguished himself by beating up the bully of his block.

So the fall and winter passed, and during the summer, Esheal sent his family to Lake Opatcon, and after Labor Day, he brought them back. And then one afternoon, the girls were playing in the car, and Celia must have leaned against the door handle or the door had not been tightly closed because it opened, and she fell out and hit her head on the curb.

Lucy ran into the store to get her father, and he came out and carried Celia into the pharmacy and placed her on the counter. When he talked to her, the child did not answer, but every so often, she shook her head as if she were waking up and mumbled something. By the time Lily came down, Celia's eyes were open and she was staring around her as if she were in a completely unfamiliar place. Esheal had an ice bag pressed to the lump on the back of the child's head, and after a while she began struggling to get down. But when he set her down, she could not seem to maintain her balance, and bumped into everything, and Lily caught her twice just before she fell.

They took Celia upstairs and put her to bed and kept her entertained by reading to her, and when she got tired of that, the girls played cat's cradle with her, and although Celia usually beat her sisters at the game, this time she could not grasp the strings properly, and finally she pulled the string from her hand and her sister's and threw it down on the covers, crying. "All you did was hit your head!" Lucy yelled at her, and from behind, she felt Lily hit her on the shoulder, hard.

By nightfall, Celia seemed to be fine, and her parents made plans to take her on a picnic to Highland Park while the girls were in school. "All alone?" Celia kept repeating; "all by myself? Without *them?*" "They'll be in school," her mother told her, while, from behind her book, Lucy made the most terrible faces she could manage at her youngest sister. Esheal took the day off, and they went out, Celia so thickly swaddled in clothes that even if she fell down in the park, she would never know it. And all afternoon, Lily watched the child as if she were in danger of vanishing into the air, and she would say, "Look at her run. Doesn't she look wonderful? There's nothing wrong with her, is there? Doesn't she look fine?"

The next day, Esheal again left the clerk and Bill in charge of the store, and again took Celia on an outing, this time to Greenwood Cemetery. Esheal loved the cemetery as he had loved the country in Russia. It shut out the city when it shut its gates, and he had taken Celia, he told himself, at the perfect time; the leaves were brilliant reds and golds, and the wind was warm when it blew, and Celia could not look enough at the "fire trees"; or call out often enough to the squirrels and rabbits and pheasants that walked around as if New York City had never grown up around their land. When they passed a statue of a dog, Celia pretended to bark, and the child's cry startled a duck which flew out of the thick foliage at the edge of a silvery-gray pond. The duck lifted heavily into the air, its huge wings rising and falling as if the air were water to it. Little frogs jumped from the flat lily leaves into the gray water, which slapped at Esheal and Celia's feet where they stood at the muddy edge of the pond.

Esheal knew that Lily, who was superstitious, would never approve of his having brought the child here, and he would not have brought her himself, if Celia had the slightest idea of what kind of place it was. But she called this cemetery the "statue park," and she loved it because it was so full of angels. She ate her lunch sitting on the lap of a huge, gray angel whose wings furled like enormous banners over both of them. "At night," Celia asked him, "do the angels fly around the sky?" "I don't know," said her father. "I think they do," said Celia; "sometimes when I'm sleeping, I see them."

"That's only a dream," said Esheal. "Which angel do you think Grandpa is?" the child asked him. "Grandpa?" asked Esheal. "Grandpa who died," the child said comfortably. "I don't know," said her father. "He's the *big* angel near the public library," said Celia; "only he's green. These angels aren't green." "That's because he's made out of brass," said Esheal. "I like green angels best," said Celia.

Esheal looked at her; she was a plump, round, beautiful blond child with huge brown eyes. He realized that he did not often look at her so closely. She looked very much like Fay, and like Fay, she had a habit of gnawing on wooden things, spoons, clothespins, anything she could get her hands on. Diana liked to say that Fay had nearly eaten up a whole piano. Fay would sit underneath it and gnaw on the large board which ran diagonally across underneath. Then she started on one of the legs, and Lily, who was afraid that the piano would fall on her, made her stop.

From the piano she went to the windowsill. By the time Fay began school, they had to have a carpenter come in to repair the sills, and while he was working, Lily heard a familiar chewing sound and found Celia under the refurbished piano, chewing on another of its legs. To everyone's astonishment, the endless consumption of wood seemed to have no effect on the girls. And his children were so bright. And of them all, Celia was the best. In spite of her illnesses, she was the calmest, the sweetest, the most secure. Esheal would not believe that anything was going to happen to her.

The next day was a Saturday, and the three girls were playing on a stoop across the street, leaning over to talk to the boys who congregated on the porch next door. Celia came over to see what they were doing and climbed up, but she caught sight of a friend of hers on the sidewalk. She started down the stairs, and Fay, who had been watching her, saw her lose her balance and fall. And she fell as if someone had thrown her. She fell down the first flight of steps, bounced onto the little landing, and off onto the second flight of steps which led to the street, and when she fell down the final flight of steps and came to a rest on the sidewalk, she did not get up. Fay flew across the street, screaming for her father, and when he came out, he picked Celia up and carried her back in without saying a word to the other two girls. Lucy and Fay huddled on the stoop across the street from their own house. They saw the doctor go in, and they waited without saying anything to one another. Finally, Fay got up and said she thought they better go find out what was happening over there, and Lucy followed her home.

No one paid any attention to them. Lily was packing some of Celia's clothes and some of her own, and Sarah was packing some of Fay's and Lucy's things. Sarah told them they were going to stay with Dinney, because Celia had to go to the hospital, and when the girls protested no one listened. Bill took them both off. As soon as Lily heard the outside door close, she turned to Esheal. "Spinal meningitis," she said; "what is it?" "An infection of the spine and brain," he said. "How do they cure it?" she asked. "They don't," said Dr. Linde, but even he could not stand up under Lily's look. "They usually don't," he said.

The doctor drove them all to the hospital, and he pleaded with Lily to come home, to get some sleep. Lily said she was staying in the hospital as long as the child stayed. What if the child should wake up and not find her there? She would never forgive herself. And Celia was in the hospital for three days, and during those three days, she was delirious and recognized nobody. Lily kept after her, trying to make her understand that she was there, trying to make her recognize her, but the child only murmured to herself and finally, Lily felt how cold the child's hand was, and when she called for the nurse, the nurse told her Celia was dead. The nurse could not pry Lily away from the bed. Esheal was called, and finally he managed to loosen Lily's fingers, one by one, from the bed's iron frame, and then he half carried her out into the hall.

"Look at that family," Lily said, staring past him; "look what kind of a family those children come from, and they're alive." Esheal felt Lily's hatred of the anonymous family down the hall, and he looked at her face, which seemed to have been twisted from birth by deformed muscles. He was frightened. She looked like a madwoman. "You'll go and stay with Diana for a while," he said to her; "you'll feel better."

But when he got home, Sarah was packing to go to Diana's. "Where are you going?" he demanded; "how can you leave her like this?" "Everyone's sick at Diana's," said Sarah; "the two children, her husband, everyone has the flu. I've got to go to her. She has no one to help her." "What does it matter?" Lily asked, continuing to cry. She had not stopped crying since Celia died. "Put her to bed," said Sarah; "I shouldn't be gone long."

But Sarah was gone longer than she intended to be, because while she was at Diana's, she caught the flu too, and finally Diana sent a note to the pharmacy saying she was desperate for some help. Could Lily come over? Lily had not come out of her room since Celia died; she sat or lay in the dark and cried steadily. There was nothing dramatic in her tears; her crying had the rhythm of her breathing and in fact seemed to be synonymous with it. The girls were afraid of her, and stayed with Dinney, or played on the street. Finally, Esheal decided he had better go see what was happening at Diana's. When he told Lily where he was going, she waved her hand and buried her head in her pillow. "Go catch the flu," she said; "leave the children without a father. The poor little orphans." And she began crying again. Esheal reminded her that the girls still had a mother, or thought they had a mother, but she did not lift her head.

He set off for Diana's feeling as if he had betrayed his own family, and when he got there, he found little enough he could do. He went out and got Diana a folding cot, and while Diana walked around the house, he talked and talked and talked, and later on, when he thought about that day, he could not understand what had possessed him. To tell Diana so much about how he felt when he knew she would not be sympathetic! But he had to talk to someone, and Diana, exhausted as she was, was there.

Chapter 44

Diana

That year, the flu was a terrible thing. It was like a plague. Whole families were wiped out; whole *buildings* were wiped out. Of course, my sister didn't have the flu in her house. She had everything else. And I couldn't go to see her because everybody in my own house was so sick. My own children got it, and my mother came to help me, and with her high blood pressure, she got it, and the doctor said she would have to stay in bed. She didn't want to go to the hospital, she was afraid of hospitals, so I said, go into my bed. So she stayed in my bed, and she developed an ear infection. They said she had water on the eardrum and seven times her ears were opened. And I was still busy with them all, all sick, my mother in the bargain. So I figured I'm walking around anyway, and I was up night and day, and Esheal came to my house, and when he saw me he said, my God, you look something terrible. And I said I haven't got a place even to lie down and I can't lie down. If one child stops crying, the other one starts, and now Momma's here, so it's impossible. If I had a folding bed, I'd put it in the dining room. So he did go and buy a bed and I lay down there.

And then when I got up he started to talk to me. I always thought he was too quiet, but I saw that when he talked, you could die from him. He told me about Celia. Well, that I knew because Mother had told me Celia died the minute she walked in the door, and then Sidney, sick as he was, made me go get him his medical book so he could look up spinal meningitis. As soon as you had an illness, Sidney got his medical book and came back to tell me what the results of that illness could be. You could drop dead from that man. Whatever the children had, he went and got the book. He fixed me good. So even before Esheal came, I knew the whole story about spinal meningitis. And I felt terrible sorry for him, and I usually didn't. I usually felt sorry for my poor sister, but this time I felt sorry for him, and he knew it, and he started to talk to me. He was going to talk to Lily after a child died? The minute I heard the child died, I didn't want to see her. I didn't want to talk to her. I was *afraid* to see her.

And what did he decide to talk about there in the house where everyone had the flu, and people were dying right and left all over the city, and on every door, a black crepe if it was an adult, and a little white one if it was a child. I can't stand to see anything black or white on a door to this day. He decided to talk about the day he took Celia to Greenwood Cemetery, the day before she died. So naturally I thought he was blaming himself for scaring the child to death, but he said, no, Celia loved it there, and she didn't know it was a cemetery; she thought it was a statue park. That's a reason to take such a sick child to a cemetery? And he started to talk about what happened there. He took Celia down to one of the ponds, and a big duck came flying out, and it was just like Russia. So good, I still didn't know what he was getting at.

And then he said she wanted to climb up a little hill near the pond so she could go sit on a little stone bench, and as they were climbing, he asks her, do you like it here? And she said, oh, yes, she loved it. And he thought to himself, you could be buried here, and he said he almost said that out loud. And he said when he thought that, he thought he was going out of his mind. And he said it was terrible, because he wanted to go on with it. He wanted to talk to the child about how she was going to die, and he wanted her to lie down on the bench and pretend she was dead, as if she were practicing.

And I said those were terrible thoughts to have, and he said they were, and that the whole time he was there, he kept thinking the same thing over again and over again: "Would you like to be buried here? You could be buried here." And he said he didn't know what he was going to do with Lily, and I said I couldn't tell him what to do with her, because once she started crying, you couldn't stop her, and it was wrong to stop her because she needed to cry. He said what about the children, and I didn't know what to say. After a while, I said, when she's feeling a little better, take her out. Make her get used to things again. I should have known better than to say anything.

And then I got sick, and my heart was very bad, and I couldn't move, and the whole time I lay there, I kept seeing this gray lake and this big black duck flying out of the swamp and the trees and across the gray sky and I kept hearing Esheal say, "You want to be buried here? You could be buried here." And how, after he thought that, he looked at her, and he knew she was going to die. It was worse than the sickness, thinking about that. And I thought about what Esheal said and how Momma said Lily wouldn't come out of her room but stayed in there crying all the time, and each time I thought about the two of them, I was sorry I had said anything at all to Esheal about my sister. I should have known better.

Chapter 45

When it became apparent that Lily would not come to visit her family, Sarah called all the children together at Diana's house. "We can't just leave her there crying," said Sarah, and the others agreed and then waited to hear what Sarah had decided. "But," said Sarah, "I can't go back to Lily when Diana is so sick." Diana nodded agreement. "So," said Sarah, "if I can't be in two places at once, it's best to have us all in one place. Dave is alone in Poppa's house; he has no one to cook for him. Bill is alone in the apartment in Esheal's house and Diana is sick here with two little children. I can't go and do like I used to, and you're too busy or too sick to come running to me. So we should all move back into Poppa's house. Sidney and Diana can take the first floor, and the rest of us can take the top floors. Lily will be right around the corner." Everyone looked at Sidney. "Fine, Aunt Sarah," he said; "it's too crowded here. No one gets any peace." "So," said Sarah, "who knows a moving man?" "Esheal does," said Bill. "When do we want the moving man?" he asked. "As soon as he can come," said Sarah; "tell Esheal to get me in the car today so I can tell Lily what's happening here, she shouldn't think I'm running away from her house."

Sarah had hoped the others were exaggerating when they spoke of Lily's condition, but when Sarah saw her, she saw things even worse than she had thought. She sat down on the edge of Lily's bed and watched her. When she put her hand on her daughter's shoulder, Lily pulled away. "It's a terrible thing to lose a child," said her mother; "I lost two. In Russia, before you were born, they almost choked to death. Then they came here and that finished them. Two on one night," said Sarah.

Lily's rhythmic crying continued as if her mother were not there, as if her mother had not spoken. "This has been going on how long now?" Sarah asked; "four weeks? Five? Maybe even six. Six weeks you haven't been to visit the grave. You let the child lay there in the cold and you don't go visit her?" Lily wriggled closer to the wall. "She lays there and she thinks, 'I never had a mother; a mother would come and see me. A mother would put flowers on my grave so I didn't have to look at the sky through dirty stones. If I had a mother, my mother would do that.' " The rhythm of Lily's crying became more irregular, as if she were pausing to listen.

"The poor little thing wants to go up to heaven, but she's afraid to go. She can't go because she drifts around this house asking if she had a mother, and if she had one, where is she? At night, in the cemeteries, you see them," said Sarah; "they look like mists and they hover around the stones when there is no other mist. A stone weighs them down. It's a terrible thing. They howl like wolves. You don't hear her at night?" Lily's blanket twitched. "She doesn't touch you with her cold hand? She doesn't blame you?" "Stop it," Lily said; "stop it and leave me alone."

"What did you say to your mother?" Sarah asked, standing up; "what did I hear you say?" Lily whimpered. "Say it again!" demanded Sarah; "I want to hear that again!" "I said," Lily repeated defiantly, "leave me alone." Sarah bent down, gripped the feather quilt covering Lily, and sent it flying across the room. Lily felt about for the quilt, but when she could not find it, she curled herself up tighter.

Sarah took hold of Lily's nightgown. "Get up, Lilian," said her mother. Lily did not move. "I said get up," said Sarah, and she tore the sleeve away from the shoulder of the nightgown. "Get up," said Sarah, "or I'll tear this from you piece by piece until you've got nothing on but your sniveling skin."

When Lily still did not move, Sarah slid her hand between her shoulder and her nightgown and ripped the nightgown down the side. "So this is what you make your mother do," said Sarah; "this is the kind of daughter you are. If you don't get up, I'm leaving this house now, and if I leave, I don't come back." Sarah started to button her coat when she saw Lily uncurling, pushing herself up on one arm, and, as if she were a creature slowly forming herself out of mud, she pulled loose from the bed and sat up, bracing herself with both hands.

"Happy now?" asked Lily. Sarah bent forward and slapped her daughter's face; she watched Lily rub the red spot on her cheek. "You look something terrible," said her mother; "that I should live to see this! Two healthy children running around without a mother and one lying cold in the ground, a husband who has nothing to eat, a sister with the flu, and you lie here taking a nap! If your father had lived to see this! So how long is it going to go on, Lily? You should come and see your sister." "Her children are alive," said Lily. "You envy the living after they close the coffin lid on them," said Sarah; "if your sister's child died, would your own come back?"

"Why did I have to go to the country?" said Lily; "if I hadn't been hit by that baseball it never would have happened." "No more," said Sarah; "she's dead and she's gone. You had her for almost five years. That's a long time to have a child. But you have two. The girls are scared of you. Do you know what that means, to be scared of your own mother?" "Why should they be scared of me?" asked Lily. "Look at yourself," said her mother. "You're shriveled up like a raisin. Your hair, I don't even know what to call it. When did you wash it?" "I don't know," her daughter said; "before Celia died."

"Before Celia died!" exclaimed her mother; "there must be rats walking in that hair. If Celia flies back to look at her mother, this is what she's going to see?" "Do you believe that?" asked Lily; "that they come back and visit?" "They do," said Sarah; "in Teray, there was a widow in the house next to ours, and she filled the skies with such lamentations the neighbors went to the rabbi to complain, they couldn't get any sleep, but he had already been to see the widow, and he decided that the neighbors should soak little cloths with oil and fill their ears with it when they wanted to sleep. He knew he couldn't do anything about her. And one night, we heard her screaming, help and murder, and her voice wasn't in the house. It was outside.

"And when we looked out the window, there she was, running this way and that in the snow, and sometimes she'd fall down in it, and then she'd get up again and start running this way and that way and it was cold as death out there, and you could hear the wolves, and the dogs were screaming, and all night, she was running back and forth. And in the morning, we went out to see what was going on, and she said her husband came back and he tossed her all around and said she was keeping him down there in the cold and if she didn't stop her lamentations, he was going to get her and throw her out in the cold every night. When the rabbi came, there were two sets of footprints, hers and a big man's prints, a man with boots. So they come back and visit, but after some time, you have to let them go."

"They don't belong?" asked Lily. "They can't keep up," said Sarah; "the living keep going. They stay the same. It hurts them." "You believe that?" asked Lily. "It's the truth," said her mother; "this is not Russia. It's so noisy here you can't hear them."

"Does Poppa come back?" Lily asked. "Of course he does," said Sarah; "but when he's ready, he'll go. I won't hold him." "He's not ready yet?" asked Lily. "There's too much going on in the family," said Sarah. "Don't say anything about this to Esheal," Lily warned her; "he'd think you were crazy." "Why should I tell Esheal?" Sarah said; "it's not his family. We're moving back into Poppa's house Sunday. I'm going over to take a look. Maybe you'll come?" Lily hesitated, sat up, and sat on the edge of the bed. "First, wash your hair," said her mother; "I'll help you."

Chapter 46

When Sarah and the rest of the family moved back into the house on Carroll Street, Esheal felt as if the floor, which had been shifting under his feet, suddenly stood still. But he saw at once that the woman who used to stand in front of his pharmacy, one hand on her hip, the other around the shoulders of one of the children, her head tilted back, smiling so happily that even her ears seemed to rise as she smiled, that woman was gone. That woman, with her narrow waist, her neat, dark skirts, her pure white blouses, who held up her children as if she had just thrown them up in the air and had just caught them, was gone.

Lily had always worn little round spectacles, but before Celia's death, he had never noticed them, or if he had (and he saw with surprise that Lily had been wearing them in her wedding portrait), they had seemed like thin, bright circles of light which illuminated his wife's eyes. Celia's death had changed her face permanently; there was a perpetual furrow between her eyebrows and her expression was a cross between puzzlement and a frown. Now she stared straight into the camera as if to ask it what more it wanted of her, and she pulled back from it. Her hair, some of which she had pulled from her head after the child's death, was thinner and strands of it were always escaping. One day, Esheal came in and found Lily sitting in a chair staring at a photograph Sarah had brought over, and when he looked at it, he felt cold.

In the picture, Lily was sitting on the grass near the dirt path, holding Celia in her lap. Fay sat next to her, and Lucy, who had just been slapped, was standing up next to Fay, sulking. When Esheal looked at the snapshot, he did not know why it had come out. The background was pitch-black and it seemed as if the picture had been taken in the middle of the night. Esheal remembered that Sarah had been standing across the road, and he had been in back of her, and he had taken the picture. Esheal had given Sarah a camera of her own, and he had been certain that her picture would not come out, so he stood behind her and used his own camera. And his picture showed Lily and the girls phosphorescent in the night, while Sarah's shadow fell like a black arrow across the road, pointing at Celia. "Then it's true," Esheal heard Lily say. "What's true?" he asked. "Oh, nothing," she said, shuffling the picture to the bottom of the heap. "What are you doing today?" he asked. "Going over to Mother's," she said.

And for a long time, that was the only place she would go. And when she came home, she and the girls would be chattering about what they had done and what they had seen and who had said what, and who had been the funniest, and occasionally, they would catch sight of Esheal, and start laughing for no reason at all, and he knew Diana had been at her imitations again. He told himself that he was lucky that Lily was going out at all, but as she began to enjoy her visits more and more, he began to resent them.

And he did not like the sound of what went on over at Sarah's house. "Isn't he gorgeous?" Lucy asked Fay one day when they came home before Lily. They were sitting at the soda fountain drinking black-and-white sodas. "He is gorgeous," said Fay. "I want to marry a handsome man like that," said Lucy. "He'll be too old when you're ready to get married," said Fay. "I don't mean him, dummy," said her sister; "I want to marry someone who looks like him."

"Who's this wonderful man?" Esheal asked the girls. "He's a friend of Dave's, and can he dance!" said Lucy; "you should see him dance with Mother!" "I didn't know Mother could dance like that," said Fay; "you should see how pretty she looks when she's dancing." "Well, how did I look when I was dancing?" Lucy asked her. "You? You looked silly. You're so short. Your head came up to his belt buckle." "Mother's a good dancer," Lucy said. "She sure is," said Fay; "maybe she could teach us." "*She* can't teach us," said Lucy; "we need a man to teach us. George said he'd teach us." "I wish Uncle Dave would teach us," said Fay; "he's the best dancer there is. Doesn't he look gorgeous dancing with Stella?" "Stella?" asked Esheal. "Another one of his girls," said Lucy; "that's who Mother said she was."

"I'm surprised your mother was dancing," said Esheal. "Oh, she always dances with Uncle Dave," said Lucy; "it's a pity you don't dance when she likes to dance so much." "Is that what your Aunt Diana said?" Esheal asked. "That's what she said," Fay told him; "Aunt Diana dances beautifully, too." "Who does she dance with?" Esheal asked. "Oh, sometimes with George, sometimes with Michael, sometimes with Leonard. They take turns. Aunt Diana likes dancing with Leonard best, because he's not too tall for her. And when Leonard went out with Mother, you should have seen what they brought back from the bakery. I'm stuffed," said Fay, who was digging the rest of her ice cream out of the glass with her long spoon. "What's this Leonard, George business?" asked their father; "don't you call them uncle?" "They said they weren't our uncles," said Lucy, "and it makes them feel too old if we call them uncle, so we don't."

Just then Lily came in. "Here," she said, handing Esheal a rose, "put this in a glass of water." "Where did you get a rose in the middle of the winter?" he asked her. "George brought some to Mother and she gave me one to take home. I always loved roses. If we ever have a garden, I'm going to have a hundred rosebushes."

"How about going over to my sister's this weekend?" Esheal asked her. "I don't want to see anyone yet," Lily said; "not anyone outside the family." "What about a movie?" Esheal asked; "there's a good one at the Brunswick." "Maybe next week," said Lily; "I have to bake some cake for Momma. Diana's in-laws, our cousins from Boston, are coming over tomorrow."

"Lily," Esheal said as they were going to bed, "I don't like you going over there and spending so much time with strange men." "Strange men?" she said; "what strange men?" "George, Leonard, *those* strange men." "They're not strange men," said Lily; "they're friends of the family." "Some friends," said Esheal; "how do I know what you're up to there?" "What *could* I be up to?" asked Lily. "Everyone's there. My mother's there, my brothers, my sister, the girls." "You went out with Leonard," Esheal said. "I went to the *bakery* with Leonard; he didn't know what to pick out." "You couldn't go alone to a bakery?" "It was his money," said Lily; "Mother asked me to go with him."

"Sarah asked you to go out with another man?" "For Christ's sake," Lily said, "she asked me to go out to the bakery with him so he wouldn't buy too much." "And you have to do what your mother asks you to do?" "I don't want to talk about it," said Lily; "it's ridiculous. I go to the bakery for some cake and already there's a whole trial. Enough of it." "Lower your voice," Esheal said; "the girls will hear you." "Maybe the girls should hear me," said Lily; "I never heard of such a jealous man!" "If you'd only stay home once in a while," said Esheal. "When I stayed home," Lily said, "you begged me to go out." "If we went places together more," he said. "And when are we going to go anywhere?" asked his wife; "you work from the crack of dawn until midnight." "I could take more time off," he said. "But you don't," said Lily.

"You could wait up for me," he said resentfully; "I'm hungry when I finish working in the middle of the night." "You're hungry," said Lily; "I ask you, what grown man with both his arms and a refrigerator full of food can't find something to eat at twelve o'clock at night? After a whole day cleaning the house and taking care of the girls, I'm tired."

"You don't spend the whole day cleaning and taking care of the girls," Esheal said angrily. "You spend most of your time at your mother's. Why don't you try doing some cooking for me for a change?" "I cook your breakfast, I cook your lunches, I send down your dinners on the dumbwaiter; how many more meals should I cook?" "But you have time to go to the bakery and get special cake for Leonard!" "I told you," said Lily; "I told you I went to buy cake for everyone who came to Mother's. It's a terrible thing, this jealousy." "It's terrible to make a husband jealous," said Esheal. "All I have to do is breathe in and out and you're jealous," she said. She flung herself down in bed, wrapped the blanket around her, and lay there motionless. "I'm telling you, Lily," he said; "this has to stop." She refused to answer him.

And the arguing went on all that winter. Lily did not stop visiting her mother, because, when she went there, she forgot everything; she forgot that Celia was dead. And one day she thought that was why she hated to come home; the house had too many memories of the little child. She spoke to Esheal about it, and when he heard that Lily was unhappy in the apartment over the pharmacy because she kept seeing Celia wherever she turned, he said of course they would move. Then he went down to the pharmacy and thought about the child's death. That Celia's death had changed his wife, he knew. One day, when he was at Sarah's, he watched Diana pasting snapshots of Lily into a photograph album, and he saw that she wrote on the bottom of each of the snapshots: "After she lost Celia." So Diana sensed it, too. None of them was the same since the death of the child.

But how was he different? He went about his business as he had always done; he worried about the children as he had always done. But his sense of the world was not what it was. Not since the day he had left the zenshina's had he felt so acutely the hostile nature of passing time which he now saw, when he closed his eyes, as a coiled cobra about to strike. He sensed the villainy loose in the world; that, he told himself, was what happened to him after Celia died. That was how he had changed. And he could not lose his sense of the world as a slow, patient opponent, a surface full of mouths waiting to swallow everything up. He had sensed this before, when he left the zenshina's, but then this awareness had left him. Now it did not. It sat on his left shoulder when he worked; it sat on the top of his head when he slept. It had caught him and its claws dug through the fabric of his clothing into his skin and would not let him go. He hoped that if they found another house and moved into it, he would somehow escape this malevolent bird which sat on his shoulder like a vulture or hawk.

And he found a house on Maple Street and told Lily that they would move into it before Labor Day, so that by the time school began, the girls would be settled in. He assumed that once they moved out of the house on Chauncey and Howard, Lily would not visit her mother's house so frequently. Had anyone asked him, he would have said that Lily promised to stop visiting her mother once they moved to Maple Street. But of course Lily had not intended to say that at all, and she would have been surprised if she had known what Esheal thought.

As that summer approached, cases of polio began breaking out all over the city, and Dr. Linde warned Esheal that the Board of Health expected such a bad epidemic that they would soon keep all trains from leaving the city. Esheal told Lily that she ought to take the children to the country. "I don't want to go to the country," she said. "It's dangerous here," said Esheal; "what if they came down with it? Isn't your sister going to Boston?" "She's going to Revere Beach," said Lily; "what has that got to do with me? She has family there."

"Ask her if you can stay with her. I heard the Board of

Health won't be letting people out much longer. Probably Boston won't be letting people in. We lost one child," Esheal said; "do I have to remind you?" "You don't have to remind me," his wife answered in a cold voice; "I'll speak to Diana. Her husband won't like it. Sidney's going to say, 'Why bother going to the beach? All the polio in New York is coming to you.'" "You're not all of New York," said Esheal; "you're her sister. Just stay away from her friends there. The Georges and the Leonards."

"I'll speak to Diana," she said, ignoring his insinuations. "And write me every two days to tell me how the girls are. I don't want to sit here all summer worrying." "You won't worry about me?" asked Lily. "If I get a letter from you, I'll know you're all right," he said. "Very nice," said Lily; "good for me. Hooray for me." "She can lie and say you live there," Esheal said. Sarah decided to go with Lily. A week later, Esheal took Lily and the girls to the train, and when she got on the train, Lily did not look back at him. His wife was talking to Sarah and the girls were waving frantically from the window.

Lily wrote three times a week as Esheal had asked her to, reporting lengthily on the health of the two girls. She said they had been the last train let in to Central Station, and that they could not have stayed if Diana had not lied and said they lived with her. The girls, she said, were fine. Almost every letter contained two or three pictures of Lily and the girls, or pictures of Diana and her children. And, as the letters began to arrive more frequently, Lily began writing messages on them. "Lucy looks much prettier than she does in this picture, the darling," or, "Fay got the hardest spanking, that's why she looks so pretty." When he saw the photographs and their captions, Esheal knew that his wife was recovering. Before she left for Boston, she had no interest in pictures. Ones he took piled up in the breakfront drawer. She had little interest in anything. Now she wrote to say that she and Diana had pooled their money and bought a mattress which they dragged out onto the rocky beach every day it wasn't raining, and that he ought to see what Diana looked like in her black bathing costume with its black stockings. She looked, Lily said, like a fat black duck. Lily wore white dresses and rested on the mattress but did not go in the water.

Near the end of the summer, Esheal got a fat envelope and when he opened it, he shook it, looking for pictures. Lily's handwriting was illegible. The day before, she said, Lucy had almost been killed by a car on the beach and she would have been killed if it hadn't been for Sarah, who had come to the beach a few weeks before. "Diana," wrote Lily, "took the children down to the beach with Momma, and then she came back, so I went down to keep Momma company. We were sitting on that great, big mattress Diana and I bought. I was lying on one end of the mattress, holding Fay, and Momma had Lucy on her lap, and for some reason, Momma picked Lucy up and put her down beside me, when all of a sudden we heard a terrible noise, and before we knew what was happening, a huge, shiny black car flew off the raised roadway that went down to the beach, and we saw it coming straight for us, and it landed right on the mattress. The car wheels landed right on Momma's skirt, just where Lucy was sitting, and if Momma hadn't decided to pick her up and move her over, the car would have landed right on her. Believe it or not, the man in the car wasn't hurt. He bounced up and down in his seat, and when he stopped bouncing, he looked at us, and his mouth was open so wide Momma said you could see down past his tonsils. And all of a sudden, Momma started to laugh, and then I started to laugh, and the man just sat there, he was shaking a mile a minute, and all the girls wanted to know was, could they go for a ride when he got the car off the mattress. And people came running out of all the houses and we had some crowd around us, and everyone looked at Momma's skirt, because she had to sit there until they lifted the car off, and everyone said she had the best luck of anyone they'd ever heard of. I think she saved Lucy's life, don't you?"

When the girls came home, school began. They went for walks with their friends, came home before dark and started on their schoolwork. On weekends, they turned Lucy's room or Fay's room into a clubhouse, and the names of their clubs changed continually. One week, they were the Order of the Golden Shield, because one of the children had some gold paper and made paper medals with that name. They spent more and more time at Sarah's. They went to the movies together. They spent so long exploring the inside of the school gymnasium that they got locked inside it and Lily had to go up to speak to the teacher, and when she came back, she threatened the girls with everything she could think of, and according to her, if the teacher had not heard them knocking at the door, they would have spent the weekend alone in the school. And it was a three-day weekend, and they would have been lined up dead like sardines Tuesday morning when the school reopened.

And time continued to pass in this way. Lily continued to say that such and such a thing had happened a year before Celia died or two years after she died. She did not lose her worried look, and the furrow between her brows became permanent and deep. Esheal felt the claws of the bird dig into his shoulder as he rang up a sale on the cash register, as he ground his powders in his mortar, and as he looked at his two daughters asleep in their beds. Lucy began high school. Lucy was thirteen; Fay was eleven. The two of them were at the head of their classes and Lily spent more and more time sewing dresses for them, going over their homework with them, although often it appeared as if the girls were going over their mother's homework for her. Lily took them over to Sarah's constantly. And to everyone who looked at the Lurias, they seemed a happy, peaceful family. Their life ran along smoothly, as if they were on a high road that had no ruts or sharp turns.

And during the next six years, the one event that stood out was Esheal's car accident. He had been driving his silvery gray car along Maple Street when, without warning, a bus plowed into him, and his car was utterly destroyed. He stepped out of the ruins of the gray Westcott without a scratch and found himself the center of an excited crowd, all of whom wanted to touch him and speak to him. He was, he saw, the victim of a miracle. "I was just lucky, I was just lucky," he kept repeating as he made his way out of the crowd, and after he talked to the police and to the bus driver, he went home to tell Lily what happened. "Death doesn't want you," Lily said, going back to her mending. Esheal said he supposed she was right, told the clerk he was going out, and took the streetcar to the Westcott showroom, where he bought an identical car, one which had, however, all the "new improvements."

Shortly after the accident, Lily was out shopping for a chicken when she caught sight of Esheal through the window. She told the woman behind her to keep her place on line, and went out on to the street. Her husband was walking away quickly in the other direction. She caught up with him and tapped him on the shoulder. "What are you doing here?" she asked him. "I needed something," he said. "What?" "Some thread," he said. "Some thread at a butcher shop?" Lily asked. "So I went out for a walk," Esheal said; "is that a crime?" "It's no crime," said Lily; "as long as you're here, why don't you wait for me and help me carry the packages back?"

The next month, Lily went into the dry-goods store, and looked up to see her husband suddenly vanish from sight. When she went out into the street, he was nowhere to be found. Maybe he was looking for someone, she thought, and forgot about it, but the next time she went into the grocery store, she saw Esheal watching her from the street. This time she stayed on line until she had bought everything she needed.

When she got home, she put away the groceries and looked in on the girls; they were both studying at the kitchen table. She found Esheal in the pharmacy. "What is it with you?" she asked him; "every time I look out of a store window, there you are. You're doing a lot of walking all of a sudden." Esheal looked down at a prescription, and took a glass bottle from the high shelf. He did not look at his wife.

"You're following me?" said Lily; "aren't you?" "Why would I follow you?" asked Esheal. "How would I know?" said Lily; "do I go around following people?" "Yesterday," said Esheal, "Mr. Appleman came in and told me he'd seen you and you said that Bill was opening his own pharmacy." "So?" said Lily; "you know all that." "I didn't know you talked to Mr. Appleman," said her husband. "Who thought of telling you?" said Lily; "it wasn't important." "If it wasn't important, you should have told me." "I can't remember everyone I say hello to all day long," said Lily. "You don't spend much time saying hello to me," said her husband; "you spent my birthday at your mother's." "I forgot!" Lily said, clapping her hands over her mouth, horrified. "I didn't forget," said Esheal; "what did your brothers tell you? That you couldn't afford a cake big enough to hold so many candles?" "I just forgot!" said Lily.

"I don't want you following me," she said; "I'll be a laughingstock." "Is that the only reason?" he asked; "I see how you talk to men in the stores." "How do I talk to them?" Lily asked, her voice rising. "How do I talk to them?" "You know how you talk to them," he said. "Don't think I don't know why you spend so much time at your mother's; you go there to meet your brother's friends."

"Not that again!" exclaimed Lily. "Is it my fault it's that again?" asked Esheal. "Am I the one who goes over to my sisters' houses and spends my time with all their single friends? What would you think of that?" "Nothing," screamed Lily; "I wouldn't think anything of that. Your sister's your sister. She's not a madam!" "That's fine talk for a married woman," said her husband. "Listen to yourself," Lily shouted; "what kind of husband accuses his wife of the things you accuse me of?"

"If you told me the truth," said Esheal, "we could start over. If you'd tell me the truth and promise not to see those men again." "What men?" shrieked Lily, beside herself. "That's what I want to know," Esheal said; "what men?"

"There are no men," Lily said. "You mean you won't tell me who they are," said her husband. "I won't tell you who they are because I can't tell you who they are; there aren't any." "If you tell me," said Esheal, "we'll forget all about it and start over again."

Lily stared at him, her expression strange, as if she were considering confessing to a crime just to restore order to her life. "How long have you been following me?" she asked him. "Long enough," he said. "You're to stop it," Lily said; "do you hear me? You're to stop it! I'll go stay with Mother." "You won't take the girls to your mother's," he said. "What kind of a woman is she? She lets them sit there while your brothers get dressed. She lets them sit at their feet, giving them a cuff link or a sock. Fay told me what she said; that she'd like it if Fay married your brother Bill. That's a decent woman? A mother who wants her son to marry her grand-daughter?"

"Don't you say anything about my family!" Lily hissed. "Why? They're perfect?" asked Esheal; "your brother will be back in jail next week. I heard all about him. He's embezzling money. This time he won't get out so fast. At least your mother won't try marrying him off to Lucy."

Lily began to cry. "Cry all you want," he said; "they're not decent people." "You're a meshuggeneh," cried Lily; "that's what you are. If you want to see what I'm doing over there on Sundays, come over yourself. If you want to hide away in the store, don't blame me. You don't see me peeping in the window trying to catch you whispering to women." "You're too busy with someone else," said Esheal; "the busier I am, the better you like it." "That's not true," sobbed Lily; "I'd like some company, too."

Just then, the bell over the door tinkled and someone came in. "I'll talk to you about this later," Esheal said. "There is nothing to talk about," said Lily. "I want to know who it is," said Esheal. "There *is* no one," Lily hissed. Mrs. Berman came up to the counter and smiled at the two of them. "In Poland," she said, "my husband, God rest his soul, and I used to work together in the store like this."

Chapter 47

The very shadows on the street came to alarm Lily. If someone jostled her while she was fighting with another woman over flannel pajamas at a sale at Gimbel's, she would jump and turn around, expecting to see her husband. She had always loved sales, and Dave used to joke about it and say she had the fastest "draw" in the West, and it was true. If there was a bargain to be gotten, Lily's hand shot out and she got her hand on it first. Now the sales made her nervous and other women were always getting things away from her. When she had to leave the store empty-handed, she concluded that she was indeed a nervous wreck as her brother Bill said she was, took the train home, and went to talk to her mother.

"I don't know what to do anymore," she told Sarah, still clutching her packages to her; "sometimes I think he's crazy. I'm afraid of him. You should see how he looks at me. You know what it's like to buy a chicken and look up and see your husband staring at you like a ghost?" "Take off your coat," said Sarah; "put down your packages." "I went to get some hair ribbons for the girls at Woolworth's, and who do I see in the candy department?" "Did you ask him about it?" "I asked him," said Lily; "he said he was buying me a box of candy." "Maybe he was," said her mother; "Meyer used to bring me candy until Dr. Linde said I couldn't eat it." "Why would he buy me candy in Woolworth's when he has a candy department in his own store?" her daughter asked. "Maybe they had something better," Sarah said. "So what was he looking for outside the girdle store?" asked Lily; "he was going to buy me a girdle?" "He was in the neighborhood," said Sarah; "there are other stores there." "He wasn't looking at the other stores," said Lily, "and when he saw me, he ran like a horse thief."

"You think he's really following you?" Sarah asked. "He

wants to catch me with some man. He's sure there's some man I'm seeing." "May his heart burn like his ears!" exclaimed Sarah; "I would never have believed it."

"He's always been this way," said Lily. "Always?" asked Sarah. "Even before Celia died," said Lily. "And for no reason. I ask him what reasons he has, and he says he has his reasons, and I know what they are. So what can I do? I'm afraid of my shadow." "Do the girls know?" asked Sarah. "They don't know anything. You think he's going to say something where they can hear it? He waits to get me alone. Hooray for me."

"So maybe you should stay home more," suggested Sarah; "until he gets over it." "He's not going to get over it," Lily said. "Maybe he will," said her mother. "He won't. He picks fights with Bill in the store. He thinks Bill brings men home to meet me. That's why Bill's leaving. He doesn't want to go out on his own. He can't take it anymore."

"But you should try," said Sarah; "except for the jealousy, he's a good husband." "Except for the jealousy!" Lily exclaimed. "He's a good father," Sarah reminded her. "That's true," Lily said. "The girls would be heartbroken if anything happened." "I know," said Lily; "but I can't stand it. My hand shakes all over." "Stay home more," Sarah insisted; "we'll come to you. If I can't come, the others will come. Then we'll see. Maybe I could talk to him." "No," said Lily. "Why not? We used to be close." "Now he things you're in on it," said her daughter. Sarah stared, open-mouthed, and then she said something in Yiddish Lily could not understand. "He should live so long that I should go to his house again," said Sarah. "You just said you would come!" Lily said. "Not to talk to him," Sarah said; "he can go sit on a tack in hell!"

Lily began to stay at home, but the more she stayed home, the angrier she became at her husband and his outrageous suspicions. She became sarcastic, and her sarcasm became habitual. One night she came down for some boric acid. "I'm sorry to keep you in in such weather," she said; "if I had somewhere to go, you could come out in the snow and catch pneumonia." Esheal ignored her. "Don't you want to know who the boric acid's for?" asked Lily; "it's for Lucy. Her eyes are red from so much studying. Look at the snow," she said, going over to the window; "if you had some time, we could take the girls sledding in the park." "I don't have any time," said Esheal; "everyone's sick." "You're the only pharmacist in the world?" Lily asked him. "Next weekend," she said, "I'm going over to Mother's for her birthday. Are you coming?" "Coming where?" he asked absently. "Wake up and smell the coffee," Lily said impatiently; "to Mother's birthday party."

"When is it?" he asked. "Sunday," she said. "Next Sunday's my day on." "Well, I haven't been out of the house in two weeks," said Lily, "and I'm going to my own mother's birthday party. She won't be having that many more." "Then go," said Esheal. "You don't mind?" Lily asked. "Why should I mind?" said Esheal. It was true, he thought. Sarah could not live that much longer.

The night of the party, the girls came back before Lily. "Where's your mother?" he asked. "She stayed to clean up," Fay said; "we have to go to bed at nine o'clock before school no matter what, so we're home. How old do we have to be before we can stay up later than nine o'clock?" "Old enough to get married," said Esheal absently. He was peering out of the door, looking down the empty street. "Don't worry about Mother," said Fay; "everybody's dancing. It will take her awhile to get finished."

The phone rang and Lily asked Esheal if he would mind her staying the night with her mother; the house was a mess and her mother was dizzy and she wanted to stay there. The boys were too drunk to be trusted with her. "Fine," said Esheal; "stay." He called up the dumbwaiter to tell the girls he was going out to deliver a prescription. Then he went out, walked over to the Romanoffs', and stood in the doorway of a house across the street. He lost track of time and had no idea how long his toes had been numb, when suddenly Sarah's door opened, and there was Lily, waving goodbye to two young men. They started down the stairs and then ran back up and hugged her and kissed her on the cheek. "Go home, already," Lily called out, and the door was closed, and the streaming yellow light cut off at its source.

When Lily came home the next day, Esheal listened to her talk about the party, about how much it had meant to Sarah, who kept saying she only hoped she'd live to have another one so nice, and how happy everyone had been, and how drunk. She said she thought her brothers were still sleeping it off, and she rattled on about how much fun everyone had had, and how Sidney sang with Diana while she played the piano and it was just like old times. She said it was too bad

Esheal wasn't there. And wasn't it sad that her father wasn't there, and that her grandfather wasn't, because if they had only been there, it would have been as if no time at all had passed. Esheal waited for her to say something about the dancing, about the two men he had seen kiss her good night, but she did not mention them. She went on and on about the party and how Dinney and Diana sang, and she played the piano, and Diana played the mandolin, and if she closed her eyes, it was like being a young girl again.

Esheal waited until dinner time was over. The girls would be studying, and when they studied, the heavens could fall and they would not notice. He took the gun he kept in his cash drawer and went upstairs. "I want to talk to you," he said to Lily. "Fine," she said, wiping her soapy hands on her apron; "let me take this off." She hung the apron neatly on the back of a chair and followed him into the bedroom.

"What's so important?" she asked him; "is your sister sick again?" "No," said Esheal; "sit down." "I'm not tired," said his wife. "Sit down!" Esheal insisted. Lily sat down on a chair. "Is this bad news?" she asked; "is that why I'm sitting down?"

Esheal took the gun from his pocket and waved it at Lily. "I know you're having affairs!" he shouted at her; "I want you to confess all of it! If you don't, I'm going to shoot you! Right now!" And he pointed the gun at Lily.

Lily looked at her husband, and she looked at the gun. "Lucy," she called out; "Fay! Come in here! Both of you!" The girls came running into the room and stopped dead in the doorway when they saw their father pointing a gun at their mother. "I want you to see this and hear this," she said to them; "your father says he's going to shoot me if I don't confess that I'm having affairs with other men."

Fay began to choke and the chokes turned into sobs. "Daddy!" said Lucy; "that's a gun! What are you doing?" "He said he was going to shoot me with it," said Lily. "Put it down!" begged Lucy; "put it down!" Esheal put the gun down on the table. "I never intended to use it," he said to the girls. "You shouldn't have called them in," he said to his wife; "this wasn't their business. The children shouldn't have to see this." Both of the girls were crying. Lily, who had an arm around each of them, was trembling violently.

"What's going on here?" Lucy asked; "what's going on here, Daddy?" Esheal mumbled something about having to go to work and went downstairs. Lily told the girls she was sleeping in their room that night because she was afraid of their father, and the two girls looked at each other and started crying again. "But what's wrong?" Lucy asked; "we didn't know anything was wrong." "Well, there was," said Lily, who trembled as if half frozen. "Go get some extra blankets," she told them; "I'm cold."

When Esheal came upstairs that night, his wife, for the first time since their marriage, for the first time since they had lived in the same house, was not in his bed. Esheal went to the girls' room and looked in. They were there. He sighed with relief. But as he turned to go, Lily sat upright, stared at him as if he had risen out of the ground, and, like a cornered animal, watched him until he went back down the hall. He was not surprised when his wife did not speak to him the next morning. It would blow over, he told himself.

But Lily was terrified of him. She was afraid to be in the same house with him. As soon as he went to work, she packed some of her clothes into her string shopping bag and went over to her mother's. When Sarah heard what had happened, she said, "Leave him. He'll kill you. Leave him." Lily asked where she would go if she left him, and Sarah said, come stay here; we'll take care of you. Lily did not go back to the house. She waited for the girls at school and told them to come over to Sarah's. "We're going to be staying with Grandma for a while," she said, and the girls, who were still frightened by what had happened the night before, did not object. "We don't have any clothes," said Lucy. "We'll worry about that later," Lily said; "hurry up."

When they returned to Sarah's house, Sarah had already spoken to Bill. He promised to call them from the pharmacy and tell them when Esheal went out, and when Bill called, Lily sent the girls over in a cab with suitcases; they were to fill them with their clothes and come right back. Dave would go with them.

When they came back, the girls were crying, but Lily told them to stop the nonsense and get their clothes unpacked. They had to go to school the next day. "I'm going to kill him," Dave threatened; "I'm going to beat him to a pulp." "Leave him alone," said Sarah; "he has enough." "He doesn't have enough," said Dave. "Don't you touch him!" Lucy cried; "don't you go near him! It's your fault! Making fun of him all the time, you and Aunt Diana! It's your fault.

He's our father and we love him. I'll call the police on you if you touch him!" "Don't be fresh to your uncle," said Lily. "Oh, leave the child alone," said Dave; "can't you see she's upset?" "That's no excuse," said Lily. "And don't you talk to me, either," Lucy sobbed, running into the bathroom and locking the door. "Well, this is a fine state of affairs," said Lily. "Don't worry," said Dave; "we'll take care of you. You don't have anything to worry about." "Someone has to tell him," said Sarah. Lily began shaking and crying. "I can't," she said; "he'll kill me." "I'll go," said Dave; "it will be my pleasure." "Behave yourself," Sarah warned him.

Dave came back an hour later. "He says he's going to change the locks," he told them; "he said if his wife wants to leave him, she's not coming in to steal his things." "Steal his things!" exclaimed Sarah. "We'll take care of you," Dave said again. "Still," said Sarah, "you have to talk to him. You have to explain." "No," said Lily. "You have to," said her mother. "I'm divorcing him," Lily said. "Then he'll leave me alone."

"You better see a lawyer," Dave said; "you need grounds for a divorce." "I have grounds," said Lily; "when a husband waves a gun at you and threatens to kill you, that's not grounds?" "You have to prove it," Dave said. "The girls will testify," said Lily. "To put them through that," said Sarah; "it's not right. Talk to him. He said he never meant to use the gun."

But the word itself was too much for Lily. She began crying uncontrollably; she was out of control. "You're safe here," Dave said. "I'll never be safe while that man's around!" Lily cried. "Dave," Sarah said; "go get Lucy out of the bathroom. She can't spend the night in there." "Maybe you better get her out," said Dave; "she's fed up with me." "It's a shock, that's all," said Sarah, who went off to plead with the child. And in the middle of the night, Sarah had to get up and take Lily out of the girls' bedroom and make up a bed on the couch for her daughter because her crying was keeping the children up.

Sarah was up early the next morning cooking breakfast. She let the pot of oatmeal bubble on the stove and went to the window trying to sift through her thoughts. In the bright gray air, the snow fell like powder through the clear air; no one had come out and there were no tracks in the snow. The buildings across the street were bluish-gray. Sarah thought she saw something move in one of the doorways, and when she leaned forward to look more closely, she saw Esheal watching her window. She knew that he had been there all night. It was like Diana and her ex-fiancé, Murray Zalman, all over again, she thought. Lily would never agree to see him. She turned the stove off and put on her coat and went across the street.

"I want to see Lily," Esheal said as soon as he saw her. "She doesn't want to see you," Sarah said; "are you surprised? You hold a gun to her head. You call her a tramp. Now you want to see her." "I never meant to hurt her," he said. "She's terrified of you," said Sarah. "I didn't hold a gun to her head," Esheal said. "Pointed a gun, held a gun to her head, what difference is it? A gun is a gun." "If she'll come back, I'll never mention anything again," Esheal said; "I swear it." Sarah looked him over. "But you believe it; you believe my daughter was with other men." "Maybe she wasn't," he said. "Maybe she wasn't!" exclaimed Sarah; "you know she wasn't!" "What does it matter what I believe? I'll never mention it again," he said. "How can she go back knowing you think things like that?" Sarah asked; "sooner or later, it will start all over again. I wouldn't tell her to go back; I couldn't. She's my child. Guns go off. She could be killed." "It will never happen again," he said. "How can you promise that?" she asked.

"Let me talk to her," said Esheal. "I'm not stopping you," said Sarah, "but she won't. If we say your name, or one of the girls says 'Daddy,' she gets hysterical crying. You can't stop her. She shakes like she's got a terrible fever." "I'll get Dr. Linde to send a sedative," he said. "No," said Sarah; "we'll do it. She'll think you're trying to poison her." "Poison her! Kill her!" he said; "I never wanted to hurt her. How are the girls?" "How do you think?" Sarah asked; "either they're silent or they cry. They're terribly upset." "Do they want to see me?" he asked. "Lily won't let them. She's afraid." "I have to talk to her," Esheal pleaded. "I told Lily to talk to you. She won't. Come over at ten. The boys will be gone. The girls will be in school. You can try. I won't stop you."

She went back across the street and when she got back into the kitchen she looked out the window again. Esheal was standing where she had left him. Where was this going to end? At ten o'clock, she let him in and sat him down on the couch in the living room. "Lily," she said, "come into the living room. I have something to say to you." She was going to tell Lily that her husband was there, and that she would stay in the room with them, and that she would be perfectly safe talking to Esheal, but when Lily caught sight of him, she ran out of the room, down the hall, and Sarah heard a window flung open.

She ran down the hall after her, and when she got to the back bedroom, she saw that Lily had climbed out onto the fire escape and closed the window after her. She went back and called Esheal, and from the entrance to the room, he could see his wife, terrified, crouched down on the windowsill, ready to try climbing down to the street below. "How did this happen?" he asked Sarah with tears in his eyes. "I don't understand it," she said; "but you can see it yourself. She's terrified for her life. It's cruel to try and see her. You have to leave her alone." "But I want her to come back," he said; "I want the girls to come back." "That she cannot do," said Sarah; "not now. You see how it is."

"I won't divorce her," Esheal said; "she can't divorce me. She has no grounds. She's the one who left me." "Why do you want to hold on to a woman who hides on a fire escape when she sees you?" "She's my wife," Esheal said; "if we live separately for a while, she may come back." Sarah looked toward the bedroom and the fire escape as if to say she thought that was impossible. "If you won't persuade her to come back," Esheal said, "will you at least persuade her to talk to me?" "You see how it is," Sarah said impatiently. "All right," she said, seeing his face; "I'll try to get her to talk to you. Don't expect it." "I suppose the boys are telling her to stay here?" he asked. "What do you think?" Sarah asked him; "they're her brothers." "What should I do?" asked Esheal. "What can you do? Go home and wait," said Sarah.

Chapter 48

The pharmacy was like a hive which hummed along of its own accord. Like so many bees, the customers came and went in the black clothes and the clerk, who was well trained, filled their prescriptions without any fuss. Esheal trimmed his window twice during the first week Lily was gone. When she still refused to see him, he called old Dr. Mandelbaum in to take charge of the store. He did not believe Lily would call him, at least not for a while. He got into his gray Westcott and drove up to Mrs. Steiner's farm for the weekend.

But the country seemed to have turned against him too. The leaves had long ago fallen and been ground to mud by the rain and the snows. Here and there, some dead leaves clung to the trees and rustled in the cold wind like dry husks of dead insects. The wind, when it blew, brought a faint, sweet smell of rot. The roads had turned to mud wallows, and sucked at the feet as if the earth itself wanted to pull someone down. The few birds who had been left behind flew cawing and screaming against a gray glass sky. Every so often, Mrs. Steiner came out to feed the chickens, to gather the eggs, to see if the hired man had milked the cows.

When he walked around the house, Esheal would see her shaking cream in a jar, making butter for the evening meal. There was no color anywhere; everything was gray, and the trees against the horizon were only gray webs, like leaves which fell to the ground whose green flesh rotted, leaving only a network of beige veins. It might have been Russia, Esheal thought, but there were no people. "It may snow," Mrs. Steiner said. She stood on the porch next to him and stared at the mountains. She crossed her arms over her thick red shawl. If she wore a kerchief, thought Esheal, she could be any woman in Pobrosk. She waved her hand through the air as if testing it. "It *will* snow," she said.

The snow began the next morning and, as the day went on,

it grew thicker and softer and within moments the country-
side was white. A thick layer of snow lay along all the arms of
the trees. The evergreens iced with the heavy snow and their
branches dropped under the weight. The poor evergreens,
Esheal thought; all winter they were the only green things,
and the eye looked everywhere for them and could not leave
them, and then in the spring, when everything turned char-
treuse and green, they looked dirty, sad, dusty, worn-out.
Green, worn-out women who had lasted the season and
outlasted it.

And the silence thickened with the snow until the landscape seemed to wait expectantly. At night, the moon shone
brilliantly; the stars were high and distant. The evergreens
cast gigantic shadows. The snap and crack of ice punctuated
the stillness, and now and then, the roar of snow falling from
the roof. Esheal felt as if he had walked around the whole
world and come back to the same place, but he had come
back too late. All the people were gone. He decided he would
write to the zenshina; who knew where she had gone in the
world?

After he wrote her, he found the loneliness of the farm
intolerable, and Mrs. Steiner helped him hitch the horses to
the sleigh and she took him to the railway station. The next
day, he was back in his own house on Maple Street. It was
snowing in the city and as each flake hit the ground, it melted
as if it had never existed. And then what he expected
happened. A process server came in with a summons. Lily
was taking him to court. She was asking for a legal separation
and support for herself and the two children. He took out his
little brown leatherette book where it rested in his vest
pocket, looked up ex-Assistant District Attorney Everett
Caldwell, and called him. "You're calling for yourself?"
Caldwell asked him; "it's your wife who wants the separation?" "It's my wife," said Esheal. The lawyer said he would
be over later that evening.

And that same night, a riot broke out in the Romanoff
house. Lily, who had been picking the girls up every day after
school, had to drag Lucy all the way home kicking and
screaming, and when she got her inside, she took a hairbrush
to her as if she were still five years old. "Leave her alone,"
Bill pleaded with his sister. "She's going to listen to me," Lily
said; "she's not going to do any damn thing she pleases."
"What does she want to do?" asked Bill; "what *did* she do?"

"She says she's going to see her father no matter what I say!" said Lily; "she wants to get killed. The man's a monster! He's a murderer! He might try to take them away from me. I don't want her anywhere near him until the court tells him he has to leave us alone. She saw all of it! Why doesn't she know better?"

"It's her father," said Sarah. "Well, do you think she's safe with him?" Lily asked, turning on her mother. Sarah shook her head. "You see?" Lily shrieked triumphantly; "you see? Your grandmother agrees with me." "I don't care who agrees with you," Lucy cried; "I don't care what she says. I'm not a child. I'm fourteen years old and I'm going to see him. You can't stop me. I'll sneak out of school in the middle of the day and go see him. I never saw him do anything so bad."

"You'd sneak out of school?" Lily asked, flabbergasted; the idea that a child of hers would contemplate such a crime left her speechless. "I will," said Lucy; "you'll see I will." "Then we'll lock you up in the room here," said Lily; "you're not going near that man." "Yes, I am," Lucy said; "if you don't like him, don't see him. I'm going. I'll jump out the window!"

"Lily," said Sarah; "you can't stop her." "I can stop her," said Lily, picking up the hairbrush and advancing on her daughter. "If she jumps out of the window," said Fay out of nowhere, "I'm jumping out with her." "Fay!" said her mother; "you'll get it next."

"Lily," said Sarah; "you can't stop them. If you can't stop them, let them go. He's not going to hurt a child." "And if he does?" said Lily. "He's not going to hurt anyone!" screamed Lucy; "he only scared you away because you drove him crazy. You had to keep on about it. You all had to keep on about it. He's so short, and so stingy and he has such big ears! And he's so old and he can't sing! You had to go on with it. Well, I don't think there's anything wrong with him and I'm going to see him." Lily started after her daughter, but Sarah caught her arm. "I want to talk to *you*," she said; even now, her hands crippled with arthritis, she had a grip like a lobster.

She dragged Lily down the hall and into her bedroom. "Close the door, Lily," she said. "Do you know what you're doing?" she asked her daughter; "can't you think anymore?" She took Lily by the shoulders and shook her. "You want to take him into court and ask for a separation and his money. And how are you going to get it? He doesn't want it. He wants to come back. You want the girls to stand up there and say their father threatened you with a gun and what are you doing? What's happening here? They're going to hate you."

Lily sat down on the edge of the bed. "You think I should let them see him?" she asked. "Can you stop them?" asked Sarah; "can you stop Lucy? And if she jumps out her window? What then? What if she goes to the court and says she wants to live with her father?" "She wouldn't," said Lily; "girls always go with their mothers." "Just keep on with that hairbrush," Sarah warned her.

"You can go see your father," Lily told the girls; "you can go see him after school. But you have to be home by six. You still have homework." "What if I want to eat supper with him?" Lucy asked. "You'll eat supper where you live," Lily said, but Sarah caught her eye. "You call me before you do anything. I'm not coming over there to look for you." "Don't worry," said Lucy; "I'll call you." "But you're not staying there overnight," said Lily, "and that's final."

And the very next day, Lily got a call from Lucy, saying that she was staying with her father for supper, and that she would be home by nine o'clock, and before Lily had a chance to answer her, the child hung up.

"As long as they're going over there," said Dave, who had drifted in, "they ought to ask for the piano." "What do we need with his piano?" asked Sarah; "we have a piano." "It's Diana's," said Dave; "she wants it downstairs where the children can practice on it. I want it downstairs. Gloria sounds like the horse cavalry when she hits the keys. Let them bring over their piano. What's he going to do with it? He can't play it anyway." "I don't know," said Sarah; "I think we should leave the man alone." "Why should the girls be deprived of their piano just because he went crazy?" said Lily; "why shouldn't they have it?" "Why start up?" asked Sarah. "No," said Lily obstinately; "I want the girls to have the piano."

Chapter 49

At the Romanoff house, the piano became the sole subject of discussion. If their father cared about them, said Lily, why wouldn't he give the girls the piano? "What does he need it for, to hold the floor down?" Dave asked them. If he cared about them, Dave told the girls, he'd give it to them. Lucy said she did not want to ask her father for anything because they were not living with him and it was not right to act as if they were still there. He'd think the only reason she came over to visit was because she wanted something. She was not going to do it, she said; she didn't even eat any ice cream there anymore; she did not want him to think she came over there to get something for nothing. Besides, she said, she and Fay played the piano so badly they ought to leave it there.

Lily said that every well-brought-up girl had to learn to play the piano, and Lucy said that she would just have to be badly brought-up. Besides, said Fay, chiming in, they could practice on the big piano when Diana's children weren't using it. Bill said it would be easier if there were two pianos; then Diana could have one in her own part of the house and they could have one upstairs to play on Sundays. "If you're going over anyway," said Lily, "how much can it hurt to ask?"

"You ask if you want it so much," said Lucy. "Look what's standing up on its hind legs and barking," said Dave. "Maybe she thinks she's big enough to support herself," suggested Bill; "it's not every girl who finishes high school. Your mother only finished public school. Diana didn't even do that. Your mother should send you out to work." "Then send me," said Lucy. "I'm not asking."

The next day when the girls stopped at the pharmacy after school, Esheal had a request to make of them. When they finished their supper, Esheal cleared the table and asked them if they had any homework they needed help with. He seemed disappointed when they said no. When he asked them how they liked it over at Sarah's, Fay stared down at her plate. "Not much," said Lucy. "I think Uncle Bill's peculiar," she said. "Why do you think that?" he asked. Esheal had his own reasons; he wondered what Lucy's were.

"I never heard of anyone getting dressed the way he does," Lucy said. "He stands there in his underwear and then he combs his hair and he puts on his hat. Did you ever hear of anything like that? Putting your hat on first? Then he dresses the rest of himself. Mother says he always got dressed like that. She says he puts the hat on to keep his hair in place. She says he's the neatest man who ever lived. And the whole time he's getting dressed, he looks in the mirror. I think he's conceited."

"Maybe," said Esheal, trying to joke, "that's why he never got married. He didn't want a wife to see him standing there in his underwear and a hat." "He'll never get married," Lucy said. "Maybe after your grandmother dies," said Esheal; "he doesn't need anybody now." Lucy nodded but Fay looked away. He was not sure he ought to be talking to the girls this way, as if they were adults.

"So you don't like it much over there," asked Esheal; "how would you like to come back here?" "We can't," said Fay; "Mother won't allow it." "She would if she came back with you," said their father. "But she won't. You know she won't," said Lucy; "she wants us to go to court and say you threatened to shoot her." "I don't want you in court," he said. "Don't worry, Daddy," said Fay; "we'll be all right." "I don't want you there," he said. "Listen," he said to Fay, "ask your mother to come back. Tell her I'll never bother her about anything again. Tell her I know I was wrong. Tell her I'm sorry."

Fay looked at her sister. "You want me to ask her?" Fay said. "And then you'll tell me what she said?" asked Esheal. "I'll ask her," said Fay. "Let's go home and ask," said Lucy. But when Fay asked Lily if she wouldn't go back, why couldn't she go back, then they could all be together in the same house just the way they were before, Lily began trembling all over and burst into tears. She ran down the hall, into the back bedroom, and the girls heard the door slam and echo. "You call him and tell him what she said," said Fay; "I asked her." And then the family started in on them about the piano.

"Maybe," said Fay, "if we asked him for the piano, and he

gave it to us, she might see he wasn't so bad." "Do you think so?" asked Lucy. "Well, how could it get worse?" asked Fay. "Daddy always used to say things can always get worse," Lucy said. "I don't think they can," said Fay; "do you? Not now." "Maybe it's not a bad idea," said Lucy, "but I don't like to ask. It's like asking for money." "I know," said Fay impatiently; "you said that before. But if we don't do anything, the hearing's in three weeks, and then if we do something, it won't make any difference." "That's true," said Lucy; "let's go. It's cold for April, isn't it?" she said, putting on her coat.

Puffed up with the importance of their mission, they marched off to the pharmacy together. "Well, look who's here," Esheal said the instant he saw them come through the door; "what are you doing here on Saturday?" "We came to see you," said Lucy, "what else?" She stopped in front of the huge jar of jelly beans to which a sign with a huge question mark had been appended. "Did anyone come close yet?" she asked. "I haven't counted them," Esheal said. "We'll help you," Lucy said; "when's the contest over?" "The fifteenth of April. I'm not sure I want your help," said Esheal; "you eat more than you count." "We don't eat jelly beans anymore, Daddy!" said Fay. "When did you stop?" he asked, laughing at her; "come in the back. I have some more jelly beans in there." They sat in the back and talked about school and ate jelly beans. Finally, Fay looked significantly at Lucy. Lucy went on munching jelly beans. "Daddy," said Fay, "Lucy has something to ask you." Her sister glared at her. "Well, what is it?" said Esheal, who was emptying some powder into a flask. Lucy took a deep breath. "We wanted to ask you if we could have the piano," said Lucy; "if you'd let us take it over to Grandma's, we could practice more." Esheal looked at Fay, then at Lucy, and stood up suddenly, upsetting the flask.

The children were frightened; they had never seen their father move suddenly before, never seen him overturn anything in the pharmacy before. "Get out!" he shouted at them; "get out! You're just like the whores on the street! You'll sell yourselves to get something you want! Get out of here! Get out of here and go back to that mother of yours!" Lucy started to cry but Fay was frozen in place, her eyes wide, her face bloodless. "Come on, Fay!" Lucy said, pulling her by the sleeve; "come on!" Fay got up and backed away from her father while Lucy tugged her toward the door. When the two girls finally reached the street, they looked at each other, and started to run, and they ran all the way to Carroll Street, up the stairs, and collapsed on the couch crying.

"What happened?" Lily asked, shaking them; "what happened? What did he do to you?" The two of them were incoherent. Sarah sat down next to the girls and tried to rock them both at once. "What happened?" she crooned; "tell Grandma what happened." "He said," sobbed Fay, "we were just like the whores on the street who sell themselves to get things." "I'll kill him," said Dave. "He's a monster," said Lily, starting to cry. "To say such a thing about your own innocent children," said Sarah; "to say it to *them*." "I don't want you going over there anymore," said Lily; "do you hear me? No more. You're not going." And this time the girls did not object.

Chapter 50

The day of the hearing came at last. Esheal had tried everything he could think of to keep the girls out of court, but Mr. Caldwell told him he thought that would be impossible since their welfare would be one of the central questions occupying the court. He asked Esheal what the girls could say against him, and Esheal told him that they would probably testify that he had threatened Lily with a gun, and after some hesitation, he said that he was afraid that they would tell the judge what he had said when they came to ask for the piano. Caldwell said he did not like the sound of that, because if Lily's lawyer could prove that he was irrational, not only in his treatment of her, but in his treatment of the children, no judge on earth would deny her a legal separation. Esheal said he did not want anyone there, not even his sisters, who had both offered to come. He hardly saw them in any case, he said, and he did not want them to see him in court.

But at the last minute, his cousin Minnie, who had moved to Philadelphia, arrived at his door, saying she would go with him, and as they drove over to the court, she said she and her mother, his aunt, had been heartbroken when they heard about his marriage. "My mother," said Minnie, "always said she was a cold woman." Was Lily cold? he wondered. He had never thought of her that way. "Mother said she wasn't a woman who was meant for marriage," said Minnie. "Well, she wasn't meant for marriage to me," said Esheal. "Get a divorce," Minnie pleaded; "you could marry someone else, someone better." "*I'm* not meant for marriage," said Esheal; "I want her back, and the girls. If she can get a divorce, that's one thing. I don't want it."

When they walked into the Supreme Court building on Court Street, Esheal hesitated in the doorway. The vast stretches of marble, the dark cool air—it seemed impossible that he could come out of this building without losing everything. And when they got to the room where the hearing was to be held, Esheal found the whole Romanoff family already seated. He sat on the other side of the room with his lawyer and his cousin, and listened to Lily testify that he had made her life a torment by his constant accusations of infidelity, that he had followed her, and how finally he had threatened her with a gun demanding that she confess everything. She swore solemnly that she had never been unfaithful and had never given him grounds for his suspicions. "Do you believe," asked the Romanoff lawyer, "that your husband was sane when he threatened you?" "No," said Lily; "I think he is out of his mind." "Do you think he is in his right mind now?" asked the lawyer, "No," said Lily, "I do not." Esheal stared at the Romanoffs, who took care to avoid his eyes.

Then Fay was called to the stand. She stood there in the new blue suit her mother had made for the occasion and stared at her father. Esheal watched her, stone cold, as if he had already died but was forced to listen to others as they heaped execrations upon his still warm body. "Now," said Lily's lawyer to Fay, "all you have to do is tell us what happened when you went with your sister to ask your father for your piano." But Fay could not bring herself to speak. Several times she seemed about to say something, but no words came out. The judge looked at her, and looked at Lily, who was frowning at her daughter, and then at Esheal, who looked tortured. Finally, the lawyer told Fay she was excused. When she sat down next to her mother, she burst into tears. Every now and then, she bent forward, looked at her father, and sank back again, her head buried in her handkerchief, crying. Esheal, whose own eyes were stinging, tried not to look at her.

Then it was Lucy's turn. When the lawyer asked her to tell the court what had happened when she and her sister went to ask their father for their piano, she stared defiantly at her mother and then turned on the judge as if she were about to say something. "Well?" said the judge. Lucy shook her head and stood there, silent. The judge could see her chest rising and falling as if she were holding back sobs, and finally, he could not stand it. "Witness excused," he said. When Esheal testified, he said he wanted his wife to come back, and that he had asked her to do so repeatedly but she either said no or refused to talk to him altogether. He also said that he had asked the girls to talk to his wife, and they had asked her to come back, but she refused.

When he was finished, the judge denied Lily the legal separation she had asked for, but he ruled that Esheal had to pay his wife fifteen dollars a week for her support and that of the children. Esheal got up to leave, and saw Lily get up, but she did not walk toward the door. Instead, she stared at the judge as if she could not believe such a person could exist. She turned to her mother, puzzled and astonished. Esheal, who was watching her, thought that this was Lily's first experience with a world which would not always obey her command. If the girls had said what they were supposed to have said, they would have won. He looked at them, standing miserably behind their mother, and realized that they were almost grown up. Lucy was fifteen. In one more year, she would be finished with high school. Fay, the baby, was thirteen. Soon they would be married.

He remembered the expression on their faces when he said that they were like women on the street, and how frightened of him they had been. He did not expect them to come over to him. He stood where he was until all the Romanoffs had gone out into the hall. He wondered what Lily would have to say to the girls. "Well, I don't see how my father was such a terrible father!" he heard Lucy say, and then they moved away, and he could no longer tell what they were saying.

Chapter 51

Esheal

The pharmacy became the whole world. It was not much of a world. After the hearing, I stared out the window at the brick wall of the building across the street until it began to seem unreal, a backdrop painted on canvas. I asked myself what in my life did seem real and not very much did. When I thought of my wife, Lily, I got angry, but she did not seem real. The girls did, but I never saw them. Times from my childhood began coming back to me, and those seemed real, the times I had visited the cemetery to talk to my father, the times I sat at the zenshina's wooden table and studied Russian, sleeping in the shed with Kopatchnik.

At times, I thought of taking my own life, but then I would think of what Lily said after the car accident. "Death doesn't want you." By now I wasn't so sure. I knew a hundred ways to kill myself. A man with a pharmacy doesn't have to worry if his ceiling will fall down when he tries to hang himself by jumping off his bed with a rope around his neck.

And in the beginning, I spent days thinking of the different ways to do it. I could drink too much potassium and my heart would flutter and that would be the end of me. I could take an overdose of sedatives and that would be the last I would hear of myself and my troubles. For a while, I got a great deal of satisfaction out of this: when customers came in, I enjoyed talking to them and thinking to myself that although they didn't know it, I would be dead in the morning. It made me feel smug to listen to their problems while I thought about how they would feel when they found out I had such problems I had taken my life.

But then I thought about the girls and what it would be like for them to go through life knowing that their father had committed suicide. Everyone would talk about them. They would be called the pharmacist's daughters, the one who killed himself. No one would marry them. I didn't want anyone to be able to point a finger at them and say their father was a coward or their father was insane. I couldn't do it. And then I thought about them, living with their mother and her family, and I knew that, sooner or later, they would need some help, not with money, but other help.

So I decided that instead of killing myself, I would get a dog. That's how the human mind works. And once I got the dog, I couldn't kill myself, because I had to take care of the dog. I kept him in the pharmacy with me after dark. People thought I kept him there to protect me, but they were wrong. I kept him for company. Once, I asked my clerk to pretend to hit me and struggle with me, and after I persuaded him I wouldn't hold it against him, I only wanted to see what the dog would do, he picked up the broom and menaced me with it. The dog jumped on me. I think he wanted to get his body between me and the assailant. After that, I knew if I was held up, I'd have two problems, keeping my eye on the criminal, and not getting knocked down by the dog. But he was company.

I began to wait for the mail, and what was so important about it? Once a week, I got a letter from my cousin Minnie, and I couldn't wait to get my hands on those letters, and then when I had them in my hands, I didn't want to open them. She and my sisters had one subject. I should get a divorce. After the separation, my two sisters, Sophy and Lizzie, were there every day, sometimes twice a day. "Get a divorce, get rid of her. What do you need her for? You're still a young man; you can get married again."

But I wasn't a young man. I was fifty years old. I had been fifty years old from the time I was born. Other men were young once; I wasn't. When I was a little boy, I was a little old man. And I didn't want to get married again. Once was enough. I couldn't go through it again. So I told them I wasn't going to go through the sham of a New York State divorce, and every two minutes, it was poor Esheal, poor Esheal. And because I was in the store, I couldn't avoid them. But when they saw I meant business, they stopped coming around so often. Then the next thing was that I should come live with one of them so they could cook for me. Well, my daughters were grown up and I was used to peace and quiet, and it would never have worked out. They were not the best housekeepers on earth; one thing you had to give Lily credit for: she kept a beautiful house. She always said you could eat

off the floor in her house. It was true. You might not be able
to walk on it because she didn't want it tracked up, but you
could certainly eat on it.

I started to go on rounds with Dr. Linde, and I liked that.
He lent me his medical books, and that kept me busy, too; I
had every illness in the order in which they appeared. Then
when I went to see patients with him, we'd see who got the
diagnosis first. I was pretty good. I won pretty often. Of
course, it was fool's luck. But the time I diagnosed a case of
parrot fever, Dr. Linde said it was too bad I couldn't have
gone into medicine. Well, a penniless immigrant who helps to
support his family doesn't become a doctor. Anyway, I didn't
think the diagnosis was very remarkable; there was a very
sick woman and a very sick parrot and I had just read a book
on tropical diseases.

Still, I was lonely. So I sold the house on Maple Street and
moved into an apartment over the pharmacy, and a Mrs.
Sugarman cooked my meals for me and sent them down in the
dumbwaiter and, half of the time, it seemed as if nothing had
happened. Now, instead of my wife cooking meals, Mrs.
Sugarman cooked meals, but the girls weren't there. The best
thing about the separation was getting rid of that idiot Bill
once and for all. As soon as he saw what was happening, he
got out of there as fast as he could.

After Lily and the girls had been gone for almost a year, I
got a letter from the zenshina, and I realized that was what I
had been waiting for all along. The letter came from somewhere in Australia and she said not to try writing to her there
because she was leaving the country. But, she said, she had
looked into her onion, and she was sure she would see me in
New York. That was a staggering idea! I had gotten used to
thinking of her as a state of mind, a place, no longer someone
real, and often, I wanted to go back to Pobrosk to see her, as
if she would somehow be hovering around in the air itself.
When would she come? Of course she didn't bother saying
when she might come, whether she had this year or ten years
from now in mind. So I forgot about it.

I got more interested in money. If I was going to spend the
rest of my life in the store, I wanted to leave a good estate for
my children. I put most of my money into gold coins and
stamps and I put the rest in the bank. I saw my wife's brothers
and Diana's husband busy with the stock market, and that
would have been enough to convince me there was something

wrong with it, but there were little things in the daily papers that made me suspicious. I wouldn't touch it. I decided that I would retire when I was sixty and travel.

In the meantime, I began to read. I put away the medical books and started reading novels. I'd never had time for them before. And because I was reading them, an old idea came back. I decided I ought to write the story of my life. This was the third time I was trying to tell it. And how far was I going to get this time? If I had a case of parrot fever, I might have been able to figure it out. But why things had worked out as they had, that was beyond me. I thought if I wrote things down, a meaning might emerge, a significance. But I have written quite a lot now and none of it seems to make any more sense than it did before I began.

Chapter 52

A year passed and Lily was still crying. Sarah's health was worsening, and Lucy graduated from high school and was said to be dating someone she had met at a dance. Lily told Lucy that, when she got a job, they could think about getting a place of their own, because then they would have enough money. All this Esheal learned from Dr. Linde who was still the Romanoff family doctor. They had, said the doctor, decided not to hold his friendship with Esheal against him. Esheal said that was very magnanimous of them, and Dr. Linde said that his status was undoubtedly enhanced by his failure to charge for his visits.

"How are the girls? What do they look like?" Esheal would ask him again and again. "Well," he said, "Fay is turning into the real beauty. She looks like a movie star. Lucy looks more and more like her mother. Fay's probably going to graduate at the head of her class, but I think Lucy will be the one to go to college. She said she was going even if she had to go at night." "Why does she have to go at night?" Esheal asked him. "Lily says she needs the money. If the girls can't contribute, they don't have enough money to get a place of their own." "Why do they need a place of their own?" asked Esheal. "The girls want it; they want a home to bring friends to. I don't think Lily likes it, being the poor daughter her mother had to take back in."

"She could get a job and let Lucy go to school during the day," said Esheal; "she used to work for Martinson's coffee." "Let's face it," said Dr. Linde, "you're getting even with Lily through the girls." "Lily said she didn't want any part of me and the girls don't want any part of me, and if that's how they want it, that's how it's going to be." "You'd be happier if you gave the girls some money for themselves," said the doctor. "How do I know they'd keep it for themselves?" he asked; "I don't want Lily to get her hands on a cent. I changed my will.

Even after I'm dead, she won't get a cent." "Have it your way," said the doctor.

Occasionally, when Esheal looked out the window, he thought he saw Lucy on the other side of the street, but he knew it was a trick of the eye and he did not stare after her. Then one day, he looked up and he was sure he saw Lucy standing across the street, looking at the pharmacy, but when he got up to go to the door and take a closer look, she was gone. And one day, he looked up and Lucy *was* standing in the doorway. The clerk, who saw her come in, stared at both of them and was astonished at how like her father she looked. "Can I borrow a dime?" Lucy asked. "Come on in," said Esheal.

It was a hot August day, and all the ceiling fans in the pharmacy were revolving lazily. Strips of sticky yellow fly-paper hung in the back of the store where Esheal worked. The boxes of chocolate had been replaced by hard candies of all description because, in the summer, the chocolates melted. Lucy knew that the refrigerator in which her father kept certain medicines was full of long, thin boxes of candied cherries. People stopped by for them on their way to the movies.

Esheal opened the register and took out a dime. "Here's a dime," he said to Lucy. She came around the counter and into the back of the pharmacy. "Thank you," she said, putting it in her pocket. "Nothing's changed here," she said, looking around the pharmacy. She sighed and without thinking, kicked off her shoes. "Does that mean you're staying?" asked her father. "Can I?" asked Lucy. "Why not?" asked Esheal; "I'm your father." "What about the piano?" asked Lucy; "are you still mad about the piano?" "Are you?" asked her father. "No," said Lucy; "I'm not." "I'm not either," said her father. He smiled at his daughter, and could not stop smiling or staring. She was seventeen and she was every bit as beautiful as Lily had been when he had first seen her. She was more beautiful. He looked at her long legs, crossed at the ankles, as Lily always crossed hers, and he was astonished at the fragility he saw. Such a delicate thing. And he had not protected her.

"You know why we did it, don't you?" Lucy asked him. "Fay thought if we asked you for the piano, and you gave it to us, maybe Mother would change her mind about you. We didn't want the piano. We haven't even touched it." "I don't know what I wanted with it either," said Esheal. They sat there silently. Lucy took a tissue from her white straw bag and wiped her forehead. It was very hot. "Here, use this," said Esheal, taking an enormous handkerchief out of his pocket. "What are you doing out on a day like this?" "Looking for a job," Lucy said; "then I ran out of money and I decided I'd walk home and when I walked by the pharmacy, I thought I'd ask for a dime in case I wanted to go out again." "It's too hot to go out again," Esheal said; "you should see your face. You look like a walking beet. You never could take the sun." "I've got to get a job," she said. "You'll get one," said Esheal; "what about school?" "I'm going at night." "Where?" he asked. "Brooklyn College," she said.

"You'll spend your life on the train," he said. "Well," said Lucy, "you always said if I didn't go to college, I'd be an ignoramus and I wouldn't even be able to get a job and everyone would look at me and know I was an ignoramus. It's the only way." "There might be another way," he said. "There's no other way," said Lucy, wiping her forehead with his handkerchief; "I don't want to hear any more about it." Esheal stared down at the counter, where he was absently drawing figure eights with his index finger. "How about going to a movie?" he asked Lucy. "Let's go," she said; "the hell with the job."

After that, both girls began stopping by the pharmacy. And in spite of the fact that Lily cried hopelessly every time the girls mentioned her husband's name, they went anyway. When it snowed, Esheal met Fay at school and took her out for lunch. They ate in the luncheonette across the street and always ordered the same thing, a huge plate of stewed mushrooms and onions, a glass of milk, and, on special occasions, a second serving of mushrooms and onions. Fay began stopping by the pharmacy to do her homework, and often she would sit in the car, which was parked outside, working. She had always loved listening to the sound of the rain on the car roof.

Lucy, who had gotten a job as a secretary, stopped in every day on her way home from work. "Does your mother like this?" he asked her, and she shrugged her shoulders. The girls were living with Lily on Elm Street, and when Esheal asked Lucy how much she was making, she said ten dollars, but she gave five to her mother. He would not offer the girls any money now, even though he knew he was depriving his daughters as well as his wife. Now that Lily had seen fit to make a home for herself on Elm Street, and advertise her situation to the world, he had no more use for her. But when the girls came to the store, he could not do enough for them. In September, when it got colder, he would pack Kopatchnik and Fay in the back seat, and Lucy rode in the front with him. Off they went to the park. Lucy could not seem to get used to the animal, but Fay, who was usually so quiet and dignified, rolled around with the dog, barked at him, even crept on all fours after him.

Esheal began closing the pharmacy earlier at night, but Jacob Berghoff suddenly reappeared and said that his wife had taken to running all over the place, and half the time she was in Florida. She stayed there so long, he told Esheal, that his youngest daughter had to go to school half the year there. Whenever he came in, Esheal ran over to the chess set and started setting up the board. He always knew when Jacob's wife came back, because the games abruptly came to an end.

Jacob had made a fortune, but he had not learned to drive, and when he came to the pharmacy, he was driven up in his chauffeured limousine, and when he was finished playing, he called the chauffeur, who took him home. "What does the man do all day when you're working?" Esheal asked him. "He works in the shop," said Jacob; "he should lay around all day in an empty car?" His son, he said, was going to law school next year, but he was going at night. "I don't know what to do with him," Jacob said. "He won't take a chance. What does it matter with the girls? They get married; they raise children. But a son shouldn't settle. Look at me. I didn't settle and I still don't have anything? So what can you get if you settle?" Esheal said that he never had been ambitious; all he had ever wanted was a happy family, and now look at him. "A man can't be too good," said Jacob; "the women walk on you. My wife, she walks on me, but I'm not there to walk on. I sleep in the Turkish baths." Esheal said there must be some men who had wives with whom they could live. "Then," said Jacob, "they were a lot smarter than we were when we were young."

Chapter 53

The story of his life, which Esheal had again begun to write, began to haunt him and drive him out of the pharmacy. To Esheal, the square white pile of paper in its neat gray cardboard box was like a half-dead animal pleading for attention he knew he could not give. Every morning after he opened the pharmacy, he looked at the box, opened it, and found it just as empty as the day before. He told himself he would write one page a day, which was not much; after all, he was not trying to write a masterpiece and he was no writer, but sooner or later, if he wrote a page a day, the pages would fill up with those neat black marks which represented a life. Every day he would take out the few pages he had written, determined to continue the story. Every day he would begin a sentence at the top of the next sheet—"After my father died . . ." or, "When we found bodies in the snow . . ." or, "When I began to study Russian . . ." and he could not imagine continuing with it. Who would care? And saying things about what went on in his family's private life seemed wrong, improper. He had not said much during his fifty-two years on this earth; words did not come naturally to him. If only, he thought, there were some other way of describing a life. But he could not draw and he knew nothing about music. Gradually, he gave up the idea of continuing his story. Still, he could not bring himself to give up the gray box or the hope that he would continue, somehow, with what he had begun.

He was sitting in the back of the pharmacy, struggling with a page which began, "After my mother left me," berating himself silently for letting his thoughts stray to Lucy, who the day before said casually that she just might get engaged one of these years, when the bell over the door tinkled. He got up to see who had come in and he was surprised to see a huge black man whom he did not know. There were not many colored people who came into the store, and those who did usually worked for one of the families in the neighborhood. He's a big man, Esheal thought. He watched the man look around the store as if he were checking for the presence of other people. The clerk was out. Esheal was alone in the store. Kopatchnik, who was lying at his feet, began to growl. That surprised Esheal; the dog never bothered waking up long enough to growl.

In the beginning, the dog had disapproved of perfect strangers entering what he appeared to think of as *his* pharmacy, but the dog soon saw there was no stopping it, and now slept peacefully on Esheal's feet. Esheal heard the dog growl again and checked his drawer: the little black gun was in its proper place. He had always had more faith in the instincts of an animal than in those of a human. He was not sure humans had instincts and, as he often told Jacob Berghoff, you never heard of a dog getting divorced.

The man was approaching the back of the store as if he were a rat in a maze who had to go through each corridor before he reached his reward. Kopatchnik was not only snarling; his ears were flat against his head and his upper lip curled back over his yellow teeth. So the dog doesn't like the man, Esheal said to himself, that's a reason to be frightened? When the man came up to the counter, he looked around again and seemed to be reassured by the silence of the store. The dog's growl was a low, throaty rumble.

"You got morphine here?" the man asked him. "Do you have a prescription for it?" Esheal asked. "Just give it to me," the man said. "If you don't have a prescription," Esheal said, "you can't have it." "The hell I can't," the man said; "I know where it is and I'll get it myself." The man started around the counter. "Stay where you are," Esheal told him; "I have a gun." "A gun, sure," the man said, and came around the corner. Esheal watched with disbelief. "Get back in the store," he said, but the man did not listen. Instead, he went toward the locked case. When Esheal saw what was happening, his sense of the world's existence vanished; the man who was going toward his locked case was a roar of outrage and evil. "You have no right," Esheal heard himself saying, and when the man did not even turn in his direction, Esheal grabbed him by the arm and pulled him back. In his other hand, he had his revolver.

The big man turned on him with surprise and placed his palm flat against Esheal's chest and sent him sprawling into the shelves on the other side of the room. "Get out of my way," the man growled, "and stay there. You can't stop me." Esheal looked down at his hand to make sure his finger was placed properly on the trigger. "If you don't stop," he said, "I'm going to shoot you." "Go ahead, shoot," said the man, who had picked up Esheal's little safe and was using it to batter the lock on the glass doors. Glass began to tinkle and fall with the sound of ice cracking and falling from a roof. Esheal fired a shot over the man's head. The man turned around, saw the gun, put the safe down, and started after him. "This is your last chance," said Esheal, and he fired another shot into the air. Esheal heard the sound of breaking glass and a cold wind blew past him. The bullets must have gone through his window, he realized; someone would see what was happening and come in.

But the big man was not frightened by the gun or by the shots, and as he kept coming toward Esheal, it seemed to the pharmacist that he stood in the middle of a howling wind in which wooden buildings and oxen and the cries of frogs and cattle and horses which reared whirled with him. And the man coming toward him was not a colored man who wanted morphine and was going to take his gun away from him; he was the center of the cloud in which all of those things whirled. Then Esheal heard Kopatchnik roar and saw the dog leap up from the floor and at that instant, the man's huge hand came toward him like a hand out of a cloud and he knew that the man was trying to take his gun from him, and he fired a third shot, and when he heard the sound of the gun, and saw the man put his hand to his head and begin staggering backward, and then crumple, the pharmacist could not seem to see him.

Kopatchnik was jumping against him and he still had the gun in his hand and he was afraid it would go off and he might shoot the dog, and he put the revolver back in his drawer, exactly as it had been before. He could not bring himself to look in the direction of the big man; instead, he heard him gasp, then make a small, choking noise, and then the thud of his body as he fell against the shelves, and a louder thud as he fell against the tiles of the floor. Who had he shot? Whose body was lying on the floor? The dog was distracted; it kept leaping at Esheal, licking his hands, yelping, as if the dog thought Esheal were dead, as if the dog thought Esheal would die if he did not look at him. The pharmacist sat down on the stool and absently put his hand on the dog's head. "Who did I kill?" he said out loud; "I never meant to kill him," he told the animal. "You saw it; he was going to take the morphine. He had no right!" The dog whined and licked his hand. "Who was he and what did he want with me?" Esheal asked the dog; "he wanted to take the drugs. I can't look at him."

Then he thought that the man on the floor might not be dead; no matter what he had done, he had to find out if the man was alive. He couldn't let him die on the floor. He slid his hand under Kopatchnik's collar and dragged the dog over with him toward the body. He found the man's arm and felt for his pulse. There was none. He was dead. He took the dog back to the stool and sat down again. The walls seemed to be breathing in and out, and the store was getting smaller. He could not get his breath, and even though he refused to look at the dead body lying on his tile floor, he saw it changing in front of his eyes; first it was one man with one face, then it was another man with another face, then it was the dead, crumpled body of a woman bleeding onto her clean, white clothes.

"I'm losing my mind," he told Kopatchnik. "Call Dr. Linde," said the dog. "And wake him up in the middle of the night?" asked Esheal. "He's used to that," said the dog. "I killed a man," Esheal said in a low voice. "He would have killed you," the dog said; "call the doctor." "Not yet," said Esheal. "A dog knows the truth," said Kopatchnik; "there are times you have to kill. And the blood tastes good. It's good and salty. And after the kill, you put your head on your paws and sleep and when you wake. up, you've been to heaven."

Esheal looked at the dog, who was sitting up, one ear cocked toward him. His body was heavy as if the laws of gravity had suddenly been suspended and replaced by something new, the kind of gravity that belonged to the bottom of the sea. He put his head on his hands and fell asleep. When he woke up, the dog was still watching him. The body was still there. Was it his imagination, or had it changed its position? He made a wide circle around the body and reached for the telephone. Dr. Linde said he would be right over, that Esheal should stay where he was, and that, when he came, he would bring a policeman with him. Esheal hung up, took the circuitous route he had followed before back to the counter, put his head on his hands, and fell asleep. —

The next thing he heard was Dr. Linde calling his name. He woke up and went out front. The policeman, whom Esheal knew immediately as Mrs. Murphy's son, asked to see the body, told Esheal he had done a good job, and went to the phone to call for the dead wagon. The policeman asked him what had happened, and he told him the story. "I'm sorry to have to ask this," said Sergeant Murphy, "but do you have a permit for the gun? We have to have a hearing when there's a shooting." "I have a permit for both my guns," Esheal said in a dull voice. "That's good," said the sergeant. "I didn't know you could shoot," said Dr. Linde. "Neither did I," said Esheal. "We could use you on the force," said the policeman. "Just get the body out of here," said Esheal; "I'll answer all the questions you want." "Can he go now?" asked Dr. Linde; "to answer questions? So we can get this over with?" "Come on down to the station," said Sergeant Murphy; "I'll fix it with the night court." "Don't you want to call anyone?" the doctor asked him; "your daughters? your sisters?" "I don't want to call anyone," said Esheal; "it's bad enough they'll have to read about it."

During the next day, Esheal answered questions at the police station, and again in his pharmacy. Reporters kept coming in, and he repeated the story again and again, and each time he told the story, he saw the body in front of him with its changing clothes. Suddenly, he thought bitterly, he was going to be a hero. The shop would be popping with people. He would have to keep Kopatchnik locked up in the apartment. And then the newspapers came out.

SLAIN IN FIGHT FOR MORPHINE

A guard employed by a private detective agency grappled with a slim undersized druggist when the latter refused to sell him morphine tablets late last night and was killed when the druggist shot him through the head.

Victim of the shooting was Fred P. Dressler, of 1140 Cummings Avenue, Brooklyn.

Police said he entered the drugstore of Esheal Luria, at 199 Howard Avenue, corner of Chauncey Street, Brooklyn, and demanded the drug, although he did not have a prescription.

When Luria, who is five feet tall, and weighs 110 pounds, refused him, Dressler, holding his hand in his pocket as though he had a gun, started to go behind the counter.

The druggist grappled with him and drew a revolver, from which he fired three shots. Two of the bullets went wild and crashed through the plate glass window. The third struck Dressler in the head. He was dead when the ambulance arrived.

Luria had a permit for the revolver.

DRUGGIST KILLS MAN IN STORE

Police today were investigating the fatal shooting by an elderly Brooklyn druggist of a man who, he said, went into his store last night and threatened him after demanding morphine.

The druggist, Esheal Luria, 52, whose shop and residence are at 199 Howard Avenue, said the man, identified by police as Fred P. Dressler, 48, of 1140 Cummings Avenue, employed by a Manhattan detective agency, attempted to help himself to the drug after being refused.

"He had no prescription for the narcotic," Luria said, "and I told him 'you just can't have it, that's all.'" To this, according to Luria, the man replied: "The hell I can't. I know where it is and I'll get it myself."

At that, he continued, the man pursued him behind the counter.

Luria said that at that point he reached for his revolver, for which he has a permit, and fired two shots into the air, without deterring the man. He then fired two more shots at the man, but missed him, he continued. But he hit him in the body with the fifth shot and killed him.

There was a crowd in the pharmacy, and everyone was determined to treat Esheal like a hero. But he hardly heard what anyone said to him; he wanted to sit in the store and think things over. The more he looked around, the more hateful the store looked. Why had he never realized how the white walls glared, how the walls, laden down with every imaginable object, seemed to tilt in as if they were going to fall? He would sell the store. In the morning, he would put a notice in the paper, putting it up for sale.

And then his daughters came in. Fay ran over to him and threw her arms around him and would not lift her face from his chest, but Lucy stood just inside the door, staring at him as if he had come back from the dead. "Let me go get your sister," he said to Fay, detaching himself from her and sitting her down on his stool. "I thought you were killed," Lucy said; "when I saw the headline, it said 'Slain in Fight for Morphine.' I thought it was you." "It was me," said her father. "Did he hit you, did he hurt you?" Lucy asked. "No, nothing like that," said her father; "he tried to get the morphine tablets. I grabbed his arm, and when he turned around, I shot him. That's all it was." "You have to close the store at night," Fay said. "And if I close the store at night, what am I going to do with myself?" her father asked. "At least get a dog who bites," said Fay. "Leave me alone," said Esheal; "how often does a thing like this happen? Now it's someone else's turn."

The cold wind blew in another gust of neighbors, none of whom wanted anything, all of whom wanted to know more details about the fight, to see where the body had fallen, to look at the stain on the tiles which Esheal had not managed to get out, to *ooh* and *aah* at the tape which held the remains of the plate-glass window together. "They're vultures," he said to the girls; "nothing but vultures." "Don't get excited," both of them said together. "Don't you have something else to do?" he asked them; "homework? a date?" "We don't have anything else to do and we're staying," said Fay. The newest wave of people retreated, leaving the store empty. Then the bell over the door tinkled and Lily walked in with her brothers. He heard the girls gasp and saw them staring at him.

"I just thought," said Lily, "that I would stop in and see how you were." "As you can see," said Esheal, "I'm fine as I ever was." "Everybody's talking about it," said Lily; "how you killed that man and he was a full foot taller than you were. You're a hero." "Some hero," said Esheal. "Come on, Doc," said Dave; "the man was twice your size and twice your weight." Esheal started to say something, but the bell tinkled again, and a new crowd of people, all holding evening papers bought on their way home from work, flooded in with new questions.

The commotion was endless, and the louder the noise of the crowd in the shop became, the more vivid grew the memory of the body on the floor with its many faces, its many outfits, its hand which seemed to have moved after the man had died. Dave said that they ought to carry Esheal through the street on their shoulders, and Esheal told him to leave him alone, but the others in the store liked the idea, and Esheal felt himself being lifted through the air and when he looked down, he saw Lily, smiling up at him.

"Put me down!" he roared at Dave; "put me down or I'll kill you! I'll call the dog! I'll kill you!" Esheal roared at him. Suddenly the shop was silent.

"Put the old grouch down," said Bill. They lowered Esheal to the floor. He looked around at the two girls and saw they were crying, but he could not understand why. Then he looked for Lily and saw her standing against the door, her face white as a corpse's, her eyes riveted on his face, tears streaming down her cheeks.

"You've gone and scared her all over again," said Lucy, hitting the counter with her fist. "It doesn't make any difference," Esheal said. "But she *came!*" Fay said. "She came to congratulate me for having killed someone," he said; "it would have been better if she'd stayed home. You're not going to tell me she came over here because she was worried about me all of a sudden?" The girls looked at each other and down at the floor. "That's what I thought," said Esheal.

Chapter 54

The stock market fell, both of the pharmacist's girls were married, he had two grandchildren, he watched the Second World War begin, and it seemed as if nothing happened to him. During the Depression, he was busier than ever; he could not complain, as the others did, of his losses because he had not invested in stocks, and when people came in who were starving, he gave them what they needed and wrote what they owed him at the end of an already long column.

Dinney was in and out of the store as she had been when he was so much younger, although this time it was her husband, not her children, who was sick. Eventually, he developed tuberculosis and was sent to Arizona, where he died before he was fifty. Diana came in for medicine, and Esheal filled her prescriptions and entered the amount in his book. Her husband had invested heavily in a Florida real estate scheme and had lost everything; few people came in to have their teeth fixed because no one could afford to pay him, and if they did come in, they paid a dollar or a dollar and a half for an extraction. His own daughters worked from eight in the morning until six at night and earned eleven dollars a week, half of which they gave to their mother. Lucy stayed in school, and did her schoolwork on the train; when she got married, she left her job and she had enough time to go shopping. She bought her trousseau three months after her wedding.

Then there was Esheal's delight at Lucy's marriage, and Lily's disgust and defeat with the man she had chosen. If she could have had her way, Lily would have had the marriage annulled even after Lucy's second child was born. Then Fay married, and she had two children.

When both girls were married, they decided that one of them would have to take Lily because she was not capable of living on her own. Lucy took her. And since Esheal was a constant visitor at Lucy's house, he again saw a great deal of his wife. They were polite to each other; they never argued. If there was one thing they agreed on, it was the importance of the grandchildren. Esheal tried living with Fay, but he did not like being a guest in someone else's house and he moved back into an apartment over his pharmacy.

When the war broke out, Lucy was terrified that her husband would be drafted, but he was not. Esheal watched her worry, but could say nothing to comfort her; he knew she was determined to get along on her own. She had no intention of accepting help either from him or her father-in-law. So his life settled into a pleasant and more varied routine than he had expected, and less and less often when he was sitting in the pharmacy did he think that he was an old man who was waiting to die.

On the day he was sixty-eight years old, on the day he had once more sworn to retire, it was snowing as if the sky intended to bury the city. Not a car passed. Nothing and no one seemed to move. The streetlights were invisible and existed only as a brightness behind the snow. Esheal had been looking out of the window for hours and had not seen a person pass. Kopatchnik, who was old and had yellow teeth, snored on his feet. A figure resembling a bundle of clothes, bent at the waist against the wind, made its way slowly down the street, stepping in and out of the little drifts that blew across the sidewalk. The wind died down and the snow began to fall steadily, whitening everything. Esheal saw it pile up in front of his door and watched it climb above the wooden frame and up the glass pane. The snow fell hypnotically and it fell so densely that it separated the pharmacy from the rest of the world. All the roads leading to it had been obliterated by the snow. All the other streets had gone under with the falling snow. People had ceased to exist; they had been buried by the endlessly falling snow. Time itself was buried by the thickly falling snow. Esheal fell asleep for a few minutes, woke up with a start, and fell asleep again.

When he next looked at the clock, it was only two, and to his blurry eyes, the hour hand looked like a black branch weighed down by snow. Time could not move forward in this weather, he thought; instead, it seemed to be going back, the snow covering the tracks of all the past years, restoring the drifts of earth and grass which time had trampled and leveled. The snow was beautiful; it was a birth and a death at once. It was too beautiful to watch. His eyes were closing and he would have nodded off again if the bell over the door had not given its familiar tinkle. Esheal woke with a start; he must have been dreaming that he was awake.

A tall, elegant woman dressed in black stood in the entrance to the shop. She wore a belted, black seal coat with a collar of little silver foxes whose little paws reached toward her full, high breasts as if they wanted to touch them, and her high, black fur hat resembled a crown. She walked toward Esheal, pulling off her gloves as she came closer. "When a war comes, it is wise for a rich woman to move," she said, laying the gloves down on the counter. "Don't stare," she said; "staring is a vile rudeness, The Countess Karalova at your service. May I sit down?" "Sit down," said Esheal. "You do not seem surprised to see me," the woman said, unbuttoning her coat. "Surprising things happen in dreams," said Esheal. The woman got up and twisted Esheal's ear until he cried out. "You are not dreaming," she said. The pharmacist rubbed his ear and stared at the woman, astonished. "You do not know who I am?" she asked; "age has changed me so very much?" "I know who you are," he said; "but it's not possible." "Yet here I am," she said. "I don't understand how you got here through this snow," he said. "I can walk on snow the way birds walk on the air," she said; "the peasants called me the Snow Woman. Of course, your people had other names." "Why did you come?" Esheal asked her. "To take you with me," she said. "Where?" "Anywhere. I am leaning toward South America. There will be few safe places once the war spreads." "My children are here," he said. "You are sixty-eight," said the woman; "I am much older than that. To be old is to be free."

"You look the same and yet you look different," said Esheal. "You are just the same," said the countess; "perhaps sadder." "Much sadder," said Esheal. "Not much sadder," she said; "now you know how sad you always were." He said nothing. "You do not answer me," she said; "do you want to live out this normal life of yours? Baby-sitting. That is what they call it here. Playing guessing games about the date of your death." "What else can I do?" he asked. "You can come with me," said the countess; "it is arranged." "No," said Esheal; "you are all I have left. If you should tire of me, it would be more than I could stand." "But I will not tire of you," said the countess; "you were my most successful pupil.

And now you should come. Your soul has already left your body and returned in another." "In my dog?" he asked, smiling. "The spirit which inhabits your dog is not your own," she said. "If I came with you," he said, "and something went wrong, I would lose everything I ever had. I would have nothing to take with me into death. I cannot take that chance." "A man who cannot take a chance is already dead," said the woman. "So be it," he said; "I am happy to observe life only. I do not want to have my hands slapped by life again." He saw her begin to fasten her collar button. "Don't go," he said; "stay. Talk to me." "Talk to you," said the woman; "when did I ever talk?" "Begin now," he said; "we are not dead yet.

"Where did you come from?" he said; "why did you come to Pobrosk?" "Such an old and tired story," the woman sighed. "I was a Liechtenstein and married to a Russian prince. I hated him and he hated me. The marriage was an affair of state. We knew there was only one way to dissolve it. One of us had to die. I chose to die. I froze to death. His family did not know I could slip in and out of trances as I chose. After I was put in the vault, I let myself out. My husband replaced my body with the body of a village woman. We made a bargain. As long as I lived, he would grant me whatever I asked for and as long as I lived, I would remain dead. We kept our bargains."

"Weren't you afraid he would kill you?" Esheal asked; "what if you had come back? What would have happened to him?" "He would have been killed. His country would have gone to war. But I had nothing to fear from him. He knew I was to be feared. I had powers. You remember the people of Pobrosk. When they came to me, I saw the strings of their lives and I learned to play on them as one plays on a harp. If I played the song of life, they lived. If not, there was much sadness." "Some who came to you died," he said. "I did not want all of them to live," she said; "it would not have been natural. I had to keep the balance." "This is all craziness," said Esheal; "it always was." "Is it craziness, Kopatchnik?" the woman asked. "No," said the dog; "it is not." Perhaps, thought Esheal, I am already dead. But if I am already dead, why won't I agree to go with her? "You are not dead," said the countess.

"Where are all your peasants?" asked Esheal. "In China," she said; "I left them there with a great deal of money. I am going to die in Russia. I am going to live long enough to see myself buried in Siberia." "Why Siberia?" asked Esheal. "The snows never melt there," she said. "They don't melt at the North Pole either," said Esheal. "I would not want to be buried in a land known for a Saint Nick," she said; "in Siberia, the sun does not come up but neither does it set. It is the right place for me." "You are not going to die," said Esheal. "But," said the woman, "I want my body in a fitting place. Am I the only one who has to tell stories? Tell me what happened to your wife."

"She left me," said Esheal. The countess raised her eyebrows. "I threatened to shoot her," Esheal said. "Ah," said the countess; "you should never threaten a woman with a gun. When you take a gun to a woman, she feels like an animal who has a broken leg and is no longer worth feeding. When you beat a woman, she knows she is important." "If I had beaten her," said Esheal, "she would have left me all the same." "Nonsense," said the countess; "a beaten woman is like a beaten dog. It comes back for more. Even if it turns vicious, it comes back. My favorite peasant beat me." "I cannot believe," said Esheal, "that you were a typical woman."

"Of course I was," said the countess; "I saw how the future of a life did not change the walls of the building. I saw no reason to spend my time polishing what did not exist." "What did?" asked Esheal. "The songs of the blood," said the countess; "they were the same songs that swept through the fields in the summer and that drove the snows in the winter. I could hear them there in Pobrosk. I knew I would go on hearing them as long as I stayed far from the town."

"But all the things of a normal life, people who will love you, children who will remember you, how could you give that up?" The countess raised her eyebrows, tilted her head, and her lips tightened. "I gave nothing up," she said; "but you, what will you have? Your children will die; your grandchildren will grow up and remember you as someone who gave them many presents and who wore a vest in which he kept a gold pocket watch, and you will leave one of them the watch, and one of them will put it in a drawer, and the watch will stay there until it is time to move the desk in which it lies, and the watch will be passed along until someone looks at its cover and sees the initials E.L. and says to his mother, who was E.L., and his mother will say, oh, I don't know; it must have been your great-great-grandfather. And the great-great-grandchild will say, what was he like, and the mother will say, oh, it was so long ago, I never knew him, but my mother said he was a good man; he wasn't really such a bad husband; he certainly wasn't a murderer, and then the mother will die, and her child, the great-great-grandchild, will die, and when the family goes through their albums, they will come to certain pictures, and everyone will say, who is that, and the oldest one will say, I don't know; perhaps it was your great-great-grandmother's David." "God forbid!" said Esheal. "Therefore," said the countess, "you should come with me."

"I can't," said Esheal; "I can't imagine myself living differently than I now live. Whatever my fate was, I lived to see it. When the pawn is taken off the board, it ceases to move." "When the pawn is taken off the board," said the countess, "it comes back to play in another game." "I will tell you why I can't come," said Esheal; "I don't deserve it. I do not deserve happiness. I deserve to be punished. I killed a man. I took a life."

"That is not why you think you should be punished," said the countess; "you took your own life. For that, you should be punished." "I never wanted it to come out this way," said Esheal. "Ah," said the countess, standing up; "the greatest delusion of all. Then you will not come?" "No," he said. "It would be like returning to Pobrosk," she said; "it would be like stepping onto the page before the words were written." "Let me keep the pages I have," said Esheal; "I cannot afford to lose them." "Then keep them," said the zenshina; "I also have those pages."

"Will you come back?" Esheal asked. "I will not be able to come back and you will not be able to come." "Have you been looking in your onion again?" he said, smiling. "Of course," said the countess. She was utterly serious. "So you will stay here and wait for your death?" she asked. "At my age," he asked, "what else do I have to wait for?" "Death waits for me, too," said the countess, "but I do not have to sit in his antechamber."

"Good luck to you," said Esheal. "Good luck," said the zenshina; "what a strange concept. You will remember me," she said, and she stooped over and kissed him on the mouth. A cinnamon-scented wind blew through the streets of an unknown place and a person who looked like Lily began whirling up from the earth toward the sun becoming smaller and smaller as she spun away. Esheal felt the same wind pulling at him, but he looked hard at the snow, and the wind died down. "Goodbye," Esheal said. He got up and suddenly embraced the countess, kissing her on the mouth, and she kissed him back as if she had never kissed anyone before. Then she was gone, and the snow was falling, and the dog watched him reproachfully, and sleep covered him as the snow covered all the tracks on the street.

Chapter 55

When he was sixty-one, Esheal sold his store and tried to retire. But he did not know what to do with himself, and he began to work part-time for a young druggist who suffered from a heart condition. The young druggist's shop was in the worst section of Brownsville, and when he was on duty, he always had a clerk or a relative with him, but when Esheal worked in the store, he worked alone. And the girls did not like it. "Why should you risk your life for pennies, for someone else?" Fay asked over and over again, and Esheal would ask her what he should do, go home and wait in his hotel room for a heart attack to take him away? And no matter what Fay said, or Lucy, he kept working in that store. Now he was seventy-eight, and a man who was seventy-eight, he said, had something to worry about when he crossed a street or when he walked on ice, but not when he went to work. But he tired more easily, and he went to the young druggist's store less and less often.

One night, he got a call from the druggist, who was ill but who said that there was an epidemic in the neighborhood; it was Friday night, and he really wanted to keep the store open. Although he was tired, Esheal said he would go. Lucy called him just as he was leaving and tried to talk him out of it. "I gave the man my word," he said, and she knew better than to argue with him.

Esheal was sitting in the back of the drugstore reading a medical book when three colored men came in. As soon as Esheal saw them, he knew what they wanted. The tallest man came up to him and pointed a gun at him. "Give me the money in the drawer," he said. Esheal took the money out of the cash register and slid it across the counter to the man. The man picked it up and handed it to the men in back of him who began counting aloud: fifty, sixty, seventy, eighty, all the way up to two hundred and forty-five. "You got any more?" the man asked him.

Esheal put his wallet on the counter, and the man took thirty dollars from it and added it to the rest. "O.K., Doc," he said, and the three of them turned to go. When the men got to the door, the big man turned around, aimed his gun at Esheal, and fired two shots. One hit him in the head and one in the abdomen. Esheal felt himself falling. With disbelief, he saw the floor rising to meet him.

"Someone will come in," he told himself, but he lay on the floor for four hours before someone came in. "Call an ambulance," he called out from behind the counter. A frightened woman came behind the counter, saw Esheal and gasped. "Call an ambulance," he said again. She went to the phone and called the police. "Call my daughter," he said; "Dewey 3-0123." When someone answered, the woman said, "hold on a minute," and asked Esheal what she should tell the man who had answered the phone. "Tell him I was shot and where I am," Esheal said. Lucy's husband said he would be right down and asked the woman if she had called an ambulance. She said she had and could he come down as fast as he could? She was afraid he was going to die while she was there. "I'm not dead yet," Esheal said from the floor.

When Lucy and Sam got to the hospital, Fay was already waiting for them with her husband. When Esheal saw her, the first thing he said was, "Who's staying with the children?" Fay said the next-door neighbor was. "Good," said Esheal. She was holding his hand and noticed it was cold. "I'm very thirsty," he said, and Fay went to look for some water, but when she came back with a paper cup, the nurse said he could not have any because he had a stomach wound; she could moisten his lips with her finger. That was all. Then the doctors came down and began wheeling him toward the elevator which would take him up to the operating room.

As he was wheeled off, he said, "I don't feel so well." Then the big gray doors closed, and the girls and their husbands went outside to wait. They had not been outside five minutes when the resident came out to look for them. "He's dead," he said; "I'm sorry." The girls started to cry, and their husbands looked at each other, and at the resident, who was so young and so miserable bringing this news. "That's all right, doctor," said Fay's husband; "we'll take care of them." "He was already paralyzed on his left side," said the resident; "he didn't have much of a chance."

"If someone had found him earlier?" asked Sam. "Who knows?" said the resident. "It's a rotten world," said Lucy. "Don't talk like that!" Fay said; "Dad wouldn't like it." "How do you know?" asked Lucy; "how do you know what he thought of the world?" "Don't fight," said Sam. "Someone's got to tell your mother," said Fay's husband. "As if she'd care," said Lucy. "Don't talk like that!" Fay said again. "Don't tell me what to say!" said Lucy; "if it weren't for her, he would never have left his own store. He would never have gone to work where he was. She killed him!" "My God," said Fay; "stop it! I can't listen to it! He's dead! Isn't that bad enough?" "No," said Lucy; "it's not bad enough. She'll live forever and drive us all crazy but he's dead." "Lucy," said Sam, "he was seventy-eight." "He was never sick a day in his life," Lucy sobbed; "he could have lived a long time." "Let's go home," said Sam. "Who's watching your children?" Fay asked. "My mother, who else?" said Lucy.

BOOK THREE

IN THE ONION

Chapter 56

Dinney

And they were such a happy family. I always used to envy them. But my husband said they were only fine when nothing went wrong. And I think he was right. Lily, Diana, the Romanoff family, they used to go to shul and my parents went to the same shul and we met as children. We were little girls together. Lily used to play the piano, and we would stand around the piano and sing, "I'll give to you a paper of pins, a paper of pins, a paper of pins, if you will marry me." We grew up together. I always loved going to Diana's house; and the only thing that worried me, their cat would follow me, and I used to sleep with Diana in the back bedroom. It was freezing, freezing, and I used to sleep there with her under the pirini. We used to go out a lot together, Diana and Lily and I. We were always together.

I was very jealous of them. They had such a lovely relationship with their mother. My mother had a very quick temper and she did not want love; she just did not want it. And when Diana got married, she was so happy with Sidney. And Lily envied her afterward; she said she didn't, but she did. After Lily was separated from Esheal, she went back to live with Sarah, and she lived there for a year or two until she made a little home of her own on Elm Street.

One day, Lily came over to Sarah's and her mother was dead. Sarah was almost eighty when she died. She hung out a line of clothes; that's what Dave told Lily, and Diana was there; she was playing the piano. The piano was highly polished and in the piano Diana could see her mother sit down to listen to her play and all of a sudden she sat back and she died. She just died of a stroke. That was the end of Sarah. And of course Lily took it hard. Her daughter, Lucy, was getting married, and Lucy said Lily could come live with her.

But when the war started, the Second World War, Lily didn't have to envy Diana anymore. Her son Michael became a dentist like his father, Sidney, and Diana worked in the office and it was the dream of their life that Michael would go into practice with them. For a while, he wasn't drafted. I don't know how he got out of it. My two boys were drafted right away and they went through the worst of it. Later on, I knew Diana hated to look at my boys because they were alive and hers wasn't. Anyway, Michael was ashamed; he saw older men going in, men with families, men with wooden arms. So he enlisted. And they took him in the medical corps, and everyone said to her, what are you worrying about, he's not even going into battle? You know, if it's not your own son, you don't worry.

When Michael got called, I remember Diana went down to be with him in Georgia for the last few days, and when she came back, she said they walked around like two sweethearts. "People thought I was his sweetheart," she said; "they didn't think I was his mother." I don't know; I think there was something peculiar there.

And Michael went down. I'll never forget that. I was afraid to see her and she was in bed and she wanted to kill herself and Sidney. It was the most horrible thing. And my two boys were all right. Michael went over on a ship full of medical people, and she used to say it wasn't even a ship worth sending anyone on. And there were five hundred men aboard that ship. Diana used to say, you don't gather five hundred intelligent human beings on a ship and blow it up. It killed her husband; it gave him a heart attack. You send away a twenty-nine-year-old handsome man, and he's drowned before he's crossed the water.

She used to say, "You realize what that means to us and what kind of man that was? A handsome man, he was a good man, and capable, everything you could hope for. I never had a day's heartache from him. I got the whole thing in one shot. Some people had dead boys come home in boxes, which was terrible enough, but he was destroyed completely." You know how many times I heard her say that? You know, I don't think she believed he was dead. Because of the way she lived the rest of her life, you know. Of course, she never looked at another man. She used to say Gloria was all she had left and Gloria wasn't too strong, and she said she was dedicating the rest of her life to her. Diana, she was great and all, but she could be difficult.

I remember I went to Gloria's house in Washington, D.C.,

for Thanksgiving, and she had a beautiful house; it wasn't a house, it was a mansion, and Gloria came down the big flight of steps there, and she was dressed to the teeth, and Gloria was always a beautiful girl. She's sixty years old today and she's still beautiful. Well, Diana's language, I don't have to tell you. She looked at her husband, he was sitting in a chair reading a paper, and she says to me, "Look how beautiful she is, and that son of a bitch doesn't even notice her."

And Lily was the same way. Even when her daughter was married and she had two children, Lily couldn't leave her alone. She never had anything good to say about Lucy's husband and Diana never had anything good to say about Gloria's. But for Diana, you could make an excuse. She lost her son and then she lost her husband. After Michael died, Sidney had a terrible heart condition, and twice he had heart attacks. He had to stay in bed eight weeks. It was terrible. Diana had to sit with him and talk to him. And they were in Gloria's house at that time, and she had three children, and children are noisy. The man was used to quiet. He never believed in God. I don't think any of us did. I don't know why, our parents were so religious. Our mothers weren't, but our fathers were. But when Sidney was dying, he said that, "Well, now I'm going to Michael, to be with Michael," and Diana used to say, "Thank God he had that thought, that comfort, that he'll be with Michael."

I remember when Gloria was going to medical school. And the dean said to Diana, "What are you doing? You're wasting your money. No man will let her get through school." And she met her husband only six months after she entered the school. Someone said to him, "Do you know the Romanoff girl is here? She's staying with her Uncle Izzie," so he came up and took her out. First she said yes, she'd marry him, and then she changed her mind ten times, and then she did marry him. But he wouldn't let her go back to school.

I like to think back about those times. I was very happy. I was very poor but I loved my life. When my boys died, of course they were old already, I couldn't look at their pictures. I was in my eighties when they died and I was in a nursing home and I taught a yoga class and I was head of the Hadassah there. And every year I'm in the paper, because even though I'm ninety, I can stand on my head. Then after a while, I felt I couldn't hide away this one picture I had of the boys; they gave it to me on my birthday. It wasn't right. Then

I began to take it out and every time, I'd see them and I'd cry, and then I'd get used to it a little more.

Now I have a boyfriend and he's very nice to me, and when we first moved in here, he took me to a double room and said, "What about it? We could have it if we were married," but I thought things were fine the way they were, so I said, "What happens if you want to read and keep the light on and I want to sleep?" So we didn't get married; we got adjoining rooms. I have grandchildren, and I love my grandchildren, but to spend all my time with them, I don't want it. That's over with. It's time.

When Sidney was in Alaska, I wrote the letters for Diana. I swear I did. She couldn't compose a letter. She just couldn't. They were first cousins. They were such close relations. How could you sleep with a first cousin? I remember one day Diana said she could take it or leave it, and she'd rather leave it. They were cousins after all. But Diana liked men. I don't think Lily liked men. Now Diana did; Diana liked men. But Lily was very difficult to get along with. I don't think she liked men at all. Her husband had a pretty good business, but she was never satisfied. She was never happy. Esheal was always very nice to me. He never charged me for anything I got there for the children. I don't think Lily was in love with him. She was not happy. She was not a happy person. Neither of her children took after him, but they didn't take after her, either.

Lily was never happy; she was never in a happy frame of mind. And yet she had a wonderful laugh, if she cared to laugh. She was altogether different from Diana. I don't think she would have been happy with any man. She wasn't happy with her girls' husbands. When she went to live with Lucy, her husband Sam had a certain chair that he sat in and there was always an argument over that lousy chair. She got mad that she couldn't sit in the chair, and she said, "As soon as he comes in, I get up out of this chair; it's his chair." Nobody could sit in it. Such a ridiculous thing, you know. As long as I knew Lily, she was always complaining.

And then she hit the children, her grandchildren, if they didn't do what she wanted. I don't think a grandmother has a right to do that. I never understood her.

I was in love with my husband, and we were poor and he wasn't so honest, but I was in love with him, and that was more than anything else. Do you know they all wound up rich? Lucy and Fay both? But with all that money, I don't think they were happy. Diana wasn't. For eleven years after Michael died, she wouldn't leave the house, and for fifteen years, she wore black. I don't call that normal. And now she sits there in her apartment looking out the window and waiting for the phone to ring or the doorbell, and do you know, they're all still terrified of her. I guess she changed when Michael died. She had no use for the rest of the world because it was alive.

And the day Lily died, I heard she was the cause of a terrible fight Lucy had with her own daughter. Her daughter wanted to go see Lily, her grandmother, but that day Lucy wasn't going. And the child was possessed; she was sure it was her last chance to see her grandmother, so Fay said she would pick her up because she was going anyway. And then Lucy threw a fit and said that her daughter never wanted to go with her when she went to the hospital, so why did she want to go with Fay? And the child got so upset, she said she would stay home. And that afternoon, Lily died. I don't think Lucy's daughter ever forgave Lucy for it afterward. Lily, she couldn't even die without causing a fight.

Chapter 57

Diana

When I was young, I was very happy. I should have known it was too good to last. Even during the Depression, I was happy. Of course, we had trouble. It was impossible to get a job. Everybody bought on margin. We didn't know a soul who didn't lose money in the stock market except for Esheal. He was too stingy to lose money. But even the boys who were errand boys invested in the stock market. Professors were looking for jobs in hotels just to clean the toilets.

Five thousand dollars I saved that Sidney never knew about. When it came time for Gloria to get married, he was crushed by the stock market. He bought land in Florida and lost it and there was no business, but I had saved every blessed week. No matter what took place, I would take money and put it away. And finally when it was time for her wedding, he couldn't borrow anymore because he had borrowed on his life insurance policy, and whatever money he got, he carried over to the stock market. He bought land with a brother-in-law and a nephew and they couldn't follow up. For two years they kept paying into the land when they were called in. I said to him, how long are you going to do it? You haven't got any fifty, sixty thousand dollars to hold that land. And then it stopped. When I gave him the money for Gloria's wedding, he cried his eyes out. He didn't think he could do anything for her.

Lately, all the children, Gloria's children, my grandchildren, keep asking me about Dave. I said, "What is this interest in Dave all of a sudden?" They've been putting their heads together over my old albums, and Joseph, Gloria's oldest, said, do you remember a fight Mom and Dad had? I said that there were so many fights, I couldn't be bothered thinking about one of them. But he said he meant the time when Robert got a call from Dave asking him to come down to New York and help him out. Robert was Gloria's husband.

The girls didn't remember. And Joseph was prompting them. He said, "Don't you remember, Uncle Dave said Dad asked him to get him a girl when he came down to New York?" That was too much for me. I stuck my head out of the kitchen and said what kind of a man would be stupid enough to ask his brother-in-law to get a girl for her sister's husband. But I shouldn't have said anything, because then they started whispering and I couldn't hear them.

Joseph put it together. He remembered Gloria saying there was nothing wrong with her family, and Joseph said his father lost his temper and said her family was the worst in the world, and then he said, "Your family! Your brother the jailbird!" Joseph reasoned it out this way: his father would never have called Dave a jailbird if he had been in the cooker for something small like a fight, and he wouldn't have said that if the amount of bail had been small. He figured Dave must have really gotten into something. Joseph went down and checked the old papers in the morgue and he found out that Dave had once run a bucket shop; he was selling stocks that weren't real. They sent Dave to jail for ten years. And when he came out, he was a broken man. Lily and I were gone; we were busy with our families, and Momma he didn't find at home anymore, and then Bill, at his age, he decided to get married. His old high school sweetheart was widowed, and when he found out she was free, he married her right away. Tootsie, that's what he called her. She was very pretty but crazy as the day was long.

Then one of the children came in and asked me if it was true Dave was on drugs, and I said, "On drugs? No one in our family was ever on drugs. It would have been good for him. He would have been calmer." But he was a very unhappy man. You can imagine how unhappy he was, he decided to go into a restaurant and died before the waiter brought him the first course. And they brought him to the morgue. Robert went down and identified him. I couldn't stand to look at him.

My sister Lily died in a nursing home. She started to wander away from the house. The police brought her back from all the streetcars. All right, so her husband had a tough life, but his was tough because he had such a disposition. Nothing pleased him. He wasn't happy. He wasn't satisfied. Lily was outdoors with the children all the time—years ago, if we had children who kept them in the house? You went out with them walking; they had to have the air. God forbid, they should not have the air. Today, they keep them inside where they belong. I don't see any babies in carriages walking in the streets until they're ready to run around. But years ago—

And dinner, at twelve o'clock midnight, that was a time for him to come up? Why did Fay get burned? She made him split-pea soup. He had to have that soup, and the whole pot of boiling soup went all over her. Lily did have an awful mess of it. He was never satisfied. And when the man was off work, he couldn't come upstairs to eat; he had to eat downstairs. And when the clerk was on, she had to have his dinner ready on the minute because he couldn't leave: the man might be stealing money. You know what goes on in business. But she never could please him no matter what she did. And in making her miserable, he made his own life miserable.

He helped his sisters. He helped that mother who left him in Russia, but when Lucy went to college, would he give her a red cent? And he could have afforded to help her. There were lots of reasons Lily had to quit. And he was jealous. For no reason. How long could she put up with it? And she had Lucy to take care of. Lucy was wild. One day I took her for a walk and she was holding onto Gloria's carriage, and for no earthly reason—cars were running back and forth in the gutter—she ran away from the carriage into the street. She used to threaten everyone, and she'd say, "I'll throw you out of the window, God forbid." But Lucy could really dance. My daughter couldn't lift a leg. Lucy did the Charleston like nobody I ever saw or knew. She used to hold onto a doorknob and practice. The whole building would shake. They were living with Momma at that time, and they were afraid that the ceiling downstairs in the ladies' apartment would come down.

Fay was quiet and sat at the piano. Celia was born sick and she was always sick. So Lily had her troubles early and I had mine late. I am ninety-two this year. My husband has been dead for thirty-one years and here I am still. Who would have believed it? My son Michael's been dead for thirty-eight years. He never had a girl; he never had anything. When he died, we broke up the office we had all fixed up for him to work in when he came back.

Then I went to live with Gloria. I lived there with her for fourteen years. Whatever I cooked was good. Whatever I made was good. I was really the head of the house, the housekeeper. Years ago, a person used to go around with a belt and keys. That was me. I was on vacation when I got a letter from my grandson. "What did you do with my gray sweater?" Mind you! I had to write back and tell him if he'd look in the closet where all his sweaters are, he'd find his gray sweater, I didn't have it with me. But never, never did I feel it was my home, at no time, no matter what I did. And I was happy to do it, because I had lost Michael and I was so terribly unhappy, I needed the work; I was like a person with a hundred hands and they all wanted to do something.

But I've lived long enough to see the cars in the sky. You know how often I remember it? I can remember standing with Dinney and Lily in the gutter and yelling at the men in the cars, "Get a horse, get a horse!" We were so surprised that something should go without a horse. And I remember Grandpa saying, "Look where it's written in the book, that carriages will ride in the skies without horses." And it happened. So much else happened I don't want to think about.

Chapter 58

Lucy

I had a very happy childhood. Really, I did. I never knew there was anything wrong between my parents until that day I saw Dad with the gun. But when Fay and I were young, our parents adored us, our grandparents adored us, our uncles, and everyone's friends. We were always black and blue from the pinching we got. Of course, our family, or my mother's family, wasn't the kind in which you grew up feeling very secure. Well, you knew you would always have them to take care of you, but they had a way of cutting you down.

Aunt Diana's apartment was like a giant classroom. She had shiny black doors and she used those doors as blackboards. I can close my eyes now and see her erasing those doors. When it came to her own children, she was perfect. She kept Michael out of kindergarten and taught him herself so that she could keep him with her. But she always managed to hurt us with that tongue of hers; we always felt like Cinderella's children when we were at her house. And I was like my father. I never could carry a tune. She used to say, "Don't ask Lucy to sing; she won't be able to make it sound like anything." Even when my children were born, I was afraid to sing to them at night. To this day, I won't sing if anyone's around to hear me. And nobody had as big a nose as I did. To this day, if I have to sit sideways, I can hardly say a word.

Aunt Diana cut us down. It was the height of the Depression, and I had gone to buy Gloria a present, and I couldn't see anything I liked, so I took the two or three dollars I had and decided to buy one good thing. And I did. I found one handkerchief reduced to three dollars, hand-embroidered all over, and it was really a beautiful thing. I was so proud of it when Aunt Diana saw it, she said, "Is this what you call a gift?" The whole evening was spoiled. And she always said something in front of everyone else.

And to me, Dave and Bill were the height of sophistication. After they changed their underwear, we used to come into their room and we literally sat at their feet and we would hand them a sock or a shoe or a cuff link and help them get dressed. They were so glamorous and the women they took out were so glamorous. The whole family emphasized looks. Uncle Dave and Bill were so dapper and so dashing. I was more afraid of them scolding me than I was of my mother or my father. I wouldn't want to get caught in their mouths because I'd be cut to pieces. So for a while, even with Aunt Diana's carrying on, everything was perfect, and then I saw Dad with that gun.

I was sure that I was never going to get married. Mother made me practice the piano one hour every day, it had to be one hour. When we went to the beach, she had rules there too. We could not go in the water one day before June first and not one day after Labor Day. On the piano, we had to practice one hour. Sometimes I would manage to push the hands on the clock ahead. And when I practiced, I used to stare at a picture Dad made. It was a model of a clipper ship in a fancy wooden frame, and I remember asking Mother, "When you die, can I have that picture?" And she said the first one who gets married will get it. But I was afraid I would never get married, and I carried on until she promised me I could have it. But I did get married first. Every girl thinks she won't get married.

Mother was an Eastern Star, and I belonged to a Junior Club of the Masons, and they were having a dance, and as usual, because I was such a good dancer, I was a hostess. And I saw Sam, my husband, standing there looking over the crowd as if it were the first time he had ever laid eyes on human beings, and, now that he had seen them, he did not approve. I thought he was so handsome that I went over to talk to him. From the time I was a little girl, I always said I wanted to marry a handsome man. I don't know why I was so set on it, but I was. Fay wasn't there that night, and after I danced with him, we talked, and he took me home. Afterward, he said he fell in love with me because of my laugh and my little ears.

Then my mother saw him. She did not like him and she did not like his family. She never did like people with accents, and his family, believe me, they were as foreign to us as the Hottentots, and they never really believed I was Jewish. Just a few days ago, his sister said I was the least Jewish person she had ever seen. Then, after they decided I was Jewish, they began carrying on about my parents, because my parents were separated, and as far as Sam's mother was concerned, a separated woman was a tramp. So I became a tramp, and there was endless screaming and carrying on because I kept their son out so late and what could I be doing? Sam was working for his father, and he was tired, so he would fall asleep, and I was working, and I would fall asleep, and by the time I woke him up, it was two in the morning. "What kind of girl are you if he comes home so late?" his mother asked me. My mother heard her and after that, she had no use for her at all. And at that time, she had no idea who Sam's mother and father were.

When I first met Sam, we had no trouble. His parents were never home. His mother was off somewhere in Florida and his father slept in the Turkish baths. But then came summer, and the ducks came home to roost, and when we invited Sam's parents to our house, Sam's father, Jacob, recognized my mother, and Jacob said to me, "Your father isn't dead." And I said, "I never said he was." "So where is he?" asked Jacob; "he should be here." "Jacob Berghoff," said my mother, staring at Sam's father; "the *same* Jacob Berghoff?" "I haven't changed," said Jacob. She didn't recognize him at first because he had so much money and he was well-dressed and he had a chauffeur. But when she realized who they were!

As soon as they left our house, she tried to talk me out of it. They were not my kind of people. They were crude. You could cut their accents with a trowel. They were ignorant people who cared only about money. She was sure my father had something to do with my meeting Sam, and that was the first I knew our families knew each other. And for a while, I thought it was really impossible.

I remember when I thought Sam was going to be drafted, his sister said, "Don't expect my father to support you," so I knew what they were talking about. It was always just a polite truce between the two families. And before I was married, Mother got after Dad, asking him to talk to me. Dad didn't believe in interfering, but he said he'd go over to the Berghoffs' with me and visit and look them over. Well, when we got there, Dad sat on the porch with me and tried to talk to Jacob's wife, but she sat there and rocked. Jacob tried to get her to talk, but she had nothing to say. She rocked and stared straight ahead through those thick glasses of hers. They were like the bottoms of seltzer bottles. Would she get up and get anyone a cup of coffee? She would not. Her husband had to do it.

When we were going home, Dad said, "Do you realize what you'll be in for there? She's not going to let go of her son. You'll never belong." But I don't know, you think the person will change, or things won't bother you, I couldn't see any problem. And Dad was right. The next thing I knew there was a riot between me and Sam. He said I'd insulted his mother. And how did I insult her? I'd never said one word to her. She said I was causing her to go blind because she cried so and she was so upset that I didn't take her with me to pick our furniture, the furniture that I was buying for our new apartment. I affected her eyes.

And I was furious. I had my family's temper. I said she was wearing thick, heavy glasses when I first met her. I said her eyes were bad then. I had nothing to do with it. And Sam carried on so I thought we were going to break it off right then and there. And when *that* riot calmed down, she insisted that she was going to buy us something. *She* was going to show us what taste she had. And Dad said, "Is this what you want to put up with for the rest of your life? I've seen women like that before. They live forever. This is only the beginning." But I was in love with Sam. And Dad said a divorce is a terrible thing, and I said I'd never get divorced. He said, don't make a mistake in the beginning; you can never go back, but I didn't want to go back.

Anyway, my mother-in-law bought us a thing which was supposed to be a breakfront about one-third the size of any other I'd ever seen. It was light tan and I hate light tan. She paid about fifteen or eighteen dollars for this monstrosity. I was lucky to be in when the telephone call came because that was the first thing I knew about it. A man called up and said he wanted to make a delivery. I said, "What are you delivering?" He said he was delivering a breakfront. "What is it like?" I asked him. He wouldn't tell me. "How big is it?" He wouldn't tell me that either. So I said, would you please not deliver the breakfront. I'm not going to be home and I want to see what the breakfront looks like first. Sam and I went down there and I took a look at the breakfront, and I said, "I'll call you back and tell you when to deliver it." And then I called him back and said, "I don't want the breakfront." He called my mother-in-law and told her, "Some-body's got to take this breakfront." She paid for it and she couldn't have her money back, so someone had to take it. It went up into her spare bedroom, and years later, not one of her girls would take it. That was another fight.

And then she criticized Sam so badly, telling me what an ungrateful son he was, that I lost my temper and I said, "You never gave him any clothing to wear, he never had any spending money. After all, where did he take me? To a neighborhood movie one night a week. What did you give him? He went to City College. He was working for a while. He certainly didn't take me anywhere. The one suit he had we burned after we got married, so what did you do for him?" And she was so insulted, between the goddam breakfront and my telling her off, that we didn't talk to her for a year. It was a very peaceful year, but in the meantime, everyone heard about the horrible daughter-in-law who would not speak to her for a full year. And through it all, my father and Sam's father played chess. When Dad tried to talk to Jacob, he said, "Women. What do you expect from them?"

Then my mother-in-law went to Europe. I'll never forget her opinion of Rome. "There's nothing there but churches." And when she got back, she sent her oldest daughter over carrying a cup and saucer. She wanted to make sure I liked the gift before she sent it over. I didn't care—I wanted peace in the family. And when Dad saw the cups and saucers, he started to laugh. I don't know when I heard him laugh last. And he said, "Come with me, and I'll buy you some china," and he really knew the best places. I didn't like iridescent anything, and her cups and saucers were iridescent and had little pictures of maidens with crooks and sheep. I never used them once in all my life. But my father bought me the breakfront I did use. He paid four hundred and fifty dollars for it. He bought my furniture and he bought my trousseau and he made my wedding. He was sorry for all those years I had gone to night school. He didn't have to do it; I under-stood.

But I couldn't understand Sam's father, Jake, and my father said not to try, not to pay any attention to him; he had a good heart. Jacob started keeping a black book, and in it, he wrote whatever the children did to displease him, and, he said, when he died, he was going to demand that this black book be read. Everything every child ever did to him would be revealed in this black book, if someone was fresh, if someone aggravated him, if someone took some money from him and didn't pay him back, he wrote it down. I don't think he ever had a black book, but we heard about it endlessly. And Sam's mother. She sat on the porch and cursed her husband constantly, wishing him dead, and criticizing him, and when he died, everybody remembered how she had cursed him and wished him dead. She never invited anyone to come to the house because she didn't want to do the work. Once, Jacob's brother came over and she couldn't or wouldn't get up off the porch to make a cup of coffee. It was the first time in twenty years that Jacob had seen his brother. So that was Sam's family. He had no kind of mother. Once, when he got sick, she cursed him because she had tickets to a Jewish show and now she would have to stay home. I wound up staying with him and she went to the show.

I didn't know what to make of them. My mother was nothing if not a devoted mother. She was more of a mother than she ever was a wife. I don't think she was suited to marriage. Aunt Diana was, but not my mother. She was too prim and proper. And she was stubborn. And that was what broke her whole marriage up. At the time, we were too young to know what was happening. If we had been older, if we had been smarter, it we had refused to go, maybe they would have stayed together. I don't think my mother ever got over my sister Celia's death. Fay and I didn't really know what was going on and children forget easily. I remember we sat on the little curb in front of the pharmacy crying and said if Celia died, we would never laugh again. We broke our word, but my mother came pretty close to keeping our promise for us. She took Celia's death very badly. After my sister died, she wanted to move, and that was when we moved to Elm Street.

I remember everything about Dad's pharmacy. There were tiles in the sidewalk before you came into the store. On the right was the showcase with the cigars. In back of that was the perfume and the powders, and behind them, the paper goods and then the counter. When you came into the drugstore, you passed the soda fountain and turned left, and then there was something like a little path, and then you went on beyond the counter, and behind there Dad worked, and he had a little safe. I would sit on the safe there, and he worked on his prescriptions and I watched him make up his pills and things he'd distill through water. And he invented a wonderful salve; he called it *P. and S. Salve: Physician's and Surgeon's Salve,* and he always wanted to patent it, but he never did.

He was held up one night and he killed a man. I don't think he was the same after that. How many people does this ever happen to? He had been held up many times. Then he was shot when he went to work for a druggist part-time. He said he gave the men the money but they shot him anyway. When I saw him, he seemed to be talking all right, but for him to call us for help—he must have known it was something serious. And what help could we give him except to stand by? He must have been frightened and wanted some support. My daughter said he seemed to have been busy with guns all of the time, and I said, what's the matter with you, Emily, druggists don't go around shooting people. In the hospital, he had no complaints. When he was going up, he said he didn't feel well. That was all. He must have died the instant we left. It was the year we moved away from Brooklyn and out to Westchester. He died. Druggists are fair game.

After he died, I couldn't get hold of myself. I took things out on Emily, and she was as distraught as I was. After that, she had nothing but trouble in school. I didn't realize. He was my father, not hers. He was a second father to her. I didn't realize how much he meant to her until it was too late. We didn't get along for years after he died. She seemed to blame me for it. I was the one who told her. I was angry and she asked if she could go out, I shouted at her and said she could go out and stay out because my father had been shot and I wanted some peace and quiet. She went out and didn't come back in and finally Jacob called and said that Emily didn't want to come home. So she became the first and only grandchild who voluntarily stayed at my in-laws overnight.

I often think about my father. When I want to fall asleep, I go over the details of the pharmacy, what you saw first, what was on the right, what was on the left, how the ceiling fans started up slowly and groggily when you pulled the metal string, the tin ceiling, the tiled walls, the beautiful soda fountain, the jars full of jelly beans, the big, brass mortar and pestle in the back, the big apothecary jars filled with red and green liquid in the front window, and people always say to me, "Lucy, how do you fall asleep like that? I'm up half the night trying to fall asleep." All I do is close my eyes and imagine that I'm back in the store.

My father was considered one of the richer men in the

neighborhood because he had his own store and a clerk. He was completely dedicated to us. If he found out that Fay or I needed books for school, he went down to Fulton Street where certain bookstores were, and he would buy the books and bring them home. He would buy the best book with the biggest print, and if the books had pictures, the ones with the best pictures. And if we came home and said, "The *teacher* said this is a good book," he ran out and got it for us. One of the rare times Mother couldn't be home for lunch, Dad picked us up and we had lunch with him in a little restaurant. And if the weather was very bad, he'd try to be at school when Fay and I came out, and he would pick us up with all of our friends and by the time he dropped everyone off, and we got home, there was no time for lunch.

And when I was a child, my sister was always sick, and Mother always took the chicken livers and fried them up in onions and put them on a roll, and that was always for Fay because Fay needed fattening up, and how I envied that chicken liver fried with chicken fat. I think I had one chicken liver in my life. Fay must have been sick so it was given to me. And one day I came home and there was a note from Mother, saying she had put some miniature sweet and sour tongues out in the window box for me, and I couldn't wait to get them, and when I opened up the box, there was a beetle in the paper and I let out a scream and I never could look at those little tongues again. I had loved them so before. And I remember that Dad never wanted us to do the dishes. He did them for us himself. "The poor little faygelehs," he used to say; "they'll have plenty to do soon enough." That's what he used to call us. The poor little faygelehs. Mother didn't like it, his letting us off that way. According to her, we'd be spoiled forever afterward because we had not washed the dishes. But if he was washing them, and he turned around and saw us doing our homework, he was really a happy man.

And I always felt disloyal when I went over to my grandmother's, although for a long time I didn't know why. But I do remember having a terrible battle with Aunt Diana once because of the way she talked about my father. I think Fay came in on it after a while. Aunt Diana had such a way of cutting you down to size, of putting you in your place. When I learned the Charleston, they showed me off for my dancing; before that, it was my small ears, smaller than anyone had ever seen.

And I remember Aunt Diana going down to Saks Fifth Avenue and just buying up everything there was on sale. And she would buy the weirdest things. I was given a peach-colored pajama set with a boa constrictor around the neck. Who gives such a thing to a fourteen- or a fifteen-year-old? But she must have gotten a bargain and so we got it. And we had to look happy about it, too. So when she was at Grandma's I wasn't too happy about going over there. I used to think, what is she going to say you did now? Or how is she going to criticize you now? And she never let up on Mother about Dad. She turned my mother against him. She tried to do the same to me, but I never resented my father for anything. Aunt Diana thought I ought to cut myself off from him because he didn't help me out with school. I knew it wasn't his fault. I worked all day, and when I got out of work, I went to school. I really didn't know what was going on after Mother left Dad. When I came home, Mother and Fay were asleep in the bedroom. I'd sleep on the couch. I would have turned heaven and earth to go to day school. In all those years I worked in the city, I never once went to lunch. I never once had a lunch hour. If my average had fallen below 3.2 I would have lost all my credits in excess of six, but I was driven to finish. And when I got through with classes, I'd get on the subway and often I fell asleep and I'd go beyond the Prospect Park station and have to get out and cross over to the other side, and then wait on the other platform for one half-hour in the cold. I needed the subway and my lunch hour to do my schoolwork. Never once in all those years could I spare the time to go around the corner and look at the beautiful buildings on Park Avenue, and I loved to look at buildings. Never once did I ever do it. I can't think about it now without crying. And then one night, I didn't have any homework, and I didn't know what to do with myself on the train, so I bought a copy of *Collier's* magazine and I made that a tradition. Monday through Thursday, I read for school, but Fridays, I read *Collier's* magazine. That was my idea of luxury.

I can still see Dad coming over to our apartment with his little bag of tools. Sam couldn't fix anything. Dad would call up and ask what the problem was, so he knew what tools to bring. He rigged up a bell system for me so that my mother and I could call each other through our dumbwaiters. I can remember falling down the steps when we were living with Grandma. They were very steep; there was a garage behind the house, and I don't know how, but I managed to fall down. I remember Uncle Bill with his soft, soft hands fixing up the bandage.

And I remember how my legs got burned in August in the country when the propane stove exploded, and the flames followed me out like a hand, just like in a cartoon. My clothes weren't even burned. Fortunately, there was one man left on the premises of the bungalow colony, and he took me to the hospital. And my mother came every day at seven to see me, and one weekend, she and Fay were there in the afternoon, and Sam and the children, and they were supposed to come back at night.

When seven o'clock came and I didn't see them, I was sure I had lost my whole family, and accident cases had been coming in all day. I got so hysterical and wild they had to give me a sedative. And then at eight, just as visiting hours were over, they all walked in. For some reason, Mother made a mistake and thought that visiting hours began at eight. I don't know how she could have made such a mistake. She had been coming for weeks at seven. Before they came, I was so glad my father hadn't been with them. He would have been all I had left. It was just a mistake. But after my legs were burned, I didn't feel beautiful anymore. Everyone used to brag about my blue eyes, but they were so weak, and I had to wear such thick glasses, so what use were they? But when I was young, I was prettier than Fay. I really think I was. And I know my father thought so, too.

I remember all those things, but now I don't like to save the old things. They take you over, all those books, cards, letters, and pictures. They keep accumulating and accumulating and it becomes a chore to sort them out and they pile up until they overwhelm you and then you get rid of them all.

Chapter 59

Fay

I was the quiet one in my family, so naturally, everyone took to me. I don't think I was so likable. I was just so little trouble. My mother said she didn't know I was there until I was fourteen. When I was fourteen, I found a boyfriend. Now that I'm sixty-nine and my sister is seventy-two, she says I was always the favorite and that she was always jealous of me, and that she used to hit me because of it. I said that I must have been doing something, and she said, "No, you weren't. You were just sitting there chewing on the piano." She says she still feels terrible about it after all these years. If anyone had asked me, I would have said that my sister and I never fought. I would also have said, like my sister, that we had a very happy childhood and that I never knew anything was wrong between my parents until the night Mother called us in and I saw my father standing there with a gun.

But I remember that whenever I had to wish, after I had blown out the candles on a cake, or after I had gotten the larger piece of a wishbone, that I would always wish for the same thing, a happy marriage and a happy family life. And the whole time I was growing up, people would say, "Fay, what's wrong? You look so sad." I didn't think I felt sad, but when I looked in the mirror, I saw what they meant. It may have been these big brown eyes, you know, tragic Jewish eyes, or I may have had some sense that things were not right.

But we never saw anything. We led such regular lives. At five o'clock we had supper, and at six o'clock we were in bed. When we came home from school, we had a glass of milk and a slice or two of bread, and then we did our homework. Once it was dark, by five, we were not allowed out of the house until the next morning. We went to school unless we had the cholera. When the snow was very high, Dad used to carry us to school on his shoulders, and at three o'clock, he would carry us back. On Sundays, we went to my grandmother's and occasionally, we went to see one of my father's sisters. We didn't see very much of them. My mother didn't like his family.

We had a Morris chair that Dad always used to sit in and if someone came over to play chess with him, that man sat in that chair. When Mother decided to get rid of it, she pulled out both cushions and we found about six dollars in coins hidden in the bottom. Over the years, when the men sat in that chair, coins must have fallen out of their pockets, so that when the chair was gone, we had quite a lot of money.

Soon after that, we had a telephone party. Dad was a pharmacist, so he had a priority, and as usual, we were put to bed at six. Lucy and I slept in one room, and between our room and our parents' was a door, and they were all so busy with the phone, we opened the door between the two rooms and we carried in our pirinis and threw them on Mother's bed and then we ran from one end of our room through theirs and jumped on their bed. I don't know what kind of time everyone else had, but we thought it was a wonderful party.

And we lived in a graystone after we moved out of the pharmacy, and all of the houses were attached, and all of them were alike. One night, Dad came home, and as usual he was very tired, and he started up the steps and let himself in. No one locked his front door in those days. A woman called out, "Esheal, is that you?" and my father said yes, it was him, and she called out, "Come on up." When my father got upstairs, he saw himself looking at the wrong woman. He had gone into his friend Esheal Littenberg's house. The part of the story that my father thought was funny was not that he had gone into the wrong house, but that he had gone into another house with another man named Esheal in it. He said that was a miracle, and he used to tease Mother, saying that maybe God was trying to tell him he had the wrong woman. After that, my mother and Mrs. Littenberg, the other Esheal's wife, locked their doors for a while.

I was always sick when I was a child, until I was nine, when I had pneumonia for the last time. And I looked worse than I was because of the way Mother dressed us. Uncle Dave used to say, "Lily, what are you trying to do to that penny? Pinch it until it screams?" and she used to say that it was her husband's money and she wasn't going to throw it out the way other women did. Everything she bought us was three sizes too large. Every winter, we got chinchilla coats; nothing else was good enough or warm enough, and when Lucy outgrew something, I got it and Lucy was a healthy, chubby child, and I was a thin, undersized child. Don't ask what I looked like. When Lucy finally reached an age of maturity and would no longer stand for another chinchilla coat, they took her down to Division Street, it was always Division Street, and they bought her a green coat with a black fox collar and I was greener than the coat with envy. Instead of getting me a green coat, they fed me. There were carts selling hot chestnuts, hot baked sweet potatoes, and hot chickpeas. They offered me one of everything but I was beyond bribery. I was in despair. I had to wait for the holidays.

Every Easter, we'd get a new outfit for the Jewish holidays and one year my mother made us the most beautiful plaid woolen skirts. Lucy had a blue one and I had a green. She bought us velveteen jackets with brass buttons and then we were taken off to the temple so Grandma could show us off to Grandpa's old friends, and we would sit there for a while, and then we would make so much noise we were sent home. We were girls. We brooded over our clothes.

There were years when I thought about nothing but clothes. And Dad was so thrilled if a sales person said to him, "This is the best we have in the store, the best money can buy," he was so happy he could afford the best, that we always got it. And one day I was going out to a dance, and I needed a little gold bag, and the salesman brought one out. This man was on Pitkin Avenue, it was always Pitkin Avenue or Division Street, and he said, "This is the best bag in the store," so I got it. After that, Dad wouldn't look at another.

And Dad was so proud of us. He insisted that we were the most remarkable children that ever lived, and then Esheal Littenberg had two girls and he thought his children were the smartest and the prettiest. And Dad could not stand it; he was going to get Esheal Littenberg one way or another. And at one time, if you asked Lucy what time it was, she would say, "Five to four." Really, she said, "Fi' to four." No matter what time it was, she said, "Five to four." Dad planned his attack. He went to visit the Littenbergs on one of his Sundays off, and he waited until it was almost five to four, and he said, "Esheal, can your daughter, Leona, tell time?" And Esheal said, "Why should she be able to tell time at her age?" So Dad said, "Well, my daughter can," so Esheal said, "Show me." Daddy pulled out his pocket watch, and it was five to

four, and he said, "Lucy, tell me what time it is," and Lucy
said, "Five to four." Esheal Littenberg was flabbergasted,
crushed, mortified, and he never bragged about his daughter
again. But he was dumb enough not to ask Lucy the time ten
minutes later. So was it any wonder that I thought we were
happy?

But looking back, half a century later, I see that there were
signs. We were at Aunt Diana's too much. At the time, it
seemed the most natural thing in the world to be there, and
we grew up with Michael and Gloria. So we must have come
under her influence more than we realized. My sister and I
both married tall men. And Lucy was so set on a handsome
man there were times I thought that she was crazy on the
subject. But I remember one thing: I had bought a beautiful
tan coat. I've never had or seen a coat so beautiful since. I
came in wearing this coat and I never felt so smart in my life,
and Aunt Diana was there, and she said, "You can't go out in
New York wearing a beige coat. You have to wear a black
coat. Wear my coat." And she took off her coat and got busy
with a needle and some thread and started letting down her
hem. Believe me, I looked ridiculous in that coat. Aunt Diana
was a tiny woman, and I was tall, and my arms and legs stuck
out of that coat like a stork's. I came in feeling so glamorous
and I left feeling like Cinderella.

And I remember I bought a brown suit, and it was really a
beautiful suit. I still have pictures of myself wearing it. And I
went to meet Dad in the pharmacy, and we went out for a
walk, and he said he didn't like the suit. I said, "But Dad,
everyone tells me how nice it is." He said, "They're all
laughing at you behind your back." And then he said that
thing to us, how we were just like the whores on the street.
And all this must have had a great effect on me, although I
didn't know it at the time. But when they were separated, it
came as a shock to me. No one broke up. Not in our circle.

When I think of that time, I often think of a doll I had. It
had three faces and its neck swiveled. One face laughed; one
face cried; one face was asleep. Everyone has different faces.
My father had a face I was not aware of until much later. He
must have lacked confidence or the strength to fight back
against his wife's family. But to see that face, something had
to happen. If I wanted to see my doll cry, I had to twist its
neck around. And my mother was not a very sensitive
woman. Very often, my father must have felt the way my doll

felt when I decided to change its face. When Mother came to live with me, she had already lived with Lucy for a long time, and I remember telling my husband, "Don't worry. She's not going to get away with the same things here that she got away with at my sister's house." I must have been angrier at her than I realized. Whatever. Those were terrible times. I remember that when Lucy first met Sam, she did not tell him Dad was alive, she was so ashamed of her parents being separated, and so was I. We were such normal people.

One night, I went to a dance at Roseland, and there was a nice man from New Jersey, an Italian fellow, who was completely cracked on the subject of astronomy. And I had the right birthday for his birthday, so then he had to take me out in earnest. I don't think he was in love with me. He believed in the signs. We made a date so that he could come home to meet my mother.

When my mother heard that I had a date with an Italian fellow, the alarms were sounded. Talk about beating the tomtoms! Within minutes, everyone in the family was calling, starting with my father. He said, "What's the matter with you, you're not good enough for a Jewish man?" My Uncle Bill called up to say that if a man's not Jewish, he's not human. My Uncle Dave called up to say, "Every morning, Fay, you'll wake up with spaghetti around your neck." That was his idea of a joke. My mother said she would not be able to hold up her head in the neighborhood if her child married a gentile, and finally, last of all, my grandmother called and said, "Fay, do you love him? Because if you love him and he loves you, marry him. A man's a man." Do you see why she was loved? She was more than loved. She was worshiped. And yet all she could pass on to her children was her charm. One night when I went out on a double date with Gloria, I turned around, and there was Aunt Diana up on the porch doing one of her imitations of the boy I was with. Of course, she was very funny, but if the boy had turned around and seen her, I'd have died.

But if Aunt Diana loved someone, and they asked her to move heaven and earth for them, she'd say, "Is that all?" She had a niece named Muriel Lemuels, and Muriel was about six feet tall and not so wonderful looking, and she never went out much. She had a talent for sewing and designing, and eventually she became a designer in Manhattan. At that time, she was staying with Aunt Diana, and she had a date. She was going with a very nice young man and she was in love with him and she wanted so badly to get him to propose to her and she asked Aunt Diana what she should do. Aunt Diana said, "Invite him home for a home-cooked dinner, and I will hide in the pantry, and I will get everything ready, and you will pretend that you cooked everything, and he'll be so impressed that he'll propose." So Muriel said fine, and Aunt Diana got dinner all ready, and then she hid in the pantry.

When it was time to serve dinner, Muriel excused herself, and when he wanted to come in and help her, she said, "No, no men in the kitchen. Please wait in the living room for me." She came into the kitchen, fiddled around for a few minutes with the beautiful tray Aunt Diana got ready, and of course, she's very nervous. And Muriel, as she's walking out, she had to go through a little door between the kitchen and the dining room, and what happens? She trips on the sill and falls flat on her face, and the food goes flying everywhere and she bursts into tears, hysterically crying. And the young man came rushing over to console her. By the time she was consoled, she was engaged. *Then* Aunt Diana came out. And wasn't that typical of her? But when she made me take off my tan coat and put on her black one, that was typical, too. She was like a coin, and both faces were hers. If you were not a member of her immediate family, you took a chance when you flipped that coin.

When she first got married, Aunt Diana kept a kosher home, but then when Gloria got married, she went up to Washington each time Gloria had a baby. She used to say Gloria couldn't have a baby without her. It was so important to Diana to keep kosher because she wanted her mother to eat at her house. But when Gloria had her first baby, and Aunt Diana was gone, Sidney and Michael brought in ham and they had the colored girl roast the ham, and Sarah came in and said she would never eat in that house again. When Aunt Diana came home, she asked them what had happened there, and Sidney said that Michael came home with a couple of goyish boys from college and they wanted ham and the girl knew how to bake ham and Sarah walked in on them. Aunt Diana said, "Now I'll have to kasheh all the dishes and the silver and I'll have to throw out certain pots," and she did. When Gloria's second child was born, Sidney and Michael did the same thing, and she did the same thing. But the third time! After that, she said, "They go for the trayf things, and it's their home. They want it." If it was her husband and her son, everything they did was fine.

They were all like that. When I gave my children milk with dinner, Grandma used to say, "If Fay says it's good for the children, then it's all right." The children came first. They certainly came before the husbands.

Mother used to take me shopping with her, shopping for chickens, and she always asked the man for a full-breasted chicken, and no matter which one the man brought her first, she did not want it. She said she wanted a young chicken, not "a chicken older than myself." And when she got it home, it had to be tender, so she used to boil the chicken, and then after it had been boiling for an hour, she would put in a little glass to boil with it, and that glass was supposed to make the chicken tender. Of course, after a chicken has been boiling an hour or an hour and a half, unless it's made of cement, it's tender. But she believed in all those things. I often think that what she was always asking the man for, she got in me. A full-breasted chicken.

Well, my mother loved us and she loved our children. If one of them had been away at school for a few months, when she saw them, she would start to cry, she was so happy. I miss her. I miss Dad terribly, and he's been dead for thirty years. Last week, Sam brought it all up again. He said Lucy and I were wrong to have gone with Mother when she left Dad. It would never have occurred to us *not* to go. Children listened to their mother. They went with their mother. But I started to cry and I felt as if it were yesterday and if there were something I could still do about it. I don't know why Sam has this bee in his bonnet, but I wish he would get it out.

In Florida, where all of us live now, old people, people like me, sometimes spend all their time talking about what they did and what they were before they came down here. They are so afraid that people won't know what they were before they retired. They want everyone to know what kind of man or woman they were in their heyday. A woman I know had a heart condition and she nearly did herself in making a dinner for twenty-six because she wanted everyone to know what kind of hostess she had been before she came down here. I don't have to bother with that. I was nobody before and I'm nobody now. All I ever wanted was to be happy. And we have been happy.

I tried going to college at night the way Lucy did, but I

couldn't take it. It wasn't important enough to me. When I was forty, and my children were grown up, then I went to college. I was never ambitious. A happy family life, that was all I ever wanted.

The worst thing I can remember is the day my youngest daughter abandoned her stuffed cat, Lizzie the Cat. The cat had been everything in the world to her, and one day, she threw it into the street and said she didn't want it. I said, "Jenny, if you don't get that cat now, you're not going to come back for it," and she said she didn't want it. She never asked for it again. Dad was staying with us at the time. It broke his heart to walk by and see that cat lying there in the street, and for some reason, the garbage men did not pick it up for a long time. Every night, when my husband came back from work, he said, "The cat is still there." Finally, Dad couldn't stand it and he said he was going out for the cat, but that night, the men had come for it. He had just missed it. You cannot imagine what I went through because of my father and that cat. Dad wouldn't look my daughter in the eye for a long time after that. But as terrible things go, that was not such a terrible thing. When the others talk about who they were, and what they did, I look around me and have nothing to say. Evidently, I took after my father.

Chapter 60

Emily

When I was a child, I went everywhere with my grandfather. I spent days walking with him. He loved to walk, and we would walk to Sheepshead Bay and watch the fishing boats go out and come in. I knew there was some mystery about him because I frequently heard my grandmother whispering to my mother about him before he came, and I thought I was at the center of it. You see, he always took my side. When I was seven, I was terrified of the wet mop. Its long gray hairs reminded me of a drowned person, and I would have done anything rather than mop the floor. But my mother and my grandmother were adamant about it; all girls had to learn to mop floors, and they would keep at me until I was in hysterics. If my grandfather was there, he would try to stop them, saying there was plenty of time for me to learn how to mop a floor, and at the sound of his sympathetic voice, I would wail even louder, thus undoing all his good work, because my outrageous wails brought my mother's and my grandmother's wrath down upon me even faster.

When I try to remember what he was like, I remember few details, few things he said, few things he did. Instead, I hear a high, clear chord which to me is the sound of his particular being. Occasionally, I hear the same sound in certain musical works or works of literature. A person is the sound of his emotions after all. I cannot hope to reproduce that sound. Suffice it to say that when I hear it it makes me at once very sad and very happy.

Since we moved out here, here where we never see another person unless we invite them, which we rarely do, where we see the shapes of deer moving against the horizon between the dip of one mountain and the swell of another, I have been hearing that sound more and more frequently. It makes me want to gather together what I have left of him. At times, my preoccupation with him seems obsessive, even to me, but it seems as if he wants something of me. I have my dog, Vidal, who I named after the dog my grandfather bought to keep his first dog, Kopatchnik, company. That was just like my grandfather. He bought Kopatchnik to keep *him* company, and then he could not bear leaving Kopatchnik alone when he had to leave the store or the house, so he bought Vidal as company for the other dog. When Kopatchnik died, Vidal had no company, and my grandfather would have bought a companion for the second dog, but before he had a chance to do that, he was shot. My Aunt Fay took Vidal, although until the day he died, she was terrified of him.

A few days ago, I was drifting into sleep over my typewriter and when I opened my eyes, Vidal was staring at me and it seemed to me that the dog began to talk. If a dog talks, he ought to have something momentous to say, but all Vidal asked me to do was get my grandfather's gold watch, it was octagonal and emblazoned with his initials, and take it to the watchmaker's and ask the man to get it going again. "I will soon be leaving," said Vidal; "I see that everything here is fine." The next day I found out that my daughter was pregnant with our first grandchild. Well, who knows? Vidal himself did not go anywhere. He is lying across my feet right now. When I look into his eyes, I see the dog's eyes, no one else's. The dog is not the same as he was. Now his eyes are like mirrors. Yesterday, when I was looking into his eyes, I saw myself and my grandfather walking along and then we stopped and leaned over the rail and looked into the water. I was asking him to tell me my favorite story, the story about one of my mother's relatives who used to beat up his wife. I never understood why my grandfather loved this story so, but he was never so happy as when he was telling it.

It seems my grandmother had a cousin Sadie and her husband drank a little too much and a little too often and when he drank, he would come home and slap his wife around a little too much. And her sons did not like this at all. The man was their mother's second husband, not their father. And they said, if Mother has to take it on the chin, he'll take it on the chin, too. So while their mother sat in the kitchen under an ice pack, they would take their stepfather out and beat him up. One day, they were very angry at their stepfather, and they dumped a big pot of borscht over his head. The soup was hot and red and he was a mess.

But he had an angel watching over him, and that day, there

had been a big train accident. The man heard the crash of the
elevated trains, and instead of sorrow and death, he heard the
knock of opportunity. He ran to the scene of the accident and
promptly threw himself down among the piles of victims. And
of course, the emergency ambulance promptly rushed him off
to the hospital, because the boys had left him in pretty bad
shape. Did they ask why he was covered with beet soup? In
their wisdom, they ignored the soup and paid him off.

When he came home from the hospital, and apologized for
his behavior, and since his pockets were stuffed with money,
all was forgiven. The upshot of the matter was that this man,
named Louis, discovered a new career. He was not what you
would call an ambulance chaser. He was an ambulance rider.
Since he never gave up drinking, and his wife Sadie ran a
saloon anyway, his life continued along in that way for many
years. But his end was sad indeed. It seems they were
summering in Marblehead when he was at the bottle again.
According to my grandmother's nephew, he drank himself
into a stupor and hung himself one night. The sons came and
cut their stepfather down. When they went through his
clothes to see what he had left behind, all they found were
bottles of all shapes and sizes stuffed into all his pockets and
even in the lining of his coat. So much for him. He came to
this country in 1869, just missed the Civil War, was born in
June 1850, and was dead in 1900. He was a glass peddler. My
grandfather used to say that his fatal mistake was getting
more interested in what was inside the glass than in the glass
itself. If Louis were alive today, my grandfather said, he
would be suffering from whiplash, and he would have a cop in
his pocket who also made neck braces on the side.

I used to love this story, but I never had any idea why my
grandfather so loved telling it. Now that I know more about
his life, I see why he so relished a story in which my
grandmother's family appeared to be such a group of oafs,
loafers, and fools. And he used to tell it with such enthusi-
asm! I thought it was the most wonderful story, filled with
ambulances, crazy people, lying and cheating, and best of all,
the shocking spectacle of a man hanging from the ceiling.
Before my grandfather started telling me this story, my
favorite had been Bluebeard, but in my wisdom, I decided
that Bluebeard could not hold a candle to this. And while I
was not listening to the tale of Louis, the accident victim, I
was listening to Grandmother Lily's inexhaustible fund of

tales about how my grandfather had threatened her with a gun and had followed her everywhere she went. I should have, according to the experts, grown up with a demented imagination. Instead, I grew up wondering at the amazing secrets of adults. Between them, the two of them fixed me. By the time I was eight, I was insatiably curious about life. And I turned my curiosity against my grandmother.

My grandfather never talked about himself. After he had been dead twenty-five years, I went to visit my Aunt Fay when she was in the hospital, and we began talking about him. It must have been the whiteness of the surroundings which started me off. I am haunted by a dream in which my grandfather and I are walking together when, suddenly, everything goes white, as if a film had broken or burned through to the radiance beneath, and when this happens I feel both bereaved and overjoyed, as if the white, milky light were trying to tell me something, and was telling me, although I did not understand what it was saying.

That was when my aunt told me that my grandfather had been born in Russia. She thought I knew. She told me about how his mother had left him behind when she remarried. When I went home, I told all this to my mother, and as she listened to me, her eyes became shiny. When I was finished, she said, "He never told me any of that." "You didn't know he was born in Russia?" I asked. "Oh, yes," she said, "I knew that. I didn't know that his mother left him." She thought for a while, and said that after she went to work, Fay spent a lot of time in the store with him, and he must have talked to her then. She was not around much after she was old enough to talk to.

I don't think that was it. My grandmother never told my mother the story because it would have upset her. She wants things steady, to stay as they are. It is strange how life molds people. When they were children, my mother, not Fay, was the wild one. But when she married, there was no room for wildness. Her in-laws watched her for signs of eccentricity. She would not give them the satisfaction of finding any. A broken marriage rivaled hell in the horrors it held for her. She tried to fit into so many places, into so many impossible nooks and crannies that all the strangeness was rubbed from her. You see flashes of it every now and then, just enough to make you mourn for it, for what was lost. My grandfather saw it all, and how, when she appeared to be doing nothing more than standing in front of the stove, she was juggling many, many worlds, all made of glass, all dear to her, and one of them was herself. Naturally he never told her.

Instead, he came over with his little doctor's bag whenever anything went wrong in the house. He could fix anything mechanical or electrical, and before he came to see us, he would call and say, "What needs fixing?" My mother said the sink needed fixing, or the lock on the door, and I had my own list, my doll, a doll's house, my skates. I could not believe there was anything he could not fix. Once he took a doll my grandmother had smashed accidentally when she was cleaning my room and he brought it back saying it was as good as new. It was. He had gone out and bought a new one.

And when my mother said that she never knew that her father had been abandoned in Russia, I realized that I could not remember anything about his death. I remember being told; after that I remembered nothing. No matter how many times I asked my mother, I have never been able to remember how old I was when my grandfather died. Finally, I memorized the date of his death: 1951. But I never believed he was dead. I refused to believe he was dead. I must still refuse to believe it. Every so often, I think I should go look at his stone and the stone carving would compel belief, but I know I will never be able to go. At times, I think what we will not believe is most important about us.

I've spent all of my life fixing things. First, I went through medical school and practiced medicine for almost ten years. Then I began to collect the pieces of the past and glue them together as best I could. I told no one here I was once a doctor, but people are always coming to me and asking me how to fix this and that, how to bandage this arm, that leg. I became interested in herbs and what their properties were, and yesterday I tried out a mixture of sage and animal fat and found it cured my headache. Soon someone with a headache who cannot take aspirin will come out here and ask me for a suggestion and I will tell them about the sage and the chicken fat. Then I will go back in and start writing.

No one here knows that I write, but if they do, they refuse to remember. Instead, they know me as the woman who knows about herbs. To them, I am still a doctor. It is impossible to change the shadow you cast before you. When we first moved here, the fall of the snows meant absolute quiet. Now the snows afford no protection. Today, people have snowmobiles and go everywhere on showshoes. When I hear the dogs barking, I know why someone has come. It is an odd thing, but no one ever calls to ask for advice or even to ask if they should come. They appear, as if they had to, as if they had no choice, as if there was no such thing as the telephone. I no longer complain about anything. I have become what I will be, and complaints are superfluous.

Today, I saw a cloud blow down the sky, and as it traveled from right to left, it grew thinner and thinner, until it was gone, erased. And I thought to myself, that is my grandfather, going home. The mistakes God made before my grandfather was born have been corrected. He can go home. I thought about how sentimental and senile I was growing. I am almost fifty. There are times I think I kept him here longer than he wanted to stay because I refused to let him go. I lived most of my life in a haunted house, but a house which never felt empty. Vidal the Fifth is barking. The children are home on vacations from school, and my husband is putting a log in the wood stove. The smoke coming out of the chimney is the color of snow, and as it rises, it thins and unravels. One lone cloud is moving down the blue sky and the moon shares the sky with the sun

Chapter 61

Sam

My wife always says I fell in love with her because of her laugh and her small ears, and it's true. Were those good reasons? They sure as hell weren't. The real reason I married her was because I fell in love with her. I damn well didn't marry her because I fell in love with her family. That whole family was living in a dream world. I was crazy about her two uncles, Bill and Dave, but Bill was not a very bright guy. Dave had more brains, just enough to get himself into trouble. He couldn't stand to earn a dollar honestly. If someone had come up to him and said, "Here, it's a million dollars," he would have said, "Take it back and let me steal it." Everything had to be a game. He had to outsmart the world. It's a warped mind.

Bill worked for me for a while when he couldn't get a job. It's hard to believe that I started him at fifteen dollars a week. That's how conditions were then. When things picked up, he went into the pharmacy business and why he wasn't sued up and down the block by every other customer I'll never know. They were not practical people, none of them. They were poor as church mice. They didn't have a cent, but they lorded it over the whole world.

Lily and I never got along. Anyhow, Lily never got along with me. Considering the kind of mother I had, I would have bent over backward to make Lily happy, if she could have stood the sight of me, that is. My own mother was no mother at all. After she overfed us, she thought she was done. She used to make me a matzoh-meal pancake in a steak pan and on it she'd put half a pound of sugar. On Friday nights, when she baked, I'd come back and take a quart of milk and I'd finish a whole pan of cake. But when she finished cooking for me, she was finished. If I was sick, she cursed me because she had to stay home. God forbid she shouldn't go out when she wanted to. She insisted on going to Europe right before the war broke out. She took my sister with her, and in Germany, they were warned not to get off the trains. There were soldiers goose-stepping everywhere. But she wouldn't put off her trip. She was a very selfish woman. She sat on our porch and rocked. Sometimes she sat and rocked for weeks without saying a word. God knows what she was thinking about. She wasn't thinking about us. I would have loved to have a mother-in-law who acted like a mother to me.

But she didn't like me from the beginning. I have no idea why. Lily was very much against my coming into the family. She was such a family woman that it broke up the deal between herself and her husband. She went to clean the house for her family; she did everything for them. I thought it was disgusting. Lucy's two uncles didn't get married because they were so devoted to their parents. Bill, he finally got married. He was sixty. I guess he wanted company when they laid him out. And did he marry an idiot! Tootsie. She looked a lot like his mother, Sarah. No one else thought so, but I saw it right away.

As a wedding gift, I got my mother-in-law. She moved right in after Emily was born. It was a family custom, apparently, but they didn't tell me about it before the wedding. Mothers-in-law moved in with their daughters when their daughters had children. It was the middle of the Depression when we got married, so we waited for two years before we had Emily, and still, I was afraid to go ahead with it. My mother said, "No child in this country ever starved to death," and she was right. So we had Emily, and the next thing I knew, we had Lily. She made fun of everything I said. One time, Emily had given her a very bad time. Everyone used to say Emily was just like her mother, but Lucy was never rude or insulting or opened up a mouth like my daughter did. Anyway, Emily spent the day imitating Lily, and Lily could never take teasing. She could hand it out but she couldn't take it, and when I got home, Lily was in tears and she had my wife in tears, all over Emily's behavior. They made me think the child was a juvenile delinquent. I don't know what started it; I think Lily wanted Emily to throw out some old doll of hers because the doll was dirty. That was some reason to throw out a child's toy? But Lily was Miss Clorox of 1944. When I got in, Emily was locked in her room, and they were threatening her with the most dire threats. So when she came out, I gave it to her. I thought that was what they wanted me to do. I was wrong. Lily came at me with a knife, a big knife she got from the kitchen. That night I told Lucy either she goes or I go. When she got wild, she wasn't responsible.

No one was ever good enough for her, only her children, and she wasn't so wonderful with them. Fay still remembers how Lily threw out all her dolls when she was at school; they were too much trouble to dust. Everything was too much trouble for her. To this day, Fay collects dolls and fusses over them. She says when she got her first job, she was working for a plumbing company, and they went to an old doll factory and came back with three dolls, and she asked the men if she could have one, and Lily was so astounded that a seventeen-year-old would spend money buying cloth to make clothes for a doll that Fay never heard the end of it. That's Lily for you. She caused so much trouble. I wouldn't know where to begin if I wanted to go over it. She said nothing good about me to the children.

For years, they didn't like me. They made fun of my cigars. She hated my smoking. She couldn't stand it when I got ashes all over my house. Every Sunday we used to take a ride in the car, and the minute she got in, she was choking. I'd stop and show her I wasn't smoking but she'd choke anyway. I'll never forget, we were going to go to the country one time, and I had bought Lucy a new car. I didn't tell Lily. We had an old Ford before that. Lily came downstairs and she saw this big, beautiful red car, this big Hudson, and she says, "That's the car Lucy should own." I said all right, you want to go in that car, we'll go in that car, and I went to open the door and she was yelling, "What are you doing, are you crazy, get out of there!" and I turned the key and started it up. I'll never forget her face.

And when Lucy got burned up in the country, I bought her a fur coat for a surprise. She didn't like it. She was like Lily in some ways; I don't think she could stand to see me spend so much money, and believe me, at that time I was making piles of it. She told me to take it back. And I said, "If you don't want a fur coat now, you're not going to get one later," and Lily said, "That's not the way a rich man acts." All of a sudden I was a rich man to her. But it didn't make any difference. Whatever I did was still wrong. So finally Lucy had to tell her to leave and she said, "All right, I'll pack and go." You know how a man feels when he enters into heaven? I know. It's how I felt the day Lily moved out.

And what did she want? What was she so unhappy about? I liked Esheal. He had a lot of mannerisms in his speech that used to drive me crazy. "You see where it comes in." That was one of them. I don't know where he picked up that phrase, but he used it all the time. I used to play two-handed pinochle with him because he loved it. He was a good soul. After he died, I was in charge of his estate; he named me as the executor of his will, and I found a letter he wrote the War Department during the Second World War.

5/8/42

U.S. War Department,
Gentlemen:—
   I remember during the Russo-Jap war, the Japs de-
stroyed the Russian navy by lying in wait for them, as the
Russian navy was passing on the other side of the island.
In the following manner.

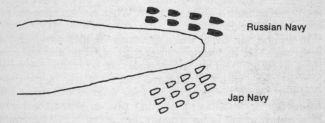

Russian Navy

Jap Navy

That being the method of the Japs, let our navy be aware
of that method.
             Yours, with deep hopes for our success,
             I am

               Esheal Luria

The poor bastard. After all he'd been through, he was still an idealist. He got back a form letter, and this letter was something to see. They had it coded fourteen ways for retrieval. They must have thought he was some kind of enemy of the state. "Your comments have been carefully noted in the Department and your interest is appreciated." I bet his interest was carefully noted. He was a good soul. And he had a right to be jealous of his wife. She was giving too much time to her family and not enough to him. I don't think theirs was a love match. I'm sure it was just that she wanted a guy to support her. For a long time, I didn't know Lucy's father was living. When we got serious, she had to tell me. Believe me, it was a relief to find out about him. He was the only sane member of the family. The rest of them were all crackpots.

Lily didn't like me and she didn't like my mother. My mother was something else again; I loved her, but I never respected her. She had terrible eyesight; she was legally blind, and something I never understood, she would sit there on the porch rocking and she would stare right into the sun. With eyes like that, staring into the sun. Maybe she was trying to stare it down. Who the hell knew what *she* wanted? She was a little like Lily. Whatever my father did, it was never enough for her. If he went to the refrigerator to take a little milk, she cursed his head off. I never understood it. A refrigerator full of food and she'd throw a fit every time. He'd drink it anyway. He was right to drink it. He paid for it. They spent their time fighting with each other. When he had enough, he slept in the Turkish baths.

In his line, my father was a salesman the likes of which I'd never seen. He had various inspectors come up and tell him the workmanship on his garments was not good and they were having trouble with this thing and that thing, and by the time they left, they'd be thanking him for what he was doing for them. But my mother he couldn't please. When the Navy came down to my father's shop, they asked him if he could possibly turn out seven hundred and fifty peacoats a week, and he said not to worry, he'd turn out seven hundred and fifty peacoats a week. In one month, he'd turn out seven hundred a day. You can't imagine how hard it was. And to turn them out without problems with delivery. That's where a lot of people lost their money. They made up the stuff and the government refused to buy it; they kept sending it back. I think if my father had stayed in the factory, he would have lived longer, but of course, my mother wanted to travel.

But I was a worker like my father. And I didn't want a life like his. I wanted a woman who appreciated me. When I met Lucy, I thought, well, this is it. But then I met her mother, and it was like my mother all over again.

The husband should always come first, not the children. When the children grow up, they owe you nothing. But when our children were little, Lucy wore herself out kissing them. She even kissed the soles of their feet, and I remember my mother telling her again and again, "Don't kiss their little feet. They'll walk all over you." It must have been a superstition, this business about not kissing their feet. But I used to worry about Lucy, and we used to fight about it because I often thought that for her the children came first. I can still hear my mother saying it. "Don't kiss their little feet. They'll walk all over you." My mother didn't wear out her lips kissing any part of us. Probably I was unfair to Lucy. I didn't know what a happy medium was. And she used to say, "Let them walk all over me. As long as I can get up afterward." I wasn't always reasonable. I didn't know what I had there. There were times I saw my wife through my mother's eyes. If she had seen me through her mother's, that would have been the end of it.

One time I was ready to drop Lucy altogether. Lily was a buttinsky. She had to get into everything. Everything was her business. I think Lucy's father had the brains in the family. Lily had no brains whatsoever. If she had any brains, she wouldn't have acted the way she did.

I was engaged to Lucy, and I was already in law school, and she and a friend of mine used to meet me afterward. Ours was already a formal engagement, and one night I called her and her mother answered. She said, "Lucy's out on a date." I said, "Is that so?" and she said, "That's so. She used to go out with this fellow before, and I felt sorry for him, so I made a date for him with Lucy." I said, "Lucy went out on a date on your say-so? Fine." And I dropped Lucy altogether. She kept calling me, but I wouldn't see her. I didn't bother with her anymore. And of course, my mother made it easier. If Lucy called, she wouldn't take a message. She wouldn't tell me. Then my friend arranged for Lucy to come down and meet us at the school. I didn't know she was coming or I wouldn't have been there. The two of them worked on me, and I started to see her again. But I was ready to drop her altogether.

And then after we got married, I began to have trouble with Lucy and money. My mother always had secret money. She used to pull it out of my father every day; one of the girls needed this or she needed that. When he went broke, she had all this money, and the whole time he was worried sick, she had a small fortune, so she didn't care. She was actually paying all the bills. Where did the money come from? She told him the butcher gave her credit; everyone gave her credit. After a while, my father woke up. But before he did, there were some times. One day, we had a terrible storm and the ice wagon couldn't get through, so my mother told me to go downstairs and chop out some ice for the icebox. And when my father saw that, he thought we had done it because we didn't have any money to pay the ice man, and he cried like a baby. But I think he was happy she hid the money because otherwise he wouldn't have had any. Of course, he had to go down on his knees to her and beg her for it, but that's another story.

Anyway, after Lucy and I were married, I went over to my mother and complained. I knew approximately how much it cost to get along and Lucy never had enough money. I had just gone into business. I didn't have much, but when you're in business, you always have money in your pocket. I went over to my mother's one day and said, "She's a nice girl, and all that, but I can't take it. She's dragging money out of me all the time." So when I heard my mother's answer, I knew what had happened. She said, "If she asks you for it, she needs it. Give it to her." And knowing how my mother wasn't so crazy about Lucy at that time, I figured that she had given her a briefing. That was my mother's doing. She had Lucy salting it away. The mother-in-law teaches the daughter-in-law. I approved of it because I remembered when we were up against it, and I knew she was saving it, and even later on, when I was on my feet, I gave her extra money because I knew it made her happy to put it in the bank. She always dreamed up extra expenses.

At least she put the money in the bank. My mother didn't trust anyone. She hid her money in the grandfather clock in the dining room, and one night they were robbed. They must have had two, three thousand dollars in that clock, and my mother was really in a corner. She couldn't tell anyone about it. My father didn't know she had the money. I don't know, with these women it's always a question. Are you supposed to be grateful to them or should you try to kill them? Anyway, what with my mother teaching Lucy, and her mother filling her ears with poison, I had something to worry about. To tell the truth, when I told Lucy it was her mother or me, I didn't know what my wife was going to do. But she had her mother's example in front of her. And her father had some things of his own to say to her. He knew I was a jealous man, and I guess he knew what that was all about.

Lucy had some things to put up with from me. Lucy had gorgeous legs and I had a fit whenever she showed them. Once, Emily bought her a pair of lace stockings; everyone was wearing them at the time, and I told Lucy that next she'd be standing on the street corner holding a red pocketbook. She cried when she had to give those stockings back, and for a change, my daughter wasn't talking to *me*. I was usually the one giving her the silent treatment. Lucy really had her hands full running the gauntlet between me and our children and her mother.

And even after all the trouble her mother caused living with us that first time (she lived with us for eight years at the beginning), when Lily became senile Lucy wanted her back again. I would never have known she was senile. She kept on talking about her mother and her brothers; she never once mentioned her husband, so I thought she was as sane as she ever was. But she set fire to the curtains at Fay's house; she didn't know what she was doing. And every doctor in the world said she had to be put in a nursing home. My wife had a second opinion. She would hire a nurse and install her with Lily in our house. Fifty-four years old and she still wanted to be her mother's favorite. If she hadn't had two children when I issued that ultimatum about Lily's leaving, I don't know what she would have done. Lucy had more sense than her mother.

I often wondered if things would have been different for Esheal if he could have brought himself to talk more to Lily. He was a silent man, and I am a silent man, and these women, sometimes you can't bring yourself to talk to them; you don't want to give them more ammunition.

I don't know how any marriage survives. Lucy had a lot to put up with when it came to me and my family. If I wasn't upset about the business, I was upset about them. Half the time, my family was involved with the business because I went into the clothing business instead of law, and there was a fight about that. They said Lucy talked me out of law. Maybe I didn't want law. I didn't like it, that pressure. I got a dose of it when I went to talk to the man who owned the buildings. And I wanted to be secure financially. I was a married man.

And my father was already in the business, so he cleared the way for me. But I paid for that, and when I paid, Lucy did, too.

During the war, my father sent me a bill. He was making the stuff up for me, and he overcharged me fifty dollars on a bill. I figured he made a mistake. So I took off the fifty dollars and sent him a check. He called me up and said if I didn't pay him the fifty dollars, he'd stop working for me and he'd sue me.

I got so mad. I used to take the car and drive him into work and take him home. That night, I didn't pick him up. I went home. I went right over to my mother and I told her what happened. And she said to me, that shows you how smart she was, she said, "Do you need the work?" I said, "Yes, I need the work." She said, "I tell you what to do. Pay the meshuggeneh the fifty dollars." You couldn't get stuff made. And that same night, my parents walked over to sit on the porch and see the children, and Dad gave Lucy a bond for a couple of thousand dollars. I said, what kind of man are you? You're going to sue me for fifty dollars and you come up here and throw money around like peanuts. I'll never forget his answer. "One thing has nothing to do with the other." And Lucy was ready to kill him, but she had to put up with him.

And she had to put up with me. I was under pressure all of the time and I couldn't stand noise or pressure of any kind, and Lucy and the children were there to get it. And my daughter was one in a million. When I gave her a licking, she called the cops. So they drove me crazy, and when I went to work, it was worse. I was like my father when it came to work. Once when a woman operator called up to say her husband died, my father tried to persuade her to come in anyway. I don't know what he said, that she should skip the funeral, or that someone else should go to it for her, but he wanted her to come in. When he hung up, he said, "How do you like that? He has to go and die in the middle of the season!" I didn't want the family having problems in the middle of my season, either. And during the middle of the season, I really had a terrible temper. Lily always used to say, "What good is a handsome man who looks like a movie star when he has a temper like that?" I didn't think I looked like a movie star, but my wife did. She said I looked like Clark Gable, only taller.

Believe me, I don't think I looked like a movie star to my

daughter, Emily. She brought out the worst in me. There were months when she couldn't go past me without getting a smack across the face. Why did I do it? She never knew. She never forgave me for it, either. I think I was so worried about her, so worried about what would happen to her if I didn't do well, that I got angry at her and hit her. It wasn't reasonable, but there it was. I would never have hit Lucy; she would have left me. My daughter was there to get it. It makes me ashamed to think about it. But I felt like a pressure cooker all the time. And Lily carried on about my hours as if I had actually moved out of the house and abandoned them. She didn't like it if I was home and she didn't like it when I wasn't. But she wanted me to be a rich man. And one thing she never got tired of whispering was that I was just like her husband. That was the worst thing she could think of to say about me after she finished calling me an animal because I smoked in my own house.

Esheal asked Lily not to bob her hair, and Lily bobbed it, and afterward, he wouldn't speak to her. Lucy's hair turned gray when she was about twenty-six and I found a bottle of hair dye in the medicine chest and I told her I didn't want her to dye her hair. She didn't. But Lily went on about it, how I was crazy jealous like her husband, and her daughter would end up worse than she had, murdered. She wound up badly enough, she was so smart. In a nursing home. She never would have believed that could happen to her.

We men are what we are. And sometimes it's not our fault what we are. Some of the things I remember when I was small, they left a mark on me. I remember once we couldn't find a room, and Dad said, "Pockets full of money and I can't find a place to sleep." Otherwise, I don't remember what was going on. I remember a fight my mother had with a landlady. The landlady threw all the garbage into the apartment. My mother must have left it in the hallway or something. Certain things stick out and other things don't make any sense. But they have their effect. I remember when Dad lost his business; he had his machine on a truck, so that they didn't get. They put a lock on his door. And when I saw him working on his machine in a little bedroom he was using for a shop, a man who had a chauffeur and a loft literally a city block long, I cried like a baby. I remember an uncle who my father helped all the time, and when we had trouble, Dad borrowed some money from him, and after Dad's business failed, this man was standing in the alley, shouting, "You crook! You took money from me and you didn't pay me back!" I never could look at him again.

And there were things I did that I was ashamed of. I went to Hebrew school, and I told the rabbi I'd pay him, but he had to give me back a quarter. If he didn't give me the quarter, he couldn't have the money. I wanted that quarter. And the rabbi was desperate for money himself. He couldn't afford to lose a pupil. And that wasn't the worst thing that I did. I told some of the other boys about my plan and they did the same thing. I must have been mad at the world and at God, too.

Life goes by. I'll never forget the day I had to go for that exam for the Army. I had to get up very early. It was pitch-dark outside and I went in and looked at my son and my daughter and my wife. Everybody was sound asleep. I walked out and there was a Greek place on Avenue U and I went there and there must have been five or six other guys and we commiserated with each other. Then we went over to the Army on Twenty-third Street, and later, Lucy couldn't get over it. I was the only one who liked the meal they gave me.

After the examination, I went out and right away I went over to the market and I was buying piece goods. I was taking a chance that I would get extra time. And I was 4F because of my weight. I ate like I never did before that exam. Then the sergeant said to me, "Sure, if you did a good day's work, you wouldn't be so fat," and I got mad, and without thinking, I said, "If you worked as hard as I did, you wouldn't be here altogether." That did it. They gave me limited service. But I appealed, and by the time they heard the appeal, the Army had a new age limit, and I was too old.

And no matter what happened, I could count on Lucy. My mother wouldn't get up to give a dying man a glass of water, and Lucy loved to entertain. We had a wonderful life. Now we're here in Florida, and it seems as if our life on Long Island never existed. Sometimes I look around and think it's sad, that people are taking one last fling before dying, but most of the time I think it's a wonderful thing that after all these years, we're here and we're happy with each other. And then sometimes, I look around and I see us all in another light, bald men with thin legs, women with tired wombs, square dancing, swimming, waiting for the children to call. But for me, it's been enough. I remember Lucy's Aunt Diana saying that when her husband died, he thought he was going to be with his son Michael. He was right. If Michael went into nothingness, he went there too. Here, when some people get old, they start praying overtime.

At night, when I can't sleep, I often think about the time my parents took me to Prospect Park, and a terrible storm came up and I got separated from them, and the crowd was impossible, and I knew I would never find them, so I borrowed a dime from a policeman and took the Tompkins Avenue trolley home. And when they got home four hours later and found me, they beat the hell out of me for leaving without them. But I think I did the right thing. I often think of myself and how lost I was that day and how I got myself home. Now I think of how I got myself and Lucy home. And the children. I hope they make it, too. So in spite of them all, Lily and my father, my mother and Esheal, we made it home. I had a hard life and maybe I should have gone into law and not the clothing business, but what difference did it make? Lucy and I wound up happy. And yet I often find myself up while Lucy is sound asleep thinking of my mother and of Lily, and wondering what the hell was it with those women? What did those women want? What were they reaching for? They must have been reaching out for something that never was. But I wish I knew. What did those women want? And was there a man on earth who could have given it to them?

The Scattering

Lucy

A vase of flowers. Such beautiful flowers! Please don't die; please last a long time. Never laugh again. Rain on the roof. A metal roof. The roof of a car. Oh, the petals edge with brown. Falling to the table, little dresses.

Going down an icy hill. We wanted to see what was at the top. A glass road. Wind. Snow like dust, erasing us. Going down backward. A breakable glass sky. Flying like a bird. The car flies. In the drift. Two men came along. They just lift the car out of the snowdrift and put it back in the middle of the road. It was scary, coming down like that. I don't like the country.

The vase of flowers on the table. Please don't die. Please last a long time. What happened, what could have happened, to bring such flowers to our home?

Fay

A blood orange. High up. Me, climbing, and it falls. Mother cuts it open. It is red. I hurt it. It bled. Hot. Can't see. Can't speak. Little sweet drops. Like rain. My father's voice. My mother's.

It rains here, sometimes for weeks. The burnt grass, my body. When it rains, he comes back. Rain is sweet. Without the rain, we are nothing but a fine dust. As the wind lifts us, we rise.

The orange, the poor orange!

Diana

A shiny doorknob. My head fitting under it. Just fitting.
Great crying. Woman sleeping. The white bed. Such crying!
What does it mean? The child! Someone close the door! The
keyhole. A Turkish shape. There it is. Three years old.
Ninety.

Deep water. Cold. The currents like scarves. Rising and
falling in the wind. The body, rising, falling. Heart. The
heart, always the heart. Mother, Dave, Bill, mine. Michael's
heart. Beating in shells. I love shells. A pearl settling in the
throat. The skull, the fragile shell. The women crying in the
room. Won't they ever stop? Won't anyone stop their crying?

Lily

Daisies. Everywhere. Bows in their hair. A horse. A monkey. A red hat. Singing. Bows. Like butterflies, such big ones. Heartbeat, so loud. Her heart. Too big. Is she coming to see me? Is Momma coming to see me? Sidney? Dave? Bill? Michael? Dinney? I saw Dinney. My clothes. They steal them. They all wear white dresses. Why is everyone old? Whose room is this? My drawer? Where am I now? Outside. Take the trolley, get out of here. Daisies. I see the daisies. Why doesn't he come get me? The gray car. He bought a black one. I won't go in it. It's raining. Inside. Come in! Don't get our dresses wet. Such nice, starched dresses.

Emily

The snow widens, covers the land. I know no one here. We live here always. We always did. The leaves turn. The leaves fall. The cold bites deep down into the earth. There is a mouse in the wall. We live out of town. Twelve miles. No one understands it. Such isolation. The sharp swallows carve the sky. The water swifting over the rocks. In the summer, building rock walls. The dog in the water. Children. The horse is loose again. Apples in the pasture. Who will find the horse? No leaves on the apple tree. The apples shine. Gold balls on the apple tree. Black shadows against the snow. How others see us move. I see him moving. The earth moves in his throat. I say, be still, I found you. A faint shape in white light. Coming clearer. I heard it all, every word. My broom, sweeping the cobwebs. I know the water runs black over the black rocks. Back where you began. That strange woman. That's what they call me. My children, running free as water. The sun sets here. Never return to the city. Stay with us. As if you could help it, in my bones.

Esheal

Rain on the roof, a killing rain. Chickens roosting on the roof. Straw roofs covered with eggs. Roofs hatching lives. The eggs freeze. Coughing. The blue snow like a huge blanket. Now I see her. She comes closer. She is who I thought she would be, and she is someone else. I wouldn't have thought I would come back as so many things.

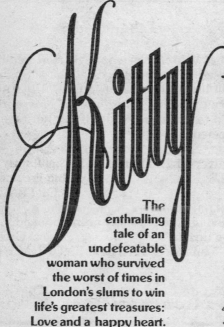

197